Praise for Santa Moi
#1 internationally bestsell

'A sweeping tale of deep love lost and fo
Brooklyn spans many decades and two continents as a woman
who lost everything during World War II learns to live again.
Filled with the color and warmth of northern Italy, the pain
and salvation of family, and the courage and determination
it takes to start life over across an ocean, the talented Santa
Montefiore's latest ripples with longing, fate, and hope. The
based-on-a-true-story twists will have you gasping aloud.'
> KRISTIN HARMEL, *New York Times* bestselling author of
> *The Forest of Vanishing Stars* and *The Book of Lost Names*,
> on *An Italian Girl in Brooklyn*

'A pleasure to read. . . . A new Montefiore novel is always a
major event.'
> *Toronto Star* on *The Temptation of Gracie*

'Nobody does epic romance like Santa Montefiore. Everything
she writes, she writes from the heart.'
> JOJO MOYES, bestselling author of *Me Before You*

'One of our personal favourites and bestselling authors, sweeping stories of love and families spanning continents and decades.'
> *The Times*

'I couldn't put this book down.'
> JULIAN FELLOWES, creator of *Downton Abbey*, on
> *Songs of Love and War*

'A superb storyteller of love and death in romantic places in
fascinating times.'
> *Vogue*

'Secrets abound, friendships are fractured, and life-altering
decisions are made in a delicious read that leaves the reader
hungry and eagerly awaiting the next course.'
> *Booklist* (starred review) on *Songs of Love and War*

Santa Montefiore

An Italian Girl *in* Brooklyn

Published by Simon & Schuster

New York   London   Toronto   Sydney   New Delhi

First published in Great Britain by Simon & Schuster UK Ltd, 2022

Copyright © Santa Montefiore, 2022
This Canadian export edition published November 2022

The right of Santa Montefiore to be identified as author of this work has been
asserted in accordance with the Copyright, Designs and Patents Act, 1988.

1 3 5 7 9 10 8 6 4 2

Simon & Schuster UK Ltd
1st Floor
222 Gray's Inn Road
London WC1X 8HB

Simon & Schuster Australia, Sydney
Simon & Schuster India, New Delhi

www.simonandschuster.co.uk
www.simonandschuster.com.au
www.simonandschuster.co.in

A CIP catalogue record for this book is available from the British Library

ISBN 978-1-3985-1696-0
ISBN 978-1-3985-1697-7 (ebook)

Typeset in the UK by M Rules

For my brother James,
with love

PART ONE

Greenwich, New York, 1979

Evelina stood back and admired the table. How pretty it looked. She'd hollowed out small pumpkins for candleholders and placed them around the three vases of sunflowers, carnations and roses that dominated the long table set for ten. She'd made her own napkin rings out of red berries and yellow sycamore leaves and put them on each plate, slotting the name card of every guest into a pine cone. The effect was charming; but it was missing one important thing.

Evelina went into the garden. The sun had almost set. The sky above Greenwich was a pale, watery blue, streaked with fiery crimson and gold. Fat-bellied clouds moved slowly across it. From where she was standing they resembled the dark hulls of ships viewed from the bottom of the sea. She stood a while making shapes out of the smaller clouds: dolphins, whales and jellyfish; waves breaking into pink foam; distant mountain ranges dyed purple. Then the twinkling of a lone star pierced the deepening indigo as the sun withdrew, taking with it its panoply of colours, and the ships and the sea creatures too. Evelina remained there, gazing into the night, watching as one by one a host of stars joined the original, glimmering through the darkness like the lanterns of little fishing boats.

She went to the herb garden and cut a handful of rosemary. She rubbed a piece between her finger and thumb and pressed it to her nose. The smell of home assaulted her senses in a flood of memory. It made her giddy with nostalgia and she closed her eyes for a moment, savouring both the pleasure and the pain, for they were equal in parts. She sighed with resignation. There was no point getting emotional over something lost in the past when the present gave her so much to be grateful for.

She returned to the dining room and sprinkled the sprigs of rosemary over the tablecloth. Sure, she'd been living in America for over thirty years, but she was still Italian in her soul. At this time of thanksgiving it was therefore fitting that, in the decoration of the table at least, she remembered the Old Country.

Evelina was lighting the candles on the table when her husband Franklin returned home. He opened the front door and stepped into the hall, letting her know he was back with a 'Honey, I'm home' as he took off his loden coat and fedora and put down his bag. Franklin van der Velden was retired now, being seventy-six, but he was still involved in college life at Skidmore where he had been, until recently, a classics professor. He was tall and lean with thick grey hair, a straight patrician nose and intelligent blue eyes. The eyes of a man who was always curious and enquiring, and patient with those less gifted than himself. He had been athletic once but now he walked with a stoop and his steps were slow and plodding.

Evelina blew out the match and untied the apron she was wearing to protect her green dress, laying it over a chair. Fourteen years younger than Franklin, she was an attentive and dutiful wife whose respect for her scholarly husband had remained undiminished since the day she had married him. She came into the hall, smiling in that sweet way of hers that rendered her face quite beautiful. At sixty-two she was not by any account an obvious beauty, but her features had character and a vivacious charm, and her hazel eyes were always bright and full of affection. They had depth, too, forged out of dark secrets and hidden sorrows that shone into them a light of empathy which people perceived subliminally and, as a consequence, confided in her secrets and sorrows of their own. Her long brown hair was swept up and fastened loosely with a clip, leaving stray wisps to float about her neck. Her shapely body was soft and comely, her Mediterranean skin forever tanned by the sun of her homeland, as if she still inhabited the olive groves and vineyards of her youth. When she spoke English, her Italian accent was thick, for she hadn't given herself entirely to this new country, but held something back for herself.

She took her husband's coat and he kissed her temple, his weathered face returning her smile with pleasure, for she was a delight to behold. Even after thirty-two years of marriage he hadn't grown complacent about the woman with whom he shared his life. He knew he was fortunate. Without her he'd never have been able to achieve the things he had or, indeed, be the man he was. She was like an anchor to his ship, securing him firmly in home and family, and giving him the tranquillity he needed in which to work.

'They'll be here soon,' she said, hanging his coat in the cupboard and his hat on the hook behind the door.

'Do I have time for a bath?'

'If you're quick.'

Franklin nodded, but they both knew he was unable to do anything in haste. He made his way up the stairs slowly, holding on to the banisters with hands that trembled slightly, pausing a moment in the middle to catch his breath. Evelina returned to the kitchen to attend to dinner. She had prepared all the traditional side dishes to accompany the turkey, which had been cooking in the oven for most of the afternoon: mashed potato, cranberry sauce, turkey stuffing, green beans and pumpkin pie. Evelina hadn't been interested in cooking before she married, but she had taught herself out of necessity. However, when she looked back to her life in Italy, to that chapter closed long ago and buried beneath so many subsequent chapters, the scent of simmering tomatoes and freshly baked focaccia seemed to dominate her memories, wrapping them in a miasma of fragrances and preventing her from recalling much else. Perhaps, she thought, it was nature's way of saving her from painful recollections. Maybe nature was being kind.

Evelina stirred the gravy in the pan, mesmerized momentarily by the whirlpool her wooden spoon created. Thanksgiving was an annual celebration of family and friends, so it wasn't unnatural, given her history, that it should bring to the surface old hurts inflicted long ago when she was young and tender-hearted. It wasn't unnatural to grieve for those she had left behind and for those she had lost. Fall was a time of wistfulness and melancholy, after all; the death rattle of summer, the mournful prelude to winter. No, it wasn't unnatural to feel thankful for what she had and regretful for what she had given up; it wasn't unnatural at all.

The first to arrive were her two sons, Aldo and Dan, with Aldo's wife Lisa and Dan's girlfriend Jennifer entering behind them with a bouquet of flowers and a box of chocolates for Evelina. Aldo was tall and handsome like his father, with his mother's dark hair and skin and hazel eyes. If it hadn't been for his Dutch surname he could easily have passed for an Italian. Dan, on the other hand, was shorter and stockier than his brother, with his father's blue eyes and thick hair. However, his dry, irreverent sense of humour was all his own and, unlike his brother, who was responsible as first-borns tend to be, Dan had an aversion to rules and resisted conformity at every turn.

The sight of her sons pulled Evelina out of her reverie and she embraced them warmly, wrapping her arms around them and kissing their cold faces, forgetting for a moment that they were thirty-one and twenty-nine respectively. To her they would always be boys. 'You look tired, Aldo,' she said, cupping his face. 'You need to sleep. Are you working too hard? Is he working too hard, Lisa?'

'Mom, I'm fine. Don't worry,' Aldo muttered, moving past her to greet his father.

'And you, Dan. If you look tired it's not because of over-working, is it?' Evelina arched an eyebrow suspiciously. 'To you, I say, work a little harder.'

Dan laughed. 'Mom, all work and no play makes Dan a dull boy.' He shrugged off his leather jacket and sniffed. 'Something smells good.'

'Dinner's a surprise,' said Evelina with a grin, aware that that joke had worn thin years ago, yet unable to resist repeating it.

'What? You've cooked a goat instead of a turkey?' said Dan, feigning horror.

'Yes, a Thanksgiving goat. I thought we all needed a change. Who needs turkey when we can have a scrawny old goat?'

Evelina greeted her daughter-in-law Lisa and Jennifer, who she knew would never be her daughter-in-law; Dan was not the settling-down type. It would be a miracle if he ever married, she thought, observing her dashing son with pride. There might be a girl out there who had what it took to tame him, but he hadn't met her yet. And it certainly wasn't Jennifer; she was much too nice.

Moments later the front door flew open again, bringing in a gust of cold wind and Aldo and Dan's younger sister, Ava-Maria, dragging a suitcase behind her. 'I'm here!' she exclaimed, and because of her loud voice and exuberance everyone turned to look at her as she knew they would. 'Hi, guys. Happy Thanksgiving! Isn't this fun? We're all together again.' She hugged and kissed her parents and greeted the others, even Jennifer who she knew wasn't really worth the investment because Dan was bound to dump her by the end of the week. Ava-Maria was dark and beautiful with a personality that demanded to be the centre of attention. Indulged by both parents and favoured by fate, Ava-Maria hadn't a care in the world.

They went into the drawing room and settled into the armchairs and sofas arranged around the fireplace, making themselves at home in the house where Franklin and Evelina had moved in the early 1960s when they'd grown tired of the noise and commotion of Manhattan. Evelina's style was cosy and unpretentious. Furniture, paintings, rugs and trinkets had been purchased because she liked them, not because they fitted into any particular colour scheme or premeditated design. Nothing matched, everything was thrown together like a vegetable stew and yet, somehow, a surprisingly harmonious flavour had been created. It was a snug, informal room, the kind of room one never wanted to leave.

Evelina was just glancing at her watch when she heard the door open and close in the hall. She got up swiftly and hurried out. There, sturdy and squat like a panzer tank, was her formidable ninety-three-year-old aunt, Madolina Forte. Beside her, helping her out of her coat, was the family friend everyone knew as Uncle Topino, which means 'little mouse' in Italian, although he was no relation of Evelina's or Franklin's and did not resemble by any stretch of the imagination a mouse. He was an old friend who had been adopted by the van der Veldens when the children were small and was so much a part of the family that no one ever asked how it had come about. They just accepted that it was so.

'Welcome!' Evelina exclaimed, taking her aunt's coat from Topino and giving the old lady a kiss.

'I can feel the damp in my bones,' Madolina complained. Unlike her niece, Madolina had not wanted to hold on to her past and had shed all but the occasional trace of Italy in her enunciation. 'It's lovely and warm in here, thank the Lord. I'll go right on in and settle myself down by the fire.' She strode with determination towards the drawing room, leaning heavily on her walking stick.

Evelina smiled at Topino. Her gaze softened as she took him in: the fluffy white hair, the high forehead, the large nose and sensual mouth. And his expressive grey eyes twinkled back at her through his round spectacles. 'You look good, Eva,' he said in Italian. Then he put his hand around her waist and planted a kiss on her cheek.

'You look good too, old friend,' she replied.

'Another year.' He shook his head and sighed heavily. 'Who'd have thought it?'

'Everything comes to pass. You taught me that.'

'The good and the bad. Life is a series of cycles and we are but mice on the wheel. I like this cycle the best. It has an air of permanence. How's the turkey?'

'Fat and juicy.' She laughed and helped him out of his coat.

It was the same coat he had worn to the first Thanksgiving dinner they'd invited him to seventeen years before. Topino did not like to waste money on things he did not need.

'And pumpkin pie?'

'Your favourite.'

He nodded and his full lips extended into a smile, curling up at the ends and endowing his face with a comical charm. 'Every year I leave with a belly full of pumpkin pie, then I spend the following fifty-two weeks dreaming of the next slice. Tonight, I'll celebrate life and pumpkin pie.'

Evelina accompanied him into the drawing room. As soon as Topino entered, the place erupted into cries of delight. Ava-Maria embraced him passionately and kissed his bristly cheeks, and the boys patted him heartily on the back. Franklin shook his hand and introduced him to Jennifer, who smiled shyly for even she had heard much of the celebrated Uncle Topino. Lisa greeted him with a kiss and laughed as he berated her for not being a good wife, for Aldo was looking tired and thin. 'The man needs to eat,' said Topino. 'What are you cooking him? Vegetable broth?'

'I eat well,' said Aldo in Lisa's defence.

'You don't look like you eat at all. Tonight, we celebrate life and good food. Mostly good food.' He shrugged. 'Life is its own celebration.'

Madolina waved her bejewelled hand from the club fender where she was warming her back against the fire. 'Put him down, you all. You're going to crush him half to death!' She watched with a ferocious gaze as they dutifully took their seats again. No one challenged Aunt Madolina, except Topino.

'I like being crushed half to death,' he replied. 'The half that survives makes me feel alive.'

'Come sit here, Topino,' insisted Madolina, patting the space beside her. 'I can feel the ache in my bones as they thaw.'

Topino sat next to her with a groan. He was only sixty-five but sometimes his bones felt like those of an arthritic old man.

Franklin handed him a glass of red wine. 'You ready for our game of chess?' he asked.

Topino grinned. 'You know me, I'll never turn down the opportunity to lose.'

Franklin laughed, for it was well known that Topino was a fiendish chess player. 'Good, that makes two of us.' Topino laughed with him. The idea of two players fighting to lose appealed to his quirky sense of humour.

'Tell me, Madolina, how have you been?' Topino asked and he listened with concentration as she told him in great detail about her hip which was inoperable on account of her great age.

'When you're as old as I am, Topino, there's no point going under the knife unless you're prepared not to come back.'

'Sure, it's a gamble,' he agreed with a shrug. 'But if you ask me, you have the constitution of a tortoise. In ten years' time you'll still be here talking about your hip.'

Madolina loved Topino's humour. 'And you, Topino?'

'I have the constitution of a cockroach. I'm pretty much indestructible.' He took a sip of wine then looked at her with a gleam in his eye. 'When the good Lord finally takes me it'll only be because I've gone begging for it.'

Ava-Maria interrupted from the sofa. 'Are you two talking about death?' she asked. 'Really, it's Thanksgiving!'

'Entertain us then,' said Topino, leaning forward, elbows on his knees, and looking at her expectantly. 'What have you been up to since I last saw you? How's college? Giving the boys a run for their money, no doubt.' And Topino did what he did best; he listened. And Ava-Maria did what *she* did best; she talked about herself. Madolina enjoyed the warmth of the fire on her back and watched Evelina who was like a daughter to her, for her niece had left Italy at the age of twenty-eight and come to live with her in Brooklyn. Madolina was proud of the woman she had become.

When Evelina announced that dinner was ready, Topino gave Madolina his arm and the two of them led the group into the dining room. Madolina caught her breath at the sight of the candles in their pumpkin holders and the flowers. 'It's gorgeous!' she exclaimed. 'That girl has style. She always had. Unique to her, it must be said, but always remarkable.' Topino pulled out the chair at the foot of the table and she sat down, handing him her walking stick to stand against the wall. 'Her mother has style. Artemisia keeps a beautiful but dilapidated house. Tani hated spending money even more than he hates society,' she added of her brother, Gaetano. 'Villa L'Ambrosiana has immense charm. That's where Evelina gets it from – her mother and their magnificent house.'

Topino was given the middle chair down the side of the table because everyone wanted to talk to him. Franklin was at the head. Evelina sat on her aunt's left. Evelina's uncle Peppino, Madolina's husband who had died six years before, had always sat next to Evelina. She noticed her aunt's gaze rest on that chair and the sudden sombre expression that darkened her face, and knew that she was thinking of him. Thanksgiving was a time for gratitude, but gratitude never came empty-handed, it always turned up with its friend, loss.

Since becoming a widow Madolina had only worn black, and while she gave thanks for Peppino's life, she could not help but mourn his passing.

Dinner was noisy. Ava-Maria's voice was the loudest as she regaled everyone with anecdotes. Topino teased her, putting her down in his usual dry and affectionate way, only for her to rebound with witty come-backs, creating a lively repartee that entertained the whole table. Dan, who worked for an advertising company in Manhattan and had plenty of anecdotes of his own, joined in and was almost as noisy as his sister, while Aldo and Franklin tried to have a quiet chat between themselves about books, for Aldo worked in publishing. Madolina complained that she couldn't follow the conversations. 'There needs to be a volume control in this house,' she said, waving her hand and instructing every-one to quieten down. Evelina looked around at the faces in amusement. It was the same every year. It was wonderful.

At last the pumpkin pie was brought to the table. Evelina had cut it into slices. She shovelled one onto a spatula and put it on Topino's plate. 'Make it last,' she said softly.

'If I could make it last a year, I would,' he replied, picking up his fork. 'But I'm too much of a glutton.'

A silence fell over the room as they tucked into the pie. Ava-Maria broke it. 'When the whole table goes quiet it means there's an angel passing overhead,' she said, lifting her eyes to the ceiling.

'How could an angel be passing overhead when she's sitting opposite me?' said Topino.

'Aw, Topino, that's so sweet!' Ava-Maria cooed.

'Angels don't speak so loud,' said Aunt Madolina.

'This one does,' Ava-Maria retaliated without lowering her voice.

'Is there more?' asked Dan.

'You finished already?' said Evelina in surprise.

'It's really good!' he exclaimed, licking his fork.

'Yes, there's more. I know who I'm catering for. A swarm of locusts!' Evelina got up with a laugh. It pleased her that they enjoyed her cooking. She never thought she'd be able to say that.

Topino sat back in his chair and patted his belly. It was getting a little round these days. 'No one makes a pumpkin pie like your mamma,' he said, smiling at Evelina.

'Would *you* like another slice?' she asked.

'You have to ask?' he replied.

'To be polite. Of course, I *know*.'

'Then I'll say yes, to be polite. Yes, please, signora, I'd love another slice.'

When there remained not a trace of pie on their plates, Franklin tapped his knife against a glass and stood up. To Madolina's relief, the room fell silent again. Topino wiped his mouth with a napkin and drained his wine glass. Evelina put her hands in her lap and watched her husband with pride. 'Tonight is a special night for Americans everywhere, but it's also a special night for those of us who have come from afar and made America our home. We celebrate together as one colourful nation built by immigrants and sustained on mutual respect and acceptance. As you all know, my ancestors came to America from Holland in the eighteenth century, Aunt Madolina and Uncle Peppino, may he rest in peace, came from Italy at the turn of the century as a newly married couple, Evelina as a 28-eight-year-old leaving Italy at the end of the war, and Uncle Topino in the 1950s.'

Evelina caught Topino's eye and her smile turned tender.

He returned her gaze with equal tenderness, and a little sadness, which, on rare occasions, leaked through the cracks in his demeanour when he let down his guard. Franklin continued to give thanks for friends, family, good fortune and prosperity. 'We are all lucky,' he said. 'And luck is a gift to be thankful for. I raise my glass to luck and to all of you, who I'm so lucky to have as my family and friends.' They stood and raised their glasses, and wished each other a Happy Thanksgiving.

After dinner Franklin and Topino sat at the card table and played chess. The two men were seasoned players and the game went on long after Madolina had been escorted home by Aldo and Lisa, and Dan and Jennifer had said goodnight and left too. Ava-Maria went upstairs to bed after helping her mother clear away the dinner. Evelina collected the rosemary sprigs and put them in a bowl by the sink. Then she went into the drawing room to see how the chess game was going.

'It appears neither of you are so keen to lose, after all,' she said, putting her hand on Franklin's shoulder. 'I think you should call it a night.'

'You're right,' Franklin replied, straightening his back and taking a deep breath. 'We can leave the board as it is and resume tomorrow.'

'You want me to come tomorrow?' Topino asked. 'Aren't you already tired of my face?'

Evelina laughed. 'Come for lunch. Ava-Maria is home for a few days and I know she'd like to see more of you, as would we.'

'Well, I can't say I'm not tempted by your cooking, Evelina, or your company.'

'Good, that's settled.' She went into the kitchen and retrieved a parcel, wrapped in brown paper and tied up with string. 'I'll see you out,' she said on her return.

Topino bade goodnight to Franklin and followed Evelina into the hall. He looked crumpled now and a little weary. The wine had made him sleepy and his eyes were heavy with emotion. She held out his coat and he slipped his arms down the sleeves and shrugged it on.

'You're a good hostess, Eva,' he said, once again falling into Italian as he was prone to do when the two of them were alone.

She smiled softly and held out the parcel.

'What's this?' he asked.

'Pumpkin pie,' she replied, her smile broadening. 'I made one especially for you.'

His eyes shone. 'You think of everything,' he said. He bent down and planted a kiss on her cheek. 'See you tomorrow.'

She nodded.

He opened the door and stepped out into the night.

Evelina returned to the kitchen to turn off the lights. She noticed the rosemary by the sink. Her heart weighted with gratitude, both for her good fortune and her bad, she rubbed a sprig between her finger and thumb. Then she pressed it to her nose and closed her eyes.

CHAPTER ONE

Northern Italy, July 1934

Evelina inhaled deeply. The scent of rosemary filled her
nostrils. How she loved it, this shrub with evergreen needles
and purple flowers that grew in every border of the villa.
The estate was bursting with flowers; there were vast terracotta pots of bougainvillea, heaps of thyme, an abundance
of oleander, and jasmine that covered the limestone walls of
the villa, exhaling its sweet perfume into the rooms. And yet
the smell that defined the place was rosemary. It was woody,
aromatic and sensual. To seventeen-year-old Evelina, it was
the smell of home.

With the sprig still held between her finger and thumb,
Evelina walked swiftly through the garden towards the
sixteenth-century villa that stood majestic but weary, in
need of repairs for which Evelina's father did not have the
means, or, it seemed, the inclination, to carry out. Gaetano
Pierangelini, known as Tani, was a hermetic writer of literary fiction, more interested in the written word than in the
upkeep of his home. He spent most of the day in his study
in a three-piece suit, chain-smoking cigarettes and typing
novels that took years to write. He earned little money but

won literary prizes and high esteem, which he valued more dearly than material things.

Tani's wife, Artemisia, on the other hand, was twelve years his junior and accumulated stuff with the tenacity of a magpie. Beautiful and bohemian, she craved those qualities in the world she inhabited, as if the villa was an extension of herself. Far from being defeated by the shabby state of the place, she saw the embellishment of it as a great challenge, knowing that there wasn't a woman alive who could do it like she did, with such panache and flair. She covered the cracks in the walls with vast tapestries, spread Persian rugs over the worn flagstone floors and masked all manner of imperfections behind enormous potted plants, extravagant flower displays, marble busts, and paintings which she had collected over the years, having a good eye for a bargain and an even better eye for quality. Inexpensive works of art had, on occasion, turned out to be works of great masters or, at least, semi-great. It was those skilful purchases that had kept Villa L'Ambrosiana and its inhabitants afloat, and enabled Tani to indulge his passion without worrying about money.

Artemisia was fortunate, for the bones of the villa, being so old, had an air of faded grandeur that was enchanting. They needed no interference. Frescoes depicting allegorical and pastoral scenes had been damaged by damp and required restoration, but they were, undeniably, exquisite. The rooms were harmoniously proportioned with tall ceilings and large windows, connected to each other by double doors framed with pink marble and *trompe l'oeil*. The place possessed a languid charm, a quiet watchfulness, as if the people moving through it were not really part of it but brief fragments of time in which their small dramas, so vital in the moment, were, in the end, reduced to dust. Generations came and went, and those walls remained as witnesses to life's transience and fragility and perhaps, also, to its apparent lack of purpose, for what did walls know of the human heart and the enduring nature of love?

Evelina skipped lightly up the steps that led from the garden to a wide terrace at the back of the villa. She slipped between giant terracotta pots of lemon trees and through wide open French doors into the cool interior of the house. She could hear her elder sister's piano playing from the music salon a few rooms away and her younger brother Bruno's squeals as he frolicked with the dog in his bedroom upstairs, while his nanny Romina sang to herself on the landing, sorting out the laundry. Deep in the coolest part of the villa her grandmother, Nonna Pierangelini, and Nonna's spinster sister, Costanza, passed the indolent hours of the hot summer's afternoon in slumber, having enjoyed a long lunch, a game of cards and endless cigarettes. Evelina continued on through the villa to the front and then stood on the step and waited. Before her an ornamental pond gleamed in the sunshine beneath a fountain of Venus that hadn't spouted water in years and was covered in moss. Two marble statues of naked men in contrapposto stood on pedestals either side of the driveway among pots of purple bougainvillea and yew hedges clipped into uneven balls.

At last she saw, at the end of the avenue of cypress trees, the sight of Signora Ferraro's horse and trap approaching slowly across the shadows. Excited, she hopped from foot to foot and then, when she could clearly see her art teacher's face, she waved energetically. Fioruccia Ferraro waved back and smiled, the ribbons on her hat floating behind her on the breeze. Evelina looked forward to her painting lessons more than anything else. Not only because she loved painting, but also because she loved Signora Ferraro. The young woman was warm, funny and affectionate, and Evelina, who was mostly ignored by her narcissistic mother, cherished the time they spent together.

The gardens of Villa L'Ambrosiana were full of things to draw. There were plants and trees, of course, but also busts and statues, stone archways, mossy grottos, fountains and arcades and Nonna Pierangelini's ornate glasshouse full of tomatoes. Hidden among the pines was a neo-Gothic chapel where the family had once worshipped in private, but which was now abandoned and forlorn, left mostly to the elements and Bruno and his friends' games. It was a wonderful place for playing hide and seek and for holding secret meetings.

The two young women placed their stools in front of a statue of a chubby harp-playing cherub and began to draw. It was quiet in that far corner of the garden, embraced by ancient trees and watched over by statues whose names were long forgotten. It was hot even in the shade and Signora Ferraro had taken off her hat and let her long brown hair fall down her back in curls. She wore a white dress with a faded pink sash at her hips and had put aside the tasselled pink-and-yellow floral shawl that she had draped over her shoulders. She had dark, almond-shaped eyes framed by thick black lashes and a full, voluptuous mouth. Her cheekbones were high and pronounced, her skin the colour of milky coffee. Besides her gentle beauty she was a talented artist. Evelina thought her the most inspiring person she had ever met and wanted to be just like her.

The two of them chatted while they drew and every now and then Signora Ferraro would look at Evelina's sketchpad and tell her how she might improve her drawing, but she always praised her for she knew first-hand how sensitive artists were about their work and how important it was to receive encouragement. Evelina was a good pupil and did everything Signora Ferraro told her to do.

'Mamma has found a husband for Benedetta,' Evelina told her.

'How old is Benedetta now?' Signora Ferraro asked, lifting her charcoal off the paper for a moment and picturing Evelina's sister who had always seemed like a woman even when she'd been a child.

'Twenty.'

'What's he like?' Signora Ferraro smiled with enthusiasm. 'Does Benedetta like him?'

'She hasn't met him yet.'

Signora Ferraro frowned. Evelina seemed not to think that this type of courtship was out of the ordinary. 'She's never met him?' Signora Ferraro repeated, puzzled.

'He's coming with his mother tomorrow, for lunch. As far as I know he works for his father in a bank in Milan.'

'Oh.' Signora Ferraro couldn't keep her dismay out of her voice.

Evelina narrowed her eyes. 'Don't you like bankers?'

'I'm sure he's nice.'

'He's rich,' said Evelina with emphasis. 'Papa knows his father because they studied together in Paris. Mamma says they're a good family and an old one too. Old seems to matter very much. At least it does to Papa. The rich part matters more to Mamma.'

'Are they coming from Milan?'

'Yes.'

'Is Benedetta excited?'

'I think she's nervous. She's been playing the piano all day. She always plays Tchaikovsky when she's nervous.'

'And if she doesn't like him?'

Evelina shrugged. 'She *has* to like him. Papa wants them to marry and so they shall.'

'Your father is very old-fashioned.'

'Old-fashioned and remote. He lives for his work. I think we children and Mamma are simply accessories to his genius. He'd be perfectly content without us.'

'I'm sure that's not true.'

'Of course it is.' Evelina flicked away a fly with her free hand. 'Benedetta and I are groomed for marriage and Bruno will one day run the estate. Meanwhile, Papa will write masterpieces and receive accolades and this old house will slowly disintegrate around him. As for Mamma, she will grow old among her flowers and plants and paintings, because those are the things she cares about the most.'

'And you, Evelina?'

'I'm not going to marry.'

Signora Ferraro smiled. 'It's nice when you love the man you marry.'

'Do you love Signor Ferraro?'

'More than anyone in the world.'

'When you have children, will you love them more?'

'I don't know. I think I'll love Matteo and our children equally.'

This satisfied Evelina who went back to her drawing. 'When you have children, will you still teach me to paint?'

'Of course, silly,' Signora Ferraro replied with a chuckle. 'You know you're my favourite pupil.'

The oldest of Signora Ferraro's four brothers owned a fabric shop in Vercellino and his wife was a dressmaker. Much of Artemisia Pierangelini's wardrobe came from there. As

Benedetta was now twenty and of marriageable age, she was allowed to have beautiful things made too, but Evelina was not permitted that privilege. She had to wear her sister's old dresses, which to Evelina looked shabby and inelegant. When the conversation turned once again to the lunch the following day, Signora Ferraro asked Evelina what she was going to wear. 'One of my sister's horrible old frocks, I should imagine,' she complained. 'But what do I care? I'm not the one who has to please.'

'Would you like to borrow something of mine?' Signora Ferraro asked. 'My sister-in-law makes me dresses for free and my brother gives me fabric he can no longer sell. I have just the dress that would suit you. Do you want to come and try it on? We can have some lemonade in my house for a change and I can show you my paintings.'

Evelina leapt to her feet. 'Let's go now,' she suggested. 'I'm bored of drawing this silly cherub. I'd love to borrow a dress and I'd love to see your paintings. I bet they're really good. Can we?'

'I don't see why not. You've done a lovely job of the cherub and, if you ask me, he's looking a little tired of being drawn. Imagine, he's had to hold that pose all afternoon.'

Evelina laughed and the two women packed up their things and walked purposefully through the garden to Signora Ferraro's horse and trap. The chestnut mare was standing in the shade of a eucalyptus tree, beside a bucket of water which one of the estate workers had provided. Signora Ferraro untied her and gave her neck an affectionate pat. Evelina wasted no time and climbed into the trap. Signora Ferraro joined her, placing her artist's bag on the seat beside her. Off they went at a trot, riding over the long shadows the cypress trees threw across the track.

It was a twenty-minute ride into Vercellino. The sky was a cobalt blue, the flat water-logged rice fields an almost phosphorescent green and on the far horizon snow-capped mountains shimmered in the mists, resembling low-hanging clouds of brilliant white. Evelina's spirits rose on the beauty of it all: the sight of small birds fluttering in the bushes, the scents of pine and wild herbs that hung in the air, the soft caress of the breeze and the warmth of the sun on her face; the rhythmic sound of the horse's hooves and the rattle of the wheels as they clattered along the dirt track towards the red-tiled roofs and church towers that gradually came into view. Evelina didn't venture into Vercellino very often, only for Mass on Sundays and the occasional outing with her mother when she wasn't being tutored. This was, indeed, exciting.

The medieval town was built on the plain of the River Po, between Milan and Turin. It was one of the oldest urban sites in northern Italy, founded, according to historians and archaeologists, in the year 600 BC. It boasted a few Roman relics: an amphitheatre, a hippodrome, and the twelfth-century Basilica di Santa Maria del Fiore, which was one of the best-preserved Romanesque monuments in Italy. However, Evelina was less interested in relics and more curious to see the people. Her life at the villa was secluded and quiet and she longed to wander the streets like the locals did, browsing in shop windows, buying food at the market stalls, eating cakes in the cafés and promenading in the town square among the pigeons. This was life, this was freedom, and her spirit yearned for it.

Vercellino was bustling with people going about their business: men pulling carts of goods, women with baskets of fruit and vegetables, small children playing, stray dogs scrounging for scraps, the odd automobile rattling noisily down the cobbled streets. Evelina was thrilled, sitting high in the trap from where she could take it all in.

Signora Ferraro pulled up outside her brother's shop which was named after him, Ercole Zanotti. 'Come, I need to pick up some fabric.'

Evelina jumped down. She had been to Ercole Zanotti once or twice with her mother, and it was a real treat. The endless rolls of beautiful silks and linens, the variety of colours, the ribbons and buttons, lace and braid, tassels, trims and fringes, and the sparkly sequins that caught the light and shone like cut glass. To Evelina it was like Aladdin's cave.

She followed her art teacher into the shop. A bell tinkled as the door opened and Signor Zanotti greeted his sister from behind the counter. 'Fioruccia!' he exclaimed, holding up his hands as if to embrace her. Signor Zanotti had thick greying hair, a woolly beard and moustache, and a pair of round spectacles perched on the bridge of his large nose, beneath fluffy eyebrows that moved animatedly when he talked. He was dapper in a three-piece grey suit, with a gold pocket watch at his belly and a gold signet ring on the little finger of his left hand, next to a plain gold wedding band. 'And you must be Signorina Pierangelini,' he said to Evelina. He smiled and his face was kind like his sister's and lively, for Signor Zanotti was a man who loved people. 'You've grown into a fine young woman,' he said. 'The last time I saw you, you were but a girl.' He put his hand in the air to show her how small she had been. Evelina laughed, delighted that he referred to her as a young woman. She wished her mother would allow her to dress like one, instead of making her don her sister's girlhood dresses. 'Ezra,' he called. 'Bring Aunt Fioruccia's fabric, will you? It's on my desk. Excuse me,' he said, turning to serve a pair of elderly ladies whose hats were adorned with so many feathers, Evelina thought they resembled exotic hens.

She ran her hand over a roll of pink ribbon. It was the most beautiful pink, like a peony, and she imagined what it would look like in her hair, or fastened to a hat. A moment later Ezra appeared from the back, holding a package wrapped in brown paper. Evelina lifted her gaze from the ribbon and glanced at him. They locked eyes for a moment and something grabbed her stomach on the inside and squeezed it hard. Then Evelina felt her cheeks burn in a deep and embarrassing blush. Horrified by this unexpected reaction she swiftly turned her attention back to the ribbon, but she no longer saw it. She didn't notice either that her fingers were trembling as they settled unsteadily onto the fabric. She was, however, acutely aware of the man with curly brown hair and soft grey eyes who was now talking to Signora Ferraro. He handed her the package and stole another peek at Evelina.

'Thank you, Ezra,' said Signora Ferraro. 'Have you met Signorina Pierangelini?'

'No, I have not had the pleasure,' he replied, those grey eyes settling on Evelina again and causing her blush to deepen.

Evelina straightened her shoulders and tried very hard to act nonchalant. She smiled politely, feigning uninterest, although it was almost impossible to hold the façade.

'Ezra Zanotti is my nephew,' Signora Ferraro told Evelina. 'He's now working here for his father.'

'It's very nice to meet you,' said Ezra, bowing slightly. He smiled shyly and Evelina felt the grip on her stomach grow tighter.

'It's nice to meet you, too,' she replied and lowered her eyes. Then her mind went blank. She couldn't think of a single thing to say. She who was never lost for words was most dreadfully lost now. She took a breath, embarrassed by her blazing cheeks.

'Signorina Pierangelini is my pupil,' said Signora Ferraro helpfully.

'Ah,' he murmured. 'How fortunate for you both.'

'She'll make a fine artist one day.'

Evelina knew she had to say something or she'd appear foolish and immature. How she wished she had worn a prettier dress. 'I like our lessons very much,' she said at last and her voice sounded alien and far away.

'So do I,' agreed Signora Ferraro. 'They're the highlights of my week.'

The two young people looked anywhere but at each other and Signora Ferraro laughed. 'Well, we'd better get going. Thank you for the fabric, Ezra. I shall make something very fine out of it.'

Evelina burst out of the shop and took a gulp of air. Her legs were trembling so much she could barely climb into the trap. She was grateful for the breeze that cooled her flushed face and brought her back to her senses. She put her fingers to her lips and felt a sudden swelling in her chest as if it had just filled with bubbles. Signora Ferraro took the seat beside her and shook the reins. The horse plodded on down the street.

'Isn't he charming, my nephew?' said Signora Ferraro casually, as if she hadn't noticed the blushes on Evelina's cheeks. 'You know, out of all my nephews and nieces, and I have many, he's my favourite. He's sensitive and kind, like my brother. Most men who are as handsome as he is are pleased with themselves, but not Ezra. He's gentle and thoughtful. You know he plays the violin and the piano too? I think he could play anything if he wanted to. He's such a talented musician. He even writes his own music. I don't understand a score, but he can read music like I read a book.'

'He'd get on very well with Benedetta,' Evelina replied, hoping to deflect the conversation from herself, afraid that her teacher might discover how much their meeting had affected her. 'How old is he?' she asked.

'Twenty,' Signora Ferraro replied.

Evelina went quiet then and remained thoughtful until they turned into Via Montebello and entered a building through a wide arch, pulling up in a courtyard where pink bougainvillea spilled from pots and geraniums grew abundantly in boxes at every window.

The Ferraros' apartment was small and intimate, with a balcony built over the courtyard and windows looking out onto Via Montebello. Signora Ferraro showed Evelina into her studio where an easel and stool were set up in the part of the room that got the most natural light. There were canvases stacked up against the walls, pots of pigments and paints and jars full of brushes lined up on shelves. Evelina was enchanted and immediately started looking through her teacher's work. There were sketches in charcoal, of faces and hands, and paintings of landscapes and flowers. One or two were surprisingly different and Evelina was mesmerized by the novelty of them. 'Influenced by Picasso,' she said, holding one up.

'It's important to learn from the greats,' said Signora Ferraro with a smile.

After they had drunk lemonade and eaten pastries, Signora Ferraro went into her bedroom and returned holding up a pretty ivory-coloured dress imprinted with small yellow flowers. Evelina could tell at once that the style was sophisticated but not too grown-up and she couldn't wait to try it on.

'You can change in my bedroom,' Signora Ferraro said and Evelina hurried inside and disappeared behind the screen.

A moment later she stood in front of the long mirror and admired her reflection. The bias-cut dress clung to the curves of her body as if it had been made for her, then floated out over her knees, finishing mid-calf. She had never worn a dress like this and was delighted at the way it made her look. She felt like a woman. No longer the child, the younger sister, the *bambina*. She wished she could go back to Ercole Zanotti and meet Ezra again for the first time. She wished he could have seen her like this and not in her sister's shapeless frock. She turned round and admired the way the dress scooped elegantly in the small of her back. She'd never considered whether she was pretty or plain. In fact, Benedetta had always been feted as the pretty daughter. But now Evelina realized that she, too, was surprisingly easy on the eye.

She returned to the sitting room to show Signora Ferraro. 'I love it!' Evelina exclaimed, doing a twirl. 'Do you think it suits me?' She knew very well that it did.

Signora Ferraro gasped in delight. 'It's darling,' she cried, tweaking it here and there, pulling the short sleeves and picking a piece of lint off the shoulder. 'You must borrow it. It's like it was made for you.'

'I'll never take it off.'

Signora Ferraro laughed. 'I'm sure you won't want to sleep in it.'

'I shall. It's like a second skin.' Evelina did another twirl.

'I hope you don't outshine your sister tomorrow. I don't think your mother would thank me if this banker decided he'd rather marry *you* instead.'

'That would never happen,' said Evelina. 'Benedetta has

always been the beauty in the family and besides, I wouldn't have him. I don't want to marry a banker.'

Signora Ferraro grinned knowingly and raised her eyebrows. 'I thought you didn't want to marry at all.'

Ezra Zanotti's face surfaced in Evelina's mind and she felt a blush flowering on her cheeks again. She turned and went back into the bedroom. 'I'm too young to think of marriage,' she said, unbuttoning the dress behind the screen. 'Besides, I haven't yet met a man I'd like to marry.' But she knew, as did Signora Ferraro, that this was no longer true.

That night when she went to bed Evelina stood by the window and gazed out onto the garden, lit up in the silvery light of the full moon. The trees and shrubs were still. There was no breeze and the smell of jasmine lingered in the balmy air, for the summer nights were hot in Piedmont. Stars twinkled in a sky as black as ink, and for the first time in her life her heart ached with a longing that was at once unfamiliar and confusing. The gardens were so beautiful, the heavens so mysterious, the moon so romantic, that she was overcome with melancholy, inspired by the unconscious yearning to share this beauty with someone she loved. Evelina knew nothing of romantic love and yet her heart recognized it like an old friend, as if it had always known it.

She put her hand against the linen curtain and rested her head there. When would she see Ezra again? she wondered.

CHAPTER TWO

The following morning Evelina was awoken by her sister playing Tchaikovsky on the piano, loudly. She must be nervous, she thought as she dressed in her usual attire and went downstairs. Her mother was in the hall, supervising a couple of estate workers who were taking down a painting of a landscape and replacing it with something modern her mother had bought at auction in Milan. Evelina was used to her mother's constant moving of artworks, making way for something she had just purchased or simply switching pictures around so she didn't get bored of seeing them in the same place. It was as much a compulsion as a hobby. Today, however, it had everything to do with Francesco Rossi and his mother, Emilia, who were coming for lunch to meet Benedetta. Artemisia was determined that the villa should reflect both her nobility and her good taste, and by extension, Benedetta's.

Artemisia stood at the bottom of the stairs giving orders as the two young men sweated in the heat. She was dressed in her usual bohemian style, thrown together with more thought than she liked people to think. A flowing silk dressing gown edged with black tassels worn over a peasant dress, a matching silk scarf wound around her head and knotted at the side so that the two ends trailed raffishly over one shoulder, accessorised by long rows of pearls. Artemisia did not care for convention. She wore what she felt best expressed her unique and flamboyant character and was confident enough to carry it off. In her early forties, she was handsome. Indeed, time had been kind and overlooked her face as it etched its unforgiving passage over the faces of her friends. With dark brown hair cut short and teased into waves, a strong, aquiline nose, vivacious hazel eyes and a determined chin, Artemisia was a formidable woman, unafraid of voicing opinions which were often quite radical; she liked to shock. Most of all, she liked attention. Today was about Benedetta, but by the extravagant vases of flowers, the moving of paintings and furniture and the smells coming from the kitchen where Angelina, the cook, was baking bread and making gnocchi for lunch, one might have been forgiven for thinking it was all about Artemisia.

Evelina knew not to get under her mother's feet. Artemisia was not in the slightest maternal. At least, she was not particularly interested in her daughters. She was, however, interested in her son. Bruno was the longed-for heir. After two girls, Tani and Artemisia had been delighted to be blessed at last with a boy and they both indulged him blindly. Tani Pierangelini did not have a vast fortune for his son to inherit, but he had an old name and an old estate, albeit rundown, and there was a certain cachet to that.

Artemisia was too busy to acknowledge her daughter, so Evelina went to interrupt her sister, whose frantic pounding on the keys was causing the house to shake. She strode through the rooms until she reached the music salon, then stood in the doorway with her hands over her ears. Her sister raised her eyes and reluctantly lifted her fingers off the keys.

The room fell into a downy silence. Evelina dropped her hands. 'Benedetta, come and keep me company while I have breakfast,' she said. 'If you play like that all morning we won't have a house left to impress them with and I will have lost my hearing.'

Benedetta sighed and put down the piano lid. Her face was set in a sulky pout, which did not render it any less pretty; in fact, it might even have enhanced it for it made her china-blue eyes shine even brighter. Benedetta was a beauty. With fine features, high cheekbones, long wavy hair the colour of hay and full lips as soft as pillows, her good looks were striking. 'I wish they weren't coming now,' she said, getting up from the stool and following her sister out onto the terrace where a long table was set up beneath a parasol and laid for four. Nonna Pierangelini and Costanza were yet to appear. The two girls sat down and Maria, the young woman who helped Angelina in the kitchen, emerged out of the shadows to serve them breakfast. 'What if he's ugly?' Benedetta asked, flicking her napkin over her lap.

'Mamma says he's handsome,' Evelina replied, thankful that it was not *she* who was having to meet her prospective husband.

'What if she's lying?'

'She doesn't lie. She's brutally honest. Of course, she might not have the same taste as you. What is handsome to her might be unappealing in your eyes. But she wouldn't lie and she wouldn't suggest you marry someone who was unappealing. Besides, you can always refuse.'

'And then what? I don't want to be left without a husband.'

'There are plenty of fish in the sea, Benedetta.'

'Perhaps, but few *suitable* fish. Francesco Rossi is a whale in a sea of minnows.'

Evelina took a sip of orange juice. 'Mamma considers herself a supporter of a woman's right to define herself, to be independent and heard. It seems out of character that she should go along with Papa's idea of an arranged marriage. You'd have thought she'd consider it old-fashioned.'

'It *is* old-fashioned,' Benedetta agreed. 'But what Mamma says and what she does are two very different things. Most of the time she just says things for effect. One stern look from Father and she's like a dog scurrying back into its basket. She's a terrible old fraud. You know that.' Benedetta sighed and popped a piece of bread and cheese into her mouth. 'Anyway, she says it's not an arranged marriage, it's simply an introduction. How else am I to meet suitable young men sitting here in splendid isolation? We weren't even allowed to attend school, but had to be tutored here in this old, ramshackle house.'

'I don't think it's because they don't want us to meet the wrong people, they just can't be bothered to give us a social life. They're too busy in their own worlds, thinking about themselves.'

'Well, I can't wait to leave it. It's stifling.'

Evelina's eyes brightened. 'Why don't we go into town, just the two of us?'

'Mother would never allow that.'

'We haven't asked her. If she's so forward-thinking she should allow us some freedoms. If you get engaged to Francesco, surely she'll permit us.'

Benedetta thought for a moment. 'Let's see. It can't harm to ask, can it? And it would be nice to leave the estate other than to attend Mass on a Sunday morning.'

At that moment Bruno skipped onto the terrace with his nanny Romina and his little dog, Dante. The two girls adored their brother, who had just celebrated his eighth birthday, and called him over to join them. Benedetta lifted him onto her knee and covered his face in kisses. Bruno wiped them off with his sleeve then reached for a grape. Romina sank into a chair and cooled herself with the fan she tucked into the belt of her uniform. 'It's too hot,' she complained. 'I feel like an ice cream melting in the sun.'

Bruno giggled. 'If you were an ice cream, Romi, what flavour would you be?'

'Vanilla,' she replied.

Evelina laughed. 'That's boring, Romi. Surely, you'd like to be something more exotic, like peach or lemon, or mint?'

'I'm vanilla,' she insisted with a grin. 'I've always been vanilla. Plain but dependable. I'm happy with that.'

'What would you be, Bruno?' Benedetta asked.

'Chocolate,' said Bruno without hesitation. 'My favourite.'

'Well, you've got chocolate-coloured hair and milk-chocolate skin. Luckily, you're not made of chocolate or we'd have eaten you by now,' said Evelina.

'What would you be, Eva?' Benedetta asked. 'I'd be strawberry.'

'Everyone's favourite!' Romina exclaimed in delight, for it was true, everyone loved Benedetta.

Evelina narrowed her eyes. 'Pistachio,' she replied with a note of defiance. 'Because I don't care that I don't appeal to everyone and I'd like to be a little different.'

Benedetta rolled her eyes. 'Typical second-sister syndrome.'

'Not at all,' Evelina retorted. 'I'm not like Mother who has to be different for its own sake. I just want to be uniquely me.'

'And you are, Evelina,' said Romina diplomatically. 'You'll plough your own furrow, *you* will.'

Bruno scrunched up his nose. 'I don't like pistachio ice cream,' he said.

'But you like *me*?'

He nodded. 'You're not really an ice cream.'

Nonna Pierangelini and Costanza emerged out of the shadows, complaining. It was too hot, or too humid, always too something. Nonna Pierangelini always wore black, in mourning for her late husband and for two of her children who had died in infancy, but Costanza, who had never married, wore bright colours and elaborate jewellery as if triumphant that she had escaped marriage and childbirth and the torments of both. When they saw Bruno, their faces transformed and they forgot about their grumbles. Nonna Pierangelini pinched his cheek and showered him with compliments while her sister ruffled his hair with her bony, bejewelled hand and told him that he was even more handsome than he had been the day before. She then rubbed her fingers and thumbs in the air and murmured 'Tuf tuf tuf' to ward off the fates that might be tempted to destroy such good fortune.

They sat down and Maria brought them fresh coffee and fruit, and pastries, which Nonna Pierangelini devoured with relish. Costanza, who was as thin as a crane, sipped her coffee and ate nothing. She hadn't maintained her figure all these years by eating pastries. It did give her pleasure, however, to watch her sister eating. The more she ate the better Costanza felt about herself and her restraint. Nonna Pierangelini had never worried about her figure and wasn't about to start now, at seventy-four. She buttered a brioche and took a large bite.

Bruno ran off into the garden with Dante, followed by

Romina. Nonna Pierangelini settled her sharp gaze onto Benedetta. 'Today is an important day,' she said. 'Remember to smile. Men like women who smile.'

'I will, Nonna,' said Benedetta, who'd been taught that it was prudent to agree with old people.

'And leave your hair down. Men like women with beautiful hair,' she added.

'I think you're lovely just the way you are,' said Costanza. 'You either have beauty or you don't, and you do, so it doesn't matter how you do your hair. But Ilaria is right when she tells you to smile. Men are easily seduced by a smile.' She grinned over her coffee cup, a grin both mischievous and wistful. 'I seduced many a man with *my* smile.'

'Madonna!' exclaimed Nonna Pierangelini with a grimace. 'We don't need to know about that over breakfast, or at all. I'm not talking about that sort of smile.'

Evelina laughed. 'How was it, your smile?' she asked, hoping to encourage her great-aunt, who was easily led into unseemly boasts about her past. 'Will you show me?'

Nonna Pierangelini gave her granddaughter a withering look. '*You* certainly don't need to know how to smile like that!' she said crisply.

'Why me?' Evelina protested with a giggle.

'Because you've got a wicked twinkle in your eye already, that's why.'

'You must take after me,' said Costanza.

'And that's *not* a compliment,' interjected Nonna Pierangelini.

'What's not a compliment?' It was Tani, stepping out of the villa with his thumbs hooked over the pockets of his linen waistcoat.

The women laughed. 'Never you mind, dear,' said his

mother, her face softening at the sight of her son. 'We're looking forward to meeting this young man today.'

'I'm staying well out of it,' said Tani. He looked at Benedetta through his spectacles. 'I don't doubt he'll find you to his liking, the question is whether you find him to yours.'

'Does it matter what I think?' Benedetta asked, looking helpless suddenly.

'It's an introduction, nothing more. I'm sure if you're in doubt you'll be guided by these two wise ladies who probably know better than you what's good for you. What is certain is that both will have a great deal to say about it.'

Evelina looked from her grandmother to her great-aunt and then to her sister, who had gone pale. She looked into the garden, to the sun rising slowly in the sky as it approached midday, and felt sorry for Benedetta.

At twelve Evelina dressed for lunch. Thrilled with Signora Ferraro's dress, she went into her sister's room to show it off. Benedetta was in her underwear, clipping on a pair of earrings. When she saw her, her mouth opened in an astonished gasp. Evelina had put up her hair. She looked every inch the woman she wanted to be. 'Where did you get that dress?' Benedetta demanded.

'Signora Ferraro has lent it to me.'

'It's beautiful.' Benedetta went over to feel the fabric. 'She's Ercole Zanotti's sister, isn't she?'

'Yes. He gives her fabric he can't sell.'

'He could have sold this, all right. He's just being kind. Shame you have to give it back.'

'I feel like Cinderella.' Evelina sighed and plonked herself on the bed. 'Tonight I'll be in rags again and this will be but a dream.'

Benedetta laughed. 'You're so dramatic, Eva.'

'You're lucky you get to have dresses made especially for you. Try being a younger sister and having nothing of your own.'

'Be patient. It won't be long before you get to choose fabric at Ercole Zanotti and have dresses made just for you.'

'One year!' Evelina threw herself back on the bed in mock despair. 'It's for ever!'

Benedetta slipped into an elegant blue dress with wide shoulders, Peter Pan collar and a narrow belt that accentuated her small waist. 'What do you think?' She turned to her sister who sat up and appraised her.

'You look like a woman who's engaged to a rich banker,' she said with a giggle. 'You might not fancy *him*, but I can assure you *he* will fancy *you*.'

This pleased Benedetta. She smoothed down the fabric at her waist and hips and turned to admire herself from behind. 'I hope he's handsome, Eva. I love the idea of going to live in Milan. Having my own home. Being a wife and raising a family.'

Evelina pulled a face. 'I'll miss you,' she said. 'I'll be alone here with Mother and Father and the two witches.'

'And Bruno. Don't forget him.'

'Of course not, but he's hardly a great conversationalist.'

'You can come and visit me.'

'As soon as you're settled. I might stay for months!'

Benedetta laughed and went to sit beside her. She took her hand. 'You can stay as long as you like. We'll find you a husband, too. A Milanese. Then we'll never have to be far from each other.'

Evelina smiled, but she did not want a Milanese husband.

*

Artemisia was pleased when she saw her two daughters in their dresses. She narrowed her eyes at Evelina's and arched a plucked eyebrow. 'I suppose that's on loan from Signora Ferraro?' she said. 'It's lovely. You look lovely, both of you.' Evelina followed her mother and sister onto the terrace where Nonna Pierangelini and Costanza were quietly playing cards at a table in the corner, shaded by a large potted palm. The ubiquitous cigarette burned slowly in Costanza's yellow fingers. Artemisia smoothed Evelina's dress where it had creased. 'If you insist on dressing like a woman, we'll have to start looking for a husband for *you*,' she said with a smile. However, at seventeen years of age, Evelina knew she was pretty safe.

Nonna Pierangelini looked up from her hand. She said something to her sister who also took her eyes off her cards. Both women stared. Evelina didn't wait to hear what they had to say about her dress and followed her mother to the lunch table. Artemisia made sure everything was where it should be, straightening a knife and shifting the vase of pale pink roses into the centre. Nonna Pierangelini called Benedetta over and the three of them talked out of earshot. Evelina glanced at Benedetta who was pale with nerves. Their grandmother was no doubt giving her some last-minute advice.

At one o'clock a blue car drew up in front of the villa, blocking the view of the Venus fountain and drive. Artemisia went outside to meet them. Benedetta and Evelina were instructed to wait on the terrace. Nonna Pierangelini and Costanza put down their cards, stubbed out their cigarettes and wandered over to join the girls.

'Can you see him?' Benedetta asked, wringing her hands nervously. 'I can't bear to look. Is he a gargoyle? You can tell me if he is.'

Evelina looked through the house to where her mother was talking to Benedetta's potential mother-in-law, but she didn't see Francesco. 'I can only see his mother,' she said. 'She's very elegant.'

'Look harder.'

'Oh, I see him now.' Evelina pulled a horrified face. 'He's like a little toad. Short, fat and exceedingly ugly. How will you ever endure it! Lord above, save my poor sister from that.'

Benedetta's face flushed crimson. Costanza laughed. 'You'll have to lie back and think of Italy.'

Nonna Pierangelini shot Costanza a disapproving look.

Evelina laughed. 'I'm joking, silly! I think he'll do,' she said and watched her sister's face slowly drain of blood.

'You're a witch, Eva,' Benedetta hissed, her eyes shining with tears.

'I'm a good witch. Oh, here he comes. Pull yourself together. He's a prince not a toad. You're saved.'

Francesco Rossi was indeed handsome. Tall and fair with a tidy moustache he looked more Austrian than Italian. His nose was straight, his eyes a chilly blue and his jawline chiselled. He had a dimple in his chin which Costanza said made a man special, and he walked stiffly, like an army officer, with his shoulders back and his chin up. When he was introduced to Benedetta he took her hand and bowed. Then he ran his gaze up and down her blue dress, resting it finally on her face with a satisfied smile. 'It is a great pleasure to meet you,' he said and his voice was deep and strong. The voice of a man who commanded respect.

Benedetta blushed but this time with happiness and not with horror. She could not have imagined a man as attractive as him. Evelina knew at that moment that she was on the point of losing Benedetta.

Francesco's mother, Emilia, wore a pale-lilac suit and hat and white lacquered shoes. Evelina could tell at once that she was a conventional woman who never said a word that might cause eyebrows to be raised. She was short and plump with a round face and a gentle, shy smile. Evelina hoped her mother would stifle her charisma for otherwise Emilia might be somewhat overwhelmed by it.

Francesco greeted Evelina politely, but he wasn't in the slightest bit interested in her, even in Signora Ferraro's pretty dress. He had eyes only for Benedetta. His mother gave Evelina more attention, perhaps aware that her son and his possible future bride needed time to get to know each other without her and Artemisia interfering. Costanza almost blushed when Francesco brought her hand to his lips and kissed it and would have given him the benefit of her beguiling smile had she been thirty years younger. Nonna Pierangelini was surprisingly quiet. She watched him warily from the end of the table like a pensive cat.

Lunch was delicious. Any stiffness on arrival was dissipated in the aromatic flavours of Angelina's cooking and the excellent wine Tani had chosen from the cellar. Tani himself remained in the depths of the house with his books, for it would have placed too much importance on this informal meeting had he chosen to attend.

Francesco complimented the gnocchi with such gusto that Evelina decided he was a man who lived for his food. Benedetta would have to learn to cook, and well, for he looked like he had high standards and wouldn't appreciate those standards being lowered. She noticed, however, that he softened with a little wine in him. He became less starched, less rigid and a bit more humorous. He wasn't funny – that would have been asking too much of a man who appeared to fulfil almost every desire – but he smiled and chuckled at the odd thing Benedetta said that amused him. Artemisia, who usually dominated the conversation with her unconventional opinions, held back, as if she had picked up Evelina's unspoken wish and sucked in her luminous personality to better match Emilia's. While Francesco talked quietly to Benedetta, Artemisia asked Emilia about her life in Milan and Evelina asked her great-aunt about her youth, which never ceased to entertain her. In spite of Evelina's attempts to divert her, Nonna Pierangelini remained silent and watchful and sombre.

After lunch Francesco and Benedetta went for a stroll around the garden. Nonna Pierangelini and Costanza retreated to their rooms for their siesta. Evelina left the two mothers talking on the terrace and took a book to the leafy grotto to read. She lay on a blanket in the dappled shade of a plane tree and forgot about her sister and the boring lunch, because in spite of the brief respite of Costanza's stories, it had been exceedingly dull. Emilia had had nothing interesting to say and for once Evelina had missed her mother's exuberance. She knew the meeting had gone well. Benedetta and Francesco hadn't drawn breath or taken their eyes off each other. Soon Benedetta would marry and Evelina would be alone with an eight-year-old boy and a dog for company. She sighed and turned the page. When would life get interesting for *her*? she wondered.

Engrossed in her book she didn't notice the passing of time. It was late afternoon when she got up stiffly and stretched. When she returned to the terrace Emilia and Francesco had left and in their place her parents were sitting at the table with Benedetta, smoking and drinking cups of coffee. Artemisia flicked ash into the ashtray. 'Come and congratulate your sister,' she said to Evelina, lifting her ebony cigarette holder to her scarlet lips. 'Francesco has asked your father for Benedetta's hand and Tani has given his blessing.'

'That was quick,' said Evelina in surprise, sitting down.

'When you know, you know,' said Benedetta happily. Her face was aglow with the excitement of it and Evelina couldn't help but feel envious. How she wished *she* could go out into the world too.

Tani looked Evelina up and down and raised his eyebrows. He hadn't seen his younger daughter dressed like a woman before. However, he wasn't the kind of man who interfered in his children's wardrobes, so refrained from commenting. Besides, he was far more interested in the marriage contract soon to be signed by two old and noble families. 'The Rossis are good stock,' he said, nodding approvingly. 'Well-connected and respected. I'm glad you liked each other, Benedetta. It is, of course, important to be able to tolerate one another.' His thin lips curled slightly and Artemisia laughed huskily.

'He's handsome, isn't he?' she said. 'Quite a looker. A little stiff at first, I thought. A little too German. But he warmed up.'

Benedetta was appalled. 'He's not German, Mamma.'

'Austrian, then. He's very northern.'

'The Rossis no doubt have Austrian blood in their veins,' said Tani. 'But I don't think we should hold it against them. The Italian side is very old, being related to the Pallavicini family. They can trace their line right back to Oberto I, in 1148.'

'We're positively nouveau riche,' said Artemisia, grinning playfully at her husband. 'Our line only goes back to the fourteenth century. We have a pope, though, which raises us up a notch or two on the food chain.'

'I don't think it matters that he's from an old family or a rich family,' said Evelina. 'It's much more important that he's nice. And nice to Benedetta, don't you think?'

'He's nice,' said Benedetta firmly.

'Did he propose? Did he go down on one knee?'

Artemisia clicked her tongue. 'Really, Evelina. This is the real world. He didn't ask her, he accepted that it was so.'

Benedetta smiled at the recollection, clearly dazed by the events of the afternoon and keen to share them. 'He spoke about what our life is going to be like in Milan. We're going to live with his parents until we get a place of our own. I'm sure I'll like that. His mother is sweet. He says his father is quite formidable, but that he'll like me.' She lowered her eyes bashfully. 'He told me *he* liked me. He said that I was beautiful.'

'Of course he did. You *are* beautiful,' said Evelina. Then she appealed to her mother. 'Now that Benedetta's engaged, she can chaperone me into town. She'll be needing new clothes for her trousseau, after all. We can go and have a look in Ercole Zanotti. Wouldn't that be fun?'

Artemisia blew a puff of smoke out of the side of her mouth, but she allowed her husband to answer. 'I don't see why not,' he said, lifting his coffee cup to his lips. 'It's not right to keep birds in cages.'

'*Pretty* birds,' said Evelina, barely able to contain herself. She pictured Ezra Zanotti and her smile broadened. 'When shall we go?'

'Tomorrow morning,' said Benedetta.

'I'll telephone Signora Zanotti and let her know you're coming,' said Artemisia. 'And, Evelina, you'll need to give that dress back.'

Evelina sighed. 'Cinderella will have to wear rags once more.' Then she grinned mischievously, her whole face glowing with excitement. 'But she can go into town.'

CHAPTER THREE

The following morning Evelina and Benedetta rode into Vercellino in the trap with Benedetta holding the reins. Evelina had barely slept for nervousness; today she was going to see Ezra again. She had done as her mother had requested and folded Signora Ferraro's dress into a bag. However, she had no intention of giving it back just yet. Halfway to Vercellino she made Benedetta pull up. She climbed down and disappeared behind a bush. A few moments later she emerged in the dress, very pleased with herself.

'Eva!' her sister gasped, astonished that she could be so disobedient.

'If you think I'm going into town dressed like a child, you've got another think coming, Benedetta,' said Evelina crisply, climbing back into the trap. 'Besides, Signora Ferraro said I could borrow it. She didn't say when I had to give it back.'

'I hope Mother doesn't find out.'

'Mamma's too busy to care. She's moving pictures, selling old ones, buying new ones and seeing her coven of friends. I'm not sure she really cares what we do.'

'I hope you're right. I could tell Papa wasn't too pleased to see you looking like that.'

'He'd better get used to it. That's what happens to girls, they become women.'

'He didn't expect you to become one so soon.'

'I'm seventeen. Lord above, I'm not a child anymore. I'm ready to fall in love.'

Benedetta laughed. 'I don't think you'll find anyone suitable here.'

Evelina cocked her head and grinned. 'You never know.'

It was thrilling to be out of the estate and in the busy town. Both young women felt an immense pleasure at being part of the bustle of a life from which they were, for the most part, excluded. They also derived pleasure from being admired, for they couldn't help but notice the men who looked their way as they drove past. Some raised their hats, others smiled appreciatively, a group of young boys ran after the trap like a tribe of competitive monkeys to see who could touch it first. Evelina and Benedetta rounded the corner and drew up outside Ercole Zanotti. They climbed down and Benedetta tied up the horse. Then Evelina took a deep breath and followed her sister inside.

Ercole was already serving an elegant-looking woman and her daughter, pulling down rolls of fabric and calculating lengths on the cutting table. Ezra was standing beside a display of embellishments and trimmings, listening attentively to an old lady who was telling him about her grandson. He lifted his eyes when Benedetta and Evelina entered, distracted by the brass bell that tinkled above the door. His gaze lingered on Evelina. She smiled at him and turned away, knowing that she had caught his interest. She was grateful to Signora Ferraro for lending her the dress. She followed Benedetta around the shop, touching the silks and cottons and running her fingers over the lace and ribbon, feigning curiosity, knowing that she was being observed. Benedetta was decisive. She knew exactly what she liked and what she didn't. Evelina pretended to listen, but her ears were picking up the conversation Ezra was having with the old lady and willing it to end so that he could serve them.

At last the old lady left with her parcel of fabric and Ezra approached Evelina and Benedetta. 'Good day to you, signorine,' he said and gave a polite nod. His grey eyes gleamed at Evelina. 'Can I help you?'

'You can,' said Benedetta confidently. She already felt like a signora. 'I'm looking to have some dresses made for my trousseau.'

Ezra raised his eyebrows and smiled. 'Might I wish you my congratulations,' he said.

'Thank you. Signora Zanotti is going to make them for me, but I need to choose some fabrics.'

'I will ask my mother to come out so that she can advise you. I think it would be better to talk it through with her.' He disappeared into the back of the shop. Evelina watched him go and felt a swell of excitement in her chest. She longed to confide in her sister, but something held her back. She didn't know why, but a small voice inside her head warned her to be cautious.

A minute later Signora Zanotti appeared from the back. She was a delicate woman with a gentle gaze like her son's and dark hair tied into a bun at the nape of her neck. Softly spoken, she asked after Signora Pierangelini and congratulated Benedetta on her engagement. Evelina left the two women talking and wandered to the other end of the shop, hoping that Ezra would find her there. She didn't have to wait long. 'Is there anything I can do for you, signorina?'

She turned to see him smiling at her warmly. 'I'd like everything in the shop,' she said with a grin. 'But I'm not the one getting married, so sadly, I'm not in a position to buy anything.'

'My aunt's dress suits you very well.' He ran his eyes over her curves and Evelina bathed in his admiration. She knew just how well it suited her.

'I love Signora Ferraro. She's an inspiration to me in so many ways. Have you seen her paintings?'

'I have. She's very good.'

'I know. I can only dream to be as good as her.'

'She says you have talent.'

Evelina laughed. 'She's paid to say that. I could be hopeless and she'd still say I had a gift.' She looked at him steadily, relishing the intimacy in his gaze. 'She told me that you play the violin.'

He gave a shrug. 'I'm not very good, but I love to lose myself in music.'

'Is there no one you can pay to tell you how brilliant you are?'

He laughed and for the first time Evelina saw his face crease into delicious lines around his mouth and at the corners of his eyes. Her heart gave a small skip and she laughed with him, for it was impossible not to. His mirth was contagious. 'Unfortunately, not. But my aunt encourages me for free.'

'Which is worth much more.'

'She's being kind. I'm not gifted, just enthusiastic.'

'My sister plays the piano.'

'And you?'

'I play, but I'm not enthusiastic.'

'Why not?'

'I don't know. Perhaps because my sister is so good, I feel inadequate by comparison.'

'Don't let that hold you back. Just enjoy it. Lose yourself in the melody. It doesn't matter if you play well or badly, what matters is that the music touches you and takes you to another place.'

Evelina smiled wistfully. 'I would love to be taken off to another place,' she said. 'How might I do that?'

He became animated now, his grey eyes enlivening with passion. 'Imagine you're a bird, launching off the windowsill. As you play, let the music carry you like wings on the wind. Wherever you want to go.' He smiled bashfully. 'It sounds silly, but I let the music take me to exotic islands in the sea, jungles in the tropics, mountains in South America, rainforests in Brazil. I'll never see those places for real, but I go there in my imagination.'

'Where else do you go?'

'Into the deep sea. I swim with dolphins and whales and shoals of multicoloured fish. The sun casts arrows of light that attract all sorts of creatures and they shimmy through it, as do I. Sometimes I'm a fish myself.' He laughed. 'You can be anything you want to be.'

'And you do all of that while you're playing the violin?' she asked.

'Music is the key that unlocks the door to your deepest imaginings.'

'I'd like that.'

'It's not hard. You'll see.'

'I'll try,' she said. 'I'll imagine I'm a bird. I'd love to feel what it's like to fly.'

If she had been taken with him before, she was now well and truly falling in love. She had never met a person who talked like he did; who dreamed like she did.

'Ezra,' his father interrupted him. 'Would you mind looking after Signora de Luca.'

Ezra gave Evelina an apologetic smile. She could tell he was sorry to have to leave her side. She wandered around the shop not minding at all that Benedetta was taking her time looking at fabrics and pictures of designs in a book that Signora Zanotti was showing her. Evelina was happy to be in the same space as Ezra, breathing the same air. Occasionally, she glanced at him and once or twice she caught his eye and their lips curled into small, barely perceptible smiles.

When Benedetta had finished, she thanked Signora Zanotti and her husband Ercole in the ladylike manner she would adopt from now on, because she was soon to be a married woman, and went to leave the shop. Evelina stopped at the door and turned to Ezra. He paused what he was doing and looked at her. 'Thank you,' she said quietly, and she hoped that he knew she was thanking him for giving her the key to unlock the door to her deepest imaginings.

The two women strolled through Vercellino with their arms linked and a skip in their step. It was a joy to be just the two of them, without a chaperone, at liberty to go wherever they wanted. They browsed in shop windows, drank coffee at a small round table on the pavement in the sunshine and sat on a bench in the square and watched life play out before them as if they were in the front seats of an enormous theatre.

It was late afternoon when they made their way home, singing songs together as the pony and trap made its way slowly down the track. They were drunk on joy. Evelina was drunk on love. She had talked to Ezra, just the two of them, and no one had noticed or cared. The moment had been hers alone, to savour. A delicious secret that she would keep to herself. She didn't want to be told that she was too young or that Ezra wasn't suitable. She didn't want anyone to ruin it, this feeling. It was as if she were floating. As if her chest were full of bubbles, lifting her feet off the ground, breaking the roots that tied her to the earth. She felt free.

Evelina was not too intoxicated to remember to change out of her dress. Once again Benedetta pulled up and waited while her sister disappeared behind a bush and emerged a moment later in the old dress she had been wearing. But Benedetta was too happy with her own plans to comment on her sister's small act of rebellion, or to caution her against it. Why should *she* care? She was going to marry Francesco Rossi and move to Milan.

As soon as they arrived home, Evelina went to the music salon and sat at the piano. She didn't bother opening a music book. Instead, she closed her eyes and took a deep breath. She thought of Ezra and placed her fingers over the keys. It didn't matter that she wasn't very good. It didn't matter that she stumbled over the notes. The point was to allow the music to take her away. That's what he'd said. With this in mind she began to play a tune from memory that she had always loved. It was in the minor key. A simple but emotive piece that moved her. As she played she noticed pictures forming in her mind. She was a bird on the wing, viewing the world from a great height. She saw palm trees, rivers, wild orchids and ferns. Monkeys and elephants, tigers and crocodiles and a fishing boat in the middle of a stream; sunlight dancing on the water, dragonflies darting on the air. She played on, slower now, and the pictures grew steadier as she held them still and sank into them. And then she was there, walking up a path in a forest, her bare feet treading over the soft ground, her fingers reaching out to touch the flowers. And her spirit filled with happiness and her eyes welled with tears. Her heart ached with the deep and urgent longing of first love.

*

That evening, Evelina found her mother at the table on the terrace with her three best friends. They were drinking Campari and playing Burraco. Since girlhood Evelina had seen those four women as birds for they clucked and chuckled and fluffed their feathers as birds do. Her mother, of course, was a black swan; she couldn't be anything less than the most beautiful. Giulia Benotti was a goose; plump and pushy with a honking laugh and a generous, maternal nature. Eleonora Maggi was an eagle; slender with an angular face, sharp eyes and a big curved nose; and finally Ottavia Sanfelice, who, with long legs, a haughty face and a superior air, could only be a heron.

Evelina greeted them then went and sat in a wicker armchair a short distance from where the women were gossiping. From there she could eavesdrop on their conversation while pretending to be engrossed in a book. They were discussing Hitler and his controversial views on race. Evelina had heard her parents discussing the issue over breakfast for the Italian newspapers were full of it. From what she understood Hitler believed in a master race of blond, blue-eyed 'Aryans' and that the Jewish people in particular were a race of inferior people who should not be permitted the same rights as their superiors. Since being appointed German chancellor in 1933 he had begun to restrict all aspects of the Jewish people's private and public lives. Since Evelina knew no Jewish people, the subject seemed remote and she listened with half an ear, as she did when her parents discussed things that had nothing to do with her.

'That kind of barbarity would never happen here,' said Ottavia. 'Il Duce is a friend of the Jews. They are Italian first, Jews second and that's an important thing to remember. They fought for their country in the Great War, after all.'

'Jews have lived in Italy since Roman times,' said Eleonora.

'They are Italians. It's as simple as that. Mussolini himself said that there's no such thing as race, only national pride.'

'What he says and what he thinks are two different things,' argued Artemisia. 'He's as slippery as an eel. Remember the poor Slavs, and as for black people, well, he certainly considers them inferior to white people. I wouldn't trust a word Mussolini says about race. His eye is trained on whichever way the wind is blowing, and the wind is coming from Germany.'

'You can think what you like, Artemisia, but Mussolini is no friend of Hitler's,' added Giulia. 'He considers the Jewish people a *great* people.'

'I wouldn't trust Il Duce as far as I could throw him,' said Artemisia and Evelina knew she was only saying that to be controversial. Her mother was never going to have the same opinion as the others. She had to be different, always.

'Oh Artemisia!' Giulia honked. 'Mussolini believes in the great traditions of Italian culture: family, religion, a person's right to be an individual. Fascism is about patriotism, not oppression. I think he's a very good thing. A strong man. A man who believes in the potential greatness of our nation.'

'Il Duce believes in the second Roman Empire,' Ottavia agreed. 'He's going to make Italy great again.'

'Through war,' said Artemisia. 'I don't care for war. I'd rather our young men lived than lost their lives in senseless battle, just to satisfy one man's ego.'

'If war is what it takes,' Ottavia continued, shaking her head to show how inevitable she believed war was, 'then so be it. It is the duty of all Italians to sacrifice their lives for their country if that is what's required.'

'I don't care to be great,' said Artemisia. 'Or to be an

empire. Mussolini is competitive. He just wants to be bigger and better than England and France, and Germany, of course.'

'Hitler and Mussolini are both Fascists, but their ideas of Fascism are quite different,' said Eleonora. 'Thank goodness. I wouldn't want to be a German right now.'

Artemisia agreed. 'This question of race is ridiculous, and religion too. Jewish, Catholic, Protestant, Hindu, Buddhist, people are people and they should just get along and accept each other. We're all different, after all.'

'Indeed, we are. We Italians are very different from the Germans. Thankfully, we have no problem with the Jews,' said Giulia.

'We can agree on that,' said Artemisia with a laugh. 'When I think of how they're being treated in Germany, my heart bleeds. I think of the Zanottis, for example, and how such intolerance would affect them.' At the mention of that name, Evelina pricked up her ears and stopped reading. 'They're good, honest, hard-working people. I'm very fond of Olga Zanotti.'

Ottavia nodded. 'Ercole fought in the war, as did his father, and is an enthusiastic member of the National Fascist Party. He's an Italian who happens to be Jewish.'

Evelina didn't hear the rest. All the while the press had been debating the differences between Italian Jews and Zionist Jews and Hitler's persecution of Jews and Mussolini's respect for the Jews, she had never known that the Zanottis were Jewish. It had never entered her mind. Why would it? Now those debates meant something. Not that she sensed danger, because what was happening in Germany wasn't going to happen in Italy. Hadn't Giulia said that Il Duce considered the Jewish people a *great* people? No, there was no threat to the Jewish people in Italy. But how very interesting that Ezra Zanotti was Jewish.

When Signora Ferraro next came to teach Evelina painting, she asked her about it. 'Does what's going on in Germany worry you?' she asked.

Signora Ferraro shrugged. 'Yes, Hitler's persecution of the Jews worries us greatly,' she replied. 'As a Jew, my bag is always packed. We never take anything for granted. It wasn't so long ago that we were in the ghettos. I'm confident, however, that nothing like what's happening in Germany will happen here. We have a tolerant government and a tolerant nation. But it makes one uneasy, and desperately sorry, of course, for our fellow Jews suffering under the Third Reich. I hope it won't last. Perhaps there'll be a change of government and things will get better again.'

This satisfied Evelina; the Jewish people in Italy had nothing to fear.

Over the course of the next few weeks, Artemisia began planning Benedetta's wedding. The date was set for the following May. In typical Artemisia style she made the occasion all about *her* and drew up extravagant designs to impress the Rossi family and friends, and to show off herself and the villa to their best advantage. Francesco gave Benedetta a ring made out of emeralds, which delighted her for it was sufficiently big and modern, and the two of them began to meet in Milan, at the Rossis' house, and at Villa L'Ambrosiana. Tani was old-fashioned and did not allow his daughter to go off with Francesco on her own. He insisted that Artemisia accompany her to Milan. On the odd occasion, both Artemisia and Tani went with her, for

Tani enjoyed spending time with Francesco's father, his old university friend.

During these excursions to Milan Evelina was left alone in the villa with Bruno and Romina, her grandmother and great-aunt and the servants, who worked quietly in the shadows and took no notice of her. She practised the piano and painted, read and strolled around the garden, and played cards with Nonna Pierangelini and Costanza. Her grandmother did not like Francesco. 'He's too neat and tidy,' she said one afternoon when the three of them were having *merenda* on the terrace, drinking cherry juice and eating almond biscuits and cake. 'I'm suspicious of men who are too neat and tidy.'

'I think he's handsome,' said Costanza, grinning mischievously at Evelina through a cloud of cigarette smoke.

'He *is* handsome, I agree, but he's controlling and rigid.' Nonna Pierangelini took an enthusiastic bite of cake. 'It's all in the moustache.'

Evelina crinkled her nose in disbelief. 'You can tell all that from a moustache?'

Nonna Pierangelini arched an eyebrow. 'You'd be surprised how much a simple thatch of hair on a man's upper lip can communicate. It goes without saying that Hitler's little tuft, for that's what it is, a tidily clipped tuft, denotes a rigid and unforgiving nature.'

'There is nothing sexy about *that* moustache,' Costanza agreed with a grimace. 'Scratchy!'

'It won't end well.'

'Hitler or Francesco?' Costanza asked.

'Both,' replied Nonna Pierangelini with certainty.

'You can't tell Benedetta,' said Evelina. 'She's really taken with him.'

Nonna Pierangelini shrugged. 'Youth is blind. It takes experience to read moustaches.'

'Are you saying he won't treat her well?' Evelina asked, worried now.

'That is exactly what I'm saying. Of course, he will at the beginning. He'll be full of romance and say all the right things. But when the honeymoon is over, and honeymoons *always* end, he'll rein her in. That's what men like Francesco do, men with tidy moustaches. They cannot allow those within their realm of control to have any freedom. He'll tell her what to wear, what to say, where to go – and, more especially, where *not* to go. No, I don't like him at all, but I won't say anything because some people just have to figure it out for themselves. Wisdom cannot be taught, you know. One has to learn it through experience and Benedetta has precious little of that because her parents have barely allowed her out.'

'I think you're wrong,' said Costanza.

'You always think I'm wrong.'

'I like Francesco.'

'You're not marrying him.'

'I think he'll be good for Benedetta.'

'We'll see,' said Nonna Pierangelini with a sigh. 'I'd so love to be wrong once in a while.'

One Saturday, while her parents and Benedetta were an hour and a half away in Milan, Evelina took the pony and trap into Vercellino wearing Signora Ferraro's dress. She was bored of finding entertainment within the walls of Villa L'Ambrosiana and set off to find entertainment on the outside. There was no chance of getting caught because her parents had planned to be away all day, and she knew Romina would not betray her. As for Nonna Pierangelini and Costanza, they were much too busy with their cards and their siestas to question her whereabouts.

When Evelina arrived in Vercellino there was a Fascist parade going on in Piazza Roma, put on by exuberant Young Fascists in their black-and-white uniforms, holding their black flags high. They were playing music and singing, and marching with great aplomb in front of a rapturous crowd of proud parents and enthusiastic locals. Evelina had seen it before. Bruno went to the local school and loved the Fascist drills, uniforms and songs, which he would come back singing: '*We are the golden dawn, Lively we grow in the light and air, We are young Italy.*'

Evelina did not consider herself Fascist or anti-Fascist. She did what she was told and read the newspapers and listened to the radio with a cool detachment, as if the things that were happening outside the walls of Villa L'Ambrosiana had little to do with her and her isolated world. Her father did not consider it ladylike for women to have opinions, and only tolerated his wife's because he knew that most of the things she said were to provoke a reaction, like a game. He believed that politics were the domain of men, and women should occupy themselves with family and home and the arts. Benedetta and Evelina were perfectly content with this. Tani was an anti-Fascist himself, although he did not advertise the fact. It was not wise to speak out against the government. He was grateful to Mussolini, he conceded, for bringing order to chaos, but he was more interested in his projects that kept him in splendid isolation in his study in one of the furthest wings of the villa where his children knew not to disturb him than in what he considered an oppressive Fascist regime.

It was with the same cool detachment that Evelina watched the Fascist parade. She wandered around the square, amused by this intensely patriotic show put on by a small provincial town of no importance. By the serious expressions on the faces of the young men and women, they believed themselves part of something great. They believed in Mussolini's imperial aspirations, in the new Roman Empire. These were the boys Ottavia Sanfelice had spoken about when she'd said that Italians should be prepared to sacrifice their lives for their nation were Italy to go to war. Evelina didn't imagine that there were any here today who would refuse.

She was delighted when she spotted Signora Ferraro watching the parade from the steps of the fountain of Diana that dominated the square. She was standing with a large group of family members, clearly enjoying the spectacle. Evelina weaved her way through the throng to join her.

'Evelina!' Signora Ferraro exclaimed happily when she saw her. 'Come and join us.' She put out her hand and Evelina took it and stepped up to stand beside her. 'I'm glad you're enjoying my dress,' Signora Ferraro added, looking her up and down with a smile.

'It's my favourite,' Evelina replied, hoping she wouldn't ask for it back.

'I hear Benedetta is engaged. She must have liked him.'

'She does. They like each other very much. He's handsome too. He's everything she could have wished for, I think.'

'Is she here?'

'No, she's in Milan with Mamma and Papa—'

'Which is why *you're* here.' Signora Ferraro narrowed her eyes. 'You're alone?'

Evelina pulled a face to show that she cared nothing for rules. 'I'm not alone anymore. I'm with you,' she said and Signora Ferraro laughed at her spirit.

'Some of my nephews and nieces are in the parade,' she

told her, pointing them out. 'Don't they look good in their uniforms? They're so proud of them. Some of them even wear them at home!'

Evelina clapped as the children marched past. Then she heard a voice she recognized.

'Hello, signorina.' It was Ezra, gazing up at her.

'Ezra,' she said in surprise, forgetting all formality. She jumped off the step to join him. 'Are any of your siblings in the parade?' she asked.

'Yes, three. Enrico, Giovanni and Damiana.'

'They're clearly enjoying themselves.'

'They like their uniforms.'

'So Signora Ferraro told me. They wear them well.'

He looked at her for a moment, an amused expression in his eyes. 'Do you want something to drink? I'm tired of watching the parade. I'd rather sit in a café and talk to you.'

Evelina was flattered. 'I'm tired of it too,' she agreed, although she'd been there barely half an hour. She glanced back at Signora Ferraro, but her teacher was too busy enjoying the parade to notice her slipping off with her nephew.

They walked through the crowd then left the piazza by way of a cobbled street of faded pink and yellow buildings. Shop fronts gleamed in the sunshine beneath scalloped awnings. Wrought-iron street lamps saluted them from above, and pots of fruit trees lined their narrow route. They slowed their pace and settled into an easy conversation. Ezra took her to his favourite café in Piazza Cavour, a pretty colonnaded square dominated by the Basilica of Santa Croce. They sat outside at a small round table, beneath a trellis of vines.

'I played the piano just like you told me to,' Evelina told him.

He smiled and looked into her eyes as if he didn't want to look anywhere else. 'Where did you go?'

'Into a tropical jungle,' she replied. 'At first I flew and then I walked. It was wonderful. Much more fun than plodding through music books, feeling dissatisfied.'

Ezra tapped his temple. 'It's all in the mind,' he said. 'You can think yourself happy just by imagining things that delight you.'

And Evelina wanted to tell him that most of all she was happy thinking about him.

CHAPTER FOUR

At the end of the summer Tani went to Paris to research the book he was writing. Benedetta continued to meet Francesco and make wedding plans with her mother, Bruno celebrated the start of a new school term and Evelina resumed her studies with her tutors, a couple of teachers who taught at the school in Vercellino and were happy to make extra money teaching her. One of them, Signor Stavola, was handsome with deep-set green eyes and light brown hair pushed off a wide forehead and held in place with a pomade that made it shine. He had a widow's peak which delighted Artemisia who thought he looked like an American movie star. The subjects he taught were Italian literature, history and French, which were Evelina's favourites. *His* favourite subject, however, appeared to be Artemisia, who detained him for a chat in the hall every morning when he came to teach. During those chats, Artemisia flirted and giggled like a schoolgirl, and he assumed a lofty, arrogant expression, gazing at her down his long nose as if she were, indeed, one of his pupils. Evelina gave him the nickname Signor Scivoloso – Mr Slippery.

Signora Ferraro resumed her art lessons and every now and then she brought a note from her nephew. Sometimes

Ezra drew a picture, other times he copied out a verse of poetry. Occasionally, he wrote a message: *I flew over Machu Picchu last night.* Or: *Old Signora Belvedere came into the shop this morning with a sprig of parsley stuck into the ribbon on her hat. She's so short-sighted, she'd mistaken it for lavender.* Evelina responded to each missive. She didn't care to show restraint. She didn't subscribe to the notion of acting coy. The fact that she was only seventeen and practically a prisoner at Villa L'Ambrosiana put her out of his reach without her deliberately making the situation more difficult. Her notes were longer than his. She wrote about where her piano playing took her and how mathematics made no sense at all so that her poor teacher was driven to distraction trying to explain how to find patterns in the numbers. Soon Ezra's notes were written to *Evelina* instead of *Signorina Pierangelini*. She kept every one of them in a box beneath her bed which she decorated with dried flowers she'd made in her flower press.

Occasionally Evelina would accompany Benedetta into town for dress fittings, not only for her trousseau but for her wedding dress, which Signora Zanotti was also making. Evelina had to be careful not to draw attention to the quiet conversations she and Ezra had in the shop while her sister was in the back room. She'd feign interest in fabrics and ask Ezra to take down rolls so that she could feel the material between her fingers. She even asked him to take them outside so that she could see the colour in daylight while snatching the opportunity to talk a little, beyond the reach of his father's curious gaze. Evelina suspected Signor Zanotti knew what she was up to. He was shrewd and observant and maybe she wasn't as subtle as she thought she was, but as she was so young she didn't imagine he believed his son's intentions were serious. Evelina did not doubt that they were. She was infatuated with Ezra. She even believed she loved him. He might have been three years her senior but from the way he spoke to her and sent her notes via his aunt, she was sure that he would wait for her to grow into a woman he could be serious about.

Evelina knew little of romance. She had never been courted and she had never been kissed. She had read romantic novels and encouraged Costanza to share her stories of what had clearly been a colourful past, but she had no idea of how the adult world really worked. Sex was something she was curious about, but it was a remote and imaginary thing that would likely not happen to her for years. Francesco had kissed Benedetta, but her sister was reluctant to share the moment with her for fear of ruining it. 'If I tell you,' she explained a little sanctimoniously, 'it won't be special anymore.' Evelina wasn't sure how that was so, but she didn't argue. She'd find out in her own good time and have her special moment too. In the meantime, she imagined what it might be like to be kissed by Ezra.

As autumn progressed Artemisia began to take the car into Vercellino two or three times a week in the afternoons for important meetings. Benedetta's wedding was a massive undertaking, she explained, and she had to discuss arrangements with the priest, among others. Tani began taking Benedetta to Milan by train, which, thanks to Mussolini, arrived and departed on time. Benedetta would spend the day with Francesco, and Tani would lose himself in the Braidense National Library, which dated back to the 1770s and was his favourite place in the world after Villa L'Ambrosiana. More and more, Evelina was stuck at home with Bruno and Romina, her grandmother and great-aunt, her books, her music, her painting and her longing.

One afternoon after a long day of tuition, Evelina left Signor Scivoloso with her mother in the hall and went to play the piano. When she played, she felt close to Ezra. She heard his voice telling her to imagine she was a bird, or a dolphin, or a lioness. To imagine she was flying, with the sun on her face and the wind beneath her wings and the mountains, treetops and streams far below her. She'd recently begun to compose her own melodies. Simple chords at first and then notes in between, building them into elegant pieces. Her formal training gave her the tools with which to play her compositions, her imagination allowed those compositions to flourish. On the waves of melody, she expressed her love.

It was nearly dark when she went into the garden. Evenings drew in early these November days. The air was cold and damp and sweet with the scent of decomposing foliage and rotting apples. She listened to the rustling of creatures and the hooting of owls. She loved the night, the glimmering of stars and the mysterious moon, playing hide and seek with the clouds. She loved the tranquillity of it and the sense of enchantment. She noticed that the light was on at the far end of the villa where her father's office was. Tani was still in Milan and wouldn't be returning until the following day. He must have left it on, she assumed, and thought no more about it.

It was only when she went back inside that she decided she'd better go and switch it off. Her father was punctilious about wasting money on electricity. Evelina wandered through the house, hastening from one icy salon to another, her way lit up by the moonlight and her own detailed knowledge of her home. When she reached the study door she put out her hand to turn the knob. Just as she was about to grasp it she heard a peal of laughter coming from within. Her hand

froze. The laughter belonged to her mother, but she wasn't
laughing alone. Something told Evelina that the person with
whom she was laughing was not her father. Her parents never
spent time together in Tani's study, and her father was, as far
as Evelina knew, still in Milan. His study was out of bounds
for everyone, even his wife. He'd always made that abundantly clear. Evelina wondered what her mother was doing
in there. Was it possible that she was showing it off to Signor
Scivoloso? Sure, there were rare books on the shelves and the
odd literary prize her father had won displayed in a glass cab-
inet, but Evelina didn't imagine there was anything in there
of enough interest to warrant bringing Signor Scivoloso all
the way through the house to view it.

She put her ear to the door. Again the sound of laughter,
the low mumble of voices and then a muffled giggle, as if
her mother was being tickled. Evelina was stunned while at
the same time burning with curiosity. Without a moment's
hesitation she ran back through the house and out into the
garden. She was in such a hurry that she didn't bother to put
on a coat or even notice the cold. She dashed across the lawn
to her father's study window where the light still shone out
onto the garden. She stood on tiptoes for the window was
high, curled her fingers over the lip on the wall and lifted her
chin. Slowly her eyes peered over the ledge, into the room.
To her horror, she saw her mother and Signor Scivoloso
lying on the sofa, kissing. It was at once so dreadful and
so fascinating that Evelina couldn't tear herself away even
though she knew she should, for her sanity more than her
self-preservation; the two of them were far too involved in
what they were doing to notice her white face at the glass.

Eventually, she stepped away from the wall. She could
only stand on tiptoes for so long and now her calves were

aching and she was cold. She hurried back over the grass and in through the front door, wondering about what she had just witnessed. What did it all mean? Why would her mother do that with Signor Stavola, and in her husband's study? What was she thinking? Evelina decided she'd sit on the step in the hall and wait for them to emerge.

She waited and waited. It was cold there sitting on the stone step with the draught slipping in under the front door. It wouldn't be long before Bruno would come down with Romina for supper, and Nonna Pierangelini and Costanza too. Would Artemisia miss it? What would Tani say if he were to find out that she'd been in his study with Signor Stavola? What would her mother say if Evelina told her what she had seen? Should she share it with Benedetta? She didn't know what to do.

At last she heard voices, distant at first and then drawing closer. Her mother was laughing, a strange, girlish laugh. Signor Scivoloso was making comments, but Evelina couldn't make out what he was saying. Eventually, they walked into the hall. When they saw Evelina, sitting on the step with her face pinched with fury, they were both visibly startled. Signor Stavola smiled to hide his embarrassment and made a lame comment about Evelina wasting time when she could be doing her homework, and Artemisia hurried him to the door and bade him a swift goodnight.

Artemisia bolted the door and turned to face her daughter. 'Why that look?' she demanded. 'Are you hungry? It's supper. Go and call Bruno. Where are Nonna and Costi?'

'Why were you in Papa's study with Signor Stavola?' Evelina demanded. Her heart was beating so fast she was sure her mother could hear it echoing around the hall.

'I wanted to show him some of your father's books.

Anyway, it's none of your business, is it. Have you washed your hands?'

Evelina noticed that her mother's cheeks were flushed and her hair tousled, as if she'd just got out of bed. 'No,' Evelina replied.

'Well, don't just sit there then. Go and wash them.'

Evelina knew her mother was not going to discuss the matter with her. In any case, she was right: it was none of her business. But Evelina had grown a little wiser from the experience, as her grandmother had said she would. Evelina knew now that her mother's trips into Vercellino had nothing to do with Benedetta's wedding.

Since Evelina had discovered that the Zanottis were Jewish her interest in the subject had been piqued. She had begun to read the newspapers more carefully and listened to the radio with an ear cocked for any references to the Jewish community. She had eavesdropped on her mother's conversations with her friends and asked her father questions, subtly of course and with care, because he did not approve of her taking too much of an interest in politics. She had become interested in the history of their people and deeply concerned about the way they had been treated.

The person with whom she could talk openly about Judaism was Signora Ferraro. Whether or not she knew why Evelina had suddenly acquired an interest in her religion and culture she did not let on, and she answered her questions with her usual patience. She told Evelina about the history of the Jewish people, the festivals, traditions and rituals that punctuated their year, and she discussed the question of race that was so topical right now and endlessly debated in the press. It did not seem likely that Mussolini and Hitler would ever agree on this question and, as far as Signora Ferraro was concerned, having such opposing opinions about a subject that was clearly of vital importance to Hitler, they were unlikely ever to form a political alliance. After all, Mussolini nearly went to war with Germany over Hitler's attempt to take power in Austria. Mussolini, Signora Ferraro affirmed, believed Hitler to be his greatest threat.

Benedetta was married in the Chiesa della Madonna del Rosario on a flawless spring day in May. Tani walked his daughter down the aisle, and Bruno, proud in his tuxedo, acted as page, offering Francesco the ring on a satin cushion. Evelina was a bridesmaid along with five female cousins. Their dresses had been made especially by Olga Zanotti and were more beautiful than Evelina could have imagined. She was given a bouquet of roses and lilies to hold and a crown of flowers for her head. She felt like an elegant young woman at last and was ready to leave her girlhood behind in the cupboard with all Benedetta's old frocks. Her sister would now leave home and Evelina would remain alone with Bruno. But as much as it made her sad to think of Benedetta moving to Milan, it made her happy to think of being the oldest child at home. Perhaps her mother would now commission new dresses for her and treat her like a young woman, the way she treated Benedetta.

Nonna Pierangelini stubbornly wore black. Even though the wedding was a happy occasion, she refused to dress in anything other than the colour of mourning. Sure, she had buried a husband, and two sons in infancy, but Evelina suspected she was revealing in her solemn choice of colour a tacit protest at Benedetta's choice of husband. 'What if

Francesco had shaved off his moustache?' she asked her as
she escorted her to the awaiting car.

'It's too late now. I've seen the man he is,' Nonna
Pierangelini replied darkly. 'And anyway, men like that don't
shave off their moustaches. They wear them like badges
of honour.'

Evelina laughed. 'I'm sure they'll be happy together,' she said.

Nonna Pierangelini shrugged. 'For the first few months.'

Costanza appeared then, tottering out in a fuchsia-pink
dress and matching hat. A scrawny flamingo with long,
skinny legs and a curved, haughty nose. 'Isn't this exciting!'
she exclaimed, smiling broadly. 'Just think of Benedetta
and Francesco on their wedding night. I was denied a wedding night.'

'But you made up for it with many practice runs,' Nonna
Pierangelini said drily and climbed stiffly into the car.

The wedding feast was held at Villa L'Ambrosiana where
four hundred guests sat down to a sumptuous banquet in
the garden beneath trellises of white roses. Artemisia's grand
designs had come off just as she had hoped, even though
Tani had paled when he had realized just how much it was
all costing. As the night's sky darkened to a rich indigo blue,
the lights of the villa shone like a magnificent ship on a sea
of flickering candles. Fireflies danced in the fragrant air as
if Artemisia had instructed them to and stars emerged one
by one to twinkle like gems. The effect was enchanting and
Artemisia was satisfied that although they did not have vast
wealth like the Rossi family, they had class and style and an
achingly beautiful home.

Tani's three brothers and their families had come from
Tuscany and Umbria, and his redoubtable older sister,

Madolina, had travelled all the way from America where she and her husband Peppino had emigrated shortly after their marriage. Artemisia had family too; her parents and a couple of younger sisters, Rosa and Lidia, who had subscribed whole-heartedly to Mussolini's call to Italian women to have twice as many children as they would want in order to increase the population and, by default, the power of the nation, and had six and eight children respectively.

Artemisia had invited Ercole and Olga Zanotti and their son Ezra. She'd also invited Signora Ferraro and her ebullient husband Matteo, and Signor Stavola, of course, who wasn't married and came alone. Evelina knew very well why her mother had invited this group, who sat at separate tables with the staff who worked in the villa and on the estate. It was all because she wanted to be close to Signor Stavola. Evelina was in no doubt now that on those thrice-weekly trips into town her mother was visiting *him* and doing all sorts of saucy things she should not be doing as a married woman. She knew because of her mother's good mood when she returned, but more specifically because that good mood swiftly turned into a bad one as soon as she saw Evelina. Her mother avoided eye contact with her and did her best to stay out of her way, as if the reproachful looks her daughter shot at her aroused guilt that perhaps piqued embarrassment. It was because of these things that Evelina knew that Artemisia was having an affair with Signor Stavola.

Tonight, however, Evelina was not thinking about her mother and her tutor. Her thoughts were with Ezra and, although his table was at the other end of the garden to hers, she could see him clearly in the gaps between the guests. He did not catch her eye in spite of Evelina willing him to do so. He was engrossed in conversation with Romina, Bruno's nanny.

The dinner was a bountiful spread of delicious food and wines which had all been brought up from Tuscany, where Tani's brother owned a vineyard. There were speeches. They seemed to go on for ever. It was as if all the Rossi men wanted to have their moment in the spotlight. If they'd known how boring they were they might have had more self-restraint. But Benedetta sat serene and happy, enjoying every moment of her special day. From the look on her face she was willing those plodding relations of her new husband's to hog the limelight for longer.

At last the band began to play and Francesco led his wife onto the dance floor. Tani and Artemisia followed and soon others joined them, Costanza, who had drunk too much, being the first, dragging one of her great-nephews into a dance, cheek to cheek. Evelina, who had been seated next to two cousins, found herself dancing with one family member after another. She tried to find Ezra among the dancers, but to no avail. She assumed he must still be at his table, talking to Romina, and with that thought she suffered a moment's anguish.

Finally, Evelina excused herself and went in search of him. However, she hadn't got very far before she was caught by Aunt Madolina. 'My dear, how you have grown,' she said, looking her niece up and down with her piercing gaze and nodding her approval. 'What a beautiful young woman you have turned out to be. I always felt sorry for you, having such a beautiful older sister, but I don't feel sorry for you anymore. I think I feel sorry for Benedetta. You're quite a beauty.'

'Thank you, Aunt Madolina,' said Evelina, wondering how she was going to manage to escape now that her aunt had captured her.

Aunt Madolina was a large-boned, strong-willed woman

who did not suffer fools. Being the eldest child, she was used
to voicing her opinions and being heard. She had not grown
up with a father who thought it unladylike for a woman to
be interested in politics. In fact, Evelina's grandfather Beto
Pierangelini had encouraged his children to have opinions
and congratulated them if those opinions differed from his
own. He had not wanted to breed parrots, he'd said. He'd
pushed them to be independent in thought as well as in
action, which had led to heated arguments with Tani, who
was more conventional. Had Beto lived, he would have
encouraged Benedetta and Evelina to question their father's
beliefs and form beliefs of their own. It was fortunate then,
for Tani, that his father had died before he could assert his
powerful influence on them.

'How old are you now, Evelina?' Aunt Madolina asked.

'Seventeen.'

'Don't let that father of yours nudge you up the aisle, will
you? Come and live with me in America.'

Evelina couldn't imagine anything worse. 'I'd love to,' she
lied, hoping the conversation would end there.

'You're far too independent-thinking to remain here. This
place is like a time warp. My brother is years out of date.
He belongs to the last century, not to this one. Europe is a
pressure cooker right now. Don't wait until the lid blows off.
Come to New York. America has more to offer women like
you. I'll talk to Tani.'

Evelina wondered how Aunt Madolina knew she was
independent-thinking. 'Fortunately, I'm too young to get
married,' she replied. 'And maybe, now that Benedetta is
married, Papa will forget about me and turn his attention to
Bruno, who's growing up fast.'

'Bruno's adorable. Those cheeks! Oh, I just can't take my

hands off them. But he's still a child. I wouldn't count on
your father taking his eyes off you, my dear. He knows just
how spirited you are, and in Tani's opinion, spirited women
are dangerous, like me.' She laughed. 'You remind me of
my younger self. Something about the look in the eyes . . .'

'If he thinks spirited women are dangerous, why then did
he marry Mamma?'

'Because she's all hot air. Like a beautiful actress, she
doesn't believe a word she says. In the end she's in awe of
her husband and does everything he asks her to. She's not as
independent as she likes to think she is. She's an Italian wife
and mother like any other, but more beautiful. Artemisia is
unique in that respect.'

Evelina thought of her tutor. *Mamma is more independent
than you realize,* she thought to herself.

Evelina finally found Ezra. He was on his way to replenish
his glass with wine. In fact, he was holding *two* glasses. When
he saw Evelina, his expression softened. 'Evelina,' he said,
looking her over with appreciation. 'Your dress suits you
well.' He knew that his mother had made it.

'Thank you,' she replied, beaming a smile. 'At last, a beautiful dress of my own.'

'You've been dancing?'

'I was, but then I got caught by one of my aunts. The
formidable Aunt Madolina, who's come over from America.'

'Every family has one of those,' he said, rolling his eyes.

'I suppose yours does too?' She laughed as he told her
about his loquacious aunt Mira, whose husband had got
so tired of trying to be heard that he had almost given up
entirely and now barely opened his mouth, except to eat.
But she was an exceptional cook, Ezra conceded, which is

why he stayed with her. 'At least she can cook and speak at the same time.'

'Do you dance?' Evelina asked, hoping he would ask her onto the dance floor.

He held up the glasses. 'I'm going to get Romina a drink and then I'll come and find you.'

'You promise?'

'I promise.'

'Then I'll wait for you,' she said, wondering exactly how long she'd have to wait.

Evelina was dragged back onto the dance floor by the two cousins she had sat beside at dinner and from there she danced with all her uncles and cousins. When she danced with her uncle Peppino, he too encouraged her to come to the States. 'You can stay with us for as long as you like,' he said, swinging her around. 'Everything's better over there, even the pizza.'

At three in the morning the bride and groom retreated upstairs to much applause. After that, the guests began to depart, their headlights disappearing down the drive. Evelina looked around for Ezra. He had promised her a dance, after all, and soon the music would end. She wandered through the gardens in search of him.

The night was rich with the scents of pine and rosemary, alive with the gentle glimmer of fireflies and the chirruping of crickets. The moon was high and pink, like a grapefruit, and the stars twinkled with more clarity than usual. It could not have been more romantic, but Evelina's heart was heavy with disappointment for she knew now that she would not get to dance with Ezra. She wasn't even sure he was still here. Unable to bear the discomfort of blaming *him* for not coming to find *her*, she blamed *herself* for having been engaged in dancing with others and wondered whether perhaps he'd given up on her. She wished she hadn't got so carried away. She wished she had waited like she said she would.

Just then she noticed a couple sitting beneath the pergola at the far end of the garden. They were shadowy figures, but Evelina could tell immediately who they were: Ezra and Romina. She tiptoed closer, then dashed behind a tree. Careful not to be spotted she peered around it to get a better look. They were talking, their heads close together, almost touching. There was an intimacy in the way they were sitting that made Evelina's throat tighten. If she was not mistaken, they were holding hands.

Evelina remained there for a long while, transfixed with both horror and curiosity. Little by little, unhappiness filled the bottom of her heart where it formed a mounting layer of silt, thick and foul.

Then they kissed. Evelina watched in despair, for their kiss was long and tender. Hot tears ran in streams down her cheeks, forming drops on her chin from where they broke free to dampen her dress. She wanted to disturb them with a shout, or expose them with a torch. Anything to break them apart. Yet, she didn't want to reveal that she was there. So she did nothing, but torture herself with the sight of them.

Eventually, she wiped her face with her fingers then hurried across the garden towards the villa. She let herself in through a back door and crept upstairs to her bedroom.

Ezra had broken his promise; she would never trust him again.

CHAPTER FIVE

The following morning during breakfast on the terrace, before anyone else had come down and while Bruno was distracted by his croissant and jam, Evelina asked Romina about Ezra. 'I'd say you got lucky with the placement,' she said, keeping her expression neutral so as not to give her true feelings away.

'He's charming,' Romina replied. A secretive smile curled her lips and Evelina was sure that the flush on her cheeks was not due to the heat.

'Handsome too,' Evelina agreed. 'I assume you both already knew each other?'

'Of course,' Romina answered. 'We go to the same synagogue.'

Evelina stared at Romina in amazement. 'You're Jewish?' she asked.

'Yes.' Romina looked surprised that Evelina didn't know. 'My parents wouldn't be very pleased if I married someone who wasn't.'

'You're engaged?'

'No, not yet. But I think we will be soon.' The flush on Romina's cheeks intensified. 'I like him very much.'

And there it was. As clear as a quartz knife to the heart.

Ezra would marry one of his own. Why hadn't Evelina thought of that? She left the breakfast table without having eaten, threw herself onto her bed and cried all over again.

In the weeks that followed, Evelina struggled to find anything in her life to be positive about. Benedetta had left and Ezra was going to marry Romina. Evelina was stuck at home with Bruno, who was adorable but hardly the companion her sister had been. She stopped playing the piano and ceased to be interested in Jewish religion and culture. Signora Ferraro continued to bring notes from Ezra, but Evelina didn't read them, nor did she write back. She added them to the box she kept beneath her bed and then, when they dried up, took the box into the drawing room and burned it in the fireplace. Nothing remained of the letters, but her love could not so easily be destroyed. If anything, the flames were fanned all the more on account of the fact that she could not have him, and her longing made her melancholy.

At the end of June Evelina celebrated her eighteenth birthday with a dinner party at Villa L'Ambrosiana. She wore the dress she had worn at Benedetta's wedding and tried to find enjoyment in the forty young people who had been invited to share her coming of age. Her mother had made sure all the suitable young men from the vicinity had been included on the list, but in Evelina's eyes they all fell short in comparison to Ezra. If she couldn't have him, she wouldn't have anyone.

Her mother suggested they go to Ercole Zanotti to have some dresses made, now that she was a young woman. Evelina was not enthusiastic. She did not want to face Ezra after what she considered to have been a terrible betrayal. However, the lure of beautiful clothes eventually got the better of her and she went with her mother, striding into the shop with her chin up and the hurt in her eyes disguised behind a cool, impassive veneer. She greeted Signor Zanotti and smiled politely at his son, then walked on through the shop to the back where his wife was ready to tend to her needs. At least, she thought, as she walked into Olga Zanotti's workshop, Ezra had the decency to look concerned.

As much as Evelina had withdrawn her interest in the Jewish people, she couldn't help but read newspaper articles reporting on Hitler's speeches against them. It was extraordinary, she thought, that in this modern world, any leader could discriminate against a people in such a brazen way, and face so little opposition to it. Didn't everyone, whatever race or creed, have a right to live in the world in peace? At least Mussolini declared in no uncertain terms that there was 'no Jewish problem in Italy'. And indeed, he was right: there *was* no Jewish problem in Italy.

On 2 October 1935, Mussolini declared war on Abyssinia. Mussolini spoke to his people via loudspeakers set up in every square of every Italian town. Tani and Artemisia protested against his decision to go to war by remaining at home and listening to it on the radio. 'A solemn hour in the history of our homeland is about to strike,' Mussolini said. 'Twenty million men at this very moment fill the streets of Italy. Twenty million men with one heart, one will and one determination. For many months the wheel of destiny, under the impulse of our calm determination, has been moving towards its goal.' That goal, of course, was the second Roman Empire.

He called upon all Italian women to give up their gold wedding rings in support of the war. Benedetta gave hers with a heart full of sorrow. Artemisia refused and wore hers with defiance. She didn't have a son old enough to go to war, but Francesco was drafted, as was Ezra. Evelina suggested she go and stay with her sister in Milan, to give her comfort. Her parents agreed. At last she was free of Villa L'Ambrosiana and all the restrictions it had imposed upon her. With her sister she was like a bird released from its cage.

Evelina did not want to think about Ezra, but living with Benedetta and her daily ritual of prayers and supplications for her husband's safe return from the battlefield only drew her thoughts towards him. The newspapers were full of the Fascist troops moving from victory to victory in a triumphant show of military prowess, but according to friends of Benedetta's parents-in-law, who had contacts in the military, the truth was very different: the armies were ill-equipped and ill-disciplined and things weren't going very well at all.

Benedetta dragged Evelina to church every day to light candles for Francesco. Evelina lit two, cursing herself for caring about a man who cared nothing for her. But her heart felt what it did and there was no point in fighting it. At least she wasn't at Villa L'Ambrosiana where Romina was sure to be shedding tears for the one man Evelina believed she would ever love.

On Christmas morning, Bruno came down with a fever. Artemisia brushed away her family's fears by claiming it was excitement, because the tree in the hall was of such beauty and the presents beneath it so red and shiny that it wasn't at all surprising that the child had got overwhelmed. But Evelina felt an uneasiness in her gut. The house was full of family, for Benedetta had come home with Evelina and two of Tani's siblings had come to stay for the week with their families. 'You should call the doctor,' Nonna Pierangelini suggested, an anxious frown deepening the furrows on her forehead. But Artemisia was determined that the festivities should not be interrupted by a little boy's inability to contain his emotions. The doctor was not called. Bruno was put to bed and the party continued.

Romina, who didn't celebrate Christmas, sat by Bruno's bedside, dabbing his forehead with flannels soaked in cold vinegar water, singing to him softly. Evelina tried to throw herself into the festivities, but all she could think about was her little brother in bed upstairs with a raging fever. Later that night, when the house had sunk into a deep and drunken sleep, Evelina tiptoed down the corridor to Bruno's bedroom. Romina was in the chair beside his bed, nodding off, for it was well past midnight. Bruno was asleep, but even without putting a hand to his forehead Evelina could tell that the fever had not broken. She nudged Romina's shoulder, waking the nanny with a start. Romina immediately checked on Bruno, fearful that she was being awoken because the child had died. 'I'll stay with him,' Evelina told her. 'You need to get some sleep.' Romina reluctantly left the room.

Evelina soaked a fresh flannel in vinegar water and dabbed the perspiration off her brother's face. Bruno looked like a little angel there, with his eyes shut and his expression serene, and her heart flooded with love. His breathing was slow, so slow that once or twice during the night she had to put her cheek to his nose to check that he was still breathing. She did not doze, but remained vigilant, as if she believed she could keep him alive by the force of her will. By the power of her wanting. If love could save him, she knew hers would be sufficient.

Dawn broke onto the grey morning, pouring its flat light through the gaps in the curtains. Evelina stood up and stretched. She was stiff and cold. The fire in the room had burned down to embers. Bruno was still asleep. She opened the window a crack to let in some fresh air, then went to use the bathroom. When she came back, he had opened his eyes. Evelina's heart gave a leap. Surely this meant that he had turned a corner. That his fever had broken. That he was going to get well.

'Gabriele is here,' he said in a voice as thin as thread.

Evelina sat down and took his hand. It was hot. 'Who is Gabriele?' she asked, feeling the fingers of dread squeezing her heart once more.

'Gabriele wants me to go with him. He says it's time.'

'There is no Gabriele, Bruno,' she said firmly. 'You're here with me, Evelina, and you're going to get well. You're not going anywhere.'

His lips curled into a small smile. 'I want to play with Gabriele,' he whispered. 'I want to . . .'

'When you're better you can play with whoever you choose.'

He looked at her with feverish eyes. 'I'm so hot.'

'I know you are, my darling.' Hastily she let go of his hand, soaked another flannel in the vinegar water and placed it on his forehead. 'Mamma will call the doctor today and he'll make you better.'

He squinted. 'It's very bright in here.'

'Is it?' She looked towards the curtains. Only a sliver of grey light was shining dully between them.

He closed his eyes. Evelina took his hand again. Her eyes overflowed with tears. 'You sleep now, Bruno. That's the best thing for you. Sleep will give your body the energy to fight the fever and break it. You'll be better soon. I know you will.' She lifted his limp hand and pressed her lips against it.

His breathing grew slow again.

Evelina was holding his hand and watching him closely

when Artemisia came in with Benedetta. As soon as his mother saw him she realized at once that it was time to call the doctor. Evelina wondered why she hadn't called him sooner. Benedetta suggested she stay with him while Evelina bathed and changed and had something to eat. But Evelina was too frightened to leave him. 'He's going to be fine,' Benedetta insisted. 'It's a fever. We've all had them and survived them. It's a rite of passage. Go. I'll stay with him.'

Evelina did as she was told. The adrenalin had kept her awake all night but now she felt raw with exhaustion. At breakfast Artemisia told the family that Bruno was fine; it was just a fever and he'd soon be well enough to open his presents. If she had managed to fool everyone then, they were no longer fooled when the doctor came and left with a grave expression on his face. It was imperative that the fever broke, he'd said. The next twenty-four hours would be critical.

Now Benedetta and Evelina went to church in Vercellino with Nonna Pierangelini and Costanza and lit candles for Bruno and those they loved who were at war. The Christmas festivities were dampened with worry, even though Tani and Artemisia did their best to pretend that nothing was awry. Romina tried to wake Bruno to give him some water, but he did not stir. He lay there like he already had one foot in the other world.

That night Evelina was not alone when she sat by his bed. Benedetta, Artemisia and Tani were with her. Four solemn people praying for the boy's deliverance. Bruno's fever had only got worse and now he was mumbling incoherently, as if struggling in a horrible nightmare. Artemisia stroked his forehead, kissed him on the temple and bathed his hot face, but nothing could bring him back. He seemed with every feeble breath to be drifting further and further away.

As daylight made a crack in the eastern sky the nightmare ended at last. Bruno sighed peacefully and his features softened. His eyelashes fluttered and his lips curled into a small smile. And then he departed, as if he had simply put out his hand and allowed some wonderful being to lead him away.

Artemisia howled and pulled him into her arms where she cradled him like a baby. Tani allowed his daughters to kiss their brother before showing them the door. Artemisia needed time alone with her child, he explained, and he would give her as much as she wanted.

Evelina, too, needed to be alone. Benedetta suggested they go to church, but Evelina knew she would find no comfort there. The only place she'd feel any measure of peace would be in the garden, among the trees and shrubs she loved, that Bruno had loved too, for he had spent many hours playing among them. She put on her coat and boots and headed out into the gloomy morning. She didn't hear the song of intrepid birds who had remained in Piedmont for the winter, or smell the sweet aroma of putrefaction as nature made way for the new growth that would come in the spring. She heard nothing and felt nothing but the pain in her heart.

Evelina had never grieved before. She had never lost anyone she loved. But this first experience of loss carved a new space into her soul, a more profound level in the still, silent caverns of her being which was irreversible. A place where wisdom would grow.

Shortly, she came upon the chapel where Bruno and his friends had so often played, and pushed open the heavy wooden door. Inside, the air was cold and stale, the frescoes on the walls stained with damp. The stone floor was strewn with crisp brown leaves and the corpses of dead insects, and the odd bird that had flown in only to be trapped inside and left to die too. It was a sad, neglected place. The perfect place for Evelina to vent her sorrow.

She sat on one of the wooden chairs which were still set out in rows from the time when the family had attended their own private Mass. She hugged her stomach and let out an inhuman cry. It came from somewhere deep and untapped inside her. A place of such hidden depths that her whole body shook at the surprise and terror of it. Yet, she couldn't stop it. Once it had started it began to gain momentum. She felt as if she might cry out her stomach for the cramps were so intense and the feeling of ejection so violent. All she could do was relinquish control and allow it to work its way through her.

Eventually, her crying grew into a quiet sobbing. Her body slumped in defeat, exhausted. Her head ached but it was nothing compared to the ache in her heart. She wondered how a person ever recovered from such anguish. Death was an impossible thing to get her head around. As much as she tried, the larger part of her felt disbelief. Her heart, however, told her the truth: Bruno was gone.

Bruno was buried in the family crypt in the cemetery in Vercellino. As his little coffin was laid to rest beside his grandfather, Beto Pierangelini, and his two uncles who had died in infancy, Evelina knew that nothing would be the same again. Their hearts had been broken, but even more than that, the heart had been ripped out of the family, leaving a gaping hole. Villa L'Ambrosiana would resonate for ever with the memory of Bruno's laughter, his playful smile, his curiosity and his love. Wherever one looked, Bruno's shadow would be there. There would be no escaping it, and every member of the family would ask themselves, over and over, could they have done more?

The evening after his funeral Evelina went to see her mother, who was in bed. She'd been given something by the doctor to calm her nerves and she lay against the pillows, staring vacantly into the darkness. 'May I come in?' Evelina asked softly.

Artemisia didn't answer so Evelina went in anyway. She sat on the edge of the bed and took her mother's hand. Artemisia's face was gaunt with misery and damp with tears. 'Who's Gabriele?' Evelina asked.

Her mother's eyes shifted and she looked at Evelina in surprise. 'Why?'

'Because when Bruno was delirious he mentioned that Gabriele was with him and that he was telling him it was time.'

'Time for what?'

'He wanted to take Bruno away.'

Artemisia gasped. She seemed to wake up suddenly. 'He said that?' she asked.

'Yes. He said he wanted to go and play with Gabriele. I wondered, perhaps, whether he's someone from school . . .'

Artemisia gasped again and shook her head. 'Gabriele was his twin. He died at birth.'

Evelina didn't know what to say. She looked at her mother in astonishment. No one had told her that Bruno had had a twin.

'Do you think Gabriele's soul had come to take his brother into the next world?' Artemisia whispered and her gaze filled with longing for herself and for her son. 'Do you think they are together in a beautiful place?'

Evelina wanted very badly to believe it. She squeezed her mother's hand. 'Yes,' she said. 'I do. I think Gabriele put out his hand and Bruno took it. I think they went off to play.'

Artemisia began to cry again. 'Thank you, Evelina,' she said. 'That's such a lovely thought.'

In the new year, Evelina returned to Milan with Benedetta. Neither wanted to be at home with the heavy pall of mourning that had fallen over the villa. Artemisia's mother came to stay for a while and her sisters took it in turns to spend time with her too. She did not need her daughters, nor did she want them. Her thoughts were only for Bruno. It seemed as if, in his departing, he had taken his mother's heart with him.

Nonna Pierangelini and Costanza did their best to comfort Artemisia and Tani, for both were suffering, albeit in different ways. Artemisia cried often and loudly while Tani buried himself in his work. Nonna Pierangelini set up a shrine in one of the salons. An altar with a photograph of Bruno and a candle that burned day and night. She decorated it with flowers from the greenhouses, rosary beads, a statue of the Virgin Mary and icons lent from her own bedroom. There she and her sister prayed. They prayed for all their departed loved ones, but now the list had grown longer and sadder. They had loved Bruno, and his death, they were certain, had robbed them of years, for wasn't it true that grief shortened the life of those who endured it?

Benedetta received the occasional letter from Francesco, telling her to have courage and patience, reassuring her that the war would soon be over and he would come home so that they could start a family and settle down to the life they had dreamed of. There was no letter from Ezra for Evelina. She imagined he was writing to Romina and a bitterness soured her memory of him so that after a while she no longer cared about him. Bruno was dead, what did anything else matter?

Spring was hot and Evelina and Benedetta returned to

spend some time at Villa L'Ambrosiana. They found their home much altered. Tani and Artemisia seemed more disconnected than ever and the villa itself seemed to reflect in its heightened air of neglect and shabbiness their lack of care for each other. The damp had spread further over the frescoes, the rugs appeared more worn, the paintings hadn't been rearranged or replaced since before Christmas. There were no plants or flowers in the house, except one enormous dying fern in the music salon beside the piano that lay quiet and sad like a coffin. It was as if time had stood still the moment Bruno left the world. Artemisia floated through the house like a spectre, her exuberance gone, her desire to be seen and admired replaced by a desire to disappear. Evelina did not imagine that Signor Scivoloso ever came to visit. Tani worked in his study and emerged only to eat and sleep and drive off to Milan, where he spent days in the library, or perhaps seeking comfort in the arms of a woman of flesh and blood. Who could blame him? His wife was barely living.

Nonna Pierangelini and Costanza seemed to have aged as well, like a pair of relics forcing the old routines of *merenda* and cards to persist, even though they seemed not to have the will to enjoy them. They were relieved to see their granddaughters, embracing them keenly, hoping perhaps that, with the girls' return, life at Villa L'Ambrosiana might slip back to the way it was.

Even though Evelina no longer took painting lessons, she went to Vercellino to visit Fioruccia Ferraro all the same, for their friendship had attained an equal footing since the roles of tutor–pupil had been removed. Fioruccia's husband Matteo had gone to war, as had most of the young men in the country. In order to help out, Fioruccia had taken Ezra's place at Ercole Zanotti's and worked intermittently in the shop when she wasn't giving lessons in the school. It was there that the two women would meet and go out for coffee, choosing a local café in which to sit and chat.

Ercole Zanotti was deeply proud of Ezra. In his opinion Italy had a right to a colonial empire like France and Great Britain and his son, his brave and patriotic son, was fighting for the glory of his country alongside his Italian brothers. Fioruccia confided in Evelina that for Ercole, his son's taking part in the war was a way of emphasizing their family's loyalty to Mussolini and Fascism. They were Italian first and Jewish second and were keen to stress the point. With Hitler's persecution of the Jewish people on the rise in Germany and anti-Semitic murmurings in the Italian press, this was not a time to be complacent. It was a time to show one's complete and unfailing allegiance to Il Duce.

'Are you afraid that the same thing will happen here?' Evelina asked her, speaking of Germany.

'Yes,' Fioruccia replied.

'What's changed your mind?'

'A feeling. I don't know. Something in the air. I sense danger in my bones.' She lifted her hand to show her naked finger and chuckled. 'I gave my wedding ring to support the war. My husband is fighting in it. Yet, I feel those gestures will ultimately count for nothing.'

'Papa says Italy will be pushed towards Germany in the light of her conflict with France and Great Britain over Abyssinia. I hope he is wrong.'

'So do I,' Fioruccia agreed. 'But if you ask Ercole, he has only praise and admiration for our leadership. He cannot imagine anything happening here that would put our people in danger. He says the government is more interested in rooting out anti-Fascists than it is in suppressing the Jews.'

'He's an optimist.'

'He is not alone. My fears seem to be exclusively my own.'

'Then you have nothing to worry about,' said Evelina hopefully, but she was inclined to believe her father's pragmatism rather than Ercole's optimism.

The Italo-Abyssinian War ended in the spring and Francesco arrived home in early summer. Far from a hero's triumphant return, Francesco was traumatized by what he had experienced and weary to his marrow. He'd lost so much weight that Benedetta didn't recognize him when he staggered through the door of their apartment in Milan and she almost shouted at him to leave. The poor man went straight to bed and slept for two full days, stirring only to eat the food his wife brought him on a tray.

Evelina tried not to think about Ezra, but the more she pushed her thoughts away, the harder they fought to be acknowledged. Ezra belonged to Romina, she told herself. He had no desire to see her. She had been an entertaining diversion for him and nothing more. The hurt, overridden by her grief for Bruno, had been stifled, but now Ezra was back in Vercellino her heart began to ache once more for him.

When she went to see Fioruccia, her friend told her that both Ezra and Matteo had returned all skin and bone and had taken days to resemble something close to their normal selves. She and Olga had cooked their favourite dishes in the hope of fattening them up, but it was the fatigue that had hit them the hardest, and the disillusionment at having fought in what they had both come to believe a futile war.

'I imagine Ezra will marry Romina now that he's back,' said Evelina, dreading the answer, but wanting so badly to hear that it was so in order for her to be able to put him behind her and move on with her life.

'Yes, I imagine he will,' Fioruccia replied softly. 'And what about you, Evelina?'

'I think I'll go to America and live with my uncle and aunt in New York,' she said, but in truth this was the first time that she had considered it. It dawned on her then that if she couldn't have Ezra there was no point in staying at Villa L'Ambrosiana and wasting away in hurt and bitterness. 'Yes,' she replied, warming to the idea. 'I'm going to go and live in America. My uncle told me that everything is better there, even the pizza.'

CHAPTER SIX

Tani was not keen on his daughter going to live in New York with his sister, not only because America was a long way from home, but because he wasn't sure his sister's influence would be good for her. Artemisia, however, thought it an excellent idea. She didn't want to have to bother finding Evelina a husband. She didn't want to bother doing anything at all except moping about mourning her son. Evelina might have been torn had her mother reached out to her for comfort, but Artemisia made it clear through her lack of interest that she would rather Evelina left her to her sorrow.

Reluctantly, Tani agreed and the wheels were set in motion for Evelina's departure. Nonna Pierangelini was saddened that her granddaughter had decided to move across the Atlantic, but she understood her desire to broaden her horizons, as she had understood when her own daughter Madolina had left with Peppino. Costanza said she wished she could go too. 'I think I would have had more of an exciting life had I lived somewhere like America,' she told Evelina, but in truth, she knew nothing about it and was basing her judgement on fantasy.

Evelina was excited to be given the opportunity to start again in a new country, as far from Ezra as was possible. She was optimistic that her heart would mend in America and that she would find a vocation to inspire her and possibly fall in love. Her life in Italy had stagnated. She needed to get back into some sort of flow. Inject some enthusiasm into her life. Find a sense of purpose.

It therefore came as a surprise when Ezra appeared at the door of Villa L'Ambrosiana, having ridden over from Vercellino on his bicycle. The maid called Evelina, who was in the garden, painting. 'Signor Zanotti for you,' she hollered. Evelina knew it wasn't Ercole. She was stunned. She put down her brush and took off her overall. As she walked towards the villa her initial excitement was dampened by the anticipation of discovering the reason for his visit. He was surely here to tell her of his marriage to Romina and to apologize, perhaps, for having mistreated her. Those thoughts caused the silt at the bottom of her heart to rise up and muddy the waters with resentment.

Evelina walked round to the front where Ezra was standing with his bicycle in a jacket and cap. She noticed at once how thin he was and how different his face looked. He no longer had the veneer of insouciance he'd had before, but a face etched with the lines and shadows of experience.

He smiled when he saw her. A hesitant smile; he was unsure perhaps of how he was going to be received. 'Evelina,' he said, and his grey eyes looked her over appreciatively. 'You look radiant,' he added.

'Thank you.' She did not want to smile. She did not want to make it easy for him. Why should she? He had hurt her. She wanted him to know how much he had made her suffer. Her lack of warmth caused him to avert his gaze. He dropped it to the ground before daring to look at her again.

'I hear you're going to America,' he began.

'Yes.'

He nodded. 'I don't blame you. Italy is changing and not in the right way.'

She frowned. 'If you mean the militarization of our country then I agree with you. The parades, the obsession with Fascism, with uniforms and pomp. The newspapers speak of nothing else. I'm sick of it too. I'm looking forward to leaving it all behind and discovering a new life in America.'

'I think Italy is heading towards an alliance with Hitler,' he said gravely.

'I'm sure you're wrong.'

'I wish I was.' Ezra sighed and shook his head. 'Mussolini is now supporting the Spanish Civil War alongside Franco and Hitler. I tell you, it's not going to end well. Will you walk with me? I'd like to talk to you.'

Evelina was about to say that she couldn't, but she was aware that this was possibly the last time she would ever see him. A heaviness fell over her heart. 'Sure,' she replied. But she wished he hadn't come. His presence just dragged her back into disappointment which she'd only just managed to overcome.

He leaned his bicycle against the wall and they set off down a path that meandered between banks of thyme and dark green cypress trees. Ezra sighed as if the sight of such beauty affected him more deeply now that he'd experienced the barren landscape of war. 'I'm sorry about Bruno,' he said.

'I am too,' she replied.

'He was a sweet little boy. I can't imagine what it must be like to lose someone you love like that.'

'It's the worst thing in the whole world,' she said and she didn't look at him because she didn't want to cry.

'I suppose going to America will help put all that behind you.'

'A little, perhaps. But Bruno's death will always be with me, wherever I am in the world. It's not something you can shake off. It's something you just have to learn to live with.'

'Of course.'

'There's not a moment in the day when I'm not thinking about him. He's always in my mind and in my heart.'

'Have you been playing the piano?'

'No.'

'I find music to be very healing.'

'It might be for you, Ezra, but it causes me pain.' She had not meant her voice to sound so hard.

He sighed heavily and Evelina knew that she was making this difficult for him. They walked on in silence. Then Ezra put his hands in his pockets and tried to steer the conversation in a different direction. 'I thought war would be an adventure,' he told her. 'I thought it would be something worthwhile, heroic even, but I was wrong. It was a disaster.'

'The newspapers were full of your glorious triumphs.'

'They lied,' he stated simply. 'Fascist propaganda. You don't want to believe anything you read in the newspapers.'

She shrugged. 'It's impossible to know what is true and what is not.'

'Of course it is. The fact is, it changed me.'

'I don't suppose you can go through an experience like that and come out the same.'

They came upon Nonna Pierangelini's elaborate glass-house, nestled comfortably in the long grasses that grew up wild and abundant around it. The glass itself was foggy with lichen and moss, the old metal frame sagging with age, and one of the roof panels positioned at an angle to catch the sun was missing. In spite of its obvious deterioration it possessed the same languid charm as the villa itself, its youth

stolen by time but rendered even more beautiful on account
of its regretful, melancholic air. 'Nonna Pierangelini grows
tomatoes in here,' said Evelina, walking towards it. 'She
swears they taste better than anywhere else in Italy, something to do with the light that has to fight its way through
the algae, I don't know.' She shrugged. 'Because of that
she won't have the place cleaned or renovated. It was built
at the end of the last century, a British design. Victorian
glasshouses were fashionable then.' She pushed open the
door and stepped inside. The air was thick and damp and
smelt strongly of the tomatoes that grew in plenty. 'You see,
magic!' she exclaimed. Ezra followed her and ran his eyes
over the clusters of bright red fruit that hung fat and ripe
upon the vines. The plants appeared too copious for the
building, filling it like a creature of many tentacles gradually
taking possession of the glass and metal designed to contain
it. Evelina plucked a tomato and pressed it against her nose,
inhaling deeply. 'I love this smell,' she said. 'It reminds me
of my childhood and of Nonna Pierangelini.' The thought
of leaving stabbed her suddenly in the chest and she felt her
heart constrict with anxiety. She didn't imagine tomatoes
smelt like this in America.

Ezra looked down at her, a frown deepening the lines on
his face. 'I'm sorry I hurt you,' he said and his expression was
one of the utmost remorse.

Evelina lifted her chin. 'You did hurt me, Ezra,' she
replied, the sense of satisfaction from his apology surprisingly
unfulfilling. 'But I forgive you. I presumed you felt something for me that you didn't. I was young and infatuated. I
wish you and Romina happiness together.' A sadness settled
upon her and she wandered down the path between the vines
so that she didn't have to look at him.

He caught up with her and put a hand on her arm. She stopped and stared at him in bewilderment. 'What is it, Ezra?' she asked crossly. 'What more do you want from me? I've forgiven you. It's fine. Let's talk about something else.'

'I was a fool,' he explained quickly. 'I put the wishes of my family above my own. My father noticed the way you and I talked together and reminded me that I was to marry a Jewish girl, not a Catholic. He made that very clear. So I did his bidding and courted Romina. I believed I was doing the right thing, but the war taught me that the only right thing is what feels right in here.' He thumped his heart. His face twisted in anguish. 'I've loved you, Evelina, from the first moment you came into the shop. I didn't stop loving you when I proposed to Romina. I just pushed my feelings aside so that I didn't have to face them. But I haven't been able to stop thinking about you. When Fioruccia told me you were leaving for America, I had to come and explain myself. I understand if you no longer love me. If you're so furious with me that you cannot. I just needed to tell you how I feel, so that you know that it had nothing to do with *you* and everything to do with *me*. You didn't deserve to be treated like that and if I could go back to your sister's wedding and do things differently, I would. I'd be the first to ask you to dance and I'd be still dancing with you when the party was over and everyone had gone home.'

Evelina's eyes filled with tears. She smiled tenderly. 'Would you kiss me in the garden?'

His shoulders dropped and he looked at her, appalled. 'You saw?'

She nodded.

'I'm so sorry, Eva.' He slipped a hand around the back of her neck, beneath her hair. 'Can I kiss you now?' he asked, and she nodded again and dropped the tomato into his pocket.

Tani and Artemisia were baffled when Evelina declared that she had changed her mind and no longer wanted to go to America. Tani was secretly pleased but Artemisia was irritated. 'You can't put people out like that. Madolina and Peppino are expecting you. I'm sure they've made all sorts of arrangements. It's rude to cancel.' Evelina suspected her mother had been rather looking forward to being rid of the responsibility of having her at home.

'I'm not cancelling. I'm just putting it off. I'm not ready to leave L'Ambrosiana,' Evelina explained.

'You needn't be afraid, you know. It's not the adventure people make it out to be. Madolina and Peppino crossed the Atlantic for Benedetta's wedding and then sailed back again. Easy. You'd hardly be left to fend for yourself. You might even find a suitable American to marry.'

'I'm too young to marry, Mamma. The truth is, I'm not ready to leave Bruno.' It was a shameful lie and Evelina winced as she said it.

Her mother caught her breath. *This* was something she understood. 'Oh Evelina,' she groaned, her face softening with compassion. She drew her daughter into her arms, wetting her dress with her tears. 'Then you *mustn't* leave him,' she said emphatically. 'We will find you a nice Italian here in Vercellino so you can remain close to your brother.'

Suddenly the world looked quite different. It was as if it had instantly become more beautiful. The trees were greener, the flowers brighter, the sky a deeper blue, the sunshine more radiant and the air more fragrant. The alchemy of love transformed everything from ordinary into extraordinary so that Evelina's heart responded to all around her with a feeling of utmost fullness.

Ezra was mindful of Romina's feelings and although he had broken off their engagement he didn't feel it was fair to flaunt his relationship with Evelina in front of her. Evelina felt sorry for Romina, of whom she was immensely fond. Bruno had loved her and she had cared for him in his final hours with the devotion of a mother. Evelina did not want to repay her kindness by stealing the man she loved, and yet steal him she had. There was no alternative. The least she could do was hide it for as long as possible to spare Romina added pain. Perhaps by the time they revealed their relationship to the world, Romina might have found someone else to love.

Ercole and Olga were unhappy that their son had decided not to marry Romina. As far as they were concerned she was a good Jewish girl from a nice family. They attended the same synagogue. They were from the same community. Indeed, they had known each other for many years. They'd been to the same school and their parents were friends. Ercole tried to reason with his son. He couldn't understand why he had changed his mind. Finally, Ezra had explained that the war had changed him. It had made him realize that he didn't want to marry out of a sense of duty, familial or otherwise. He wanted to marry for love. Ercole had insisted that love grew if the seeds planted were watered properly. But Ezra argued that the seeds had to be planted in the right soil in the first place. In the end Ercole had put up his hands and shrugged. 'I used to understand you, Ezra,' he said, shaking his head. 'You're looking for something you may never find.' Ezra couldn't tell him that he'd already found it.

Evelina and Ezra were therefore careful to keep their relationship secret. The only person in whom they could confide was Fioruccia. They both knew that they could trust her, and they needed her, for without her help they had nowhere to go. Fioruccia was not surprised that they had come together. She had known all along how Evelina felt about Ezra and was pretty sure why Ezra had got engaged to Romina. In her opinion, it was right that they were together for they complemented each other like music and dance.

Fioruccia confided in her husband Matteo, who was happy to keep the secret. He was an easy-going man who did not care for religion. It mattered not to him whether a person was Catholic or Jewish or an alien from Mars, it only mattered that they were kind and good and preferably had a sense of humour. He was not an observant Jew. He barely went to synagogue, never said the prayers on Friday night and considered himself Italian above all. Had Fioruccia been Catholic he would have married her all the same. He wasn't an atheist, but he was agnostic. He just wasn't sure and he didn't really want to waste time thinking about it. If there was a God, he'd find out when he died. If there wasn't, he wouldn't care because he wouldn't be conscious. 'Was I caring before I was born into the world? No, I wasn't aware I existed,' he'd explain when the question of God was raised – and Ercole would go pink in the face and try to convince him otherwise.

Ezra and Evelina enjoyed dinners at Fioruccia and Matteo's apartment on Via Montebello. Fioruccia was a good cook, which for Matteo, who loved food more than anything, was an important quality in a wife. War had been hard for all the obvious reasons, including the fact that there simply wasn't a good enough reason to have embarked on it in the first place, but the hardest part, according to Matteo, had been the lack of good food. He was now eating for the present *and* the past, he said. Making up for all the meals he'd missed while in Abyssinia. His belly was already round. He patted it with satisfaction, like an old friend he had lost and re-found, and piled his plate high with spaghetti.

Evelina loved her evenings at Fioruccia's. It felt natural to be there with Ezra. On Via Montebello she felt they were a proper couple because Fioruccia and Matteo saw them as one. Evelina helped with the cooking, even though she lacked skill, and she helped clear away and wash up while the men remained at the table, smoking cigarettes and drinking grappa. Her parents never asked her where she was. Ever since Bruno died, they had both lost interest in her. Tani worked and Artemisia prayed and neither noticed when she left the villa and when she returned. She'd take her bicycle and head into town or into the hills where she'd meet Ezra. They'd walk and talk and lie in the long grasses and poppies, basking in the sunshine and each other. On Saturday nights they joined the locals in the main piazza, and no one knew that they were a couple because Evelina was Fioruccia's friend and Ezra was her nephew and it was natural that they should be together.

By the end of the summer Benedetta was pregnant. She and Francesco came to Villa L'Ambrosiana to share the exciting news. Artemisia was drawn out of herself at last. The thought of having another child to love lifted a little of the weight of grief that she'd been carrying and she embraced Benedetta with enthusiasm, congratulating her with something of her old exuberance and letting her know that she hoped it was a boy. 'If it's a boy, Mamma, we will call him Giorgio, after Francesco's father, and Bruno.'

Artemisia was beside herself with joy. She hadn't felt joy like this since before Bruno died and she drank it in like a woman dying of thirst. 'Giorgio Bruno,' she gushed, gently putting a hand on her daughter's belly. 'I pray that he is a boy. A beautiful, healthy, happy boy. Giorgio Bruno.'

Evelina was delighted for her sister. All Benedetta had ever wanted was a husband and children and now she was on the brink of having both. Francesco was deeply proud and treated her as if she were made of porcelain. Benedetta bathed in his attention, inciting more of it by becoming increasingly fragile. One would have thought she was the only woman on the planet to have ever been pregnant.

In her excitement, Evelina confided in her sister about Ezra.

They were sitting outside on the terrace after lunch. Artemisia, Nonna Pierangelini and Costanza had gone upstairs to sleep a siesta. Tani had taken Francesco off around the garden to show him where he planned to plant the new arboretum. The sisters were alone. 'Ezra Zanotti?' Benedetta asked in surprise.

'Yes, you remember him?'

'Of course, I remember him. How could I forget. Wasn't he engaged to Romina?'

'You knew that?'

'His mother told me they would marry while she was fitting my dress. They were really excited about it.'

Evelina sighed. 'Romina doesn't know we're seeing each other.'

'That's for the best.'

'But we will have to come out of hiding at some stage.'

'I don't suppose you've told Mamma and Papa.'

'No.'

'You know they'll disapprove, don't you?'

'Not because he's Jewish. They won't care about that.'

'Because he's not rich,' said Benedetta. 'He's the son of a fabric merchant and a dressmaker. Mamma will look down her nose at them and Papa will want someone with money and connections like Francesco. Why don't you let them find someone for you?'

'Because I don't want *someone*. I want Ezra,' said Evelina, feeling hot suddenly and wishing that she hadn't confided in her sister. Now that Benedetta was married she had acquired an air of superiority that Evelina did not like. 'I love him. I'll never love anyone else.'

Benedetta laughed. 'You're only just nineteen, Evelina. What can you possibly know of love?'

'If you have to ask me that, Benedetta, then you know less than I do.'

Her sister was offended. 'Don't tell me what I do and don't know about love.'

'If you truly loved Francesco you would understand that no one else will do.'

'Very well. You love him. I think you'll find there are many obstacles in your way to happiness. For one, Ercole and Olga Zanotti will not approve. From what I understand, having spent time with Olga, their religion is important to them. Do you know any of them who has married out? No, I didn't think so.'

'We'll go and live in America.'

'You might have to.'

'Good.'

'Yes, good.'

They sat in silence for a while, both feeling equally uncomfortable. Evelina went to pour herself more orange juice but found the jug empty. 'I thought I could tell you everything, Benedetta,' she said eventually. 'I thought you'd be on my side.'

Benedetta sighed. 'I am on your side. You can marry whoever you choose. I'm only saying it's not going to be easy.'

'Life isn't easy.'

'You can make it as hard or as easy as you like, by the choices you make.'

'I don't have a choice, Benedetta,' said Evelina firmly. 'I'm fully committed to Ezra now. There's no changing course. There's no giving him up in order to accept someone I don't love just because he's rich and well connected. What sort of life would that give me? A comfortable but empty one with endless days wishing I was with Ezra. I think I'd rather be dead.'

'Don't say that.'

'Life without love isn't worth living.'

'There's not only one man for you, Evelina. It's a myth that your soulmate is somewhere on the planet and all you have to do is find him to be happy. Depending on where you go, you'll open up avenues that will present you with opportunities. If you go to America, you'll open up a new avenue *there* that will present you with people who'll play important roles in your life. If you go to England, you'll open up avenues *there* and meet different people who'll play those roles. Ezra is not the only man on the planet you can love. You are here and he is here and you love him. But if you leave and go somewhere else, you'll very likely find some other man to fall in love with.'

Evelina folded her arms defensively. 'I don't agree with you and I don't want to talk about it anymore.'

Benedetta stood up. 'I hope I'm wrong and that everyone approves and you get to marry the man you want.'

'So do I,' Evelina snapped, watching her sister put her napkin on the table and make for the door into the house. 'You won't tell anyone, will you?' she asked.

'No, I'll keep your secret. I hope it won't be a secret for much longer. Secrets like that bring all sorts of problems.'

Evelina was happy to watch her go.

Evelina had taken to playing the piano again. Now that she was angry with her sister she went to the salon to express her annoyance through music. She sat on the stool beside the dying fern and began to play. It felt good to hit those minor chords, to let the harmonies and disharmonies release her frustration. She found that when she felt something strongly the melodies she composed were more poignant. When she felt happy they didn't attain the same depth or drama. Unhappiness took her deeper into herself, to a part that only music could reach, and, in so doing, inspired her to bring forth something special. She never wrote down the tunes, she didn't need to. They remained in her head and somehow her fingers knew where to go. They were more adept when she followed her imagination, when she was inspired by her emotions. Somehow her fingers grew clumsy when following someone else's score.

That evening after dinner Francesco brought up the subject of politics and Tani sat back in his chair and lit a cigarette. Artemisia, having come out of her self-imposed exile, while not completely restored to her usual feisty, controversial self, was at least awake to the arguments. Nonna Pierangelini and Costanza had gone into town for dinner and cards with friends, which was just as well because they both thought Mussolini a menace. Benedetta agreed with everything her husband said and Evelina remained quiet, absorbing it all fearfully. They were talking about Mussolini's edging towards an alliance with Hitler. After Great Britain and France turned their backs on Italy following Italy's invasion of Abyssinia, Mussolini looked to Germany for an alliance. Francesco thought it would be a good thing and would make Italy stronger. Together they would be the most powerful countries in Europe, he said. Tani argued in his quiet and serious way that it would be a disaster. Hitler and Mussolini were both expansionists, which meant war and conquering. 'The world has yet to recover from the last war,' he said.

'What would it mean for the Jewish people?' Evelina asked, taking care not to catch her sister's eye.

'Mussolini has said time and again that he does not agree with Germany's racial doctrine,' said Francesco.

'And you believe him?' said Artemisia, arching an eyebrow cynically.

'Of course,' Francesco replied. He was a proud Fascist and admirer of Il Duce. 'He has given me no reason not to.'

'I suspect that, if an alliance is made, Mussolini will find himself stepping into line with Hitler,' said Tani, flicking ash into the ashtray. 'I'm not sure how he'll be able to avoid it.'

'The Italian people would never allow it,' said Evelina with passion. 'It simply wouldn't be allowed to happen.'

Tani smiled at her. 'History is marred by countless examples of racial persecution, my dear. It's happened before and it will happen again. No one ever learns from history.'

'I just refuse to accept that something as abhorrent as Hitler's discrimination against the Jewish people could happen here,' said Evelina, her voice rising with fear.

'What do *you* care?' said Francesco with a chuckle. 'You're not Jewish.'

'I'm human,' Evelina snapped.

Francesco shrugged. 'We're all human and we all think Hitler's anti-Semitism is a disgrace. However, I respectfully disagree with you, Tani. Mussolini considers Italy a healthy blend of races. That's what makes us great. If Mussolini forms an alliance with Germany, he will not bow to Hitler's views on race. He won't be dictated to by anyone. He'll make a puppet out of Hitler.' He drained his glass of brandy and replaced it loudly on the table. 'He'll have Hitler wrapped around his little finger.'

Benedetta laughed with admiration for her brilliant husband. Evelina smiled too. She didn't always agree with Francesco, but right now she wanted to. Tani and Artemisia remained quiet. What did the younger generation know about anything?

CHAPTER SEVEN

Giorgio Bruno was born in the spring of the following year. Any residual resentment between Benedetta and Evelina evaporated in the joy that accompanied his birth. It was as if this child brought with him a power to heal. Artemisia returned more fully to the world, Francesco softened and showed himself to be a doting father. Nonna Pierangelini and Costanza clucked like a pair of hens. Tani rarely spent time in his study when his grandson was in the house and like a magnet the baby attracted family members from all over Italy to Villa L'Ambrosiana, filling it with the cheery sound of chatter and laughter and the smell of cooking.

Evelina thought about Bruno. After his death she didn't think she'd ever have a child of her own, for fear of suffering loss. She didn't think her heart could endure such pain a second time. But now, looking into her nephew's little face, her heart swelled with love and it was so blissful, this feeling, that she realized she'd endure anything in order to experience it.

Those months were imbued with charm, cherry blossom and the scent of spring. Evelina spent as much time as she could with Ezra. They bicycled into the countryside, lay entwined in fields of poppies and kissed and talked and gazed up at the clouds. 'What do you see?' he asked.

'Clouds,' she replied and laughed.

'I see lions.'

'Lions?'

'Look! Can you not see them?' He pointed. 'There's the head with the mane. The nose and one eye.' He traced his finger along the body to the tip of the tail. 'Now tell me you don't see a lion.'

'I do,' said Evelina in surprise. 'And there's another one.'

'No, that's a tiger.'

'It's not a tiger. It has a mane.'

'That's not a mane, those are its whiskers.'

'Where have you ever seen whiskers like that?'

He rolled over and kissed her. 'You don't know your tigers from your lions!'

She laughed until he was kissing her deeply and the laughter was pushed down into her heart where it filled it with suds of happiness.

Evelina and Ezra dined at Via Montebello and tried to talk about other things besides Hitler and Mussolini's alliance, and the persecution of the Jewish people. Evelina wanted to remain in her bubble of endless sunny days, blossom and bougainvillea, and carefree evenings with Ezra. She wanted to bask in sunshine, beauty and love and not notice the grey clouds gathering on the horizon, edging their way slowly towards her, threatening to cover the sun and everything beautiful. She wanted these days of nonchalance to last for ever.

But nothing lasts for ever.

In July 1938, ten months before Mussolini signed the Pact of Steel alliance between Italy and Germany, the Italian newspapers published the 'Manifesto of Race', a pseudo-scientific article written by Fascist scientists that argued that race was purely biological, the Italian race was Aryan and the Jews did not belong to the Italian race, which should be kept pure.

Tani read the article over breakfast. He shook his head in dismay and looked at his wife and daughter over his glasses. 'How does one define race?' he asked with a shrug. 'That question has been debated for hundreds of years and no one has yet to give a satisfactory answer.'

'How would you define it, Papa?' Evelina asked. She was so upset by the article that she could no longer eat her breakfast.

'Racism assumes a link between biology and culture, otherwise it is simply ethnicity,' Tani told her. 'One cannot say that Italy is made up of people of one biology and culture. If the Aryan people settled in Italy in the Iron Age, then what happened to the original Italians?' He shook his head for he found the very question he was asking ludicrous. 'There are Nordic people and Mediterranean people and many in between. Various scholars have concluded that race only exists in the context of communal identity. If Mussolini wants to unite the Italian people in a common identity then the Jewish people are a part of that diverse mix that makes Italy what it is.' He folded the paper and put it on the table. 'During these times of uncertainty Il Duce should be encouraging his people to find strength in unity, not driving a wedge between them and fostering hate. You want to know my opinion? I don't believe in race.'

Artemisia and Evelina were so incensed by the manifesto that they drove straight over to Ercole Zanotti to show their solidarity. They found the shutters down and the shop closed. When they knocked, a pale-faced Ercole pulled back the curtain. When he saw it was Artemisia and Evelina, he unbolted the door and allowed them in. Evelina looked around for Ezra, but he wasn't there.

'We are ashamed to be Italians,' Artemisia told them, embracing Olga who quietly cried against Artemisia's breast. She was fearful that this was only the beginning and, with Mussolini keen to show his loyalty to Hitler in order to strengthen their alliance, he might allow anti-Semitism to go even further. But Ercole was adamant that Mussolini was not a man who saw distinctions between races. 'In fact, I would go as far to say that Mussolini will take a very dim view of this manifesto. These scientists don't know what they're talking about. One of them is a zoologist! It's laughable.'

'What are you going to do?' Evelina asked.

'Do?' Ercole shrugged. 'There is nothing to do, but what we have always done. Put our heads down and continue to work as good Italians.' He glanced at his wife. 'It will pass,' he added, but Evelina could tell from the fear on Olga's face that she didn't believe him.

Evelina met Ezra later at Fioruccia and Matteo's. She was shocked to find them all so upset. She had hoped that they would take the same philosophical view as Ercole, but they did not. 'There's a German man I work with,' said Matteo gravely. 'The things he tells me that are going on in Germany would make your blood run cold. It's only a matter of time before the poison seeps into Italy.'

'We need to *do* something,' said Ezra with passion.

'But what?' Fioruccia asked. 'What can we do? We have no money, no power, no voice.'

'We need to think about leaving.' He looked at Evelina and took her hand. The reassuring smile he gave her did nothing to soothe her fears.

Matteo shrugged. 'We have nowhere to go.'

'And our lives are here,' Fioruccia added, looking incredulous. 'Our businesses, our homes, our friends. We just need to keep quiet and hope the storm passes.'

'You sound like your brother,' said Evelina with a smile. 'Maybe it's too soon to think about leaving. After all, the Italian people will be appalled by this manifesto. I can't believe anyone will support it. There'll be an uproar. Just you wait.'

'It's not the Italians I'm worried about,' said Ezra. 'It's the Germans, and every day their influence grows stronger.' He kissed her hand. 'You only have to look into our history to know that when you sense danger it's because there *is* danger. It's not the time to sit it out and wait for the danger to pass. When it comes it will be too late.'

Ezra's words echoed in Evelina's ears when, in September, foreign-born Jews were banished from Italy and Jewish children and teachers expelled from Italian schools and universities. Evelina's first thoughts were of Fioruccia, who was a teacher in the local school. Her second thoughts were for all the refugees fleeing Germany and Austria who would have to find somewhere else to take them in. Where could they go? Unable to take more than a paltry sum with them, what would they live on?

Inter-racial marriages between Jews and non-Jews were also prohibited. As appalling as this law was, Evelina was sure that, by the time she was ready to marry, Mussolini's government would have been replaced by another, or she and Ezra would have gone to live in America. She did not, for one moment, believe she wouldn't marry Ezra.

To her horror, Francesco agreed with much of the race manifesto. Evelina knew that her brother-in-law's admiration for Il Duce was such that, as Il Duce withdrew the support he had in the past given to the Jewish community through his many speeches and interviews, so did Francesco. 'Perhaps it's a good thing to weed out those in our nation who are unhelpful to our Fascist ideals,' he said one evening over dinner at Villa L'Ambrosiana.

'What do you mean by that?' Evelina asked, trying to restrain her temper. When she looked at Benedetta, her sister avoided catching her eye. The pink stains on her cheeks, however, revealed her discomfort.

'Citing Paolo Orano's book *The Jews in Italy*,' Francesco replied in the pompous tone of one who claims absolute knowledge on a subject while in reality knowing very little, 'the Jews are essentially a subversive and revolutionary people who aim to undermine and ultimately control the nations in which they settle. The Jews have brought their troubles upon themselves.'

At this outrageous declaration, Tani spoke up, this time in a voice that was not his usual quiet and patient tone. 'While I welcome debate in this house, and have had many discussions with you where we do not agree, I draw the line at this. This kind of talk is not welcome here.'

Francesco's face went the colour of bull's blood. He inhaled through his nostrils. 'I'm not saying I agree with what Hitler is doing in Germany, I just think their control needs to be curbed.'

'Control?' Tani exclaimed. 'What control? They're being terrorized in Russia, denied any civil rights in Germany, suffering unspeakable conditions in the Balkan states and in Poland they're trying to send three million Jews into exile. Yes, you do need to worry about the Jewish people's growing power,' he said sarcastically. 'If you're not careful they'll take over the world!'

No one had ever seen Tani so furious. Evelina, Benedetta and Artemisia and the old sisters stared at him in astonishment. Francesco's jaw hardened. 'This is anti-Fascist talk,' he said and drained his wine glass. 'I think we should leave,' he said to his wife. 'We're not welcome here.'

'You're very welcome here, Francesco,' said Tani softly. 'It's your opinions I object to.'

Francesco said goodnight stiffly and left the room. Benedetta, her eyes shining with tears, followed after him dutifully. The following morning they packed their bags and left for Milan, cutting their stay short. Evelina wondered whether they'd ever come back.

On the 17th of November, the second series of racial laws was passed. Jews were fired from all public jobs, as well as from the army, navy and air force. They were expelled from the National Fascist Party, which hit Ercole hard because he'd been very proud of his membership. They were not allowed to own businesses with more than a hundred employees or businesses related to national defence. They were forbidden from employing non-Jewish domestic help.

Matteo was directly affected by these laws because he owned a textile company that employed over a hundred people. With great sadness he was forced to sign over his business to his foreman and hope that he'd be honest and sign it back when the troubles ended. Olga employed a young Catholic girl to help in the house. Now she had to let her go. The new laws affected every one of Ercole and Olga's family members.

Once again Ezra tried to persuade Ercole to leave. He told Evelina that his father was adamant that they stay. He didn't want to give up his business and his home for something that might not happen. 'I told him that Hitler will return all the Jews to the ghettos. It's already happening in Rome. They're forbidden to work in their professions and have nothing to live off. Italy has turned against them and they are being left to rot. German Jews are being sent to labour camps in Poland. It's only a matter of time before things get worse here. We have time to run away, but we have to go *now*.'

'But where will you go?'

'America. We can get entry visas for a sum. But Papa won't hear of it. He's as stubborn as a mule. He says he doesn't want to leave. He's Italian, he says, as if that's going to protect him from the anti-Semites. He continues to have faith in Il Duce.'

'Even after these racial laws?'

'He's mad. Hitler won't leave a single Jew alive.'

Evelina's throat grew tight. She stared at him with wide, incredulous eyes. 'You think he'll *kill* you?' she said hoarsely.

'I think he wants to annihilate the whole lot of us.'

'But he can't do that. He can't murder people and get away with it?'

'He'll do whatever he likes and no one will have the power to stop him. The only place we'll be safe is in America. People are leaving in their droves already. I don't want to be left behind.'

'Then go! We'll go together. We can stay with my aunt Madolina. Leave your father here to weather it out and go.'

Ezra shook his head. 'I'm not leaving my family behind. It's either all of us or none of us.'

Evelina wrapped her arms around him. 'Oh Ezra.'

He buried his face in her neck. 'I won't take it lying down, Eva,' he said. 'I'll fight in the Resistance. There are already quite a number, you know.'

'It might not get to that,' Evelina said hopefully.

'It will,' Ezra replied.

Evelina now saw the world through the eyes of the Jewish people and it was a frightening, hostile place. Fascism had acquired a deeply threatening face. The Roman salute that had replaced the handshake symbolized the militarization of her country, the banishment of compassion and empathy and the surfacing of coldness, intolerance and an ugly greed for power.

The following summer Jews were banned from skilled professions. Doctors, dentists, engineers, accountants, architects, journalists, lawyers and many more were prohibited from working. Children of mixed marriages were exempt from the racial laws and there were stories of Jewish mothers signing affidavits stating that their children were the result of extramarital affairs with Catholics in order to get them Aryan status. Still, Ercole Zanotti did not want to leave. In spite of these further restrictions he believed that if he kept his head down, remained quiet and got on with his business, life would eventually return to normal and he and his family would be left in peace.

Those who could, left. Ezra begged his father to follow the exodus. Ercole dug in his heels. 'I'm Italian,' he repeated. 'And no one, not even Mussolini, can tell me otherwise.' Ezra told Evelina that he felt like a pariah, because people now crossed the street to avoid him and were unable to look him in the eye. Shops even put notices in their windows stating: *No dogs or Jews.* And the news from Germany only got worse.

'I want to tell everyone that I love you,' Evelina told Ezra one afternoon when they were alone in Fioruccia's sitting room. It was raining hard against the windowpanes and almost as dark as night. Inside, the fire was lit and its golden light danced across the walls like demons. 'I don't want to hide anymore. Everyone should know.'

Ezra kissed her temple. 'I don't want to hide either, but it's imprudent, Eva. If the police find out, we could both be in trouble.'

'Then at least allow me to tell my parents,' she said.

He looked at her with tenderness. 'All right. I'll tell mine too. My father will be very disappointed. He wants me to marry a daughter of Israel.' He laughed. 'In the light of what's going on right now, I don't think he's in any position to demand anything of me. Love is a fragile and precious thing and we're lucky to have it.'

'Whatever happens, Ezra, I'll never stop loving you. You know that, don't you?' Evelina's eyes filled with tears.

He cupped her face and kissed her lips. 'I'll never stop loving you, either.'

'I'm frightened.'

'Me too. I'm not frightened of the Fascists or the Nazis, I'm frightened of losing *you*.' They held each other close. 'I don't want you to ever regret loving me.'

'Why would I do that?'

'Because if I were Catholic you'd have nothing to be afraid of.'

'If I learned one thing from Bruno's death, it's that love hurts. It hurts so much that the head tells you not to love, to protect yourself from pain. The heart, however, yearns to love. It will do anything for it. It will suffer gladly for the smallest taste of it.' She squeezed him harder. 'I'm enjoying a *feast* of love, Ezra, and even my head is not telling me to stop.'

He couldn't argue with that.

*

Evelina decided to tell her parents, Nonna Pierangelini and
Costanza over lunch the following day. The five of them
were alone at the dining-room table. It was still raining. It
looked like it would never stop. 'I have something important
I need to tell you,' she began.

Tani put down his knife and fork and wiped his mouth
with a napkin. 'What is it, my dear?'

'I'm in love.'

Artemisia looked surprised. She arched her eyebrows.
'With whom?'

Nonna Pierangelini looked at her with interest. 'At last,'
she said with a sigh.

Evelina took a breath. 'Ezra Zanotti.'

Both parents were startled. Ezra was not one of the young
men in Evelina's circle. They hadn't ever considered *him*. The
name meant little to the old ladies, who frowned, trying to
work out where they'd heard it before. 'The same Zanotti
as the shop?' asked Nonna Pierangelini.

'Is he a shopkeeper?' asked Costanza with a grin. 'Very
modern.'

'Jewish,' said Nonna Pierangelini, pulling a sympathetic
face, foreseeing trouble.

'For how long has this been going on?' Tani asked.

'Over three years.'

'Three years!' Artemisia was horrified. Evelina could
see her doing the maths and trying to work out how it had
flowered without her noticing.

'I see, so it's serious then,' said Tani, nodding to himself.

'But you can't marry him. The law won't allow it,' said
Artemisia, visibly flustered. 'I mean, even if he were suitable,
which he isn't, the racial laws prohibit inter-racial marriage.
Surely you know that?'

'Of course, but that won't stop me loving him. You can't choose whom you love. It just happens.'

'How romantic,' sighed Costanza.

'Not if he's carted off and imprisoned,' said Nonna Pierangelini wryly.

'Jewish men are wonderfully sensual lovers,' Costanza added with a grin. 'I should know.'

'Does he want to marry you?' Tani asked, ignoring his aunt.

'He does.'

'Then you only have one choice. You must both go to America.'

Evelina shook her head. 'Ezra won't go because his father won't go.'

'Well, that's ridiculous!' Artemisia cried.

Evelina shrugged. 'Ezra has tried to persuade him, but he's adamant that he's Italian and that he has as much right as anyone to be here. Besides, his business is here. What would he do in America?'

'Start a new business,' said Artemisia simply.

'There's so much opportunity in America,' said Costanza, who knew nothing about it.

'I understand his reluctance to leave,' said Tani. 'No one wants to be a refugee. His family has lived here for generations. It's devastating for them to contemplate giving up their home and livelihood.'

'We'll sit it out,' said Evelina firmly. 'After all, Fascism won't go on for ever, will it? I'm only twenty-two. There's no rush.'

'I was married at nineteen,' said Nonna Pierangelini.

'I'm nearly eighty and I've never married,' said Costanza. 'There are many roads to Rome.'

Artemisia was relieved by this decision of Evelina's to wait. 'No, there's no rush,' she said with a smile. 'You're absolutely right, darling. Who knows what the future holds.'

Tani inhaled deeply. 'Has Ezra told Ercole and Olga?'

Evelina nodded. 'He's telling them today.'

'I doubt they'll be very pleased,' he said with a wry smile. 'I dare say they'd have preferred Romina. However, be that as it may. If the two of you are determined that you won't go to America, then you have no choice but to wait it out here. In which case, you must be very careful.'

'We'll keep it secret,' Evelina reassured him.

'Have you told Benedetta?'

'Yes, I told her a while ago. She didn't approve. We had a row. We haven't spoken about it since.'

Tani narrowed his eyes. 'I don't like to speak ill of anyone, least of all my son-in-law, but I wouldn't trust Francesco.'

'I told you,' said her grandmother. 'It's in the moustache.'

'What do you think he'll do?' Artemisia asked, worried.

Tani shrugged. 'I don't think he'll do anything, but he's not a friend of the Jewish people. That's all I'll say. Be careful.'

Ezra reported that Ercole and Olga were not happy to hear that he intended to marry Evelina. Olga had cried. She had wanted a nice Jewish girl for her eldest son. Ercole had lost his temper. He was worried that the police would find out that the two of them were seeing each other and send Ezra off to prison. 'You must obey the rules, Ezra, and not draw attention to yourself. You have no idea what they do to people who go against the regime.' Ezra had told him that he knew very well what they did and that he wasn't about to go and flaunt his love. He asked his father once again to change his mind and emigrate to America. His father refused.

The following year, on 10 June 1940, Italy entered the war on the side of Germany. Mussolini had dithered and dawdled, but with Great Britain on the retreat and France on the brink of surrender, Il Duce dived into the war in the hope of having a place at the winners' table when Hitler divided up Europe.

Francesco enlisted immediately. He was confident the Rome–Berlin Axis would defeat the Allies. In his eyes Il Duce was invincible. Still Benedetta did not return to Villa L'Ambrosiana and Giorgio grew into a little boy without knowing his mother's side of the family and the enchanting delights of her home.

Life for the Zanottis continued in spite of the war. Fioruccia taught at the Jewish school which had been established by the community following the racial laws. Her nephews and nieces studied and slowly came to terms with their new life, even though they missed their friends. Ercole sold fabric as usual and Olga made dresses, although business was thin on the ground. Matteo's factory still manufactured army uniforms but the demand was in decline and fuel was scant. Ezra worked very little in the shop and spent more time away. Evelina knew he was working with the Resistance, but when she asked him directly, he simply answered that he had friends who were involved and he liked to give them his support.

Evelina and Ezra were now able to spend time together at Villa L'Ambrosiana. Ezra's home above the shop was not an option on account of his five siblings coming in and out, which prevented them from finding space in which to be alone. In the salons of Villa L'Ambrosiana they read the newspapers and listened to the radio. Ezra gleaned information from German-speaking contacts of the horrors happening to the Jews in Poland and Eastern Europe and the camps designed to destroy them. So terrible were the stories that Evelina refused to believe them.

In July 1943 Fascism fell. Mussolini was voted out of power by the Fascist Grand Council and, with his arrest, twenty-one years of Fascist rule in the Kingdom of Italy came to an end. Ercole was ecstatic. 'I was right all along,' he declared, wiping the dust off an expensive bottle of wine. 'Now the war will end and Badoglio will lift the racial laws.' Ezra felt foolish for having tried to persuade him to leave. 'You see, my son, experience always knows best,' Ercole continued as Olga took glasses down from the cupboard. 'Now let's drink to freedom.'

There was dancing and singing in the streets outside the shop and the Zanotti family finished their wine and celebrated with the rest of their community, soaking up the wonderful feeling of optimism that filled with air with bubbles. As soon as he could get away, Ezra cycled to Villa L'Ambrosiana to make merry with Evelina. When she saw him pedalling up the drive she flung open the door and ran down the steps to greet him. He dropped his bicycle to the ground and pulled her into his arms. 'It's time to plan our wedding,' he said, and Evelina laughed with relief and excitement. 'Papa was right,' he added, kissing her. 'I should never have doubted him.'

Their euphoria turned quickly to terror, however, when the German tanks moved swiftly into Italy. Badoglio, Mussolini's successor, fled and the Italian army floundered with no leadership. The Germans freed Mussolini and took control of the northern part of Italy, calling it the Italian Social Republic and reinstating Il Duce as the leader of the reformed Republican Fascist Party. The Jewish people were now left to the mercy of Nazi Germany. There would be no wedding for Ezra and Evelina and it was too late to leave for America. The expensive bottle of wine that Ercole had opened in celebration remained on the sideboard as a reminder that experience doesn't always make a person wise.

CHAPTER EIGHT

Ercole Zanotti stopped saying 'What's happening in Germany would never happen here' the night he and his family were arrested. The Germans now occupied the town and those who could leave had left. Many had tried to flee to Switzerland, only to fall prey to unscrupulous guides who traded them to the Germans. Those who made it across the border were often sent back, or languished in refugee camps. The lucky ones who had money and connections found freedom after having bribed guides, border officials and hoteliers. But it was too late now for Ercole and Olga Zanotti and their family.

Evelina heard the news from Ezra who cycled across the countryside to Villa L'Ambrosiana in the middle of the night. He threw stones at her window and, when she appeared, whispered loudly to meet her in the chapel and to come at once. Evelina knew something terrible had happened and dressed hurriedly. She sneaked down the back stairs and out through the kitchen door. She ran as fast as she could through the balmy September night to where the chapel shone like a secret jewel in the moonlight.

'The Fascists have taken everyone,' Ezra told her

breathlessly when she entered and found him pacing agitat-edly back and forth across the stone floor.

'Everyone?'

'Mamma, Papa, Enrico, Giovanni, Damiana, Alessandra, Maurizio.'

Evelina put a hand across her mouth in horror. 'What happened?'

'There was a massive crash as the shop window was shat-tered. It was so loud I thought part of the house had fallen down. Before any of us could make sense of our thoughts they were banging on the door with their rifle butts and ringing the bell. Papa went to open the door and they stormed in. I hid upstairs in the back bedroom. They were shouting at us to pack our suitcases with clothes and books . . .'

Evelina noticed blood glistening on his cheek. 'How did you get away?'

'I threw myself out of the back window and escaped over the roof. I should have taken the others with me, but there was no time and they were too far down the corridor. When I heard what was happening, I followed my instincts and fled. Had I waited longer they would have seen me. There was no time.' He put his hand to his forehead. 'I could have at least tried to bring Maurizio . . .'

'Where are they taking them?'

'I don't know.'

'Oh, Ezra. What are you going to do?'

'I'm going to hide out here until it's safe to find my friends in the mountains.'

'Okay, I'll bring you everything you need.'

He pulled her against him and held her tightly. 'We should have left,' he groaned.

'There's no point looking back. You need to look forward

now and work out how you're going to survive. You know I'll do anything I can to help you.'

'I know you will.'

'Mamma and Papa would happily hide you in our attic—'

'I'm not going to hide like a rat. I'm going to find the Resistance and join them. That's the only thing I can do to help my family and others like them.'

'Do you think they've taken Fioruccia and Matteo?'

'I imagine they've rounded up all the Jews.'

'Oh God. This isn't happening!' Evelina felt dizzy with terror.

'I'm afraid it is. But we have to be strong.'

Evelina tried to find something positive to say. That they'd be imprisoned for a while and then released, but she couldn't lie. She'd heard rumours of what the Germans did to Jews and had refused to believe it. Now it was happening to the Zanottis and the Ferraros, she feared those rumours might be true. She held on to Ezra ever more tightly.

Evelina had never been so afraid in her life and yet fear translated into decisive action. She ran back to the house and gathered things she thought Ezra would need: blankets, water, bread, cold meat and a couple of books. She also brought candles and a box of matches, but Ezra said he wouldn't light them in case anyone came looking for him. 'They're not going to come all the way out here,' she told him, but Ezra wasn't so sure.

'I'm not going to take any chances,' he said. 'Don't tell your parents I'm here. Don't tell anyone, do you understand? You can't trust a soul. Not a soul.' Evelina knew she could trust her parents, but she agreed to keep him secret all the same. 'Tomorrow the town will be talking of nothing else. They must believe that I've gone too.'

Evelina nodded. 'Is there anything I can get you from the apartment? Papers, money, anything?'

'I imagine Papa emptied the safe. He will have taken everything important with him.' He swore, spitting the word out with fury. 'He should have listened to me.'

'I know, he should have.'

'He should have taken the chance when it was offered. We could have all been in America by now.'

Ezra slumped against her then and sobbed. Evelina had never seen a grown man cry and it made her feel more afraid than ever. She held him close, trying to absorb his pain so that he would suffer less. Then they were kissing. A passionate kiss, heightened by the terror of his flight and the fear of what tomorrow might bring. Neither knew what the future held, or if there would be a future at all. Their uncertainty fuelled their desire and thrust them into the moment with an intensity neither had ever felt before. Evelina gave herself to Ezra not as a woman on her wedding night, but with the hunger and craving of a woman on the brink of losing the man she loved.

Dawn was seeping into the night's sky when Evelina went back to the villa and climbed into bed. She didn't try to sleep. She stared up at the ceiling, feeling only the panicked beating of her heart and a terrible sticky fear in the pit of her belly. How could this be happening? In the morning she joined her parents at the breakfast table and tried to appear normal. Artemisia noticed her pallor and commented upon it, but her father was too engrossed in the newspaper to notice. After breakfast she rode her bicycle into Vercellino to find the place practically deserted. No one walked the streets, shops were closed. A dreadful silence hung over the piazza. She leaned her bicycle against the wall on Via Agnello and walked over to Ercole Zanotti's shattered shop window. There was broken glass all over the cobblestones, glinting in the sunlight. It appeared as if nothing had been stolen, however. Rolls of fabric remained on the shelves. Trimmings and lace on the counter alongside fashion magazines and a vase of yellow flowers. One of the neighbours appeared, scratching his balding head. He was middle-aged with an unshaven face and a sad look in his eyes. He told Evelina that he'd heard the glass shatter at about two in the morning and had peered out of his window to see what the commotion was about. He saw the family being taken away in a police van. 'They're good people, the Zanottis,' he said.

'They'll be back,' Evelina told him firmly.

The man shrugged and pulled a face. He didn't believe it. 'I'll get my sons to help me board it up so no one takes off with his merchandise,' he said. 'Then, if they do return, they'll find they have a business to come back to.'

Evelina nodded. 'You're very kind.'

'It's the least I can do. I'm ashamed of my country.'

'It's no longer our country, it's Hitler's,' she said and turned away so that he didn't see her tears.

For the next few days Ezra hid out in the chapel. Evelina brought him food, water and cigarettes and told him what she'd heard on the radio. The Germans had taken over Vercellino and four of them had arrived at the villa in a big black car, in their bottle-green uniforms and peaked caps, and talked to her father in private. Artemisia had feared they were going to requisition the house and steal her paintings, but they didn't. They were polite. They didn't speak a word of Italian so they'd communicated in English, which Tani spoke fluently. They'd simply come to introduce themselves, they said. Tani told Evelina later that they'd come to show him who was boss.

As soon as Ezra was able to flee into the mountains to fight alongside the partisans, he did. He promised Evelina that he'd be back and he was true to his word. In the months that followed he returned every week. She managed to give him one of her father's old woollen sweaters, a few pairs of thick socks and heavy leather boots. She hoped Tani wouldn't miss them. Occasionally Ezra would come with a group of two or three men and they'd eat the food Evelina brought from the kitchen, smoke cigarettes and sleep under the blankets she provided. Soon, they were hiding arms in the small room at the back of the chapel and coming more often. Artemisia and Tani were oblivious, retreating further and further into their turgid worlds so that they, like the villa itself, seemed to sink into a timeless stupor.

The partisans Ezra had joined were Jewish like him who hadn't the money or the contacts to flee, young men avoiding conscription, released prisoners of war and anti-Fascists. They were well armed, efficient and full of swagger. In spite of the dangers, it seemed that they relished the sense of brotherhood this adventure gave them, and the feeling of heightened patriotism and purpose.

They had found out that Jews had been rounded up throughout Italy and been taken to a detainment camp at Fossoli. This military base had originally been used for British prisoners of war, but when Italy had surrendered in September those POWs had been moved to Germany and the camp had been adapted into a concentration camp for Jews. At the end of every month cattle cars of prisoners were sent off to Auschwitz in Poland. Ezra was devastated, but hopeful

that the Allies would advance north, end the war and liberate
them. He did not entertain the idea that he would never see
his family again. That thought was unthinkable.

Evelina heard little from Benedetta. Since Francesco's
argument with their father, they hadn't been back to the
villa. Artemisia was distraught that she wasn't allowed to
see her grandson and begged her daughter to come and stay
for Christmas. Evelina didn't want her sister to come, for
while she was at the villa Ezra would have to stay away. It
was simply too dangerous. But Benedetta agreed and brought
Giorgio on the train from Milan.

When Evelina saw her sister, her resentment lifted and
they embraced with regret that they had allowed so much
time to pass without seeing each other. Giorgio had grown
into a cherubic little boy. He was now six years old and full
of curiosity and joy. Artemisia found traces of Bruno in his
features but as hard as Evelina tried, she did not; he looked
just like his mother. Benedetta, on the other hand, looked
tired and drawn and strangely shifty, jumping at every
sudden noise, like a timid mouse.

Francesco was in the south with the Italian army, fighting alongside the Allies. Benedetta confided in Evelina one
evening that after his fight with Tani his pride had prevented
him from coming back. 'He believed in Fascism as if it
were a religion and Il Duce a god,' she told her. 'Now the
south has fallen and Mussolini is but a puppet of Hitler's, he
won't want to admit that he was wrong. When it's all over I
imagine he'll be a very angry, disillusioned man.' Benedetta
turned her eyes to the fire and smiled softly. 'It's good to be
home,' she said.

'We've missed you and Giorgio,' said Evelina, her feet
curled beside her on the sofa.

'I know, and I've missed you too. It wasn't right to keep Giorgio from seeing his grandparents and his aunt, not to mention his great-grandmother and great-aunt. You can imagine how much he sees Francesco's parents.'

'I can.' Evelina raised her eyebrows. 'He's a strong man, your husband.'

'Not the sort of man one contradicts,' Benedetta said slowly. Her face darkened, as if she was distracted by an ugly thought. 'Still, for better or for worse!'

'Are things okay between the two of you?'

Benedetta sighed. 'He has quite a temper.'

Evelina didn't like the way the conversation was turning. 'What sort of temper?'

'Well, you know, he drinks and then he behaves in a way that isn't gallant.'

'Has he . . .' Evelina hesitated, not wanting to intrude on their married life.

'Hit me?' Benedetta finished the sentence for her. She nodded. 'Of course. He's good with the back of his hand.'

'Benedetta!' Evelina was horrified. She remembered what her grandmother had said about his moustache.

'It's okay. Don't tell Mamma or Papa, please. I can handle it.'

'You shouldn't have to.'

'He thinks it's his right.'

'No one has the right to hit another, however much they're provoked.'

'I probably do provoke him. We have very different views of the world.' She looked at Evelina and her eyes turned sad. 'I feel terrible about the Zanottis,' she said. 'Just terrible.'

'Mamma told you?'

'She did. Ezra was taken too?'

'They were *all* taken,' Evelina lied.

'Will they ever come back?'

'I hope so. If the Allies win the war and liberate them. Who knows what their fate will be?'

'Let's go into Vercellino tomorrow and light some candles for them.'

'Yes, that's a good idea. I'm afraid I've turned my back on my faith.'

'Now is the time you need it most.'

'It's hard to have faith when there's so much misery in the world. The stories one hears are horrific. I think God has taken His attention off the world. Perhaps it's too much even for Him.'

'I'm sorry about what Francesco said about the Jews.'

'I know you didn't agree with him.'

'Some of our biggest arguments have been about that.' Benedetta touched her cheek gently as if to nurse an existing bruise. 'I've paid for my opinions, but it's a price I'm willing to pay. No one should treat other human beings in that way. It's despicable.'

'I'm sorry you married him, Benedetta.'

Benedetta shook her head. 'I'm not. I have Giorgio. I wouldn't change that for anything in the world.'

The following morning they drove Tani's car into Vercellino. Benedetta was saddened but not surprised to see the Zanottis' shop boarded up with planks of wood. The broken glass had long since been cleared away but an eerie silence pervaded the street, as if the spirit had left, leaving the body to decay. 'Do you remember the excitement we used to feel coming here?' Benedetta asked wistfully.

'Of course,' said Evelina with a shudder, envisaging the

family being taken away in a police van. 'Olga was such a sweet, gentle person, and Ercole . . . Well, they were just the nicest people.'

'I hope they come back.'

'Benedetta, no one is going to come back.'

'How can you possibly know that?'

Evelina started walking away. 'I don't, I just fear it. I hope I'm wrong.'

They wandered through the town to the church. The medieval building cast a long shadow over the piazza and reached its tall, ornate tower skywards in a silent supplication to the God Evelina believed was no longer listening. They wandered through the giant wooden doors. Inside, various people were sitting on chairs, kneeling in prayer and lighting votive candles up at the front, in the transept. Old people mostly, men, hats in hand, and women dressed in black, mourning the fallen. The atmosphere was sombre and sad. There was little gold on the altar for most of it had been melted down to fund Il Duce's war in Abyssinia, but there were candles, flickering through the gloom. The place smelt of warm wax and centuries, and reverberated with the tremor of prayer that seemed to be embedded in the frescoed walls.

They walked up the aisle and stood in front of the table where small votive candles burned, cradling in their golden flames the hopes and appeals of those who had lit them. Evelina and Benedetta added their supplications to the table, closing their eyes a moment to concentrate on their prayers. Afterwards they genuflected in front of the altar and left the way they had come. Once outside, Benedetta turned to Evelina and asked, 'Do you still love Ezra?'

'Yes,' Evelina replied. 'With all my heart.'

'I lit a candle for him.'

Evelina smiled. 'That makes two of us.'

The night before Christmas, it snowed. Giant flakes tumbled from the sky, rapidly forming a thick quilt that covered the estate. Giorgio was beside himself with excitement when he awoke in the morning and looked out of the window. He loved snow and couldn't wait to go outside to play in it. As it was early, Benedetta took him out before breakfast. She watched him run about the gardens, delighting in the fluffiness of it, sticking his tongue out to catch the few smaller flakes that twirled on the wind.

They wandered through the trees and Benedetta recalled those times in her youth when she had wanted nothing more than to leave. Now she wanted nothing more than to stay. Shortly, she came upon the clearing where the chapel sat in the dim light of dawn like a beleaguered ship, its roof blue-white with snow. She thought of Bruno then for he had loved to play there. How he would have adored the snow. Giorgio ran ahead. He didn't notice the chapel. He was more interested in the footprints that came out of the trees, went across the clearing and stopped at the big door.

Benedetta frowned. She looked to the wood and then at the chapel. These footprints were recent, perhaps only minutes ago. Her heart began to beat wildly. She called Giorgio over and took his hand. Together they walked to the door and pushed it open. It was dim inside and smelt of cigarette smoke. She entered. 'Hello!' she called, her voice sounding braver than she felt. There came no reply. She continued on, past the wooden chairs to the end where the bare altar stood among crispy brown leaves and dead spiders. Then she noticed blankets strewn in one corner. They were blankets from the villa. She didn't imagine her mother had put them there. Curiosity drove her into the room at the back. When she saw the quantity of guns lined up against the wall and wooden boxes piled on top of one another, her heart stalled. These belonged to partisans.

Giorgio followed after her. Before he saw what was in there she managed to divert him and nudge him back into the main part of the chapel. 'Let's go and have breakfast,' she said, trying to keep the tremor out of her voice. The child was only too pleased to get out into the snow again and began to kick it in delight. Benedetta felt sick.

As she stepped across the threshold, she noticed a sealed white envelope with Evelina's name on it. She hadn't noticed it before. She was tempted to open it, but as she put her thumb beneath the flap, she stopped herself. It wasn't her business, after all. No, she'd take it to Evelina and ask her to explain herself.

When she got back to the house, Artemisia was already at the breakfast table. 'Happy Christmas,' she said brightly. Then she spotted the anxiety on her daughter's face. 'Are you all right, darling?'

'I just feel a little nauseous. Can you look after Giorgio for a moment while I go upstairs?'

Artemisia gave Benedetta a knowing look. 'You don't think you're ...?'

'I don't know.'

Artemisia smiled. 'Oh, I do hope so. It's about time. Now that would be the best Christmas present, ever.'

Benedetta hurried up the stairs to her sister's bedroom. Evelina was at her dressing table brushing her hair. 'Happy Christmas!' she exclaimed. 'Isn't it gorgeous, the snow!'

'Evelina.'

At her sister's harsh tone, Evelina stopped brushing. She turned to look at her. 'What? Has something happened?'

'I've just been to the chapel.'

Evelina lifted her chin. 'Oh,' she said. She was quite sure Ezra and his men would not have been near it since Benedetta had come home.

'And there are footprints all over the snow. I went inside and found . . .' She lowered her voice. 'Guns!'

Evelina got up and hurried to close the door. 'Yes, I know, I can explain.'

'You'd better.'

'But you must swear not to tell a soul.'

'It's a bit late for that. I don't have to swear to anything. I've seen them with my own eyes.'

'All right. Ezra wasn't taken the night his family was arrested. He escaped and joined the partisans. He's been hiding out in the chapel.'

'It looks like he's been coming with his friends.'

'He has.'

'And you've been supplying them with food and blankets?'

'Yes.'

Benedetta began to pace the room in agitation. 'Do you realize how dangerous this is? You could get us all killed.'

'It's fine. No one comes out here.'

'Yet.'

'They don't even know the chapel exists, and why would they search the place anyway? We're safe, I promise you.'

'You'd better be right. If Mamma and Papa hear about this, you'll be in serious trouble.'

'They won't. No one goes into the chapel. No one except Bruno has been in there for years.'

Benedetta sighed and stopped pacing. 'I won't tell anyone,' she said quietly. 'But I'm scared.'

Evelina was relieved. It felt good to share her secret. 'It's all right. I was scared at the beginning too. But Ezra is fighting the Germans. He's helping the Allies. When the war is over he'll have played his part. His family will be released and everything will be good again.'

Benedetta looked at her sister with pity. 'You're such a dreamer,' she said, but her smile was full of affection.

'I have to dream. It's the only way I can survive; to believe that the war will end and Ezra and I can marry and have children and do all the things normal married couples do.'

'I didn't think you wanted marriage.'

'I do with Ezra. I want to give myself to him body and soul.'

'Then, I should give you this.' Benedetta took the envelope out of her pocket. 'It was on the floor as I went into the church. I think it must have been attached to the door and fallen off.'

Evelina tore it open and pulled out the paper. *We were ambushed by German soldiers in the night. I'm sorry to tell you that Ezra has been captured. Carlo.* Evelina's legs gave way and she collapsed onto the floor.

Benedetta took the letter out of her hand and read it.

There were no possible words of comfort. Nothing she could say would bring him back. She sat beside her sister and drew her into her arms.

CHAPTER NINE

Evelina walked through the snow to the chapel. The pain in her heart was unbearable. She had only ever felt such desolation once before in her life and that was when Bruno died. She hadn't thought it was possible to hurt so much and survive, yet she had; she knew now that she could survive this. Snow began to fall again in large wet flakes, settling into the footprints of the men who had come in the night to leave the grim message on the door. Soon those prints would be gone, covered up and hidden, as if they had never been.

Evelina pushed open the door. The place was empty. It was cold. The air misted on her breath. Everything was as they had left it when they had last spent the night. Blankets folded and placed in the corner, books Evelina had brought for Ezra in a tidy pile, flasks of water, the odd plate, forks, things they didn't really need, but which Evelina wanted them to have, to give them a sense of normality and comfort.

She sat on one of the wooden chairs and put her head in her hands. A sob was disgorged from the core of her, forced out by a strange contraction that is particular to grief. She had dwelt in this dark tunnel before, but its familiarity only made the experience all the more painful. She held her stomach and moaned. It sounded alien to her ears, more like the groan of a beast than the cry of a human. But she was alone so what did it matter? She allowed it to be drawn out of her in a long, agonizing howl, until there was no breath left in her and she had to inhale sharply to restore the air to her lungs.

Ezra, Ezra, Ezra . . .

Where would they take him? Would he, too, be sent to Fossoli? Would he be reunited with his family? Would they survive? Might the partisans rescue him? What could she do to help?

When Evelina returned to the villa her sister was at the breakfast table with their parents. Giorgio was playing with a paper aeroplane his grandfather had made him. Artemisia stood up when Evelina entered. Her face was full of compassion. She pulled out a chair. 'Come and sit down, my dear,' she said gently.

Evelina looked at her sister and frowned. Had she told them? Could she? Benedetta gave her a reassuring smile. Evelina sat down and looked from one parent to the other in bewilderment. There was a brief moment of silence before Artemisia spoke. 'This is a difficult time of year for all of us, Evelina,' she said. 'I think about Bruno every day, but at Christmas it hurts all the more.' Evelina started to cry. Her mother put her hand on hers. 'It's all right. There's no shame in showing your feelings, Evelina. It's natural. I understand.'

Tani smiled sympathetically. 'Bruno would not want us to be sad at Christmas, and in the snow. He loved snow, just like Giorgio does. Eat something, you'll feel better with a full stomach.'

Evelina wiped her eyes with her napkin. 'I'm sorry,' she mumbled, taking a breath. 'I'm just so desperately sad.'

Artemisia seemed to delight in her daughter's emotion

for it united them in their love for Bruno. She squeezed her hand. 'It's going to be a beautiful day,' she said. 'Bruno will be with us, for he wouldn't miss Christmas. We'll take strength from each other. That's what families do. We support each other during these difficult times.'

As soon as Benedetta was able to get Evelina on her own, she explained herself. 'I had to tell them something, otherwise you'd have been put on the spot and what would you have said was the reason for your tears?'

'Oh Benedetta. I'm going out of my mind. I don't know what to do. I don't know how to help . . .'

Benedetta put a hand on her shoulder. 'There's nothing you can do but wait. The war will be over soon and he'll be released.'

'What if they shoot him? They shoot partisans, you know.' Evelina began to cry again. 'What if he's already dead?'

'Don't say such things. You have to hope. That's all you can do.'

The sisters embraced and Evelina drew comfort from Benedetta's arms around her. 'I love him so much, Benedetta. I don't think I can live without him.'

'You won't have to. In the meantime, we must help the partisans.'

Evelina pulled away and looked at her sister in puzzlement. 'You want to help them?'

'Yes, anything to end this war. To bring Ezra back to you.'

'But you disapproved of Ezra . . .'

'If you love him, Eva, then he's the right man for you. I married a "suitable" man and look where it's got me.'

'Oh Benedetta . . .'

'Don't pity me. I chose him. Suitable doesn't count for anything if it just brings unhappiness. I don't think Francesco ever truly loved me. He just liked what I represented. I should have waited for a man like Ezra.' She smiled sadly. 'It's too late for me, but it's not too late for you. How can we help the partisans?'

Evelina felt a swell of empowerment, replacing her sense of impotence with action. 'I'll introduce you to them when they return after Christmas. They'll let us know what they need. The fact that we allow them to store arms in the chapel is a big help. I'm sure we can do more.'

'They'll need money. I have money.'

'Won't Francesco question where it's going?'

'No. He's generous. I want for nothing.'

'Very well.'

'And while he's away fighting, I can do what I like.' Benedetta sighed. 'To think I was once desperate to leave. Now I'm desperate to stay. I don't ever want to go back to Milan.'

After Christmas, Evelina introduced her sister to the band of men Ezra had fought alongside. The leader was a man in his fifties called Gianni Salvatore, from Turin, who had been imprisoned for four years in Regina Coeli prison in Rome. He'd been a member of the Giustizia e Libertà, an anti-Fascist resistance movement, and fought against Franco in the Spanish Civil War. He was ruggedly handsome with shaggy brown hair, intelligent brown eyes and a smile that turned up at the corners, which gave his face an irresistible charm. Benedetta took to him immediately, finding in him the romance and heroism her husband lacked. From that moment on she would do anything for their cause.

Gianni told Evelina what had happened to Ezra, how they'd been surrounded by German soldiers in the woods while they slept. Gianni hadn't been with them that night, but one of the men had managed to escape and was able to report back. Five of them had been taken off at gunpoint and they later found out that they'd been taken to Fossoli Camp where Ezra's family had gone. Evelina hoped they'd been reunited, but Gianni shook his head; he wasn't a man to sugar coat the truth. He said he imagined Ezra's family had been transported long ago to Auschwitz in Poland. As to their fate, he couldn't say.

Evelina prayed hard for the war to end and for Ezra and his family to survive. In the meantime, she and Benedetta supplied the men with food, enabled them to use the chapel as a safe house and bought cigarettes, medication and other essentials as and when they needed them. They sewed clothes that required mending and occasionally tended the wounded. As winter thawed and spring turned the land a lively, innocent green, Evelina realized that Benedetta was in love. Her sister's eyes sparkled, her gait was bouncy, her spirits buoyant. Gianni was sometimes away for weeks, other times he came to the chapel often. Benedetta waited for those moments like a loyal wife, praying for his safety as if she no longer had a husband to light candles for.

If it hadn't been for the partisans, Evelina would have pined with grief. Helping Gianni gave her a sense of purpose and the belief that she was helping Ezra. With every day that passed she felt a day closer to his release, and with every small comfort she was able to give to Gianni and his men, she imagined someone somewhere doing the same for Ezra. She knew they'd stopped sharing the news that was trickling in from survivors about the horrors of those prison camps in Poland and she was grateful to them for their discretion. She didn't want to hear. The mental torture would have been unbearable.

Evelina and Benedetta believed they were keeping their activities secret from their parents until one afternoon in June. They were finishing lunch on the terrace. The maid was clearing away the plates. Giorgio had gone to play in the garden with his nanny. Tani put his napkin on the table and lit a cigarette. He leaned over and held the match steady while Artemisia lit hers. Then he inhaled and let out a stream of smoke, sat back in his chair and lifted his chin. 'I think it's time that you girls told us exactly what's going on in the family chapel,' he said. He looked from one daughter to the other and his expression was inscrutable.

'I don't know what you're talking about, Papa,' said Benedetta.

He looked at Evelina. 'Perhaps you'll tell me then.'

'There's nothing going on in the chapel, Papa,' Evelina replied, eyes wide with innocence.

He smiled in amusement. 'I hope you'll be better at lying when the Germans come sniffing around here and asking questions.'

'And why would they do that?' Benedetta asked.

'Because it's inevitable,' interrupted Artemisia. 'Someone will sneak, they always do.'

Tani flicked ash into the ashtray. 'You're helping the Resistance,' he said. 'Don't think we haven't noticed.'

Artemisia shook her head. 'I'd have to be blind to miss the food being taken from the kitchen or the two of you rushing into the garden all the time.'

'We support you,' said Tani. 'In spite of the danger you're putting yourselves in, and us of course, you're doing the right thing.'

'We are?' Benedetta said, her shoulders dropping with relief.

'We support you,' Artemisia agreed and an old, forgotten light danced in her eyes from the time before Bruno's death, when she had relished being outspoken and controversial.

'You do?' Evelina was astonished.

'There's no running water in the chapel and it's not very comfortable,' their mother continued. 'If those men need a bath, a bed to sleep in and some proper food, you must bring them here.'

Tani nodded. 'Yes. The sooner we rid the country of the Germans the better.'

'And the sooner Eva gets Ezra back,' said Benedetta, glancing at her sister.

Tani and Artemisia looked at Evelina.

'He wasn't taken when they took Ercole and Olga,' she confessed. 'I harboured him in the chapel until it was safe for him to leave. Then he fled into the hills and joined the Resistance.'

'But they captured him at Christmas,' Benedetta added. 'He was taken to Fossoli.'

'Oh Evelina. I'm so sorry,' said Artemisia with feeling. 'And you've been hiding this from me for all these months?'

'I couldn't tell you.'

'Well, now you have, we must share everything. No more secrets. We're in this together.'

'What about Nonna and Costi?' Evelina asked.

Artemisia grinned. 'Helping the Resistance will give them something to do besides playing cards.'

Benedetta laughed. 'It'll give them a new lease of life,' she added. 'It wouldn't be fair to deny them that.'

'So, tell us, what's going on in the chapel?' Tani asked. As Benedetta and Evelina shared their clandestine activities with their parents, Evelina noticed that both Tani and Artemisia seemed to emerge out of their soporific worlds and step eagerly into theirs.

Over the summer months that followed, Gianni and his men took refuge in the villa. Tani enjoyed talking to them and hearing stories of their adventures. Nonna Pierangelini mothered them and Costanza flirted with them, and both women were grateful for the enthusiastic card players among their number. Artemisia organized the maids to help with the washing and sewing of their clothes and instructed her daughters to help Angelina in the kitchen. She floated about, relishing her new role, chatting up the men and flirting with Gianni, for she too was taken with this rough partisan who reeked of danger. But in spite of her beauty and the fact that she was closer in age to Gianni than Benedetta was, it soon became apparent that he cared only for Benedetta. Artemisia, who had enjoyed many affairs of her own, encouraged it. 'Life must never be boring,' she said, running her fingers down her daughter's face and smiling knowingly. 'As soon as it gets boring you lose your sense of self in the tedium of domesticity. Sometimes a woman just needs a man for the sheer pleasure of him.' But Benedetta needed Gianni for more than pleasure; she needed him for love.

Evelina watched her sister and Gianni with envy. Not the kind of envy that eats away at the soul, but the kind that fills the soul with longing. How she wished Ezra were there so that she too could walk hand in hand around the gardens and make love in the secret silence of the night. She watched them sitting on the same bench beneath the pergola where she had spied on Ezra and Romina kissing, and she watched them laughing together as she had laughed with Ezra. There wasn't a moment in the day or night when Ezra wasn't in her thoughts. There wasn't a moment when he wasn't in her heart. And his name was forever in a whisper upon her lips as she prayed to the God that never listened for his safe return.

Evelina lost herself in music. She played the piano at every opportunity, disappearing into the lush landscapes of her imagination as Ezra had taught her to do. She lost herself too in the clouds, lying on the grass for hours and gazing into the puffs of white and watching them transform into animals, boats, fish, mountains and palaces. And then she reached out her hand to find that she was alone. In those moments her sorrow overwhelmed her and she could do nothing but give in to tears and allow her grief to gradually work its way through her.

At the beginning of September Fascist police turned up at the villa. They had reason to believe that the Pierangelinis were shielding partisans on their property. They brought with them two enormous German shepherds that sniffed about the house and then set off into the gardens. Tani and Artemisia invited the police inside, feigning ignorance and politeness. Artemisia poured three glasses of grappa, offered them cigarettes and lit one for herself. She smiled in that beguiling way of hers and the men relaxed a little and told her that partisans were operating in the area and hiding out in farmhouses in these hills, being supported by the local community. 'I can assure you they haven't been here,' said Tani.

'I'm sure you are right, but we have orders to search all the properties in this area. We apologize for the inconvenience.'

Evelina and Benedetta joined their parents in the hall. They knew the police would find no partisans in the grounds, but if they went into the chapel they would certainly come across evidence to prove that they'd been there. The girls kept their chins up and made a concerted effort not to catch their parents' eyes. Artemisia laughed and flirted and Tani frowned as if he found the whole encounter bewildering.

Evelina's heart was pounding against her ribs. She knew that, if they found the arms stored in the back room of the chapel, they'd all be arrested. She didn't regret helping the partisans, but she did regret the false sense of security she had felt over the months since Ezra's arrest. Perhaps they should have been more careful to conceal the evidence.

It seemed like an eternity before the police came back with their dogs. They declared the place clean and the whole party left, thanking Tani and Artemisia for their hospitality. As soon as they'd disappeared down the drive the girls ran to the chapel. They wondered whether the police had somehow missed it. The gardens were large, after all. But when they entered, they discovered, to their astonishment, Nonna Pierangelini and Costanza sitting on chairs like a pair of roosting hens. When they saw the girls, they hissed, 'Have they gone?'

'Yes,' said Benedetta. 'What are *you* doing here?'

Costanza was trembling with excitement. 'I saw the cars coming up the drive from the window, so I suggested we head straight here and pretend to be praying . . .'

'That was *my* suggestion,' said Nonna Pierangelini. 'I suggested we pretend to be praying.'

'We thought the police might respect old ladies in prayer. So that's what we did.'

Nonna Pierangelini pushed herself up stiffly. 'And it worked.' She did not seem in the least surprised. 'They came with their dogs and—'

Costanza cut her sister off. 'I said, "Do you mind!"'

'And *I* said, "This is a place of worship and that is what

we are doing. Have you come to arrest us for praying for our sons and grandsons and for the end of this dreadful war?"'

'What did they say?' Evelina asked.

'They apologized,' said Nonna Pierangelini.

'They glanced about and the dogs lifted their noses, and then—'

'And then I told them that, if they waited outside, we'd be through in twenty minutes or so and they could come in then if they wished.'

'Nonna! That was a gamble,' said Benedetta with a gasp.

'I know, but the young man who seemed to be in charge had a very untidy moustache and a weak chin. He also had watery eyes. I suspect he has a dominating mother and a formidable grandmother. He nodded, said sorry again, and left.'

'You saved us!' Benedetta cried, the relief turning to tears.

'We do want to be useful,' said Nonna Pierangelini with a bashful smile.

'We haven't had so much excitement in decades,' said Costanza breathlessly. She did seem to have suddenly acquired a new lease of life.

Nonna Pierangelini looked serious. 'Now we must give thanks.' She dropped her chin and closed her eyes.

The two old ladies prayed for an end to the war. Evelina prayed for Ezra and his family. Benedetta prayed for Gianni and his men. Then, she prayed that Francesco would never come home.

When the war finally ended the following May, Benedetta's prayers were answered. Francesco, wounded in battle, died of an infection in the days before the Germans surrendered. After laying him to rest, Benedetta was free to marry Gianni.

Evelina waited with excited anticipation for Ezra's return.

She fully expected Ercole and Olga, Matteo and Fioruccia to come home with him and for life to go back to the way it was. She and Ezra could marry at last and settle down to the kind of life Evelina had once believed she'd never want. Every day she cycled into town, but every day Ercole Zanotti remained boarded up, until, at the end of the summer, the boards were taken down and the foreman in whose name Matteo had re-registered his company following the racial laws of 1938, took it over. 'That family is never coming back,' he told Evelina when she asked him. 'They're all dead,' he stated simply and without emotion. 'The Germans did away with the lot of them.'

The newspapers reported the fate of the Jews in the camps the Germans had set up to work them to death, or simply to put them to death. The stories were extraordinary and Evelina could not bring herself to believe them. Then survivors returned home and the full horror of what they had been through could not be disbelieved or denied.

Still, Evelina waited for Ezra. She waited as spring gave way to summer and summer faded into autumn. She waited with hope in her heart because she could not bear to relinquish it. She could not bear to give up. She had held on to it for so long that she didn't know who she'd be without it. When she had told Ezra that she'd love him for ever, she had meant it.

In September she learned that the rabbi from Ezra's synagogue had returned to Vercellino. He had survived eighteen months in Auschwitz and a few months in a refugee camp before finally making his way home. Evelina cycled into town to see him. Rabbi Isaac Castello, old beyond his years and painfully thin, confirmed with deep regret that Ezra and his family had been murdered. 'I'm sorry,' he told her, taking her hands in his bony ones and looking into her eyes with such compassion that Evelina was overcome. She sank into a chair. 'Ezra is at peace now,' he said.

Evelina did not want to believe it. She could not. Ezra murdered? It wasn't possible. There must be some mistake. She returned home in a daze, lost. The beauty of the rice fields and olive groves were an affront to her sorrow. How could the world continue now that Ezra was no longer in it? When she arrived home, she did not go inside. She went to the chapel and knelt before the altar. 'You saw fit to take Bruno, Lord,' she prayed. 'And now you see fit to take Ezra, too. But I ask you, in your infinite wisdom, to give him back. I cannot live without him, you see. I cannot. Please, let the rabbi have made a mistake. Let Ezra have lived and bring him back to me.'

A week later Romina appeared at Villa L'Ambrosiana. She was much changed. No longer the plump, pretty girl who had played with Bruno in the garden, but older and haunted and afraid. The horrors she had known were unspeakable. Now she was alone in the world. 'I didn't know who to turn to,' she explained when Artemisia brought her into the house. 'I've lost everyone and everything. I have nothing.'

Artemisia took her hand. She would never forget how Romina had loved Bruno. 'You have *us*,' she said firmly. 'And you can stay here for as long as you want.'

Evelina helped nurse Romina back to health. It was the least she could do after the tenderness she had shown Bruno during his short life and in his final hours. For a while Evelina derived a certain fortitude from her work. It gave her a reason to get up in the morning. An incentive to carry on.

It gave her someone to care for. The girl didn't talk about the camp. She couldn't. Even though Evelina wanted to know, she knew better than to ask. Romina spent her days quietly, doing needlework beside the fire in the sitting room or walking in the gardens, savouring the sounds and smells of nature, allowing the vibrations of life that pulsated through the trees and shrubs to heal her broken spirit.

In spite of Romina, Evelina didn't think *her* broken spirit would ever heal. She had lost Ezra and therefore her reason for living. She felt like a husk of a person, simply breathing out of habit, moving slowly and numbly through endless days with no purpose, like a spectre. Benedetta, who now lived locally with Gianni, fell pregnant again. It was agreed that Romina would help Benedetta look after her children. Romina was happy to do so; she too needed to find a sense of purpose. Evelina found herself alone in the villa with nothing to do. It was then that she realized she had a choice. She could either waste away over her lost love or grab life by the collar and refuse to allow grief to destroy her.

She wrote to Aunt Madolina, requesting that she go and live with her in New York. When she received her enthusiastic reply, Evelina told her parents of her plans. Neither saw any reason why she shouldn't go. In fact, they encouraged it. Perhaps life would be better for her in America, they thought. She could start again. Find a sense of purpose and a reason to be happy. Happiness was what Tani and Artemisia wished for her, after all.

Evelina left for America by boat just after Christmas. She stood on the deck and watched the Italian coastline retreat into the mist and with it her hope: Ezra was gone. She looked to the heavens. The clouds hung fat and heavy in the winter's sky, but she did not look for lions and tigers. She could not bear to look for them. From now on clouds would just be clouds. There would be no magic or fanciful imaginings. Ezra had taken the magic with him and now life was simply life, with no colour or music or charm. A very different future waited for her. It had to be so; it was the only way she would survive.

PART TWO

The Hamptons, New York, 1980

Evelina felt the pull of the past upon her heart in increasingly insistent tugs. What had once been a gentle tweak, inspiring reminiscences of Villa L'Ambrosiana, Nonna Pierangelini, Costanza, her parents and Benedetta, was now a definite wrench, reminding her of things she had taken great trouble to forget. Sometimes they took her breath away, these recollections, with their ugly faces and bitter taste. After all these years living in America, why were memories from long ago rising up like bodies of the dead to haunt her?

Evelina hadn't thought of Bruno in years. Of course he had crossed her mind many times, fleeting images of his laughing figure skipping through the snow or playing with his dog, like reels of old film replaying the same footage over and again. But she hadn't allowed herself to travel further down that particular path of memory, because what lay at the end of it was raw and tender and dark; painfully dark. She avoided thinking about the night he passed away, or of his burial in the family crypt, or of the struggle they had all faced of having to live on without him.

Nor did she think about the morning she'd learned that Ezra had been captured, for the same reason. If she allowed herself to dwell on that horrifying episode, even for a moment, it would lead to the conversation she had later had with Rabbi Isaac Castello, and she couldn't bear to hear those words again, for they were still as sharp as knives and would cut just as deeply as they had the first time. She didn't allow herself to wander down that twilight path into what had been Ezra's fate for her imagination would seek out the worst possible scenario, and she couldn't live with that.

However, some years ago, she had come across a book in a second-hand bookstore quite by chance. It was written by an Italian called Primo Levi, entitled *If This is a Man*, about his experience in Auschwitz. Evelina knew as she reached for it with a trembling hand that it would only deepen her anguish. It was seriously unwise to dig into Ezra's experience and unearth what might have been his torment, and yet a macabre curiosity took her over. She was unable to stop, as if she was driven by the shadow side of herself. She carried it home to her apartment in New York like a thief, holding her handbag close as if it contained something at once precious and forbidden. Then, while the children were at school and her husband Franklin at work, Evelina lay in bed and started to read it. By the fourth page she was crying so hard she could no longer see the words. Levi's story was too close to Ezra's for her to be able to separate the two. She wondered whether they had known each other, either in Italy fighting with the partisans, or later, in the camp. The experience Levi wrote about, made all the more heartrending by the dispassionate style of his prose, was way beyond anything Evelina's imagination could have invoked. There was no return now up that twilight path; she knew too much to ever be able to disregard it.

Evelina hid the book beneath the mattress to read again a few days later when curiosity overrode prudence and she delved once more into the horrors of Ezra's imprisonment. She knew he would not want her to know – indeed, through her experience helping refugees who had managed to settle in Brooklyn after the war, she knew that for the most part they did not discuss what they had been through with outsiders. She'd overheard conversations they'd had among themselves, and gleaned various snippets of information, but this book told her the whole story. The whole, unabridged truth, which, had it not been for Primo Levi's extraordinarily brave testimony, she would not have believed. How could she? It was beyond the realm of her experience. Beyond even her most gruesome nightmares.

Evelina was sixty-three which was not old. Yet she felt, with every year that passed, the weight of memory growing increasingly heavy. As her three children grew up and away, she spent more and more time with Franklin, just the two of them. They'd travelled to Europe and South America, and seen something of the world together. And their love for each other had deepened. She loved Ezra still, she would never stop loving him, but she loved Franklin too. It was, indeed, possible to love two men in very different ways. She realized now, in her wisdom, that there were many faces to love.

Franklin was now seventy-seven and older than his years due to ill health. They no longer travelled, or at least, not very far afield. Aunt Madolina had a house in the Hamptons and they liked to go there. It was close to the beach and they both enjoyed the tranquillity of the sea and the sight of birds on the sand, chasing waves. This year, for Thanksgiving, Madolina had invited them to spend a few days with her there, with Uncle Topino, of course, and Dan, who had had a series of girlfriends since Jennifer. Aldo and Lisa were spending the holiday with Lisa's family, and Madolina's daughter, Alba, with hers, having married for the third time and moved to Colorado. Ava-Maria had a serious new boyfriend and she'd chosen Thanksgiving to introduce him to the family. Evelina suspected they'd marry. Franklin said that any man brave enough to marry Ava-Maria was, in his eyes, both a hero and a fool.

In her nineties, Madolina did not seem to be slowing down. Her mind was as quick as it had always been, and she was just as outspoken, opinionated and blunt. Sometimes even her walking stick appeared to be struggling to keep up with her. Madolina loved to entertain. It was easy for her, for she employed Miguel and Monica, a Hispanic couple, to cook, clean and look after the place, setting them up in the annex so that they were on call for whenever she needed them.

The house was typical in style of the classical Hamptons 'cottage': pale grey clapboard walls and tiled roofs, white window frames and shutters, and a round 'ox-eye' window in the triangle of the central gable that looked lazily out over the sea. It was large and airy with a wide veranda and a sumptuous garden. However, it being November, the hydrangeas were long over and the trees had shed their leaves. The wind whipped off the water, cold and damp, yet inside, the fires were lit and the central heating was on full blast. Madolina did not like to be too hot in summer or too cold in winter, and every effort was made by Miguel and Monica to get the temperature just right.

A velvet-topped card table had been set up in the drawing room for Topino and Franklin's chess game, which was tradition. Both men claimed to be lacking form, which was tradition too. 'I'm going to be an easy conquest,' said Franklin as they settled down to play.

'You'll decimate me in record time,' said Topino. 'I don't even know why we bother.' Yet the two of them were as competitive and sharp as they were every year, and the match went on for hours and sometimes days.

Dan arrived with Ava-Maria and Jonathan, her boyfriend, just before lunch. Madolina was dozing by the fire when they burst through the door. Ava-Maria's voice rang through the house. 'We're here! Mom, Dad, Madolina, Topino ...!'

Madolina awoke with a start. 'Good Lord, has Hell opened its gates and let all the demons out?'

'You stay here, Madolina,' said Evelina, putting down her needlepoint and getting up. 'It's Ava-Maria and Dan.'

'And the long-suffering lover,' added Madolina with a grin. 'I'm looking forward to getting an eye-load of him.'

Franklin and Topino suspended their game.

Ava-Maria rushed into the room still in her coat. Her cheeks were pink with excitement, making her blue eyes even more pronounced. 'Isn't this exciting!' she cried, throwing her arms around her mother. 'We're all here together. You must meet Jonathan. Jonathan!' she shouted and a moment later Jonathan and Dan appeared in the doorway.

'Well, he's obedient at least,' said Madolina under her breath.

'Jonathan, meet my family,' said Ava-Maria proudly. She subsequently introduced him to her mother, Topino, Franklin and Madolina.

'Ah, Uncle Topino,' said Jonathan, shaking his hand. 'I've heard so much about you.'

'I wouldn't believe anything Ava-Maria tells you,' said Topino. 'She sees the world through rose-tinted glasses.'

'In which case, she has an idealistic view of me as well,' Jonathan replied, smiling at her affectionately. Ava-Maria smiled back at him with delight.

'I suggest you take advantage of it for as long as you can,' Topino added. 'It would be nice if she always looked at you like that.'

Madolina put out her hand. 'I'd like to say we've heard a lot about *you*, but Ava-Maria has been uncharacteristically secretive.'

Ava-Maria laughed. 'That's not true, Aunt Madolina. I just wanted you to form your own opinion.'

'I would have done that anyway,' said Madolina. 'Welcome, Jonathan. It's a pleasure to meet you. I must say, you're a brave man taking on Ava-Maria.'

Topino shrugged. 'You're a far braver man taking on all of *us*.'

Jonathan laughed. 'If a person is better understood in the context of her family, I'd say I like Ava-Maria more already.'

'Well said!' Evelina exclaimed.

Franklin stepped forward. 'Do you play chess?' he asked.

'I do,' Jonathan replied, looking over to the chess board.

'Good. Topino and I are tired of playing each other,' he added.

Topino grinned at Franklin. 'Who says I'm tired of playing you? I'm not *tired* of playing you, I'm *sick* of playing you. It's a tradition, you see, Jonathan. A tiresome tradition and neither of us has the heart to stop it. Every year Franklin and I face each other at the chess board and every year we do our best, which is really quite pitiful. Perhaps you can show us how it's done.'

'Don't listen to him!' said Ava-Maria, taking Jonathan's hand and leading him towards the door. 'They're like fiends in the guise of hopeless old men. Come, I'll show you your room. He's in the blue room, isn't he, Aunt Madolina?'

'Until you make it official, my dear, he is, indeed, in the blue room,' Madolina called after her.

Dan flopped onto the sofa. 'So, what do you think?' He looked at his mother.

'He's handsome,' Evelina replied. Indeed, Jonathan was. He had an open, friendly face, a humorous smile, straight white teeth and sensitive, sage-green eyes that twinkled behind glasses.

'I'd be careful inviting him to play you at chess, Topino,' Dan warned. 'He's very clever. He studied business at Harvard.'

'Business studies has never guaranteed a good chess player,' said Topino. 'But a good brain certainly does.'

'Is he a banker?' asked Madolina.

'An investment banker,' said Dan.

Franklin arched an eyebrow. 'Good. He'll earn enough to keep her.'

'Oh Franklin,' said Evelina. 'Ava-Maria is a joy. He's lucky to have won her affection.'

'That is true,' Topino agreed seriously. 'Ava-Maria is a gift.' He looked at Evelina, his grey eyes full of tenderness. 'Like her mother.'

Evelina smiled.

Dan chuckled. 'I'd say *you* see the world through rose-tinted glasses, Topino.'

'Not when it comes to the women in your family,' Topino replied. 'When it comes to the rest of the world, however, rose-tinted glasses is the only way to see it. Why look at grey when you can lift your eyes and see a rainbow?'

Franklin and Topino resumed their game. Dan talked to Madolina and his mother while they waited eagerly for Ava-Maria and Jonathan to come back downstairs. 'How about you, Dan?' Madolina asked. 'Every time I see you, you have another girl on your arm. When are you going to find one you can keep?'

Dan laughed. 'I'm in no hurry to settle down, Aunt Madolina. I like my freedom too much.'

'You're thirty years old. Don't leave it too long or you'll be an old man.'

'People don't rush to marry like we did in our day,' said Evelina. 'Benedetta married at twenty. Anything beyond twenty was almost considered too old.'

'You married at thirty,' Madolina reminded her. 'But that was because of the war. Had the war not happened, you would very likely have married at twenty as well.'

'Had the war not happened, my life would have been very different,' said Evelina, thinking of Ezra. She glanced at the two men playing chess.

Topino slapped his thigh and laughed loudly. 'Sorry, old friend, but you took a gamble and it didn't pay off.'

Franklin caught Evelina's eye and smiled. 'I'm being taken to the cleaner's,' he moaned.

'That's what you always say,' she replied.

At last Jonathan and Ava-Maria emerged. Madolina declared it was time for a drink. Topino said checkmate and the game was finally over. The two men shook hands.

'You're a better man than I,' said Franklin.

'Not better,' said Topino. 'Just lucky.'

Franklin frowned. 'There is no luck in chess.'

'Some say there is no luck in life,' Topino added. 'We make our own luck. In which case, I am a winner in the great game of life. If I had a glass, I would raise it to that.'

Franklin went to the drinks room and opened a bottle of wine. Jonathan didn't drink alcohol. He and Ava-Maria both drank Coca-Cola with lemon. Dan had a beer. After lunch, Franklin went upstairs for a rest. He tired easily and wanted all his strength for dinner. Madolina nodded off again in front of the fire. She would never have admitted to being tired and siestas were for Spanish people, sick people and old people who had given up on life. She fell into none of those categories and therefore only retreated to her bedroom at the end of the day. Ava-Maria, Dan and Jonathan decided to watch a video.

Topino asked Evelina if she felt like going for a walk.

The two of them set off down the garden towards the beach. Evelina wore a woolly bobble hat and sheepskin coat, Topino the shabby overcoat he had had for years and a Russian ushanka hat made from rabbit fur that he'd been generously given at the end of the war by a liberating soldier.

It was mid-afternoon but the land was already darkening. Purple-bellied clouds sailed across the sky like clumsy barges on a translucent sea. The sun was gradually making its way south, leaving a streak of pink in its wake. When they reached the bluff, they linked arms like an old married couple. Together they stomped over the dunes where the wind had made ripples in the sand and long grasses grew in tufts, like the unkempt face of a weary old man who has long given up on caring how he looks. Leaning on each other for support they finally reached the beach. It extended for miles and was almost empty. They stood a moment, watching the light dance bewitchingly upon the waves and orange-billed terns pecking the shallow water for fish.

For a long while neither of them spoke; theirs was the silence of two people who were completely at ease with each other. They began to stroll, listening to the sound of the sea and the wind, and enjoying the emptiness of their own thoughts. At length, Topino looked across at her and smiled. 'I think Jonathan is The One,' he said.

'Isn't it a bit early to tell?'

'I can tell a person just by looking at them. He has a nice face.'

'My grandmother could tell a person by looking at his moustache.'

'Really?'

'Yes, really.'

'What did she think of Hitler?'

'Not much. She didn't rate Stalin either.'

'She was right. What incredible powers of divination.'

Evelina laughed. 'She was right about Benedetta's husband Francesco. He used to hit her, you know.'

'That's not good.'

'No, it wasn't. Nonna Pierangelini claimed she knew he was no good the first time she saw his moustache. It was too neat and tidy, she said.'

'I think she had a point.'

'I'm glad Jonathan doesn't have a moustache.'

'It's the '80s. Men have better taste.' He grinned. 'Have you ever kissed a man with a moustache?'

'No, and I don't think I'd like to.'

'Franklin has never had facial hair?'

'What do you think?' They laughed.

'I like Jonathan,' he said seriously. 'I think he'll be good for Ava-Maria. She needs a strong hand and he's strong but kind. I think kind is one of the most important qualities a person can have.'

'I agree. People are always looking for beauty, but beauty fades, or at least one grows accustomed to it. Kindness endures.'

'Franklin has been kind to you.'

'I've been lucky.'

'*He's* been lucky.'

Evelina nudged Topino playfully. 'You would say that.'

'You're a good woman, Eva. There are various paths you could have taken and yet, you chose the one of most integrity. I say it again. He's lucky to have you.'

'I'll never forget Aunt Madolina telling Alba that life is not designed to give us what we want. That sometimes we can't have everything we desire. That it just isn't possible. The older I get the more wisdom I recognize in her words. Life is about learning, isn't it? It must be. Why else are we here if not to grow in some way? If life gave us everything we wanted, if we were happy all the time, we'd have no opportunity to grow. We'd be selfish creatures, looking out only for ourselves and our own gratification. Suffering drives us deeper. It makes us more compassionate. More understanding of other people's pain. It makes us kinder. Bruno's death changed me. It dug down into my being and broke through to another layer, one I never knew was there. I'm a better person because of it, I know. Sure, the world became a place of darker shadows, but the light became brighter too. I learned to appreciate love, because previously I had only ever taken it for granted.'

Topino put a gloved hand over hers. 'You said that so beautifully.'

Evelina smiled bashfully. 'Do *you* think there's a reason for suffering?'

'I think life is easier to manage if you believe there is. Ultimately, it doesn't really matter what is true and what isn't. If believing in a purpose to life makes living more tolerable, then that can only be a good thing.'

'What do *you* believe?'

He sighed. 'As you know, after the war, I went through a time of not believing in God. I lost my faith as so many did. But now I'm older and wiser, I don't think like that anymore. I cannot look at a sky like this one and not believe in a higher power. Look at it. How beautiful it is. The reds and golds, that clear, innocent blue, as pale as a duck's egg.' They stopped and turned their faces to the horizon. 'God is love and love is present in everything of beauty. I think God is the wrong word anyway. I'd rather think of a divine power of which we are all part. All of us. Whatever race or creed. We are all part of something so much bigger than ourselves and yet we see ourselves as separate, different, isolated and alone. But we are not alone. Our souls are all divine sparks. Out there somewhere is a giant bonfire which is where we're all headed.' He chuckled. 'The truth is I don't know. What I do know is that you, Eva, are a part of me.' He squeezed her arm with his. 'You'll always be a part of me.'

'And you'll always be a part of me,' she replied. 'The older I get, the more I understand the value and meaning of true friendship.'

'We've travelled a long road, you and I.'

'We certainly have.'

'Franklin is not the only lucky one. I am lucky to have found you,' he said.

'If I hadn't left Italy for New York, I would never have found you.'

'*I* found *you*,' he reminded her.

'No, *I* found *you*,' she argued.

'All right, if you're going to be pedantic, we found each other, by chance.'

'It wasn't chance, it was fate.'

'Or the Universe. However you like to put it.'

'It was meant to be.'

'Well, of course. That's for certain.'

Evelina looked at Topino then, her eyes full of affection. 'I'm grateful to be here with you now,' she said.

'As am I.'

'Who'd have thought that the path taking me *away* from love would be the very path to lead me straight back to it?'

'That sounds like a riddle.'

'Well, it is, isn't it? A paradox. We survived against all the odds. No one had odds stacked against them like you and I did.'

'You never told me what happened when you arrived in New York.'

'Didn't I?'

'No. You told me you got on a boat in Genoa and left. So what happened when you got here?'

'You really want to know?' Evelina asked.

'I'd really *like* to know. We've got nothing else to do on this beach besides talk.'

'Very well.'

'What was it like arriving in America after having survived German-occupied Italy? What did the Universe have in store for you as you put your first foot on the path that led you to *me*?'

CHAPTER TEN

New York, 1946

Peppino and Madolina Forte lived in a large brownstone house on a tree-lined street in Brooklyn, a short walk from Prospect Park. Peppino owned a thriving air-conditioning company and had done well for himself over the thirty-odd years that he'd lived in America. He told Evelina that New York was unbearably hot in summertime and everyone needed air conditioning. In fact, he boasted, he couldn't make enough units to supply the demand – and everyone wanted *his* brand because it was the most reliable. As his business had grown, so had his bank account. He and Madolina had moved from the small apartment next to the railway line, which had been their first home in America, into a series of increasingly bigger houses, eventually upgrading to the home of Madolina's dreams in the most refined area of Brooklyn. The jewels on her plump fingers and ear lobes had grown larger and more ostentatious to reflect their changing status and the fur coats that kept her warm in the winter months became progressively more luxurious. Peppino was proud of his wealth and was keen to show it off. This was the land of prosperity and opportunity, after all, and he considered himself one of the many success stories that had come out of Italy; the epitome of the American dream, the embodiment of the ethos that hard work results in success and upward mobility. The more his wife sparkled and wrapped herself in fine fur, the more American he felt – and the desire to feel American was what drove Peppino Forte to steadily amass his fortune.

Madolina was no second fiddle to her husband's concertmaster. On the contrary, she was a success in her own right. Formidable and fearless, Madolina Forte said what she thought and because of the confident way she went about it people listened. In fact, they listened so keenly that over the years she had become one of the leading voices in her community. And she had much to say. She held regular salons in her drawing room where the women of her neighbourhood discussed politics, women's rights, played cards and arranged charity fundraisers for the poor, especially Jewish immigrants who had escaped persecution in Europe. She had a weekly and very popular show on the local radio called *Mamma Forte* where she talked about everything that concerned women, from advice on how to cook the perfect pizza to sex before marriage, living in sin and juggling work and family life. Madolina had an opinion about everything, usually surprisingly modern and open-minded for a Catholic woman of her age, and she didn't always please everyone. In fact, the radio station had to hire a secretary specially to respond to the many letters Mamma Forte received each day. Madolina was not averse to criticism. In fact, she relished it. She enjoyed reading the unfavourable correspondences just as much as she enjoyed the appreciative ones for her main objective was, ultimately, to instigate debate and get people talking, and not only about the comfortable subjects. Her most ardent critic was Father O'Malley, the fiery local priest, who listened to every show with a face swelling with indignation. He made a point of cornering her after Mass on Sundays and giving her his opinions on the outrageous points she'd made. Madolina listened with patience. She was a good Catholic, but it was a challenge to maintain a balance between being true to herself and being true to the Church, which she considered woefully outdated. Sometimes, there was just no way she could please both. In those cases, Madolina didn't hesitate but to please herself, much to Father O'Malley's consternation. It was a brave woman who took on the Church, but Madolina was intrepid, and set on her course like a boat with a fixed rudder; not even the will of God could alter it.

Madolina needed little sleep and started her day at five every morning. She was a fireball of energy and drive that blazed through life with the determination to make it as interesting and fulfilling as possible – and to help as many less fortunate souls on the way as she could. It was into this whirlwind of activity that Evelina arrived. To her relief, it was just what she needed to take her mind off her profound loss.

Madolina and Peppino had three children, a son and two daughters. Joseph, who was now thirty, had travelled to Australia in his twenties after graduating in engineering. He'd married a local girl and decided to remain in Sydney and raise his family there, joining an engineering firm and working on some of the most exciting projects the city had to offer. Their eldest daughter, Jane, was an activist. She had inherited her mother's drive and her father's good business sense. However, in her determination to be all things American, she had smothered the Italian effervescence in her nature, which her parents had in abundance, and become serious and worthy. She had fulfilled her parents' dream, however, and married a wealthy attorney from Washington. They lived in a big white house in Forest Hills where she entertained her husband's political friends and associates as a good American wife should. There was never a sign of pasta or a plate of gnocchi on the menu; the Italian sun never shone on that refined corner of Washington.

Their youngest daughter, Alba, was the opposite. At twenty-five she was as lazy and spoiled as a beautiful pussycat lying purring on a windowsill. She had no desire to do anything or be anyone in her own right. Her ambitions went as far as marriage, and her husband had to be rich, handsome, indulgent and preferably Italian-American. Her mother's dynamism and her sister's seemingly gilded life had only served to turn her into an apathetic creature lacking in any sense of purpose besides that of preening her beauty and finding entertainment in frivolous pursuits.

Madolina and Peppino believed that Evelina would be a good friend for Alba. They hoped she would inspire Alba to raise herself higher than her meagre aspirations, for Evelina had opinions, interests and a curiosity about the world. Little did they know that besides emigrating to America Evelina had no idea what she was going to do with her life. Alba's ambitions might not have satisfied her parents, but at least she had them; Evelina had none.

When Evelina arrived on the boat from Italy she spoke little English, in spite of her former tutor's enthusiasm and ability. Having thought she had no reason to learn another language besides French, which she had mastered with ease, she now realized with regret that English was essential if she was going to lay down her roots in America. Madolina was appalled by this lapse in her education and arranged for her to attend English classes at once. She tutted furiously at her brother's lack of attentiveness where his daughters were concerned, complaining that he'd only ever been interested in his writing, even as a boy, and failed to notice the world around him. Evelina thought nothing of her father's lack of interest; after all, she'd known no different. However, she was grateful to have something constructive to do for four hours a day; if she was busy she would have less time to pine for Ezra. Thanks to her keen and agile mind, and a great deal of hard work, it wasn't long before Evelina began to speak English with fluency.

The Fortes attended Mass every Sunday at the local Catholic church and Evelina lit candles for Ezra's soul where once she had lit them for his life. Alba talked endlessly of men and marriage, but Evelina never wanted to love another and marriage was out of the question. She did not confide in her cousin, however. She couldn't bring herself to speak about Ezra in the past tense. If she didn't mention his name, perhaps she could fool herself into believing that he still lived. She could endure not having him for herself if she could believe that he walked the planet somewhere – that he breathed, ate, slept and talked. It was the thought of him not existing at all that terrified her. So she pictured him alive, in another country far away, and because of that denial of his death she was able to live.

There was a grand piano in the Fortes' drawing room. Alba played badly, Madolina not at all. Jane had played, of course, her thin white fingers fluttering over the keys with a dexterity that came from hours of hard practice, but now the piano sat in silence, dusted and polished by the maid as a thing of beauty but not of usefulness. Evelina couldn't bring herself to touch the keys. She knew that music would transport her back to Villa L'Ambrosiana and to Ezra, to a time when she had found boats and beasts in the clouds and flown like a bird through valleys of rainforests and rivers. That part of her was dead like a tree in winter and the best she could do was focus her thoughts on reality. She no longer had the heart to dream, but a heart as closed as a walnut.

Evelina found a friend in Alba, who spoke enough Italian for the two of them to make themselves understood with a mixture of both languages. They were very different, but perhaps it was because of those differences that they so enjoyed the novelties they found in one another. Evelina thought Alba funny. She had a dry sense of humour, an irreverence and a refreshing disregard for authority. Alba thought Evelina charming and innocent, if a little eccentric. To Alba, Evelina's upbringing had been strange in its isolation and antiquated way of living. The fact that Tani and Artemisia had chosen a husband for Benedetta so riveted Alba that she made Evelina tell her the story of their meeting over and over again, which certainly helped improve her English. Evelina did not tell her how Francesco had hit her sister, abused her and disrespected her; for a start, she did not have the vocabulary. She told her instead that he had died a hero's death in the war and that Benedetta had later fallen in love and married a partisan.

Alba was a beauty, which was baffling because neither parent, nor sibling, had been so blessed by nature. Her father was bullish with a thick neck, a barrel chest and small, weaselly eyes, and her mother was large-boned and stout with a strong jaw and a lumpy nose. They were both undeniably intelligent, witty and gregarious but they weren't by any stretch of the imagination beautiful. Alba's prettiness was therefore a surprise. It was as if she had inherited the best of both and then refined those qualities by some strange alchemy into a lithe, sensual body and a wide, attractive face. Her green eyes were feline, her lips pouting and her nose a little upturned. She might not have had her sister's ambition or her brother's acumen, but she had something neither of them had, charm. Armed with that, Alba didn't believe she needed anything more to secure herself a comfortable and cosseted future.

Although Peppino and Madolina had told Tani that they'd look after Evelina as if she were their daughter, Evelina knew that she had to earn her keep. She was no longer a child and it was fitting that she found some kind of employment. With this in mind she threw herself into her aunt's philanthropic life with enthusiasm. Every dollar she raised for the Jewish immigrants was money that would go to families like the Zanottis. Had Ercole and Olga listened to Ezra they might have started a new life here in Brooklyn and been helped by Aunt Madolina's wonderful initiatives that gave much needed aid to so many.

Alba did not have Evelina's empathy for the poor, but fundraisers required people with money, so there was always a chance she might find among their number a suitable man to marry. The two young women got dolled up and went out, and while Alba had her eye on the wealthy young gallants, Evelina made a concerted effort not to draw their attention. The only thing that interested her was the amount of money raised at the end of the evening and the thought of how far that money might go towards enabling a family in need to forge a new life.

Evelina dreaded the stories that were coming out every day about the horrors of the Nazi concentration camps. She had turned her back on Italy and the war, but the war still managed to find her in America. The refugees she met through her charitable work did not speak about their ordeals, but she overheard snippets of terrible things that kept her awake at night, for they spoke to each other. The news was full of the Nuremberg Trials and the heinous crimes committed mainly against the Jewish people. Every time Evelina heard or read something she thought of Ezra, Olga, Ercole, Matteo and Fioruccia. She thought of the Zanotti children in the Fascist parade in Vercellino, marching up and down the square with pride, and she wept. It was better not to read at all, to close one's ears and focus on living in the moment and finding distraction in it. After all, suffering on account of their tragedy would not bring them back, and compared to what *they* must have endured it was shamefully self-indulgent to allow herself to feel burdened.

Madolina's heroine and role model was Eleanor Roosevelt. She had a photograph of her on her desk in her study and one on the wall in the hall, and had even bought a Scottish Terrier just like hers and called him Buster. 'A better woman you will not find,' she liked to say before listing her many great qualities, her causes and her fearlessness in the face of opposition and criticism. Madolina had met her once, in 1939, when the First Lady had attended a tea for Women's Day in New York. She had shaken her hand, looked into her eyes and seen such deep wells of compassion and intelligence that Madolina had been struck as if by an angel. She liked to tell the story – and *had* told it many times during her *Mamma Forte* radio sessions. She never tired of praising Eleanor Roosevelt or using her as an example of a thoroughly modern woman. 'She's an inspiration to all women who want to carve out a role for themselves beyond the realms of the kitchen and nursery,' she'd say. But her exaltation of

Eleanor Roosevelt was lost on her daughter, because Alba had no intention at all of carving out a role for herself.

In spite of the many suitably rich and well-connected men who presented themselves to Alba Forte, the kind of man who really appealed to her was of a less scrupulous variety. She liked men who smelt of danger, rode motorbikes, wore leather jackets, smoked marijuana and drank beer. And she knew exactly where to find them. She let Evelina borrow her clothes and showed her how to apply make-up so she didn't look like she was fresh off the boat from Genoa. Then she took her to Dixieland clubs to listen to bands playing jazz, to dance and to flirt with the kind of young men her mother disapproved of: Italian men. Men who were connected to the Mafia.

Evelina was happy to go along with her. After all, she'd had such a sheltered life in Vercellino that the lamp-lit, noisy streets of Brooklyn were otherworldly and exhilarating. Evelina was swiftly gathered up into Alba's group of afflu-ent young people whose sole focus in life was on pleasing themselves and spending their parents' money. Evelina loved to lose herself on the dance floor and it was thrilling to be admired. But she didn't let any of the men get too close. Perhaps she never would.

In the spring Alba acquired an unsuitable boyfriend. His name was Antonio Genovese and he was everything Peppino and Madolina would *not* want for their daughter. For a start he didn't have what they would call 'a proper job', nor did he have any intention of getting one. His parents were of Italian descent, from Sicily, and he claimed he worked for his father, but what he did exactly was hard to tell. He drove a sky-blue Buick convertible and would take Alba to drive-in movies where he'd roll the seat back and make out with her. Alba told Evelina proudly that she'd gone the whole way. 'You don't go out with a guy like Antonio Genovese and not give him what he wants,' she told her excitedly. 'Otherwise he'll just ditch you for someone who does.' There was no point in cautioning her to be careful. Alba did not welcome advice, from anyone, and besides, who was Evelina to disapprove of sex before marriage when she had given herself to Ezra?

One warm Saturday, Alba suggested they go to Coney Island. 'Antonio has a date for you. You'll love him. He's real handsome, just you wait.' Evelina adored Coney Island with its vast beaches and boardwalk, fairground rides, freak shows, parades and circus acts. It was a place such as she had never seen before. A place built especially for fun and entertainment. Even though she wasn't very enthusiastic about her date, she did not want to miss out on what was so far her favourite thing about America: Coney Island of blissful forgetfulness.

Antonio and his friend Mike Herrington turned up in Antonio's Buick at five on a particularly hot June afternoon. Mike was indeed handsome, with short, sandy blond hair and light brown eyes. He had a raffish smile and a pair of sharp wolf teeth that gave his face a mischievous charm. He wasn't of Italian descent like Antonio and had a proper job in an advertising company, selling, as he put it, 'the idea of a golden youth to America's young'. As he sat in the front of the Buick, one arm resting on the window frame, a cigarette smoking between his finger and thumb and listening to Nat King Cole singing on the radio, Mike seemed to perfectly embody the image he was being paid to sell. He was confident and had an air of sophistication his friend Antonio lacked. Whereas Antonio looked like he'd borrowed his father's car, Mike looked like he could have bought it. Alba and Evelina climbed into the back and with the roof down and the wind in their hair the four of them headed out to Coney Island.

The place was packed with people. Antonio put his arm around Alba's neck and drew her in for a kiss. Evelina smiled shyly at Mike, who asked her about herself. She deflected his questions – she had no wish to share her past. 'Tell me more about the golden youth,' she suggested and Mike was only too happy to explain why the youth of today's America was different from its parents' generation, who'd suffered deprivations during the Great Depression years, and how he'd been working on advertising campaigns for cigarettes, make-up and fashion, creating through pictures a gilded, glamorous world of luxury and prosperity of which every young American wanted to be a part. He was good at it and Evelina found herself wanting to be part of it as well. She wanted to forget the war and her loss and the archaic, somnolent world of Villa L'Ambrosiana, and give herself entirely to this new world of bright lights and jazz.

They bought hot dogs and thick ripple-cut French fries from Nathan's and tickets to watch the Tiger Rag. Alba thought the show disappointing. 'What's so exciting about seeing a man put his head between the jaws of a tiger? It would be far more entertaining if the tiger bit it off!'

'You can see from its eyes that's exactly what the tiger wanted to do,' said Evelina and Mike smiled at her because he liked her thick Italian accent and the way she gave a little murmur of concentration before starting a sentence.

'Let's go on the Cyclone,' Antonio suggested, taking Alba's hand and setting off towards the roller-coaster. Evelina loved anything that moved fast, and nothing moved as fast as the famous Cyclone.

'Don't hesitate to hold on to me if you're scared,' Mike told her as they climbed into the car and sat side by side.

But Evelina laughed. 'I'm not scared of speed,' she replied, failing to notice his disappointment.

'Then what are you scared of?' he asked.

She shrugged, implying that she wasn't scared of anything. Then, in a moment of candour, she replied, 'The real world. There is nothing more frightening than that.' Before he could ask her what she meant, the car had begun to move and they gripped the bar in front of them to prevent themselves from falling out. Evelina squealed with delight as they raced around the track, climbing up and whizzing down, the feeling of exhilaration taking her over and making her laugh out loud. Behind her, Alba and Antonio screamed and kissed and held on to each other as if their lives depended on it. Evelina thought of Ezra and how she might have pretended she was afraid just like Alba in order to get him to put his protective arms around her. Then the car whipped round a corner and Ezra was left behind as Evelina's thoughts turned once again to the present moment and with resolve she immersed herself in it.

After the roller-coaster, they threw themselves down slides, drove into each other in the bumper cars and had a go on the carousel. Eventually, dizzy from the rides, they wandered into a fortune teller's tent. The woman with the crystal ball, tarot cards and candles was Romanian and called herself Mystic Marica. She had thick red hair that fell over her shoulders in tight curls, scarlet lipstick and large eyes the colour of peat. She wore a black shawl embroidered with red roses and an amethyst pendant hung between her creamy breasts. Her hands were white, her nails impossibly long and painted the same colour as her lips. She was a cliché and Evelina had no intention of letting her read her fortune.

One after the other Alba, Antonio and Mike sat at the little round table and allowed Mystic Marica to read their cards. Evelina did not believe in the supernatural and had no desire to be convinced otherwise. However, when she suggested she leave the three of them to it and meet them outside, Alba persuaded her to stay. 'It's only fun,' she said. 'I'm going to marry a rich man and live in a palace. Let's see what Mystic Marica says about you.'

'Go on, Evelina,' said Mike. 'If you don't believe it, what does it matter what she says?'

Evelina had no choice but to take the chair and shuffle the cards. While the others waited for her outside the tent, Evelina split the cards into three piles with her left hand then restored them to one pile with her right hand, just as Mystic Marica told her to do.

The crone started taking the cards off the top and placing them on the table, picture side up. Evelina saw the Tower, the Four of Swords and the Hermit. In her thick Romanian accent, Mystic Marica began to speak slowly and deliberately. Evelina wasn't convinced she was, in fact, Romanian. It was far more likely that she was putting on the accent for effect. She was probably from Brooklyn. 'You have suffered a very great shock,' she said. 'Your world has been turned upside down. You have travelled a long way and now you are in a state of pause. You are taking a deep breath and allowing your soul to recover. Going within, retreating into your inner world. Finding a sense of peace and tranquillity in your spirit.' Well, considering Evelina's Italian accent she didn't think it was hard for a fortune teller to guess that she had just arrived from war-torn Europe. Mystic Marica then picked three more cards with her long white fingers: the Six of Swords, the King of Swords and the Lovers. 'You need to let go of the past,' she continued. 'But the past will not let go of you. You will find happiness with an older man, a kind, intelligent, scholarly man who will remind you very much of your father.' Mystic Marica frowned then and her nose twitched like a cat. She picked another card and placed it beneath the Lovers card. It was the Seven of Swords. 'The card of deception. Be careful, my dear, what you wish for. We are the creators of our reality and no fortune teller can predict how your life will go, only how your life *might* go, following the choices you make today and your thoughts that manifest, whether you want them to or not.' Mystic Marica looked into Evelina's eyes with her dark, unfathomable gaze. 'You have a big capacity for love, my dear. Bigger than you know. It will surprise you. If the decisions you make come from the heart, you will find happiness, but if they come from the ego, you will destroy everyone around you, like an anchor tossed into the sea that sinks the entire ship.' She tapped the King of Swords with her scarlet talon. 'He's a good man,' she said. 'He will know you better than you know yourself. Don't underestimate him.'

Evelina thanked her, although she wasn't entirely sure that she'd said anything revelatory. A lot of mumbo-jumbo — words which thrown together sounded wise, but actually meant nothing at all.

'Did she tell you you're going to marry a prince and live in a palace?' Alba asked with a giggle.

'No, she told me a lot of nonsense,' said Evelina. 'I'm going to die unhappy.'

Mike looked appalled. 'I'm going to ask for our money back!' he exclaimed.

'It's a joke,' said Evelina with a smile. 'I don't believe a word she said. Come on, let's go and find something to eat. I'm feeling hungry again. How about a corn on the cob or an ice cream?'

As they made their way through the crowd, the skies over Coney Island darkened and the twinkling lights of the fairground shone brightly, promising a golden future to the gilded youth of America. Evelina thought nothing more of Mystic Marica and her strange predictions. Instead, she bathed in those dazzling lights, in the music and the street entertainers, and let Mike take her hand.

CHAPTER ELEVEN

There was undoubtedly chemistry between Evelina and Mike. Evelina could not deny it, although she rather wished there wasn't. She felt guilty for looking at another man, as if she was betraying Ezra with every lustful glance. But Ezra wasn't ever coming back. Evelina needed to live her life, not shrink from it. She couldn't reach Ezra where he was and there was no point in wishing she could. Those kinds of wishes were beyond the abilities of even the most gifted fairy godmother. Ezra would want her to be happy. And with Mike, Evelina *was* happy. He made her laugh. He was interesting to talk to. He was attractive, confident and kind – and he wasn't Italian, which was crucial. She didn't know whether she'd ever *love* him. Whether she was even capable of feeling that depth of emotion again. But she knew for sure that she could never love him in the way she loved Ezra. Ezra would always occupy the greater part of her heart. It simply couldn't be otherwise. Ezra had occupied it for so long and now, in death, he would remain eternally there, like a beautiful fossil that would never deteriorate or lose its form. He would be for ever young and handsome. He would be for ever hers.

That summer Evelina and Alba regularly went out with Antonio and Mike as a foursome. They went to the movies, to the baseball, to Coney Island and to dances. Evelina's command of the English language was improving with every lesson, but she learned the most with Mike, Alba and Antonio. She wrote regular letters to her parents and to Benedetta, and was thrilled when she heard the news that Benedetta had given birth to a baby girl, who they'd named Pasquala.

Evelina did not miss home, at least, she didn't allow herself that indulgence. Home was no longer Villa L'Ambrosiana and her family, but Ezra and Fioruccia, Matteo, Olga and Ercole too. They were intertwined, tragedy and joy, like two sides of the same coin, and she couldn't think of one without thinking of the other. It was better not to think of either, for each thought was laced with sorrow. Better to leave them all in the past and let the dust settle over them, blanketing both the pleasure and the pain.

Evelina gave herself to the present moment and to her future. Her life would be in America now. She had no intention of ever going back to Vercellino. As she settled into a comfortable routine of helping Aunt Madolina with her charities, going out with Mike, Alba and Antonio, she slowly began to shed a skin, and it felt good.

The first time Mike kissed her did not feel as strange as she'd feared it would. She'd worried that she'd compare him to Ezra, that she'd hanker after the familiar feeling of Ezra's touch, but instead, she relished the novelty of Mike's. He'd invited her to his home for dinner with his family, and afterwards, they'd sat on the roof beneath the stars. 'You never talk about yourself,' he said.

'There's not much to say,' she replied with a shrug.

'That's not true. You're just holding back. You don't have to hold back with me, you know.'

She sighed. How could an American possibly understand what she had been through? 'I left Italy because I wanted to leave it behind,' she said. 'Talking about it only brings it back.'

'I can't imagine it was easy living through the war.'

'No, it wasn't easy at all.' She took a sharp breath, knowing that even if she'd wanted to share it with him the words wouldn't come, but stick in her throat like thorns. 'But it's behind me now,' she added and she closed the subject with a smile.

Mike took her hand. 'You're in a good place here,' he told her. 'America's the finest country in the world. And you're with me. I'll keep you safe.' He kissed her then. It felt warm and gentle and she put her hand to his face and felt a fondness expand inside her chest. As his kiss deepened she felt an anchor fix her ever more securely in the moment. She didn't think of Ezra or wonder what he would make of her; with Mike; she didn't think of home at all. America was home now and Mike was part of this new chapter of possibility and change.

At the beginning of September Evelina returned home from a fundraising tea she'd attended with her aunt to find Alba curled up on her bed, crying. Her first thought was that Antonio had broken up with her. But it soon transpired that Alba was pregnant. 'What am I going to do?' she whispered.

Evelina didn't know the answer to that. She perched beside her on the bed and put a hand on her shoulder. 'Have you told Antonio?' she asked.

'No, I'm too scared.'

'Are you going to tell your parents?'

Alba was horrified at the thought. 'Of course not! I'm going to get rid of it.'

Evelina stared at her cousin in shock. 'You can't do that, Alba. Besides the fact that it's illegal, it's dangerous! You could die.'

'I can't lose Antonio over this.'

'How do you know you're going to lose him? Perhaps he'll marry you.'

'Hardly! I haven't even met his parents. You've met Mike's—'

'That doesn't mean anything,' said Evelina quickly.

'It means that Antonio isn't serious about me. That's what it means.' She sat up and wiped her nose with the back of her hand.

'Are you sure you're pregnant?'

'I've missed two periods, Evelina. What else can it be?'

'Do you feel sick?'

'Only with fear.'

'No morning sickness?'

'Nothing. I don't feel sick at all. But I've missed two periods. That's not normal.'

'You need to see a doctor.'

Alba began to cry again. 'Will you come with me?'

Evelina took her hand. 'Of course,' she replied.

Alba booked a doctor's appointment through a friend, because she couldn't possibly go to her family doctor for fear of her mother finding out – and if anybody was going to find out something as sensitive as this, it was Madolina.

The morning was hot and sticky when Alba and Evelina left the house together. Rainclouds hung low over the city and the air was thick with the smell of car fumes and street cooking. They took the subway to downtown Manhattan. Neither spoke. They were much too nervous. Alba was as pale as oatmeal. Her eyes were dark with dread, her usual exuberance subdued. By the time they reached the grey-stone building of the doctor's surgery it was pouring with rain. The two women hurried inside and took the elevator to the second floor. Alba had booked her appointment under a fake name. When the receptionist called out that name neither Alba nor Evelina reacted, until the woman was on the point of giving up and calling out the next name on the list. Then Alba came to her senses, apologized and disappeared into the consulting room, closing the door behind her. Evelina waited. She tried to read a magazine, but was unable to concentrate. She flicked through it, glancing at the pictures, hoping that Alba was wrong and that she wasn't pregnant.

Twenty minutes later Alba emerged, even whiter in the face than before, and Evelina knew that her cousin's instincts had been right. But what was she going to do about it? They found a diner around the corner and ordered hamburgers and chips and Coca-Cola. Alba lit a cigarette. 'That damned fortune teller, what was she called?'

'Mystic Marica,' Evelina replied.

'Mystic Marica,' Alba chuckled bitterly. 'She warned me, you know.'

'She did?'

'She didn't say I'd marry a prince and live in a palace.'

'She didn't?'

'I lied.'

This didn't surprise Evelina. 'What did she say?'

Alba blew smoke into the room. 'She encouraged me to find a deeper meaning to my life and that Antonio offered me material pleasures but could offer me nothing spiritual.' She shrugged. 'Who needs spiritual? Spiritual doesn't sparkle or keep you warm in winter like fur does.'

'How did she warn you?'

'She said I was in love and being careless. She told me to be careful.'

'She told me to be careful too. She probably tells everyone to be careful.'

The waitress brought their drinks. Alba took a drag and watched her put the glasses and Coca-Cola bottles on the table. 'So, what am I going to do about it?'

'You only have one choice,' said Evelina.

'Which is?'

'To have the baby.'

'Jesus, Evelina! Is that the best you can come up with?'

'It's the only thing I can come up with.'

'And where am I going to have the baby so no one finds out about it? It's not easy to hide a growing belly, you know!'

'You have to tell your mother.'

'We *are* talking about the same mother, aren't we?'

'I agree, she won't be happy. How about you tell Antonio first?'

'I can't tell Antonio. I told you. He'll ditch me.'

'He's going to find out about it sometime. As you said, you can't hide a growing belly.'

'Can't I just get rid of it?'

Evelina was appalled. 'It's a baby, Alba! A living thing. You can't kill it.'

'It's not a baby. It's a lump of cells. It won't know.'

'*Santa Maria, madre di Dio,*' said Evelina, filling her glass. 'I'm not religious and it's your body, but the baby inside you is a life and it belongs to Antonio too. You cannot make this decision alone. You must tell him. He has a right. He's the father.'

Alba groaned. She stubbed out her cigarette with a trembling hand. The waitress brought their food. Alba stuffed a chip into her mouth and chewed anxiously. 'Okay, I'll tell him. I'd rather tell *him* than Mom.'

Evelina smiled. 'She might like a grandchild. My mother went crazy over Benedetta's son.'

'She's already got grandchildren, what's one more? No, she'll kill me.'

'She'll be angry at first, but she won't stay angry for long. Aunt Madolina is a practical, energetic woman. Problem solving is what she's good at.'

'She damned well better be a magician then because this will be the biggest problem she's ever had to deal with.'

Alba did not want to be on her own when she told Antonio that she was pregnant, so she arranged for the four of them to go out on the Saturday night. They'd go to the movies first and then dinner. After dinner Evelina would take a walk around the block with Mike so that Alba could tell Antonio the bad news. At least then, if he lost his temper, she'd have Evelina to walk home with.

Alba was in a bad mood all Saturday. Madolina, who did not abide bad tempers, sent them off to Fulton Street to do some shopping for her while she entertained her friends in the sitting room with tea and cards. Evelina was happy to get out of the house. Often, Madolina would call her down to make up numbers after one of her guests had had to leave early or simply hadn't turned up. As much as Evelina enjoyed playing cards, she didn't relish being stuck in her aunt's salons, unable to leave until the game was over. Sometimes their games went on well into evening.

By the time Antonio and Mike swung by in Antonio's car, Alba was at her lowest ebb. 'What's wrong, baby?' Antonio asked when he saw her face.

'Nothing, honey,' she replied, climbing into the back. 'Just had a bad day. You'll cheer me up.'

Mike had got out to open the door for Evelina. 'You okay?' he asked, putting a hand in the small of her back and kissing her.

'Sure,' she said. 'Alba just needs to be distracted.'

'Then *Blue Skies* is the perfect movie. Nothing like a musical to lift the spirits.' Evelina wasn't sure anything could lift Alba's.

The movie theatre was packed with people. They sat in the middle of a row with Coca-Cola and cartons of popcorn. As the lights went down and the programme started, Alba leaned in to Evelina and whispered. 'I can't go through with it.'

'You have to,' Evelina replied.

'I'm scared.'

Evelina squeezed her hand. 'It's going to be okay, I promise you. Antonio's a good man.'

After that Mike pulled her into his arms and began kissing her and Evelina didn't see much more of Alba or the movie.

Alba managed to pull herself together during dinner. They went to a popular diner and, encouraged by the attention Antonio had paid her during the movie, Alba cheered up. It was only at the end of dinner when Alba lost her appetite and didn't touch her ice cream that Evelina suggested she and Mike go for a walk.

It was a warm evening. Summer still lingered, staving off autumn with a heat and humidity that refused to lift. The leaves had barely started to turn, but the street lamps were golden and the skies above Brooklyn blush pink. Mike took her hand. 'What's all this about?' he asked. Evelina didn't want to tell him, but she knew she had to explain why she'd

asked him to walk around the block with her before they'd
even finished their desserts.

'Alba has something she wants to tell Antonio,' she said.

'She's not breaking up with him, I hope.'

'No, of course not. She really likes him.'

'Good, because he really likes her too.' Silence. 'So, what
is it she wants to tell him?'

'I'm not sure I should tell you.'

'Evelina, you have to tell me. We're a couple. We tell each
other everything.'

For some reason that declaration made Evelina feel
uncomfortable. 'Well, if you promise not to tell . . .'

'I won't let on that you told me, I promise.'

'She's pregnant.'

Mike stopped walking and turned to look at Evelina in
horror. 'Jesus! Really?'

'Yes, really. I accompanied her to the doctor. There's
no doubt.'

He rubbed the back of his neck and gasped. 'That's bad.
That's really bad.'

'What do you think Antonio will do?'

'I don't know.' Mike took a packet of cigarettes out of his
pocket and popped one between his lips. 'You want one?'

She shook her head. 'He won't break up with her, will
he?' she asked anxiously.

He struck a match and the little tip of the cigarette glowed
scarlet. 'I don't know,' he replied. 'Antonio's all fun and
jokes. I don't know what he's like when he's serious. And
this is serious.'

'It certainly is.'

Mike pulled Evelina towards him and kissed her lips. 'I
want to make love to you,' he said.

Evelina brushed off his comment with a laugh. 'Oh Mike, Alba's pregnant. This isn't the time to talk about that.'

'Of course it is. It's exactly the right time. We'll be careful.' He grinned. 'There are ways to avoid getting knocked up, you know.'

'I know, but I'm not ready for that.'

Mike assumed she hadn't done it before. 'I'll look after you,' he said gently. His eyes shone. 'It's fun, you know. You'll like it.'

'I'm sure I will, when the time is right.'

He sat on a stoop and patted the step beside him. Evelina tucked her skirt under her and sat down. 'And when is the time going to be right?'

'I don't know. I just don't want to rush into anything.'

'Then let's get married.'

Evelina was speechless.

'Don't look at me like that,' he said and laughed. 'I love you, Evelina.' When she didn't reply, he frowned. 'You do love me, don't you?'

'Of course I do,' she replied, but she knew what love felt like and this wasn't it.

'Then let's get married and we can make love as often as we want.' He put an arm around her waist.

'Oh Mike . . .'

'Are you turning me down?' He looked hurt.

'No, just saying not yet.'

'Not yet, not yet. I don't want to rush into anything. Now is not the time.' He imitated her Italian accent. 'Well, when is it going to be the time? We've been dating all summer.'

'All summer? You think that's a long time?'

'Long enough to know that I want to spend the rest of my life with you. Long enough to know that I don't want anyone else.'

Evelina stood up, flustered. 'Don't rush me, Mike,' she said, trying not to let her panic show.

'It's hardly rushing,' he argued.

She folded her arms. 'You know nothing about me.'

'How can I know anything about you when you don't tell me anything?'

'We should get back to the diner. Antonio might have walked out and left Alba on her own.'

Mike got up but he didn't put his arm around her or take her hand. They walked a foot apart, but the distance felt bigger. 'I won't rush you,' he said eventually, dropping his cigarette onto the pavement and crushing it beneath his foot. 'But I'll take a "yes" any time you're willing to give me one.'

When they returned to the diner Alba and Antonio were still at the table deep in conversation. Evelina gave a tentative wave as they walked in and to her surprise Alba waved back enthusiastically. 'Come and sit down,' she said happily and Evelina could tell from her pink cheeks and sparkling eyes that the conversation had gone well. Alba looked at Antonio and said, 'Shall I tell them, or do you want to?'

Antonio took her hand and grinned. 'You tell them, baby.'

'We're getting married!'

Evelina was so relieved, she threw her arms around her. 'This is the most wonderful news!' she gushed. 'I'm so happy for you.'

'We won't tell anyone about the baby,' Alba said in a low voice. Then to Mike, 'I'm pregnant.'

Mike pretended he didn't know and Evelina was grateful to him for that. 'Congratulations!' he said. 'A marriage and a baby. What'll be next?'

Antonio laughed and shook hands with Mike. 'We'll get

married in November,' he said. 'And when the baby comes, no one will be any the wiser. I mean, who's going to count?'

Alba caught Evelina's eye and they both laughed. 'Madolina!'

Evelina didn't tell Alba that Mike had asked her to marry him, not because she didn't want to steal her cousin's thunder, but because she'd then have to explain why she had refused him. Evelina wasn't really sure herself. It was just a feeling. A sense of something not being right. She was fond of Mike. *Very* fond of him. But she didn't love him. Was it, perhaps, unrealistic to expect to experience again the kind of love she felt for Ezra? Or even a fraction of that love? After all, Benedetta couldn't have loved Francesco when she'd married him. She'd barely known him. She might have found him attractive and charming, but she hadn't known him long enough to really love him. That had come later. Or had it? As Evelina thought harder about her sister's marriage she wondered whether Benedetta had ever really loved Francesco or whether she had loved the *idea* of him, which had shattered after she'd made her vows to love and obey and he'd lifted his hand to strike her. The real man had been a brute.

Evelina knew Mike well enough to know that he was kind. In fact, if she had to write a list of all his good qualities she'd need more than two sides of paper. If she had to write a list of his faults, she'd probably only need one line: he wasn't Ezra. But she was never going to find Ezra in another man and the real Ezra was gone. Maybe she'd have to compromise in order to carve out a decent life for herself. If she didn't marry, what would she do? Who would she be? She had learned, in the last year, that in order to feel secure and find a sense of belonging in this new country she needed a family. A family of her own. So, why didn't Mike fit the bill?

The following day Antonio parked his car outside Alba's house and, dressed in a suit and tie, knocked on the front door. Alba had told him that her father liked to enjoy a long tea on a Sunday afternoon, reading the papers and listening to the wireless. That would be the perfect time for Antonio to come and ask for her hand in marriage.

Alba ran to answer the door. Evelina stood watching on the stair. Madolina walked into the hall, wondering who would be ringing the bell on a Sunday afternoon. When she saw Evelina she frowned, sensing something was afoot. 'What are you two cooking?' she asked them.

Alba opened the door. 'Antonio! Come in. Come in.'

Antonio walked in looking brushed and polished. 'Good afternoon, Mrs Forte,' he said politely and put out his hand. 'I'm Antonio Genovese. It's a pleasure to finally meet you.'

Madolina, who had never met her daughter's boyfriend, smiled, clearly disarmed by his good looks and obvious charm. 'Very nice to meet you too, Antonio,' she said. 'And not before time,' she added wryly.

'I've come to see Mr Forte,' he said and a tinge of nervousness broke through his slick veneer.

'Have you, indeed. Well, I'll go and see if he's available.' Madolina left them in the hall.

'Don't worry, honey, she's friendly when you get to know her,' said Alba, straightening his tie.

'How do I look?' Antonio asked, grinning down at her.

'Handsome,' she replied, patting the tie. 'You look mighty handsome.'

A few seconds later Madolina returned. 'He'll see you,' she said. 'Come with me.'

Antonio followed her to the drawing room where Peppino was sitting in an armchair, spectacles on, reading the newspaper. When he saw Antonio, he folded the paper and put it down. 'Come on in, Antonio,' he said, getting up. He gave the young man's hand a vigorous shake.

When Madolina left the room, she found Alba and Evelina by the door, ready to eavesdrop. 'Oh no you don't,' she said, shooing them away like a pair of chickens. 'You're coming with me.'

'Oh Mom . . .'

'You're not to listen. It's men's business.'

'What do you think?' Alba asked, following her mother through the house.

Madolina smiled. 'I think you should invite him to stay for dinner – and then I'll let you know what I think.'

Antonio stayed for dinner. Whatever Peppino thought privately about a young man who had no proper job and a dubious family name, he didn't let on. He opened a bottle of champagne and raised his glass to the happy couple. Evelina knew that Antonio's family was rich and if there was one thing her uncle respected almost more than anything else, it was money. He couldn't dispute the fact that Alba would be as well looked after by the Genovese family as she had been by her own. As for her aunt, Madolina would have preferred an East Coast American Columbia graduate with a good job and an old family name, but deep down Evelina knew that she just wanted her daughter to be happy.

At the end of dinner Antonio announced that they wanted to marry as soon as possible.

'Why the hurry?' Madolina asked.

Antonio took Alba's hand and looked at her with devotion.

'You've been in love, Mrs Forte. You know what it's like to have to wait.'

Madolina sighed. 'Well, I suppose when you know, you know, and there's no point hanging around just so your mother can arrange the party and the flowers and the dinner and the dress—'

'Oh Mom!' Alba interrupted with a laugh. 'You'll manage. Besides, Evelina will help you. She can be your assistant, can't you, Evelina?'

'I'd love to be your assistant, Aunt Madolina,' said Evelina, wondering whether her aunt was beginning to sense, in the rush to get up the aisle, a bun cooking in the oven.

'If you insist,' said Madolina with a sigh. 'I'm sure I can arrange things in time. But we'll have to start tomorrow. There's not a moment to waste.'

'If anyone can whip up a wedding in a couple of months, *you* can,' said Peppino, draining his glass. He opened a mahogany cigar case and lifted out a beautifully wrapped Montecristo. 'It'll be the grandest wedding Brooklyn has ever seen,' he said, putting the cigar beneath his nose and sniffing it. 'No expense spared, Madolina.' He pushed the case across the table to Antonio. 'Go on,' he said. 'Help yourself.'

Madolina watched as he copied his future father-in-law and put a Montecristo beneath his nose. 'I look forward to meeting your mother,' she said.

Alba giggled. She was now tipsy on happiness. 'So do I,' she agreed.

CHAPTER TWELVE

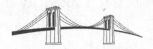

Madolina undertook the task of arranging her daughter's wedding with the brisk efficiency of a colonel. Evelina was her lieutenant and never in her life had she been so busy. Jane's wedding, eight years before, had been an extravaganza, but this was something else entirely. Alba was their youngest and, Evelina observed with increasing certainty, their favourite, for Madolina saw to every minute detail of the ceremony and supper with an almost religious zeal. She wanted everything embossed or embroidered with entwining 'A's. From the order of service and the bride and groom's hassocks in the church to the menus, place cards and napkins at the wedding feast. Unlike Artemisia whose attention to detail at Benedetta's wedding was done solely to promote herself, Madolina's was done to celebrate her daughter, and to express in gestures both tender and sweet a wistful goodbye.

When the day arrived, Evelina was more nervous than the bride. It was *she* who had arranged everything, following Madolina's orders, and if anything went wrong or was other than perfect, it was *she* who would be blamed. The dress, at least, could not have been more beautiful, nor Alba more beautiful in it. Made especially for her in white silk and lace, it was both elegant and glamorous with a small waist and a full skirt, offset with the diamond and sapphire suite of jewels Antonio's father had gifted her at their engagement party. Peppino had appreciated that gesture and at the first family meeting at the Genovese mansion in New Jersey the two men had discovered that they had much in common. They both smoked the same brand of cigar and put their good health down to cold showers every morning and grappa the Italian way, with coffee. They'd shaken hands and forged the beginning of a firm friendship. Madolina had warmed to Antonio's mother the moment she said she was an avid listener of the *Mamma Forte* radio show. The fact that the woman was brash and talked too much did not put her off. Madolina was the kind of woman who found the good in everybody, even when it was rather well concealed.

Alba's belly was only slightly rounded, looking more like the result of one too many celebration dinners than a night of careless sex in the back of Antonio's Buick. Madolina dabbed her eyes at the sight of her daughter, the emotion being too much. 'I can't believe my little girl is getting married,' she said, and Alba kissed her and told her that even though she was moving out she wasn't moving too far away.

'I'll still need you, Mom,' she said, her smile faltering a moment.

Madolina blended a smudge of make-up on her face with her thumb. 'Thank goodness for that,' she replied. Then she turned to Evelina and added, 'At least I'll still have you.'

'Not for long,' Alba teased. 'It'll be Evelina and Mike next.'

Evelina pulled a face, which made them all laugh, but inside she didn't feel merry at all.

Mike was an usher. He looked handsome in his suit with his hair brushed off his clean-shaven face. His eyes, however, betrayed his lack of gratification. He did not like to be turned down and instead of backing off and giving Evelina time to get used to the idea of marriage, he kept bringing it up. Each time more urgently, as if he was more concerned about his damaged pride than the precious time with his beloved lost in indecision. 'Next time us,' he told her when the service was over and they were reunited at the hotel where Evelina had organized the wedding feast.

Evelina laughed as she always did. It was her default mechanism now, a way of brushing off his comments and not having to respond to them. 'You haven't told me how good I look,' she said.

'You look beautiful. You always look beautiful. I'd say you outshine the bride, but then I'm biased.'

'That would be a terrible mistake for a maid of honour to outshine the bride.'

Mike chuckled. 'Alba won't allow anyone to outshine her on her day, even you.' He pulled her towards him and kissed her. 'You drive me crazy, you know.'

'Oh Mike—'

'You do. You don't let me make love to you and you won't marry me. What's a man to do? What'll it take? Tell me and I'll do it. But don't string me along.'

'Not now, Mike. This is Alba's day—'

'It's always something, isn't it?'

'Let's talk about this later. Let's get something to drink.' Evelina took his hand and led him through the throng of people, for Peppino and Madolina knew everyone who was anyone in Brooklyn and the room was full.

At dinner Evelina was seated next to a cousin of Antonio's and a man called Franklin van der Velden, who had come with Alba's sister, Jane, because her husband hadn't been able to make it. Jane's husband and Franklin had met at Columbia

University where he now worked as a classics teacher. He was tall and slim with intelligent blue eyes the colour of forget-me-nots, light brown hair and a wry, humorous smile. 'It's a pleasure to meet you, Evelina,' he said, looking at her through a pair of glasses. 'Your aunt has done a fine job. This is a splendid party.'

'I'm glad you think so.' Evelina swept her eyes over the extravagant flower displays and felt a warm sense of satisfaction. 'She had a very short time to arrange it.'

He took a sip of champagne. 'I'm sure Madolina didn't do it all on her own.'

'No, she had an assistant,' Evelina replied with a grin.

'Then I should compliment you.' He raised his glass.

'I have to earn my keep,' she said.

'Is that what you do? Work for Madolina?'

'Unofficially, yes.'

'If you'd like a proper job, I could help you.'

'Doing what?'

'Charity work.'

'I already help Madolina with her charities.'

'Does she pay you?'

'No, but I live in her house for free.'

'So you should, you're family.'

'Well, I'm happy to help her. I enjoy it and there are so many refugees who need help.'

'How long have you been in America?'

'Since January.'

'How did you find it? It must have been hard leaving home.'

Evelina frowned. 'It was hard, but I wanted to leave. I'm happy here. This is home now.'

'What makes a place home, do you think?'

Evelina was surprised by his question. It wasn't the usual

thing people asked her. She sighed. She wasn't quite sure. 'Family and friends,' she replied hesitantly. 'Being happy somewhere.' He didn't interrupt, but watched her closely as she worked it out. 'I suppose feeling a sense of belonging. Familiarity. I've been here eleven months and although at first I was a little homesick, I'm used to it now.'

'I think love makes a place home.'

Evelina felt silly for not mentioning the obvious. 'Well, of course, love. That's what I meant by family and friends.'

'It's carving out a life that has a sense of purpose and fulfilment.'

'Yes, that also.'

'But if there's no love then the house is just a house and the community one lives in is empty and cold. Love is the propeller and without it we simply stand still and isolated, marking time.'

'I wouldn't want to live like that,' said Evelina. This talk of love made her feel morose, suddenly.

'Do you have a nice fella?' he asked.

'Yes, his name is Mike. He's here.' She pretended to look around, but she didn't want to find him.

'That's good. It would have been difficult to leave Italy if you'd had a fella there.'

She dropped her eyes to the plate of food that had just been put in front of her. 'I couldn't have left in that case,' she said softly. She sighed then, a sigh laden with unspeakable things.

'Jane tells me you've become a great friend of Alba's. A steadying influence, is what she said.'

Evelina was relieved to change the subject. 'I'm not sure I've been a steadying influence, but we are good friends, that is true. Now she'll be leaving to live in New Jersey.' She sighed again.

'That's not far.'

'No, it isn't. And knowing Alba, she won't want to be too far from Madolina. She complains about her mother all the time, but really she needs her very much.'

'Madolina will miss her, but at least she'll still have you. Until you leave too.'

'I'm not going to leave. Not yet.'

'This Mike—'

'And you, Franklin? Do you have a nice girl?' she interrupted with a smile that told him she did not want to talk about herself anymore.

He tucked into his dinner. 'No,' he replied. 'I don't have time for that right now.'

After dinner there were speeches. Peppino spoke touchingly about his daughter, which made everyone cry. Mike, who had drunk too much, told a few slurred anecdotes about Antonio that made everyone laugh. Then Antonio told the room how much he loved Alba and there was silence. 'Alba in Italian means sunrise,' he said, gazing tenderly upon his bride. 'And with every sunrise comes hope, possibility, novelty, beauty and love. That's what she is to me, and more. My own perfect sunrise.' Madolina wiped away tears. Peppino raised his glass. Antonio's family cheered loudly and Evelina was glad that she wasn't sitting next to Mike, who would use this moment to nudge her closer to accepting his marriage proposal.

The band started playing and Antonio took his bride's hand and led her onto the dance floor. Mike found Evelina and they too began to dance. Soon everyone was dancing and it didn't feel like America anymore, but Italy, with all the exuberance and emotion of a grand Italian wedding.

It wasn't long before Evelina noticed how unsteady Mike was on his feet. His hands were damp and beads of sweat glistened on his forehead. He pushed his hair off his face and it stuck up in tufts. He'd taken off his jacket and she could feel how hot he was as he pressed his body against hers. 'Why don't we go outside and get some air?' she suggested.

'No, I have a better idea.' He stopped dancing and dragged her towards the band.

Evelina felt something cold squeeze her heart. 'No, Mike . . .' she protested, but he was already speaking to the conductor, who suddenly halted the music. Bewildered, everyone stopped dancing. A murmur rippled through the room.

'I have an announcement to make!' he exclaimed.

Evelina went hot. Every eye in the room was upon them. She wished there were somewhere she could hide.

'Evelina and I are getting married!' he shouted, raising their hands in the air.

Evelina wanted to vomit. A roar of applause erupted and everyone cheered. The music started up again, this time with more vigour. Mike pulled her into his arms and kissed her full on the lips. She heard clapping. A moment later Alba and Antonio were embracing her. She saw their mouths moving but she didn't hear what they were saying. It was as if she were under water, as if she couldn't breathe. Madolina found her and enveloped her in her strong arms, kissing her loudly. Peppino came next and then it was one after the other, people she didn't know, shaking her hand, patting her, speaking to her and all was noise and touch and smiles and voices and Evelina felt dizzy and disorientated and gripped with panic.

She made for the door.

She didn't know where she was going, she just knew she had to get outside to breathe some cold air.

As soon as she was in the street she took a deep breath. It was cold and the pavement was slippery with ice and snow, but she didn't care. She stood there in her strapless dress and high heels, trembling with fury. 'Are you all right?' came a voice behind her. She spun round. It was Franklin. She didn't know what to say. 'Do you want a smoke?' He flicked open his silver cigarette case.

Evelina didn't, but she took one anyway. He struck his lighter and their hands touched as they shielded it from the wind. 'You're going to get cold out here,' he said as she took a puff, then coughed. 'Here, take my jacket.' He slipped out of it and hooked it over her shoulders. It was warm against her skin. 'I take it the announcement wasn't welcome?'

Evelina took another puff and didn't cough this time. 'I cannot believe he did that to me,' she fumed.

'He might have asked you first.'

'He's been asking me for weeks and I tell him every time that I'm not ready.'

Franklin hesitated a moment, narrowing his eyes in thought. 'Come, let's go somewhere warm where we can talk.' He offered her his arm so she wouldn't slip on the ice.

They found a diner in the next block and sat in a booth on opposite sides of the table. Franklin ordered two hot chocolates. 'That'll warm you up. You're not exactly dressed for the cold.'

'I'm too cross to be cold,' she said.

'He's drunk. He'll feel rotten in the morning and you'll forgive him.'

Evelina shrugged. 'I don't know that I can.'

'Men behave stupidly sometimes when they don't get what they want. He's young and foolish, but I'm sure he's not bad.'

'No, he's not bad.'

'If I may be so bold, why don't you want to marry him?'

'I don't want to marry anyone.'

He raised his eyebrows in surprise. 'Never?'

Evelina stared into her hot chocolate.

'Pass me my cigarette case and lighter, will you? They're in the inside pocket of my jacket.' She did as Franklin asked and he opened the case, took out a cigarette and placed it between his lips. She watched as the smoke clouded the air between them.

'A pretty girl like you not wanting to get married doesn't add up.'

She cupped the mug and sighed. 'I loved someone once,' she said quietly, without looking at him.

He nodded and by the expression on her face he guessed at some sort of tragedy. 'I'm sorry. I didn't mean to . . .'

'It's all right.' She sighed again and the weight of sorrow shifted a little in her chest. 'He was killed in the war.'

'Is that why you came here?'

'There was nothing left for me in Italy. I lived in a small town in a remote part of the country. I didn't want to be there without him. Everything reminded me of him. Everything.'

'And you don't feel you can love anyone else?'

Her eyes filled with tears. She didn't know Franklin at all, and yet she felt she could talk to him. Perhaps, knowing that she would probably never see him again made it easier for her to share her story. Like a confessional with a priest; whatever was said would be instantly forgotten. 'I like Mike very much. He's funny and interesting, but I don't love him. I don't think I will ever love like that again. I cannot. And maybe I don't want to. Ezra was the world to me but now he is gone.' Saying those words out loud made the tears spill onto her cheeks. She wiped them away with her fingers. 'I'm sorry. I really shouldn't be troubling you with my problems.'

'They're not problems, Evelina. They're burdens and I'm sorry that you're carrying them.' Franklin smiled gently. 'It takes time to learn to live with grief and everyone learns at their own pace. Nothing prepares you for it and there's no manual to guide you through it. You just muddle through and find your own way of coping. It'll never go away, but you *will* eventually reach some sort of acceptance and with that comes release.'

'You sound like you know what you're talking about.'

'I too have suffered loss,' he said. 'My father died when I was eleven and it hit me very hard. I don't think you ever comprehend it – death is so final, it's impossible to comprehend – but you do reach a point where you accept that it is what it is. Then you lift your chin up and carry on. That's all you can do.' He flicked ash into the ashtray.

'And the hole in your heart is never filled?'

'Not really, but your heart is bigger than you know and it's very good at compensating.'

'Do you believe in God, Franklin?'

'I believe in something bigger than myself. I also believe in purpose. I don't know what mine is and I suspect I'll never know, but I do believe I have one. Whatever it is, we're all here for a reason. Your Ezra was here for a reason and so was my father. They completed their lives and departed. I don't know where they are now, but I sense they're present. Energy can neither be created nor destroyed. Their consciousness is out there somewhere and I like to think I'll recognize Dad when I see him again. But who knows?' He watched her sip the hot chocolate. 'Don't be too hard on Mike, Evelina. I can understand why he wants to marry you.'

She gave a small smile. 'That's very sweet of you.'

'He's a good guy. Who can blame him for being in love with you?'

'He would be better off loving someone else. Someone who can love him back.'

'Perhaps you will, in time.'

She drained her mug. 'I don't know. What I do know is that I won't be pushed into marriage. I'm going to have to tell Aunt Madolina that there is to be no wedding.'

'She'll be happy. She likes having you around.'

'I might be with her for ever. She won't be so happy then, will she?'

'Your heart will heal and you'll fall in love again. You're young . . . and the heart is stronger than you realize.'

Evelina did not want to agree with him. She didn't ever want to love anyone else. She thought she could but she had been mistaken. She could not.

Evelina had thought that, after his rash announcement at the wedding and her rebuff, it would be *she* who ended their relationship, but to her surprise, it was *Mike*. No one could understand why she didn't want to marry him, least of all Madolina. 'He's from a good family. He's got a good job. He's handsome, you can't deny that, and he's interesting to talk to. What's more, he's got a sense of humour. I always think people who laugh live better and longer. And he loves you. That's not something you should turn your nose up at.'

'But I don't love him in the way he wants me to,' Evelina explained.

'That'll come. Some people just take longer. If all the ingredients are there, you'll get a good cake. In my day our parents chose our spouses for us.'

'Like Benedetta and Francesco,' said Evelina, wanting to add that, as it turned out, it wasn't a particularly good match.

'I'm older and wiser than you and I can see that you and Mike are a good fit.' Madolina narrowed her eyes. 'You let him go and you'll never get him back.'

'It's not a case of *me* letting *him* go, Aunt Madolina. He's let *me* go.'

'He'd have you back in a heartbeat if you agreed to marry him.'

Evelina shook her head. 'I can't do that.'

'What are you waiting for? Prince Charming?'

Someone who will never come, Evelina thought to herself. 'I don't know,' she said out loud. 'But I'd rather not marry at all than marry the wrong person.'

Madolina looked exasperated. 'Then you'd better look for a job, because if you're going to be alone, you need to have something to live off. You can't live off air, you know.'

Evelina remembered that Franklin had offered her a job working for a charity. She got his telephone number from Jane and called him one evening when he was home from work. He didn't appear to be at all surprised to hear from her and offered to arrange a meeting with Mrs Spellman who ran the business. The following day he called her back with a date and time for an interview. The charity's office was in downtown Manhattan so Evelina took the subway and turned up for her interview in a smart skirt and jacket with a row of pearls at her throat. She was excited. She'd never had a proper job before and the feeling of independence that trip into New York gave her was exhilarating. It reminded her of the time she'd ridden into Vercellino with Benedetta. She thought of Ezra then but pushed the memory away. Now was not the time for nostalgia or sorrow.

Mrs Spellman was an elegant woman in her forties, with short blonde hair styled into fashionable waves and a direct gaze that seemed to look right through her. Full of energy and purpose she wore grey slacks and a white shirt and had rolled up her sleeves to show she meant business. Franklin had told Evelina that Cynthia Spellman was the wife of a wealthy stockbroker and had been brought in to head the charity, which dated back to the middle of the eighteenth century, some five or so years before. Its main purpose was the education of underprivileged children but had recently expanded to give support to unmarried mothers in those poor communities of New York.

Mrs Spellman offered Evelina a seat then sat back in her chair, lit a cigarette and smiled at her. 'Any friend of Franklin's is a friend of mine. So when would you be able to start?'

'As soon as you need me,' Evelina replied.

'I need you now. We're desperately short-staffed and there's so much to do. I can only pay you forty dollars a week, but I can promise you that the work is rewarding.'

Evelina accepted immediately and agreed to start in two days' time.

That evening she telephoned Franklin to thank him.

'I already heard,' he told her. 'Cynthia liked you a lot.'

'She's a nice woman,' said Evelina.

'She sure is.' There was a brief pause. 'Let's celebrate with supper and a show. There are some good plays on at the moment. What are you doing tomorrow night?'

CHAPTER THIRTEEN

Evelina loved the theatre, a love that had been enthusiastically encouraged by both her parents throughout her childhood. Artemisia had maintained that if she hadn't married Tani she would have been an actress. Tani had maintained that she'd been *born* an actress and that Villa L'Ambrosiana was a perpetual stage upon which she performed her many daily dramas. He was not wrong, although it was adulation Artemisia craved, and the audience in that isolated old place was never big enough or loud enough in its appreciation to satisfy the diva that inhabited her. However, both Tani and Artemisia adored theatre in all its forms and, as an annual treat, on a birthday or perhaps at Christmas, they had taken their children to the famous La Scala or Il Piccolo Teatro in Milan. As a result, Evelina had grown up with the impression that opera, ballet and plays were the highest forms of art expressed in movement, music and dance, to be treasured and appreciated, unlike cinema, which was within everyone's reach and therefore primarily for the uneducated masses. The theatre was special.

Evelina was excited. She didn't care what play she was going to see, she was just thrilled to be going at all. She chose the prettiest dress in her closet, a black sleeveless frock with a

small waist and a full skirt, accessorized with the pearl necklace and matching earrings she'd worn for her interview with
Mrs Spellman. She swept her hair off her face and curled it at
her shoulders. It was a more sophisticated, fashionable look,
but since her relationship with Mike had ended she'd wanted
to be someone different. Someone new. After all, she had a
job now and was going to earn her own money, it seemed
the right time to cultivate a new persona.

Franklin was quite a bit older than Mike. Evelina wasn't
sure how much older he was, but she assumed he must be
in his late thirties or even his early forties. He wasn't looking for a girlfriend, that much he'd told her, and she wasn't
looking for a boyfriend either, that much she'd told *him*. So
tonight was simply about friendship and that suited Evelina
very well. She'd just got out of a romance, the last thing she
needed was to jump into another.

When she came down the stairs Madolina was in the
drawing room with her friends, playing cards. Cigarette
smoke wafted into the hall and filled the house, along with
the women's chatter and the occasional peal of laughter.
Among the women was Taddeo Paganini, Madolina's closest
friend and confidant. Taddeo was the only man permitted to
join this hallowed group of philanthropic females, but he was
no fox in the henhouse. A confirmed bachelor with red hair
and a penchant for flamboyant ties and socks which he wore
with pinstriped suits, he was acerbic and witty, with an eye
for the ridiculous. A journalist by trade, he was passionate
about Madolina and followed her around like a bridesmaid,
quoting poetry in her honour. Evelina adored him because
he made her laugh. Whenever she felt down she could count
on Taddeo to lift her spirits with his irreverent comments
and dry asides.

The double door from the drawing room into the hall had been left ajar so that when Evelina stepped into the hall, her movement caught Taddeo's attention. He immediately excused himself from the card table and swept out to see her.

'Well, if it isn't Lauren Bacall!' he exclaimed, looking her up and down with admiration. 'My dear, you look simply sensational.'

Madolina followed him out. 'You know what would make it, a brooch,' she said, narrowing her eyes.

'You're right, Madolina. She's like a Christmas tree without its star,' Taddeo added.

'I don't have a brooch,' said Evelina.

'I have one you can borrow. It'll be perfect.' Madolina went upstairs.

'Who's the lucky man?' asked Taddeo.

'Just a friend.'

He arched an eyebrow. 'And you dress up like that for a friend, do you?'

'We're going to the theatre.'

'And for dinner, I suspect.'

'We're celebrating my new job.'

'Well, it's not like you've made it into the boardroom, is it.'

Evelina laughed. 'There's no romance,' she said firmly. 'We're just friends.'

'Famous last words, Eva,' said Taddeo.

Madolina came down the stairs with a diamond and pearl brooch in her hand. Carefully, she pinned it to Evelina's dress, then patted it with satisfaction. 'Now you look finished.' She stood back to admire her. 'Yes, now you look every bit a lady.'

The brooch was in the shape of a bee. Evelina went to the

mirror to admire it. 'Thank you, Aunt Madolina,' she said, caressing it. 'It's beautiful.'

'Peppino gave it to me on our first Christmas. I've always loved bees.' She smiled tenderly at the recollection.

'That's because you're a queen bee,' said Taddeo. 'Buzz buzz buzz.'

Evelina laughed. Madolina rolled her eyes. 'And if I'm the queen bee, what does that make you?' she asked.

'A poor, tireless worker bee, gazing longingly on his queen from a far corner of the hive.'

'Oh really, Taddeo. You're incorrigible.' Madolina turned to her niece. 'Now, you have a good time tonight. Franklin's a nice young man. You couldn't really do better than him.'

'He's called Franklin, is he? I hope he lives up to his name in both beauty and brains,' said Taddeo.

'He might not be Franklin Roosevelt to look at,' Madolina replied. 'But one can grow bored of beauty. One never grows bored of intelligent conversation.'

'Thank the Lord for that,' interrupted Taddeo, sweeping a hand through his thinning ginger hair.

'Beauty fades but the mind only grows livelier with the years,' Madolina added.

Taddeo sighed. 'There is some justice, after all.'

There was a knock on the door. Evelina grabbed her coat. Taddeo took it from her and held it up so she could slip into it. 'You have a nice time, my dear, with your Franklin. Perhaps, if you play your cards right, he'll buy you a new coat. This one has *got* to go.'

Evelina opened the door to find Franklin on the step. He smiled when he saw her and his eyes lit up with pleasure. Noticing Madolina and Taddeo behind her he could not avoid greeting them without being impolite. He strode into the hall, kissed Madolina's plump cheek and shook Taddeo's hand, then put his arm around Evelina's waist and escorted her to the car.

Taddeo turned to Madolina. 'That's going all the way,' he said and Madolina nodded.

'I think you might be right, Taddeo,' she agreed. 'The funny thing is that he reminds me of my brother, Tani.'

Taddeo chuckled. 'How deliciously Freudian!'

The play was *Cyrano de Bergerac* and it was showing at the Alvin Theatre on West 52nd Street. The sight of the dazzling light bulbs thrilled Evelina who remembered those nights in Milan when she'd gone to the theatre with her parents and Benedetta. She'd felt the same sense of anticipation and wonder then.

She and Franklin settled into the red velvet seats in the centre of the stalls from where they had a square-on view of the stage. The curtain was down and people were slowly making their way into the aisles and being escorted to their seats by the usherettes. Franklin had bought a programme and they sat together reading it, discussing the actors and the plot. Franklin explained that the play was based on a true story about a man who had a large nose and thought that, because of it, he would never be loved. 'It was written in 1897 by Edmond Rostand, a French poet and playwright,' Franklin told her. 'And beautifully translated into English. I think you're going to love it.'

'I just love being here,' Evelina said, almost trembling with pleasure. 'The friends I've made prefer the cinema.'

'There are some really good movies, but nothing beats theatre. Seeing actors on stage is much more powerful, I believe.'

'The atmosphere is wonderful, don't you think? Everyone here together, excited about what they're going to see. It must be fun being an actor.'

'Terrifying. I'm very happy I'm sitting here and not waiting behind the curtain.'

Evelina laughed. 'I rather fancied myself as an actress when I was growing up. My mother is a real diva, her whole life is an act, and my sister and I used to put on plays.'

'Did you act at school?'

'I didn't go to school.'

Franklin looked horrified. 'You didn't go to school?' he repeated in amazement.

'We were home-schooled.'

'That's very old-fashioned.'

'My father is from another age. He should really have been born at the beginning of the nineteenth century.'

'What does he do?'

'He's a writer and a good one. He wins prizes.'

'Did you manage to make any friends, not going to school?'

'A few. Children of our parents' friends. We were very isolated.'

'You and your sister. Just the two of you?'

'I had a brother. He died.'

The lights dimmed. Franklin whispered, 'I'm so sorry to hear that, Evelina.'

'It was a long time ago,' she replied softly.

Evelina adored the play. They drank wine in the bar during the interval and Franklin introduced her to a couple of friends who, by coincidence, had chosen to come the same night. Evelina felt good in her dress and knew that she was being looked at and admired. It was a very different crowd to the one she was used to in Brooklyn. More sophisticated and elegant. She didn't get to come into Manhattan very often, although, with her new job, she'd be coming in every day. She looked forward to that.

When the play was over, Franklin took her to an expensive restaurant nearby. She hadn't been to such a place since she'd arrived in America. With Mike, Alba and Antonio they'd eaten in diners and cafés, or at home. This was something else. Evelina felt like a sophisticated lady. There was a woman at the reception desk who took her coat and hung it up in a cupboard. It looked a little sad among the fine furs and men's camelhair overcoats. Franklin knew the maître d' who showed them to a round table in the corner with a view of the dining room. On the table a candle glowed beside a small lamp with a crimson shade. Franklin ordered wine and tasted it with the attention of a connoisseur before nodding his approval and lighting a cigarette while the sommelier filled Evelina's glass first. She studied the menu and Franklin told her what was especially good. 'You come here a lot,' she said, noticing that he hadn't even glanced at the menu.

'I love the theatre and this is where I come after the show. I know the menu well. The lobster wasn't very good the last time I was here, but the crab salad is sensational.' Evelina ordered the two least expensive dishes on the menu, aware that Franklin would be paying and not wanting to appear greedy.

'Tell me, Evelina, besides putting on plays with your sister, what else did you do?'

Evelina smiled and took a sip of wine. She hadn't talked much about her life in Italy. She'd told Mike nothing. But for some reason it didn't feel strange telling Franklin. 'I painted,' she said, picturing at once the sumptuous gardens of Villa L'Ambrosiana.

'Are you any good?'

'I thought I was *very* good.' She laughed. 'I thought I was Michelangelo.'

'Do you paint now?'

'I haven't painted in years.'

'I suppose you had a tutor for that too.'

'I had a tutor for everything.' She lowered her gaze as Fioruccia's face surfaced in her mind like a reflection on water.

'You should take it up again, if it gives you pleasure.'

'I don't have anywhere to paint. I used to paint in the garden. There was so much to paint there.' Evelina's eyes gleamed in the candlelight as she told Franklin about Villa L'Ambrosiana. She told him about the grottos and statues, ornamental stairways and colonnades, and she told him about the villa itself, with its shabby, run-down charm. 'It's a little like an old actress of the theatre,' she told him with a grin. 'You can tell she was once a beauty, but her skin is now cracking with age and she covers her balding head with a wig. She wears fine furs and pearls, and yet she craves the glory days of her youth when she was applauded and admired. That is the villa. My mother is crazy about plants so the walls are covered with honeysuckle and jasmine and everywhere there are big pots of bougainvillea.' Her thoughts wandered then to the paths that meandered through the property. 'There is rosemary everywhere. In the summer when the evenings are hot, the air is thick with the smell of it. The scent is wonderful.'

'It sounds beautiful. What happened to your paintings?'

Evelina shrugged. 'I don't know. They must be still in the villa somewhere.'

'Your mother didn't frame them and put them up on the walls?'

'If you knew my mother, you'd know how ridiculous that sounds.'

'What's she like?'

Evelina told him about Artemisia. The food came and their glasses were refilled. Franklin listened. He gave her his full attention and Evelina enjoyed remembering the good times. In the recent past she'd focused her thoughts so intensely on the sad times that she'd forgotten the fun and the laughter, of which there had been plenty. She told him about Benedetta, how they'd gone into Vercellino on their own and how she'd changed into Fioruccia's dress in the bushes. Then she told him about Francesco and how he'd been cruel to Benedetta. 'He died in the war and I wasn't sad,' she confessed. 'He was an ardent Fascist and a misogynist. Benedetta was loyal and put up with him as she'd been taught to do. She was a good wife to him and mother to their son Giorgio. Then she fell in love with a handsome partisan, much older than her, and very brave, and I realized then that she was never going to go back to Francesco. It was just as well that he died. Benedetta is happy now with Gianni and they have a little girl called Pasquala, who is half-sister to Giorgio. I think their life is peaceful. It must be a great change for Gianni who was imprisoned by the Fascists and later fought for the partisans. But I imagine he likes the tranquillity.'

It was during dessert that Franklin asked about Ezra. The mention of Ezra's name gave Evelina a jolt, but there was no reason not to talk about him. Perhaps it was healthier to remember him than to bury his memory as if it were something seedy or unpleasant. She took a spoonful of ice cream and chocolate sauce and realized that her relationship with

Ezra had been like a mountain. The tip, which was his death, was very small in comparison to the time they had spent together, which was the greater part of the mountain. So she told Franklin about the first time they met, the notes they'd sent to one another through his aunt and then, shortly before she was due to leave for America, when he cycled up to the house to find her. She told him about the summer before the rain came. Of the seemingly endless days of sunshine. Of the love. 'He was Jewish,' she said. 'The racial laws of '38 were a terrible blow, but they did not endanger his life. When the Germans occupied Italy in '43, everything changed. They had had the chance to leave, but his father, Ercole, never thought things would get so bad. He didn't want to leave his home and his business. He'd lived in Vercellino all his life, as had his parents and grandparents. He saw no reason why he should leave it.' She shook her head and sighed. 'But they were all murdered in the camps. All of them. Even the children.' She lowered her eyes and frowned, the old feelings of sorrow and regret filling her chest once again.

'How terrible,' said Franklin with feeling. 'And you lost the man you loved.'

She nodded. A lump had formed in her throat and she strained every muscle to prevent herself from crying. 'I've never talked about this before,' she said in a thin voice.

'I'm glad you feel you can talk to me. You know, it's not good for you to keep it all in. It might prevent the tears, but it won't allow you to heal. The only way you can heal is to allow light into the dark places. Talking about it and sharing it lets the light in.'

'I'm sure you're right. It is still so raw.'

'He must have been a very special man to have been loved by you.'

'He was, very special.'

'You know, some people go through their whole lives and never love like that. Sure, they marry and have children and build lives together, but they never know what it is to really love someone. You didn't get the chance to build a life together, but you got the chance to love one another. And that's quite something.'

Evelina was so moved she didn't know what to say. She put her glass to her lips and took a final sip. As she put it down she noticed that her hand was shaking.

It was snowing when they left the restaurant. Fat flakes fell softly like feathers and twirled playfully in the golden glow of the street lamps. It had already settled onto the pavements, covering the street in a velvety white quilt that hid the city's flaws and transformed it into a dreamlike world of glitter and sparkle. Evelina put her hand in the crook of Franklin's arm and they walked to the car.

He pulled up outside Madolina's house and escorted her up the steps to the front door. 'I really enjoyed tonight,' she said, putting the key in the lock. 'Thank you, Franklin, for inviting me.'

'I enjoyed it too,' he replied. 'Good luck tomorrow. I'm sure it'll be fine. Cynthia Spellman is a nice woman.'

'She seemed very nice.'

He bent down and planted a kiss on her cheek. 'Say, would you mind me asking you out again sometime?'

She smiled. 'Of course not. I'd like that.'

'Good. I'll call you.' With that he skipped down the steps to the car. Evelina unlocked the door and went inside. Just before she closed it she noticed Franklin was waving at her. She lifted her hand and waved back.

*

The following morning Evelina took the subway into Manhattan. She was nervous about her new job, but excited too. How far she had come from the girl who had swapped her dress in the bushes on her way into Vercellino. How much the world around her had changed. There were no horses and carriages in New York. There were sleek cars and bright lights and noise. It was exhilarating to be a part of it. To have left the dozy world of Villa L'Ambrosiana behind her. She didn't ever want to go back.

Evelina sat on the train and thought of Franklin. She'd had the most wonderful evening at the theatre. The play had been excellent and the dinner afterwards a real treat. But the most prominent recollection of the night was talking to him. Just talking. Sharing her thoughts and feelings, and being listened to with compassion and interest.

As she walked up the snowy sidewalk towards the office building, she found herself thinking of Franklin non-stop. She thought about him as she went up in the elevator and she thought of him during the many times in the day when she paused her work, looked out of the window and let her mind drift. And when she got home in the evening, the telephone rang and it was him. She took off her earring, put the receiver to her ear and sat down. 'Tell me,' he said. 'How did it go?' And she knew, as she took him through her first day, that he wasn't asking simply to be polite, but because he really wanted to know, and because he cared, and the warm feeling that gave her was like the breath of spring on the branches of a winter tree.

CHAPTER FOURTEEN

Christmas with Peppino and Madolina was noisy. Alba and Antonio, Jane and her husband Richard and their three children celebrated with them, and Taddeo Paganini, who'd dressed up as Santa Claus to entertain the children, for the festivities would not have been complete without him. He helped Madolina put up a big Christmas tree in the drawing room and decorated it with fairy lights and tinsel and glass baubles containing tiny figurines sprinkled with frost. On the top he fastened an enormous gold star. At the foot the presents were laid out in their brightly coloured paper and ribbon, and Madolina had spared no expense.

The day before Christmas, Evelina met Franklin. They went for a walk in the park while everyone else went ice skating, even Madolina who was unexpectedly good, breaking her steady flow with the odd, stately twirl. Night fell early. Street lamps shone through the gathering mist and in their golden halos small flakes of snow could be seen twirling too. Franklin and Evelina walked hand in hand. It was cold but Evelina's hand felt the warmth of Franklin's through the wool of her glove, along with the solid feeling of dependability. They'd spent a lot of time together recently; dinners, opera, ballet, the occasional movie and the odd lunch. It had become obvious that Franklin had changed his mind about having a girlfriend, and Evelina, to her surprise, had changed hers too. Franklin treated her like a lady and Evelina raised herself up so that she became one not only in his eyes, but in her own as well. She liked the person she was when she was with him. There was a tranquillity and an effortlessness to their dynamic that left no room for doubt in Evelina's mind that Franklin was The One. Mike had been young and insecure; Franklin was a man.

They stopped under a street lamp and Franklin gave Evelina a gift wrapped in red paper and tied with red velvet ribbon. He told her to put it under the tree to open on Christmas morning. Evelina held it against her chest. 'You really shouldn't have,' she said. 'But I'm glad you did. It will be my most special present.' She smiled. 'How silly of me. I should have bought something for you.'

He looked at her with tenderness. '*You* are all the gift I need,' he said, and she laughed, pleasure painting her cheeks with a flourish of pink.

Franklin bent down and kissed her. It was the first time he had kissed her lips and Evelina closed her eyes and let him wind his arms around her in a warm embrace. It felt good, his kiss. It felt right. Franklin was tall and strong and his enfolding of her gave her a pleasant feeling of security. A sense of having arrived at a long-awaited destination and not needing to go any further; a sense of coming home. Evelina knew then that they belonged to each other and that she was no longer a rudderless sail boat directionless upon the sea, but a boat with a fixed route and a steady compass.

The following day when the family sat around the tree, opening their gifts, Evelina pulled the bow on Franklin's present and unwrapped the red paper. She pulled out a big box of watercolours. 'Who's that from?' asked Taddeo, looking over her shoulder and studying the box carefully.

'Franklin,' said Evelina.

'Do you paint?'

'I did, in Italy, but I haven't painted in years.'

'What a thoughtful present,' interrupted Madolina. 'Although, I'm not sure where you're going to find the space to set up your easel here.'

'He likes you a lot,' said Jane with a smile.

'It's kind of him to think of me.'

Taddeo arched an eyebrow. 'Darling, I don't imagine he's thinking of anything *but* you. A gift speaks a thousand words, you know.'

'So, what does that gift say?' asked Alba.

'Well, it's very obvious. You see, the desire to paint comes from inside of one. By giving Evelina such a beautiful box of watercolours, he's telling her that he sees her, not just on the outside, but on the inside too, and that he understands her and cherishes her. He wants to inspire her to rekindle an old passion.'

'How romantic!' exclaimed Alba. She turned to Antonio. 'I hope you've got *me* such a thoughtful present!' Antonio laughed for it wasn't so much thought that mattered to Alba, but cost, and his had cost a great deal.

'It's *more* than romantic, Alba, it's touching.' Taddeo put a hand to his heart. 'A box of paints tells me more about his heart than a piece of jewellery ever could. This man is for keeps. I hope you know that.'

Evelina blushed.

'As long as I've known Franklin he's never been smitten,' said Jane in her serious and thoughtful way. 'But I think he's smitten now.'

Evelina wasn't comfortable with all the attention, so it came as a relief when Alba stood up and declared that she and Antonio had an announcement to make. The room fell silent. Madolina caught Taddeo's eye and they both smiled expectantly. 'We're going to have a baby!' Alba immediately looked at her mother to see her reaction.

Madolina was thrilled. 'What wonderful news!' she cried, standing up and pulling her daughter against her bosom, enveloping her in a cloud of Givenchy and maternal love.

'And you've waited all this time to tell us?' Evelina heard Taddeo mutter under his breath. He glanced at her and gave a little shrug. Evelina said nothing, but she wondered whether Madolina and Taddeo had known all along.

Peppino, who clearly hadn't known, patted Antonio on the back and shuffled off to get more champagne. 'This calls for a celebration!' he said, as if they weren't already in the middle of one. 'I'm going to open my finest bottle.'

The following spring Alba gave birth to a little girl and Franklin asked Evelina to marry him. The baby was christened Chiara and Evelina said yes.

Evelina prepared to write at once to her parents but Franklin felt that wasn't enough. 'We should tell them in person,' he said.

'You mean, go to Vercellino?' Evelina asked, suddenly feeling conflicted.

'Yes, I want to meet them and I'm sure they'll want to meet me. I'm marrying their daughter. It's the correct thing to do.'

'You know Mother will throw us a party. There's nothing she'd love more than a party, with her at the centre of it all.'

Franklin laughed. 'I don't see why that's not a good thing.'

'If you're sure you don't mind. Italy is not at all like America.'

'I can't wait.' He pulled her into his arms and kissed her. 'I want to see where you grew up, Evelina. I want to meet the people who brought you into the world. I want you to show me the gardens, where you painted, and the town where you used to ride in the pony and trap. You've told me about it, but it's not the same as seeing it for myself. It'll be an adventure.'

'That crossing can be pretty rough,' she warned him.

'We'll be in first class.'

'We will?' Evelina perked up at the thought. 'First class?'

He grinned down at her and Evelina knew that Franklin wanted to give her everything she ever desired. 'Of course, my darling. You don't think I'm going to let my bride travel in steerage, do you?'

When Evelina told Madolina of their plans, she was horrified. 'You must marry first,' she said firmly. 'I'm all for young people spending time together unchaperoned, you know I don't live in the dark ages like that old fossil Father O'Malley, but it's not proper to travel on a ship together without being married. Besides, it's awkward and first-class tickets don't come cheap. No, much better to share a room. I'm sure Franklin will agree with me. As for Tani and Artemisia, I can tell you they won't mind missing the ceremony.' She thought about it a moment. 'In fact, I've got a splendid idea,' she continued excitedly, rubbing her chubby hands together. 'You can marry here in a small and private ceremony and then have a church wedding in Vercellino. Your mother will love that, won't she? No one enjoys a party more than Artemisia. And Peppino and I will give you a party here to celebrate. How does that sound, my dear?'

*

And so it was, on a fair morning in July, that Franklin and Evelina boarded the sleek Italian liner *Saturnia* to Genoa, stopping at Gibraltar and Naples on the way. Newly married, this was their honeymoon and they enjoyed every blessed moment with the enthusiasm of teenagers. Evelina knew she had to let Ezra go. To gently release him into the depths of her memory along with Bruno, to lie in rest in the conflicted waters of love and pain like broken treasures. Evelina had made a conscious decision to give herself to the now, to the new and intact, and find in it a different kind of happiness.

She had never given herself to Mike because instinctively she had known that they had had no future together. With Franklin it had been different right from the start. When they had finally made love on their wedding night she had given herself to him with all of her heart. She'd held nothing of herself back. With Franklin she had rediscovered the joys of sensual pleasure. She didn't compare him with Ezra or even feel guilty that she was betraying him, unlike the first time Mike had kissed her, because it felt so right with Franklin. As they explored each other's bodies during the long hours on board the *Saturnia*, Evelina marvelled at the soul's capacity for love. Like a winter tree that sprouts green shoots in the spring, the heart's ability to regenerate itself left her humbled with awe and gratitude.

Besides making love, they enjoyed promenading along the deck, playing cards in the lounge with fellow travellers and gazing out to sea in the evenings, when the setting sun leaked liquid gold onto the surface of the water. It was a tranquil time and one that they'd look back on in later years as being charmed.

Approaching Genoa, Evelina began to feel nervous. It started with a feeling in her stomach like the stirring of bees.

A vibration, a buzz, a growing sense of trepidation. She'd left Italy broken-hearted, pining for Ezra and their stolen future. She'd been quite a different person then. She was American now, with a new husband and a new future. Was it perhaps too soon to face the past? Had enough time lapsed for it not to hurt her anymore?

Franklin held her close as the Italian coastline emerged from the haze and gradually deepened in colour until it was clearly visible; the horseshoe bay, the yellow and orange houses clinging to the cliffs like clams and the hills, adorned with inky green trees. Small boats motored out to greet them and a waving crowd gathered on the quay, welcoming relatives home with all the ebullience and hysteria one would expect from a nation at ease with public displays of wild emotion.

Franklin and Evelina took the train to Vercellino. They sat in first class, watching with rising excitement as the countryside whizzed past their window. Franklin had never been to the north of Italy. He'd been to Rome and Florence on various European trips before the war, but had never travelled to Lombardy or Piedmont. He was thrilled to be there, his eyes wide and alert, taking in every ravishing detail with interest. It was all so familiar to Evelina. She felt as if she had never left. As if she were crawling into her old skin. She wasn't sure that it fitted her anymore.

Tani and Artemisia had come to the station to meet them in Tani's ancient Fiat. Evelina only realized how much she'd missed them when she saw them through the steam, standing on the platform, her father in a pale linen suit and panama hat, hands in pockets, while her mother, in a floral dress and sunhat, her hair loose about her shoulders, waved madly. Evelina climbed down from the carriage and flew into their arms, giving and receiving more affection than she had ever done before leaving for America.

Tani recognized a fellow scholar immediately. The two men shook hands and it was only then that Evelina realized how similar they were. In a flash of memory, she recalled Mystic Marica telling her that she would marry a man who was very like her father. But the memory was quickly drowned in the flood of questions. Tani spoke good English but Artemisia's was lamentable, so the two men sat in the front of the Fiat so they could talk while the two women sat on the seat behind, chatting almost without drawing breath, in rapid, staccato Italian.

Artemisia admired Evelina's diamond and ruby ring which she and Franklin had chosen together at Tiffany. She also admired her clothes and her new hairstyle, and the general air of America that she had brought with her. She wanted to know everything and Evelina was happy to tell her for never had her mother shown such an interest in her life.

They went quiet when the car turned into the drive. Villa L'Ambrosiana sat like a retired old diva at the end of the long avenue of cypress trees, her harmoniously proportioned walls clothed in jasmine, her world-weary eyes gazing sleepily at the mottled statue of Venus and the reflection she made in the stagnant water at her feet. Evelina felt a lump lodge itself in her throat. It was beautiful. Exactly as it always had been. As it always would be, both in her imagination and in reality, because some things are too set in their ways to ever change. Her eyes misted and she felt a swell of happiness. Once, she had dreamed of leaving, of flying like a bird to exotic new places, to break free from her gilded prison, but now she was thrilled to be coming back, like a homing pigeon that knows where it belongs.

On the steps of the villa was a small group of people, standing in the sunshine to welcome her home; Nonna Pierangelini, dressed in a long black frock and pearls, like a plump magpie, her skinny sister Costanza in scarlet, Benedetta and Gianni with their children, and Romina. Evelina could barely wait for the car to stop before she scrambled out to greet them. While she hugged and kissed her family, Tani introduced Franklin, and Franklin, who had studied Latin and had learned some Italian since meeting Evelina, was able to converse a little and understand what they were saying if they spoke slowly.

Nonna Pierangelini took Evelina's hand and squeezed it as they walked through the house to the terrace. 'He's handsome for an American,' she said, her small eyes glowing warmly in her wizened face like grappa. 'And an intelligent expression, which is important. A girl must never marry a man less intelligent than herself, but a man she can look up to and admire. I think Franklin is that sort of man. Am I right?'

'You are, Nonna. He teaches classics at Columbia University,' she told her proudly.

Nonna Pierangelini gasped. 'Then he's the best sort of man,' she added, shivering with pleasure. 'Just like my Tani.'

Costanza sidled up on Evelina's other side. 'I hope he's a good lover,' she said, winding her nicotine-stained fingers around Evelina's arm. 'That's important too.'

Evelina laughed. 'He's a very good lover, Costi.'

'Then God will bless you with lots of babies.' She cackled. 'God can only do His thing if the husband does his.'

They settled into the wicker chairs and the maid brought out jugs of iced lemonade and chilled wine. The two old women spoke no English at all and Benedetta's was as limited as Artemisia's, so the women formed a group apart and settled into conversation. Gianni spoke English fluently, which surprised everyone except Benedetta, who knew how erudite her husband was. He talked to Tani and Franklin about the civil war and the part he'd played in it, and Franklin listened with fascination as Gianni told him how they had used the chapel here on the estate and how vital it had been.

Romina took Pasquala from Benedetta and went into the garden with Giorgio. She turned to look at Evelina as she descended the steps. Evelina lifted her eyes and smiled. Romina smiled back, and Evelina remembered how sweetly she had looked after Bruno. How tenderly she had cared for him in his final hours. She recalled then how she and Ezra had been engaged – she could still see them on the bench in the moonlight, kissing – and how he had broken it off because of *her*. She wondered whether Romina had ever found out about that, or whether Ezra had managed to keep it secret. His capture and imprisonment and finally his death ensured that Romina would probably never know that Evelina had loved him too.

That evening Evelina walked around the gardens arm in arm with Benedetta. Cards were a universal language and Franklin had been sucked into a game with Nonna Pierangelini, Costanza and Artemisia. The four of them looked very content there on the terrace with half-empty glasses of grappa, Franklin's bourbon on the rocks and an ashtray full of cigarette stubs.

Crickets chirruped in the long grasses and birds twittered in the pine trees as the two women ambled slowly down the path that weaved its way through the estate. Evelina inhaled the familiar smells of home and felt a heavy sense of nostalgia settle upon her heart like a comfortable old blanket. It was warm and reassuring. She knew every corner of the garden. Every statue, fountain and stone stair, each one mottled with moss and lichen and time, each one home to a memory replaying now in her mind like dancing nature spirits. The shadows lengthened and grew damp, and she remembered how she had painted with Fioruccia in these shady nooks and played with Benedetta as a little girl among the trees and bushes. That was all gone, but strangely she could still hear the echo of their laughter reverberating through the years.

'He's lovely,' said Benedetta. 'I'm glad you found happiness, Eva.'

'I never thought I would. I thought I would mourn Ezra for ever.'

'Life is a long time. It contains many chapters. Ezra was one. Franklin is another. There is time to live many lives.'

'Do you feel that about Francesco?'

'I do. I was happy when that chapter ended. I thought I was happy, at least in the beginning, but with hindsight, I realize now that I was miserable most of the time. I just didn't know it. I knew no better. But I'm glad we married. I would never have had Giorgio otherwise, and he's one of the great loves of my life.'

'He's grown so big. I can't believe he's ten.'

Benedetta laughed. 'He's always been big. He's like a prize pumpkin at a village fair.'

'Didn't we have a strange upbringing?' Evelina shook her head. 'I mean, Francesco was chosen for you.'

'You're lucky you were able to make your own choice.'

'I'm very lucky,' she agreed.

'But I got to choose Gianni.'

'And he's made you happy.'

'Very.' Benedetta smiled at her sister with affection. 'I miss you though, Eva. You weren't just my sister, but my friend too. I miss my old friend.'

'And I miss you too. Alba's a shallow thing, like a beautiful hummingbird. She's taken your place as far as she can, but she's not you and never will be. Perhaps one day you'll come out and visit me.'

'I'd like that so much.'

Suddenly the chapel was before them. They'd stumbled across it without even noticing. Evelina moved away from her sister and walked towards it, as if it had a dark, magnetic pull which she was powerless to resist. Benedetta gave her space and remained where she was.

The chapel was shrouded in shadow for the sun was sinking low in the western sky and only the tops of the tallest pine trees caught the light and glowed golden, like candles. Evelina felt a tightness in her chest as she approached. She knew she shouldn't go inside. It would be better to walk on and leave it to the nature spirits. But like the tongue that seeks the aching tooth, she pushed open the old door and stepped across the threshold into the past.

The place was exactly as she'd left it. It smelt the same too and she sniffed the air as if trying to pick up Ezra's scent among the layers that had settled there over the years, one on top of the other. She walked towards the altar at the far end, her senses alert to every tone and hue. She could almost see the blankets and books she had brought Ezra discarded on the stone floor among the crispy old leaves the wind had blown in and left to pulverize with the dead insects that had met their fate in the same careless way. She could almost see Ezra there and feel the passion of his embrace and the tenderness of his kiss. She sank into a chair and put her head in her hands. Here she had made love for the first time. Here in this very room. It now seemed like a lifetime ago. As old and forlorn as those dry leaves and insects. She had told him she loved him, and he had looked deep into her eyes and promised her that after the war was over they'd marry and settle down to a simple life together. And she had believed him, because their love was so intense and so strong that she hadn't imagined that anything or anyone, not even the Germans or the Fascists, could snuff it out. She'd thought they were blessed by God, protected by the angels, shielded by fate which had already carved out their future in the great book of life. Yet, there was nothing left of it now but memory, not even dust.

She heard footsteps and lifted her head out of her hands. It was Benedetta, her face full of concern. 'Come,' she said softly. 'Leave Ezra where he is, Eva. He's at peace. He'd want you to be at peace too.'

Evelina stood up. She sighed and wiped her eyes.

Benedetta put out her hand. 'Let's go back to the house. Franklin will need rescuing.'

Evelina nodded and took her sister's hand. She walked out into the dusk and closed the door behind her. They left the chapel in shadow. The sun sank lower and the tops of the trees were left in shadow too as the first star twinkled dimly in the sky.

CHAPTER FIFTEEN

Artemisia had arranged a blessing for Franklin and Evelina in the basilica in town, followed by a small party in the garden. It wasn't the extravaganza that Benedetta's was, and the family's relations did not travel from far and wide to be there, but it was nonetheless a splendid occasion. Everyone made a fuss of Franklin, and he danced with Costanza, Benedetta and Artemisia and even managed to get Nonna Pierangelini onto the dance floor too. Nonna Pierangelini wasn't keen on dancing and preferred to sit somewhere quiet where she could talk, but once she was in Franklin's arms there was no stopping her. She smiled happily, her small eyes twinkling with pleasure as he held her firmly, one hand on her back, the other holding her hand, and moved in time to the music. She was much shorter than he was and they made an incongruous couple, but everyone delighted in the spectacle, surprised that Nonna Pierangelini had such a sound sense of rhythm and such light feet.

Evelina was having too much fun to think of Ezra. The chapel was hidden in the middle of the wood, cloaked in forgetfulness and the advancing night. She did not allow her mind to drift back there, but concentrated on the now where she and Franklin were embarking on their new life together with confidence and love. Villa L'Ambrosiana once again vibrated with life. Gone were the shadows that Bruno's death had left behind and with them the darkness of war. Optimism blazed in the effervescent sunset, the glowing moon, and in the hundreds of flickering candles that had been scattered around the garden like fallen stars. The children stole the dregs of champagne from discarded crystal flutes, the band continued long into the early hours, there was singing as well as dancing, and laughter rose on a tide of goodwill.

At last Evelina found herself in the arms of her husband. The band began to play a love song and Franklin pressed his cheek to hers. She smiled softly and closed her eyes, swaying gently to the music. She was grateful to have found love when she had thought it had died with Ezra. She held Franklin close, aware that she had been given a second chance. She resolved then that she would never take him for granted, but treasure him for the gift that he was.

Franklin and Evelina stayed for a week at Villa L'Ambrosiana. From there they were due to travel to Rome and Florence, finishing their trip with Naples and finally the Amalfi Coast. On the last day, Evelina awoke at dawn. She felt strangely wide awake. If it hadn't been for the semi-darkness she would have thought it was morning. She climbed out of bed, careful not to wake Franklin, and tiptoed into the bathroom. She closed the door and opened the shutters. It was a beautiful dawn. The sun had not yet peeped over the edge of the world but sent her glow ahead to alert the birds and animals to her arrival. The trees were full of twittering and the garden, so peaceful in the blushing half-light, was slowly emerging from the night. The scents of rosemary and jasmine were so strong that Evelina felt an overwhelming desire to be out there. To experience the dawn with nature, to soak up the beauty before leaving it. Who knew when she would return?

She dressed quietly and crept out of the room. She left the villa by the back door, excitement rising in her chest with the anticipation of a solitary walk in this paradise. As she was about to head off across the lawn she noticed a bicycle leaning against the wall. Inspired suddenly, she climbed on and pedalled down the drive. She inhaled the scent of the cypress trees, felt the warm breeze in her hair and on her face, and savoured the sense of exhilaration that made her laugh out loud, scattering birds into the air. She left the estate and found herself cycling towards Vercellino.

She took the track that cut through the countryside, weaving her way across rice fields that shimmered in the light of the sun, now rising over the horizon and flooding the plains with gold. It was all so familiar, her heart ached at the thought of leaving it. Alone on her bicycle she couldn't help but think of Ezra and her heart ached for him, too.

The streets of Vercellino were quiet, the residents yet to awaken to the new day. The silence of sleep still hung over the houses whose shutters were closed and only the odd early riser and stray dog prowled about the indigo shadows where the sun had not yet reached. Evelina cycled to Ercole Zanotti's old shop as if by default, the wheels of her bicycle rattling over the cobbles just as they had always done when she had come to find Ezra.

When she saw it she caught her breath. It was no longer a shop but a café. Instead of the words *Ercole Zanotti* in gold writing above the window, there was a very different sign: *Caffè Franchetti*. Evelina stopped and placed a foot on the ground for balance. The sight was so unexpected that she was unable to move. She stood staring at it as if expecting it to change back to *Ercole Zanotti* at any moment. It didn't. It remained just as it was, a café built on the grave of a once thriving business. Built on the ashes of an entire family.

Eventually, she leaned her bicycle against the wall and pressed her nose to the window. The room was very different now. What had once been a shop was now a place to eat and drink with a long counter where Ercole's had been, round tables and chairs and shelves of bottles, glasses, cups and saucers and jars of biscuits. She swept her eyes about the room in search of something that might have been left behind. A trace of Ercole or Olga, or Ezra, but there was nothing. It was as if they had never been there.

She only realized that she was crying when the glass misted. She pulled herself away and wiped it with her sleeve. Perhaps it was a good thing that she was leaving today, she thought as she climbed back onto her bicycle and pedalled away. Vercellino would only haunt her. She had a new life now, there was no point in trying to find the old one. It had gone. No amount of searching would ever find it, and it would only bring her pain. She was married to Franklin now and she was happy.

When she arrived back at the villa she found her grandmother on the terrace in her habitual long black dress, draped in pearls. 'Good morning, Nonna,' she said, pulling out the opposite chair. 'You're up early.'

'I couldn't sleep,' said Nonna Pierangelini with a shake of the head.

'Why not?'

'You're leaving today. How can I sleep knowing I might never see you again?'

Evelina was horrified. 'Oh Nonna, that's a terrible thing to say.'

'But it's true. I'm old. I'm not long for this world. You won't be back for years. Perhaps never. America's the other side of the world.'

'You have many years left in you,' Evelina protested.

'I doubt it. I've lost too many people for it not to have shortened my life.'

'You have a strong heart and a strong faith.'

'Oh, I'm not afraid of dying, because I don't believe in it. How can I be frightened of something that doesn't exist? But I'm tired of suffering loss. There is no loss in the next world, and I'll be thankful for that. There's too much of it in this one.' She smiled sadly at her granddaughter. 'We lost dear Bruno and we have lost you, perhaps not in such a final way, but we have lost you all the same.'

Evelina's eyes filled with tears. 'Don't say that, Nonna.'

'I know you have to live your life and I'm happy you've found a nice man to take care of you. I like Franklin. I like him very much.'

'No moustache,' Evelina said with a grin.

Nonna Pierangelini grinned back. 'Of course not. He's the good sort. You hold on to him, won't you?'

'Of course, I will.'

'Life is full of temptation, Costi can tell you that, and it's easy to take each other for granted. Don't you fall into any traps.'

'I won't, Nonna.'

'The world is full of traps. The devil puts them in your way to test you. You know that, don't you?'

Evelina nodded, although she didn't believe it.

'He does and it's a wise woman who knows how to dodge them. A moment's pleasure is not worth a lifetime of regret.'

Evelina thought of her mother and Signor Stavola and wondered whether she ever regretted her affair.

'The reason I'm telling you this is because I'm a wise old bird and I know more than you do, and because you're beautiful and men will fall in love with you. It's just the way it is.'

'I'll be careful, Nonna.'

'I know you will, my dear. But I wouldn't be doing my job as a grandmother if I didn't alert you to the dangers. Every wife has the opportunity to stray from the marital bed. Even I had one or two, but nothing could lure me away from my duty. The vows I made before God I kept. Every one. Because I have always known the right path to take. It's really very easy. You only have to ask yourself one question: who will I hurt? If you can navigate your way through life without hurting anyone, you'll find your life in the next world to be a very pleasant one.'

Evelina nodded again. She wasn't quite sure why her grandmother was telling her all this. She had no intention of committing adultery.

'Now, you be sure to write often and tell your old grandmother how you are and what you're up to.'

'I will.'

Nonna Pierangelini smiled. 'Good girl. You've always been a good girl, Evelina, even when you were naughty. Which you were, often. But your heart is where it should be and that's the key to Heaven.'

It was hard saying goodbye. The family stood on the steps as Tani drove Evelina and Franklin away to the station. They waved and Evelina thrust her arm out of the window and waved back. Then she watched with a constricted heart as the villa receded until it was a small toy house at the end of the long avenue of cypress trees. She could still make out her grandmother in her black dress, waving a white handkerchief, until that too was gone.

The rest of the trip was the honeymoon they had intended it to be. Evelina welcomed every new place with enthusiasm and joy. She relished being Signora van der Velden and staying in hotels. It was a novelty and she delighted in the beautiful rooms, the room service and the staff who were there to indulge her every whim. She loved waking up to Franklin every morning and talking long into the night. She loved roaming the cities together, visiting churches and museums, dining in restaurants beneath the stars and strolling through moonlit squares. They held hands, they kissed, they made love and they laughed. It was perfect, just the two of them, and Evelina did not want their trip to end. But end it did. Too soon they were back in New York and moving into their new apartment in Manhattan near the university so that Franklin didn't have too far to travel for work.

Franklin insisted on Evelina making one of the rooms into a studio for her painting. It wasn't large, but it was big enough for an easel and had a south-facing window. Evelina enjoyed the tranquillity of that little room and the view onto the leafy street below. At first she wasn't sure what she was going to draw. It wasn't quite the same as sitting in the shady corners of the gardens at Villa L'Ambrosiana, sketching cupids. Then she knew. Fioruccia's face surfaced in her memory, beautiful and young. She smiled at her with affection, brown eyes shining with encouragement, and Evelina felt a wave of sorrow flood her chest. She put the charcoal to the paper and endeavoured to find her old friend and bring her back to life upon the page.

It wasn't long before Evelina was pregnant. Franklin was

elated and fussed about her as if she had suddenly become a fragile and helpless creature. Evelina gave up her job at the charity and Aldo was born in the spring. She cradled him in her arms, cocooned in the love he had brought with him, and thought of Bruno. She pressed her lips to his forehead and understood her mother's pain as if a veil had been lifted, revealing a whole new landscape. The landscape of motherhood which would change her irrevocably.

Evelina settled into her new role with enthusiasm. Dan was born a couple of years later and four years after that Ava-Maria came screaming into the world with the determination and fanfare that would define her life. Ava-Maria would never do anything quietly. Evelina sent photographs home and long letters describing her life in Manhattan. Her grandmother wrote to her regularly, and Costanza rarely. Artemisia managed the odd letter, but she was more involved in the lives of Benedetta's children, which was understandable, for she saw them all the time. Evelina did not expect her to be very interested in children she didn't know. Out of all her grandchildren, for Benedetta had now had three more, Giorgio Bruno would always be Artemisia's favourite on account of the name he carried and of the love he had inspired in her when she had believed Bruno had taken with him all she had.

Evelina missed her family, but she had a family in Madolina and Peppino, and in Alba who was like a sister to her. She'd become close to Taddeo Paganini, too. He made her laugh and had become something of a confidant. Taddeo was interested in everything. That was just the way he was. Life fascinated him on every level and in every form. With a sharp eye for hilarity and a love of the absurd, he not only chronicled Manhattan life for his column in the

New York Times, but for Evelina, too, who enjoyed regular lunches with him in his favourite Italian restaurant. He was entertaining and funny, but he was also a good listener. Even though Evelina had a nanny to help look after the children, she had her gripes like anyone and Taddeo encouraged her to air them, then to find the humour in them and, eventually, to let them go. 'It's all in the way you look at things,' he said wisely. 'If you can laugh at your troubles, they'll never really trouble you.' And most of the time he was right.

Franklin worked hard. He came home late, and often, when he was at home, he disappeared into his study to mark his students' work or to prepare lectures. Evelina didn't mind. She was used to the man of the house being absent, but she missed him. Franklin, she knew, would never ignore her by choice – he was just passionate about his job and invested all his energy in it. There was nothing he loved more than inspiring inquisitive young minds and, in turn, his students adored him. He was becoming more important within university life and, as his importance grew, so did the demands on his time. When they did sit down together for supper he told her with relish about his students, his colleagues and his plans to improve the courses he ran and the excursions. He planned to take a group to Italy the following year on a field trip to Rome. He didn't shut her out but included her in all his ideas. Evelina couldn't complain. She had the children to keep her busy and they delighted her. She had a growing group of female friends, whom she'd met through the children, and she had Taddeo, of course, who had the time to listen to her in the way her husband didn't. But sometimes, when they turned out the lights to go to bed, she wished Franklin had, at some point, asked her about *her* day.

*

Then one rainy day in October 1959 everything changed.

Evelina dropped Aldo and Dan off at school, handing them over to their teachers and wishing them a good day. Ava-Maria was at home with the nanny. Evelina didn't have to rush back. In fact, she'd arranged to meet Alba at a café in Brooklyn. Evelina took the subway. She was early, so she wandered into a bookshop. She loved everything about a bookshop; the smell of paper, the sight of spines lined up in tidy rows on the shelves, books arranged in neat piles on the tables. She loved the different jackets and fonts, the wealth of images and designs, the thought of the billions of words written by industrious minds. She could lose herself for hours, but today she only had fifteen minutes, so with one eye on her watch she allowed the other to lead her through the rows of titles.

Eventually, it was time to leave. She bought a copy of Dr. Seuss's *The Cat in the Hat* for the boys and Edith Wharton's *The Age of Innocence* for herself. Then she hurried to the café, for now she was a little late. She wasn't surprised when Alba hadn't yet arrived. This was not unusual. Alba was vague and usually turned up in a rush, having only just remembered they were meeting. Evelina chose a table in the far corner, and took the seat in the nook of the wall so she could view the whole room. She liked to watch people come and go. People were endlessly fascinating. Although she had now lived in America for thirteen years she still felt like an outsider, looking in. She knew that if she were to go back to Italy she would feel the same sense of dislocation. She was neither fish nor fowl but somewhere in between. And in between sometimes felt a little rootless.

Evelina sat down and ordered a cup of coffee and a bagel. She hadn't had time for breakfast. She wondered what her life would have been had she remained in Vercellino. She would have married an Italian and Benedetta and she would have raised their children together. Life would have continued along a familiar track and there would have been few surprises. It would have been nice to remain close to her family. As she sipped her coffee Evelina wondered at the way her life had gone. She also wondered at how late Alba was. She was now fifteen minutes late. Evelina opened her new book and began to read.

It wasn't until she had finished her bagel and ordered a second cup of coffee that she realized Alba wasn't coming. She had obviously forgotten or been delayed while visiting her mother. Evelina wasn't irritated, although she was a little disappointed. She'd been looking forward to seeing her. However, she had another cup of coffee to drink and a book to read and she rather relished the thought of being able to spend the morning in a place where she knew no one and was unlikely to be disturbed. She settled into her seat with a sigh of pleasure.

She was distracted suddenly by the door opening. In that split-second she did not expect to see Alba, but something about the movement in the doorway drew her attention. She lifted her eyes off the page.

Her body froze. The restaurant fell away. The tables and chairs and all the people faded and disappeared, swallowed into insignificance, leaving her alone in the spotlight of her own incredulity. There, staring at her with same look of astonishment, was Ezra.

Evelina could barely breathe. She could barely think. She just sat there, petrified by shock, blinking at the man she loved who had returned from the grave.

Ezra was no longer a young man. His hair had receded and

was quite grey. His skin was lined. There were purple shadows beneath his eyes and in the hollows of his cheeks, and his shoulders were a little stooped. But he was still Ezra. *Her* Ezra, and the emotion that swelled in her heart and snatched the air from her lungs was proof that time had done nothing to diminish her love.

He was now walking towards her. Slowly, as if fearful that perhaps she wasn't who he thought she was, but a lookalike. Or maybe fearing that if he moved too quickly she would run away. But she wasn't a lookalike and she didn't flee. Evelina was neither aware of her body nor conscious of her decision to stand. But she found herself on her feet, edging round the table, stumbling against a chair.

Ezra said nothing. He didn't have to. His eyes, his mouth, his breath communicated a million sentiments that words could never express. And, as he drew her into his arms, the ferocity of his embrace spoke of a million prayers finally answered.

She pulled him against her, pressed her face into his neck, and wept.

PART THREE

Greenwich, New York, 1981

'How fast the years go,' said Madolina with a sigh. 'Our children grow up and have children of their own. Then *they* grow up and before you know it, you're sitting at the top of the pile with a VIP ticket to Heaven.' She was at the card table with Taddeo, Topino and Evelina. Franklin wasn't well enough to play the traditional game of chess this year. Instead, Jonathan, who was engaged to Ava-Maria and planning to marry her in the spring, was due to take his place. Topino had suggested they suspend the game; after all, he claimed his brain ached even at the thought of it. But Franklin had insisted. 'Thanksgiving was all about tradition and it wouldn't be right to break this one,' he'd said, especially as Jonathan had turned out to be an exceedingly good player. 'Every year we get a little older,' Madolina continued. 'But this year I feel every one of my ninety-five years.'

'Nonsense,' said Taddeo, examining the cards in his hand. 'It's all in the mind.'

'No, it isn't. It's in the knees, the joints, the back, the hips . . .'

Evelina laughed. 'You're pretty good for your age, Aunt Madolina.'

'It's a slippery slope,' she said. 'I'm telling you.'

'Life is a slippery slope,' said Topino. 'It's littered with banana skins. But you seem to have a gift for avoiding them. If you ask me, Madolina, you'll outlive us all.'

Madolina laughed. 'Really, Topino, I'd have to have learned the secret of eternal youth. No, my time is nearly up. Every Thanksgiving I think it's going to be my last.'

'And yet, you're still here, Madolina,' said Taddeo, peering at her over his spectacles. 'Let's not talk about the final curtain before the play is over.'

'I enjoy talking about death,' said Topino. 'It reminds me that I'm still alive.'

'And it *is* part of life, isn't it,' said Evelina. 'You can't have one without the other. They're just different sides of the same coin. I like to think we'll all meet again at the great card table in the sky.'

Topino arched an eyebrow. 'You think we'll still be playing cards? In that case, I might prefer the alternative.'

'Which is what?' asked Taddeo. 'Playing Grandmother's Footsteps with the devil?'

They laughed heartily. 'Oh, you do delight me, you know,' said Madolina, looking at them all in turn. 'I might be about to go, but at least I'll go laughing.'

'That's the spirit,' said Taddeo.

Madolina patted Evelina's hand. 'You've been like a daughter to me, Evelina dear. Ever since you came to live with me all those years ago, you've been a delight. My own children were a disappointment. You know, I haven't spent Thanksgiving with them for years. They're so busy with their own families . . .'

'And you don't like to travel,' Evelina added pointedly.

'Well, I'm not going all the way to Australia, if that's what you mean.'

'Or Washington.'

'Washington should come to *me*.'

'As for Alba . . .' Evelina rarely saw her these days.

'Oh, I lose count of her husbands! Which is it now?'

'Three,' said Taddeo.

Madolina waved her hand as if to wave away the problem. 'I don't know where we went wrong with that one. But we did, spectacularly.'

'She's finding her way,' said Topino philosophically.

Taddeo chuckled. 'There are many roads to Rome,' he said. 'But I think she's on her way to Naples!'

'She's happy and that's all that matters,' said Evelina.

'As long as she's looking outside of herself for happiness, she'll never find it,' Topino said wisely. 'Happiness is a state of being.'

'And you're a wonderful example of that,' said Madolina, patting his hand.

'At least, she won't find it in a man,' Topino added.

'Rubbish!' exclaimed Madolina. 'I've found happiness in Peppino, and I've found happiness in you, Taddeo. Topino, you too have brought me happiness. You don't know what you're talking about. Evelina understands. She's a woman. Don't tell me you haven't found happiness in Franklin.'

'I certainly have,' said Evelina. 'And I too have found happiness in Topino and Taddeo.'

'You're a bachelor, Topino. You don't know what you're talking about. You should have allowed yourself to find happiness in a good woman and settled down. That goes for you too, Taddeo. You both have more in common with each other than you know.'

Taddeo looked at Topino and grinned. 'Some of us just aren't willing to compromise, isn't that right, Topino?'

Before Topino could answer, Evelina cut in. 'You're silly old fools, the both of you. Now, shall we get on with the game or we'll be here all day?'

'And I might not have all day,' said Madolina, sucking in her cheeks. She caught Taddeo's eye. He pulled a face. 'Well, you never know,' she added.

Franklin made it downstairs for Thanksgiving dinner. He was thin and frail, but he managed to dress, with Evelina's help, and sit at the head of the table. He looked much older than his seventy-eight years. His left hand shook so he had to hold his glass with his right, and he barely ate a thing. Ava-Maria and Jonathan talked about their wedding plans. Aldo and Lisa were expecting another child. Dan had brought his latest girlfriend, who was petite and feisty with hair cut short like a boy's and a strong personality. Evelina wondered whether he'd found his match at last. Franklin spoke little, but he listened with pleasure, not worrying about keeping up with the various conversations going on all at once.

Madolina talked about dying, but Franklin *was* dying. Evelina didn't know how much longer he had. The doctors had various theories as to what was ailing him, but he and Evelina were both tired of tests and pills and theories. Evelina didn't ever want to see another hospital again, or another specialist. She would take care of her husband and make sure that he was comfortable. He needed her and she was happy and willing to rise to her duty, as his wife and friend, and respond to that need.

Evelina's mother was still alive at eighty-eight and living at Villa L'Ambrosiana. Costanza had died years ago at the great age of one hundred and two, joining her sister no doubt at Heaven's pearly gates. Tani, too, had passed away. Benedetta wrote often, and very occasionally they spoke on the telephone. Benedetta had never come to visit Evelina, but from the tone of her latest letter, she and Gianni were growing increasingly nostalgic and Evelina sensed they might be persuaded. The world was only large if one allowed it to be.

Evelina, too, was nostalgic about the past, but Franklin would never return to Vercellino. He would probably never leave the house again except for the odd special occasion. Evelina knew that and had accepted it. She wondered whether she'd ever go back to Villa L'Ambrosiana herself. Whether she'd ever again wander through those gardens she had loved so much in her youth, linger in the chapel which had been at the centre of so much drama, taste Nonna Pierangelini's enchanted tomatoes and sit on the terrace at sunset with a cool glass of wine, contemplating the past. How she had longed to leave it, the repressive, sleepy villa she had once considered a kind of prison, and yet now, at sixty-four, she looked back on it with affection. It had acquired a golden glow, as if bathed in a sacred light. As much as America had become her home – she'd lived here now more years than she had lived in Italy – Vercellino was a part of her soul. The tug on it was growing ever stronger.

'I hope Daddy makes it to our wedding,' said Ava-Maria quietly, drawing her mother away from the general conversation and looking at her father with concern.

'Oh darling, of course he will,' Evelina reassured her, but she wasn't sure.

'I can't bear to walk down the aisle without him.'

'You won't have to. He'll be there. I promise you.'

'He looks so old now, doesn't he?'

'Well, he *is* nearly eighty.'

'Madolina's nearly a hundred and she looks younger than him.'

'That's because she's built like a tank – and she's not ill.'

Ava-Maria took a deep breath. 'I'm glad you're looking after him, Mom. I'd hate him to have to go into hospital and—'

'I'll always look after him,' Evelina cut in. 'Don't worry. Your father's in safe hands.'

'I know. You've always looked after him.'

'Well, I never had a job of my own. You could say that *he* was my job.'

'Why didn't you ever try and sell your paintings? You're a really good artist.'

'Not good enough.'

'You could have painted portraits. You're especially good at those.'

'Oh, I'm not sure I'm so good.'

'Who was Fioruccia?'

Evelina was surprised. Ava-Maria never went into her studio. At least, she had thought she didn't. 'She was my art teacher when I was a girl. She used to come to the villa and teach me. She later became my friend.'

'What happened to her?'

'She was killed in Auschwitz.'

Ava-Maria was shocked. 'That's horrible.'

'Yes, it is.'

'Topino was in the camps too, wasn't he?'

Evelina frowned. She didn't know what to say. It wasn't something Topino had ever talked about with her children.

'He has that number on his arm.'

'Yes, he does.'

'Would he tell me about it if I asked him?'

'I don't know.' Evelina felt uneasy. 'I imagine it's a time he would rather forget.'

'I don't think the world should forget what happened. The only way to avoid it happening again is to tell people about it. The only people who can do that are survivors, like Topino.'

'Well, darling, if you want to ask him, of course you must. He's perfectly capable of saying no.' Evelina looked at Topino. He was listening to Madolina. He was a good listener. Evelina wondered whether he'd be a good talker, if Ava-Maria asked him to be.

At the end of dinner, Franklin invited Topino to give the speech. Topino stood up and the table went quiet. 'Madolina said a little earlier that with every Thanksgiving she feels a little older. She's right, of course. We all get older, in spite of our efforts to defy time. But time will not be defied. The first Thanksgiving I celebrated with Franklin and Evelina was back in 1962. It was here in this very house. They'd bought it that spring and you children adored it. Dan, you built a tree house.'

'It's still there,' he laughed. 'Or what's left of it.'

'And Ava-Maria, you loved the pool.'

'Still do!' she exclaimed. 'Just not in winter.'

'Every year we get a little older, but we grow a little wiser, and we enjoy watching life unfold. Jonathan and Ava-Maria are going to marry. This is an exciting development. I raise my glass to you both and your happiness.' Topino lifted his glass and everyone else did the same. 'Dan has brought the lovely Lucille to celebrate Thanksgiving with us this year and I hope, Lucille, that you'll be here to celebrate with us again next year. Because Thanksgiving is about tradition and while circumstances change all around us, it's traditions that knit them together so that we enjoy the comfort of the familiar while welcoming in the new. Jonathan and I are

going to play chess tomorrow afternoon and I am going to
be badly beaten.'

'Oh Topino!' Ava-Maria cried, pretending to yawn.
'Change the record!'

'No, no. I'm prepared for defeat. There comes a time when
the old have to make way for the young. When I am finished
with the game, perhaps someone will stand in for me so that
the tradition may continue. Perhaps she will be a woman.
Perhaps you, Lucille?'

'I play,' said Lucille with a shrug. 'I'll take anyone on.'

'There, you see, we already have a taker.'

Dan caught Lucille's eye and they laughed.

Topino continued. 'When I look back over the years, I
realize that *you* have been my family. I had a family once,
of course. We all start off with one. But I lost mine along
the way. At one point I thought I could survive without
one. Who needs a family, I said to myself, when I have my
own company. Really, how could I possibly do better than
that? But life is not worth living if there's no love in it, and
one cannot survive by simply loving oneself. *That* I know
for sure. Life without love is simply a gaping hole of point-
lessness. More than anything, Evelina has taught me about
the value of family. She made it so comfortable for me that
I never went out and found one of my own. I adopted hers.
You. So, I raise my glass to you, Franklin, and you, Evelina,
and thank you, at this time of thanksgiving, for welcoming
me into your family all those years ago and for not regretting
it, because I've kind of lingered.' He pulled a comical face
and everyone laughed and raised their glasses with him. 'And
finally, I look back over my life, to the many chapters I have
lived, and am grateful to the relentless passage of time for all
the things it has taught me. Without time there would be no

past to look back on, no memories to savour and no growth of spirit. I am grateful, also, to time.' He nodded and lifted his glass again. '*L'chaim*,' he said. 'To life.'

After dinner Ava-Maria helped her mother clear away the plates, then she went and found Topino, who was outside on the terrace smoking a cigarette and looking up at the stars. 'Aren't they beautiful tonight,' he said as Ava-Maria joined him.

'Yes, they are. It's a particularly clear night.'

'I had to come out and have a look. It's easy to take them for granted.' He inhaled through his nostrils, savouring the smell of the garden. The scents of the night.

'I don't think you ever take anything for granted,' said Ava-Maria. 'You know, you've taught me many things in my life, but one of the most wonderful things you've taught me is appreciation. By example. You appreciate everything. You always have.'

'It's easy to become the voice in your head and to fail to see the beauty of everyday life unfolding around you.'

'Topino, will you tell me about that number on your arm?'

Topino put the cigarette between his lips and rolled up his sleeve. 'This?' he said. 'If I ever forget to appreciate a day, I only need look at this and it reminds me. It never fails.'

'What happened in the camp?'

'You don't want to know, Ava-Maria. It was a dark time. It's best left in the past.'

'I think you're wrong. If everyone who went through it were to leave it in the past, the world would never learn from history. And it has to learn, so that it never happens again.'

'Human beings rarely learn from history. The lesson is lost after a few generations. You don't need to be a historian to understand that. Humankind makes the same mistakes over and over again.' He tapped his temple. 'Its memory is short.'

'We have to try, at least.' She looked at him and frowned. 'I've known you all my life, Topino, and yet I know nothing about you. You're like an uncle. Like my mother's brother. You're as much part of the family as Alba, more so, because we see you all the time. Yet, you're a mystery. Why are you a mystery? Because I've never asked you any questions. I'm always telling you about myself.'

'I'd rather be the one asking questions.' He chuckled and drew on his cigarette. The little end glowed brightly then a curl of smoke floated into the air. 'And I enjoy listening to you talk about yourself.'

'It's silly, but I don't even know your real name.'

'You don't?'

'No. You've always been Topino. Uncle Topino.' She laughed. 'It's absurd. That can't be your real name.'

'Why are you suddenly so interested?'

She sighed. 'Because I'm growing up. Or maybe, I'm tired of talking about myself. Or perhaps because Daddy's life is fading away and I'm suddenly aware of how precious people are. I've always taken everyone for granted, even you. But now I'm curious about that number. I'm curious about your life before you became one of us. I want to know why you never married. Have you ever been in love?'

Topino chuckled. 'Everybody's been in love,' he said.

'I don't want to know about everybody. I want to know about *you*.'

'Very well, my dear. I'll tell you about me, although I might send you to sleep. I'm not very interesting.'

'Like you're not a good chess player.'

'That too. Everything's relative.'

'Beauty is in the eye of the beholder.'

He shrugged. 'Then maybe I won't bore *you*.'

Ava-Maria linked her arm through his. 'Let's walk around the garden in the moonlight,' she suggested. 'It's so lovely. I don't want to go inside. If we go inside, I'll lose you to Dan or Aunt Madolina or Mom. I want to have you all to myself for once.'

'You have my undivided attention. What do you want to know?'

'What are you really called?'

'Ezra,' he said. 'Ezra Zanotti.'

Evelina watched Topino and Ava-Maria disappear into the darkness and wondered what they were talking about. Whether he had agreed to tell her his story. If he did tell her, she wondered how much he would divulge. It was a miracle that he had survived the war, a miracle that he had moved to New York, a miracle that he had walked into the café that morning in Brooklyn, when she'd been waiting for Alba. It had been a miracle, too, that Alba hadn't turned up.

Ezra Zanotti, back from the dead. After all those years, Evelina still couldn't quite believe the miracle of it.

CHAPTER SIXTEEN

New York, 1959

The café was no place to speak of life after death. Ezra took Evelina's hand and led her out into the wet street. It was still raining. Cars splashed down the tarmac and people dashed up and down the sidewalk beneath umbrellas. Neither Ezra nor Evelina had an umbrella. They almost ran. Evelina didn't know where he was taking her and she didn't care. She was crying and laughing, and in the turmoil of her emotions pulsated a thousand questions.

Ezra stopped in front of a brownstone building. Once inside, he put his hand in the small of her back and guided her up the narrow staircase to his apartment. It was a small place, in need of a lick of paint, but clean and spartan. It was not the apartment of a man who was concerned about decoration or material things. Books were strewn over the surfaces and piled on the floor, and music scores lay on the table by the window alongside a music stand and his violin, as if he had only just put it down to run out for a cup of coffee.

Evelina stood in her wet coat, gazing about her, trying to take it all in. Her Ezra, here in Brooklyn. How long had he been here? How ...?

They stood gazing at each other, not knowing where to begin. How could they possibly bridge the gap between knowing and not knowing with words? Words were unbearably inadequate. Clumsy and shallow and small.

'Ezra,' she said at last. But tears caught in her throat and she was unable to continue.

'Eva.' He drew her into his arms again and this time it was with sorrow and regret that he held her. 'My Evelina.' He inhaled deeply, breathing her in, savouring the scent of her. He looked into her eyes and there was so much tenderness in his gaze that Evelina began to weep again. He wiped the wet hair off her face with a gentle hand. 'I never stopped loving you, you know. Not for a moment.' His words, spoken to her in Italian, brought back home to her in a torrent of memory. He smiled and his eyes were so full of shadow that something snagged in her heart. 'And yet, here you are.' He shook his head, barely daring to believe. 'Here you are.'

When he pressed his lips to hers it was with a ferocity that took her by surprise, while at the same time pulling her into its vortex. Evelina kissed him back. She kissed him fiercely, as if she needed confirmation that it was truly him, a man of flesh and blood, and not a ghost who might suddenly dematerialize into light. Urgently they shed their coats then turned their hurried fingers onto their clothes; unbuttoning, unzipping, undressing each other with the rush of two people who had waited years and did not have the patience to wait a second more.

They tumbled onto the bed and then Ezra was inside her. Evelina wrapped her arms and legs around him yet still she could not get close enough. She wanted to dissolve into him, for their bodies to blend, for their souls to merge. She wanted to somehow fill the vacuum his loss had created with every fibre of his physicality and in so doing erase all the suffering she had endured.

Yet nothing could erase that, for it lay deep and rooted. She closed her eyes and gave in to the sensual gratification that gradually overpowered her longing and allowed her thoughts to melt away.

At last they lay exhausted upon the sheets, entwined. For a long while neither of them said anything. Both knew that to speak about the last decade was entering a vale of thorns.

'The rabbi said you were dead. I gave up on you because I thought you were dead,' Evelina said eventually, propping herself up on her elbow and looking at him reproachfully.

She cried again. She cried for having been lied to, or misled, and she cried for the lost years, which she would never get back. 'I'm married, Ezra. I have children. Why didn't you come back to Vercellino?'

'I did,' he told her. 'But you'd already left for America.'

She stopped crying. 'When did you come back?'

'In February 1946.'

'You must have just missed me. Who told you I'd left?'

'Romina.'

'Romina?'

'I came to your house and Romina was there.'

'Yes, she came to live with us. She lost everyone in the war. She had nowhere to go, so Mamma invited her to stay.'

'Your mother is a good woman,' he said.

'Why didn't you ask for an address? You could have written to me.'

'I could have, but I didn't.'

'Why didn't you? I would have come back for you.'

'Romina told me you were married.'

Evelina sat up. 'She told you *what*?'

'That you were married.'

Sorrow turned to fury. 'I wasn't married. I had just left broken-hearted, believing you were dead, Ezra. I wasn't married. I was broken.'

Ezra got up and walked to the window. He knitted his fingers behind his head, staring out onto the wet street below. 'She told me you'd married a man from Milan and gone to live in America,' he said and there was a sharp edge to his voice.

They remained lost in thought for a moment, both trying to understand what had happened, neither willing to get their heads around the fact that they had been deliberately sabotaged.

'Romina knew about us?' Evelina asked.

'I didn't know she did.'

'*How* did she know?'

'Perhaps she worked it out when I showed up at your house. A decision made in haste without a thought for the consequences. A decision made out of jealousy and bitterness and because she had lost everything.'

'If anyone else had answered the door you would have been told the truth.' Evelina put her head in her hands and sighed heavily. 'Of all the people, it was Romina. And to lie after all we had done for her. How could she?'

Ezra said nothing. He stood by the window, looking out.

Evelina went up behind him and wound her arms around his waist. 'Oh Ezra,' she groaned, resting her forehead against his back.

He turned round and cupped her face in his hands. 'But we found each other, didn't we?'

'We did.' She smiled as he bent down to kiss her again. 'What do we do now?'

'I don't know.'

'I do. We stay like this.' She held him close and put her head against his heart. 'We stay like this and we never let go.'

'You still play the violin,' Evelina said. It was now past midday. They had spent the entire morning in bed. She picked up the instrument and put it beneath her chin.

'I make them,' Ezra told her. He was lying naked on the sheets, his body partially covered with a sheet, one arm behind his head, smoking a cigarette.

'That's incredible. Where did you learn to do that?'

'I met an old Italian luthier when I moved here who agreed to take me on as an apprentice. Our workshop is just around the corner.'

She plucked a string. 'When did you come to New York?'

'Five years ago.'

She stared at him with wide, incredulous eyes. 'You've been here for five years, in the same city as me, and I never knew?'

He nodded.

'Did you find someone else? Have you a woman?' She tried to keep the jealousy out of her voice for what right did she have to be possessive?

'You ruined love for me, Eva, because after you, I could never love anyone else.'

That should have satisfied her, but she found herself asking, 'But you've had women . . .'

He smiled wryly. 'I'm a man, Evelina, not a saint.'

She laughed, feeling foolish. 'Where did you go after Vercellino?'

'I went to Israel.'

Evelina put the violin down. She climbed into bed and snuggled against him. 'Why did you go to Israel?'

'I'd lost everyone, Eva. I couldn't stay in Vercellino. There was nothing left for me there but memories. I went to Israel, fought against Palestine, then emigrated here.'

'You fought against Palestine?'

'I had nothing else to do.' He chuckled. 'I like to keep busy.'

He stubbed out his cigarette and Evelina noticed the number tattooed on his wrist. She took it in her hand and ran her thumb across it. 'What happened, Ezra? After you were taken to Fossoli?'

He sighed and pulled his wrist away. 'Let's not talk about that, Eva.' He rolled her over and buried his face in her neck. 'The past is gone. I want to enjoy *you*. After all, it's taken me over a decade to find you.'

'Oh really, Ezra, you didn't even look.'

'You belong to another man. What could I do?'

'Look,' she said.

He held her gaze, his face serious, that unfamiliar darkness in his eyes. 'One gets tired of hoping, Eva. Sometimes, one just has to accept things as they are and move on.'

'Is that what you did? You moved on?'

'Didn't you?'

'I suppose I did.'

'We both moved on, but we found each other anyway. Let's be grateful for that.'

Evelina left Ezra's apartment in time to pick up the boys from school. As she walked past the café she remembered that she had forgotten to pay the bill. Embarrassed, she dashed inside and explained. The woman behind the counter had no recollection of her ever having been there, but Evelina paid anyway. She took the subway back into Manhattan and arrived at the school gates five minutes early.

The boys rushed out of school with their usual exuberance. Aldo had got a gold star for his homework and Dan had hit another boy and been reprimanded. Evelina told him off but he still managed to find it funny. When she got home she handed them over to Zofia, the Polish nanny, and went upstairs to her bedroom. She sat on the bed and breathed heavily as the full impact of the day began to sink in: she'd just committed adultery. Mystic Marica and the Seven of Swords surfaced in her mind. She pushed the image away, not wanting to believe there was any truth in it.

Evelina showered and changed. She was about to take a walk around the block when the telephone went. It was Alba. 'I think I stood you up this morning,' she said. 'I'm sorry. It totally slipped my mind. I've only just seen it in my diary. Will you forgive me?'

Evelina had forgotten all about Alba. 'Of course I forgive you. It's fine. I sat reading and had two cups of coffee. Really, it was very pleasant.'

'But you came all the way out to Brooklyn for nothing.'

'It's not so far on the subway. Besides, I like being there. It reminds me of when I first arrived here.'

'You could have popped in to see Mom.'

'I could have, but I didn't want to bother her. You know how busy she is.'

'Can you make it tomorrow? I'd really like to see you.'

Evelina's mind whirred with possibilities. 'Yes, let's meet tomorrow,' she replied, thinking of Ezra.

When she put down the phone, she felt a wave of guilt and bit her lip anxiously. She had betrayed Franklin and he didn't deserve that. She sat on the bed again and put her head in her hands and sighed. What was she going to do? Of all the cafés in Brooklyn, Ezra had walked into hers. What were the odds? How many millions of people were there in New York? And he'd walked into her café! It was fate.

But fate had not taken the Ten Commandments into account.

It had stopped raining and a sprinkling of stars could be seen twinkling in the dark patches between the cloud. Evelina put on her coat and went for a walk. Evening crept in early these days. The pavements glistened with streaks of gold beneath the street lamps and the air was thick with damp. She pulled her woollen hat low over her forehead and thrust her hands into her pockets. What was she going to do? It was a question that had no answer. She loved Ezra with all her heart, but she was married to Franklin, and she loved him too.

What was she going to do?

She strode down the sidewalk, her gaze on the piece of tarmac in front of her, the hypnotic rhythm of her shoes drawing her further into herself. It was hard to take it all in. Ezra was alive. Alive! She had prayed for his return, but she had never believed her prayers would be answered. How could the rabbi have made such an error? Why would Romina want to hurt her? Ezra must have thought she hadn't waited for him. He must have left the villa with the impression that she had given up on him, and so quickly. He had been captured in December 1943 and turned up at Villa L'Ambrosiana just over two years after. How hurt must he have been to have believed that she couldn't even have waited two years! That thought was so horrific it knocked the breath out of her.

She found a phone booth and punched in his number. Blinded by tears she could barely make the numbers out on the piece of paper he had given her. 'Ezra,' she said when he picked up. 'I never gave up on you. Never. At least not in my heart.'

'I know you didn't, Eva,' he replied.

'No, you don't. You don't know.' She wiped her face with her glove. 'You don't know how I grieved when I was told that you had died. I grieved for you, for your parents, for Fioruccia and Matteo ...' Her breath caught in her chest. 'For the children ...'

'It's okay, Eva ...'

'No, it's not okay. You've spent the last thirteen years believing I didn't wait for you. After everything you went through, and I know something of what you went through, you came home to find that I had gone. I can't bear it ...' She pushed some coins into the slot with trembling fingers.

'Eva, it's in the past.'

'But it's haunting me, Ezra. There wasn't a moment of the day when I didn't think about you. When I didn't miss you and pine for you. I ached for you. And then, there came a moment when I realized I had to live. I couldn't waste away holding out for a man who was never going to come back. Who was dead. I believed you were dead. Oh God ...' She leaned her forehead against the glass and closed her eyes. 'You were dead and now you're alive and I'm married.'

'It's okay, my darling,' he repeated. 'It's okay.'

'I was living without you. I had found happiness, and now ...'

'We'll muddle through.'

'But what does that even mean? How can we muddle through? I want to be with you, Ezra. Every night and every day. I just want to be with you.'

'Eva, you have to calm down.' There was a long pause as she took a breath and tried to pull herself together. She pushed more coins into the slot. 'How many children do you have?' he asked.

'Three.'

'How old are they?'

'Five, nine and eleven.'

'Do they look like you?'

'A bit.'

'Then they must be beautiful.'

'Oh Ezra . . .'

'You have a family. You have a husband. You have a home. I had a family too, but I lost it. Family is precious, Eva. More precious than you and me.' Ezra chuckled and there was resignation in it, as if he had learned to accept life as it was and feel gratitude for whatever it gave him. 'I'm grateful to have found you. I thought I had no one left in the world, but you appeared like a gift from the blue. We've found each other. It doesn't matter what tomorrow brings. We don't have to *do* anything. We're in the same city. We're breathing the same air. We're free.'

'When I think about what you must have gone through—'

'Don't. Don't think about things that don't matter.'

'You're right.' Evelina sniffed and wiped her face again. 'I need to pull myself together.'

'I'm not going anywhere, Eva. I'm here.'

'I know.'

'Where are you?'

'A block from my home. In a phone booth.'

'Then you need to go home to your children.'

'I know.'

'What does your husband do?'

'He's a classics teacher at Columbia.'

'I'm glad you married someone with a good brain.'

'Yes, I'm glad too.'

'Does he treat you well?'

'Very.'

'What's his name?'

'Franklin.'

'Like the ex-President.'

'Like him.'

'You need to pull yourself together and go home now, Eva.'

'Can I see you tomorrow?'

'You can come to my workshop.'

Evelina had forgotten that he had a job. 'Of course, you make violins. I'd love to see where you work.'

Ezra gave her the address. 'Come tomorrow morning.'

'I'm meeting my cousin for coffee. I'll come after that.'

'Good.'

'Okay. I'm feeling better.'

'Listen, it's going to take a while for this to sink in. It's not every day that the dead rise – in fact, I think it's only happened once before and, as a Jew, I'm inclined not to believe it. That makes me the first.'

'You're forgetting Lazarus.' She laughed.

'I don't believe that either. I'm still the first. Don't take my first place away from me. I'm enjoying it.'

'Oh Ezra, how can you laugh about such a thing?'

'Because I've found you, Eva. That makes me the happiest man in the world.'

Evelina walked around the block to dry her face and compose herself before going home. She did not want her children or the nanny to see that she'd been crying. Her whole world had suddenly turned upside down and she didn't know how to deal with it. She just wanted to curl up and cry. But Ezra wanted to laugh. His was a glass half full. She knew she needed to see it that way too; she would try.

When she got home, the children were having tea in the kitchen. Zofia was supervising Ava-Maria while the boys looked after themselves. Evelina joined them for a while, putting on a good show and smiling at the funny things they said. Looking into their sweet faces she knew that Ezra was right. Family was precious. She didn't want to do anything to risk hurting them, or losing them. She tried not to think of Ezra, but half her mind remained attached to him, afraid perhaps that if she let him go for a second she would lose him, while the other half did a good job of being a mother.

After bath time she read Ava-Maria a bedtime story. Her little daughter always wanted the same story about a cat. Evelina knew the words by heart, which was just as well, because she wasn't aware of what she was saying. She kissed her goodnight just as Franklin came through the door. He took off his coat and hat and put his bag down by the stairs. 'Am I too late to say goodnight?' he called.

'No, come on up. Ava-Maria is ready for bed. The boys are reading in their rooms, but I'm sure they'd love you to read to them if you have a moment.'

Evelina stood in the doorway. Her husband kissed her on the cheek and then went into Ava-Maria's room to kiss her goodnight. Then he went to see his sons. Evelina watched as he opened *his* favourite story book by Oscar Wilde and read them 'The Happy Prince'. Evelina went downstairs to see to supper. She hadn't given it a thought. She opened the fridge and was relieved to find some chicken and vegetables. Although she didn't feel like eating, she knew Franklin would be hungry. She picked up a tomato and cradled it in the palm of her hand. The sight of it transported her back to the first time Ezra had kissed her in Nonna Pierangelini's glasshouse. She pressed it to her nose. It did not smell like her grandmother's, but then it had not been cultivated in a place of enchantment. Her vision blurred with tears.

Franklin disappeared into his study until supper time. When he emerged, he looked at Evelina with a frown. 'Are you all right, darling? You're pale.'

'I don't feel well, actually. I think I might have a slight fever.'

Franklin put a hand to her forehead. 'You don't have to stay up for me. If you want to have an early night, I'll sleep in the spare room.'

'You don't mind?'

'Of course not. I'll be working late tonight anyway. You go on up and I'll eat as I work. I've got a load to get through.'

She kissed him. 'You work too hard.'

'I know, but I enjoy it.'

She took off her apron and hung it on the back of the door. 'See you tomorrow,' she said, but Franklin was already putting his dinner on a tray, his mind on other things.

Evelina lay in bed thinking of Ezra. She took herself back to the first time they had met at Ercole Zanotti. He was older now. The lines had dug deep around his eyes and mouth and into the furrows on his forehead, but he was still handsome. He'd always been handsome. She imagined she was in his arms. She imagined so hard that she could almost smell him. Almost feel him. He was so familiar, it was as if they had never been apart.

Evelina's body ached for him. She curled into a ball and

tried not to think about the future. She tried to feel gratitude like he did that they had found each other. It was a miracle, after all. The kind of miracle that rarely happened. Yet, now she wanted more. She never wanted to be parted from him again. But that was a prayer too far, one she knew she could never ask for. One that God, in His wisdom, would not grant. For in granting her that wish, He would crush four innocent hearts.

Ezra was right: family was precious.

CHAPTER SEVENTEEN

The following morning Evelina took the subway to Brooklyn and met Alba in the coffee shop. Alba was on time and waiting at a corner table when Evelina pushed open the door. In a white mink coat and hat Alba looked elegant and expensive. Only when she was sure that Evelina had seen her furs did she take them off. 'A gift from Antonio,' she said breezily. 'He's guilty as hell. That's the thing. He thinks I don't know. He thinks he can give me presents and I'll turn a blind eye. Men.' She sighed with exasperation. 'Why do we waste our time?' She gave her cousin the once-over. 'Well, you look nice. Is that for me?'

'I decided I needed to make more of an effort. It's easy to let our standards slip when we're married with children.'

'Speak for yourself. I need a little glamour in my life. If you were competing with girls ten years younger than you, you'd be darn sure not to let your standards slip, I can tell you!'

Evelina sat down and they ordered coffee and pastries. Alba ordered a glass of champagne. 'Is it bad?' Evelina asked.

Alba shrugged. 'Let's just say I'm coping.'

'That doesn't sound good.'

'You marry a man like Antonio, you have to accept a roving eye as part of the deal. I get expensive jewellery and furs and he gets to sleep with other women.'

Evelina was appalled. 'Alba!'

'It's true. I can say it to you.' She gave her cousin a reproachful look. 'You want me to lie?'

'Of course not.'

'Then don't be so innocent. Not everyone has a bed of roses marriage like you do.'

'I wouldn't say it's a bed of roses.'

Alba chuckled. 'It's a bed of roses, Evelina.' She delved into her purse for her tortoiseshell cigarette case, opened it with a talon and popped a cigarette between her scarlet lips. 'Look.' She was now speaking out of the side of her mouth and flicking the lighter. 'I knew what I was getting into when I married him. Well, I knew some of it. Not all of it. But I wasn't naive.'

'Do you still love him?'

Alba blew smoke into the air between them. 'Love, what's that? I don't know. I'm too close to know the wood from the trees.'

The waiter brought their drinks and pastries. Alba took a swig of champagne. 'I suppose I love him. He's the father of my children. I look at the wives of his brothers and colleagues, if you can call family members you work with colleagues. They're all the same. We've made identical beds and we're lying on them.'

'That's depressing,' said Evelina, sipping her coffee and thinking of Ezra in his workshop, waiting for her to appear.

The champagne began to take effect and Alba's shoulders relaxed. 'I shouldn't complain. I have a nice life. Look.' She lifted her wrist to show off a sparkling diamond bracelet. 'He

spoils me. I can't say he doesn't do that. I have everything I
want. Everything money can buy.'

'Then what don't you have?'

Alba cackled. 'Antonio.'

Alba stayed longer than Evelina expected. She drank another
glass of champagne and smoked a couple more cigarettes.
She didn't ask Evelina about herself, which was typical, but
held forth about her own troubles, offloading them onto
her cousin and then skipping out of the restaurant at eleven,
feeling lighter.

Evelina embraced her and saw her into a taxi, then turned
on her heel and headed to Ezra's workshop. She couldn't
believe that she was here, in Brooklyn, on her way to seeing
Ezra. It felt surreal, like she was living a dream.

She found the shop easily. *Gandolfi's Lutherie* was announced in an arc of big gold letters on the window, beneath
a scalloped green awning. Displayed on a platform behind
the glass were guitars and violins and an enormous cello.
Evelina's heart began to race. She took a deep breath and
pushed open the door. A bell tinkled just like it had done at
Ercole Zanotti. A woman chewing on the end of a pencil and
flicking through a ledger looked up from behind the counter. 'Good morning,' she said and smiled. She had hooded
eyes and an aquiline nose and a thick accent Evelina didn't
recognize.

'I've come to see Ezra Zanotti,' said Evelina, trying not
to look guilty, even though the woman had no idea who she
was, or that she'd committed adultery the day before and
would likely do so again today.

'He's downstairs.' The woman slipped off her stool.
'Come, I'll show you.' She led Evelina to the back of the

store and pointed down a narrow staircase. 'Ezra, I have a lady here to see you,' she shouted. Then she indicated with a nod that Evelina should go on down. Careful not to slip on the steps in her enthusiasm, Evelina took it slowly.

Ezra appeared at the bottom. He smiled and held out his hand. Evelina's chest expanded with joy. She put her hand in his and looked at him with wonder. Ezra, who'd come back from the dead. She wanted to throw herself into his arms, but she noticed an old man with a white beard in a brown apron looking up from a work bench, and drew back.

'Let me introduce you to Giuseppe Gandolfi,' said Ezra in Italian.

'The proprietor. It's a pleasure to meet you,' said Evelina, mastering her self-control.

'The pleasure is all mine,' said Giuseppe, green eyes lively with interest. 'Ezra has told me all about you.' Evelina wondered how much he had said and frowned. 'How long has it been since you last saw each other? Ten years? That's the thing about New York, it's a big melting pot of immigrants and yet, old friends somehow find each other. It should be called the City of Miracles.'

'Where are you from?' she asked, recognizing his northern Italian accent.

'I was born in Casale Monferrato.' Evelina nodded. That wasn't far from Vercellino. 'Then I moved to Milan.'

'He learned how to make violins under Leandro Bisiach himself, in his workshop in Milan,' said Ezra. Evelina didn't know who Leandro Bisiach was, but she assumed from the admiration on Ezra's face that he was important. 'Come, look at this.'

Evelina followed him to a wall exhibiting flat wooden pieces shaped like the bodies of violins. 'This mould belonged to Bisiach himself,' he said, lifting it off its peg. 'It's taken from his studies of a Stradivarius.' He ran his long fingers over the curves. 'Isn't it beautiful?'

Evelina wanted to agree with him, but it just looked like a piece of old wood. 'I think this entire room is beautiful,' she said. 'It's a wonderful cave of creativity.' It was an artist's workshop with work benches and shelves of tools – so many tools in various shapes and sizes, she couldn't imagine what they were all for. There were violins, cellos and guitars in various stages of development, pots of varnish and oil, jars of brushes, pieces of machinery and shelves of maple and sycamore piled neatly, piece upon piece. The place smelt of wood and varnish, like a carpenter's workshop.

'Do you play these instruments too?' she asked Giuseppe.

'When I get the time,' he replied and grinned, revealing crooked yellow teeth. 'The trouble is we have too many repairs. I don't know what people do with their instruments. Perhaps they use them to bash each other over the head with.' He sighed. 'I'd like to have more time to make new ones, but the repairs keep coming and I don't like to turn anyone away. Sometimes we get an interesting old piece, and then it gets exciting. You know, a man brought in a Raffaele Fiorini for restoration not so long ago.' He paused his work and inhaled through his nostrils, kissing his fingertips. 'Sublime.'

Evelina laughed. 'What are you doing now?' she asked, wandering over to his work bench to take a closer look.

'I'm working on a new violin. We have to keep up with the demand for new instruments as well as repair and restore old ones. I'm carving the scrolled head from a piece of maple, which I will then glue to the body.'

'It is such a skill and you do it beautifully!' she exclaimed, watching Giuseppe chip away thin shavings of wood.

'You could say that, at seventy-five, I have learned my craft.'

She laughed again. 'I think you have. It seems to be second nature.' She turned to Ezra. 'Do you get to make new violins or are you always repairing old ones?'

'I make them too,' he replied, coming up behind her and putting a hand on her shoulder. That hand, placed so casually on her coat, drew all her attention. 'It's fantastic to make such a beautiful instrument. And every piece is different because it's carved by hand. I cannot imagine doing anything else.'

'Have you heard him play?' asked Giuseppe. Then he chuckled. 'Of course you have. He plays like a professional, but we don't want his head to swell, so let's keep that to ourselves.'

Ezra laughed and patted Evelina's shoulder. 'I'm going to take my friend here out for an early lunch. Can I bring you anything?'

'No, my long-suffering wife has made me a focaccia sandwich. If I don't eat it, she'll be hurt. And she makes good sandwiches. Better than anything you can buy in a store.'

'It's been fun talking to you, Giuseppe. I hope we meet again,' said Evelina.

Giuseppe nodded. 'You can come any time you like,' he said. 'As long as you're not too much of a distraction.' He smiled and watched them head up the stairs.

Once out in the street, Ezra spun Evelina round and kissed her full on the lips. She was terrified she might be seen by someone she knew, even though she'd never been in this street before. 'Ezra, we mustn't,' she said, gently pushing him away. 'It's dangerous.'

'I think we're quite safe here.'

'You can't be sure.'

'Come then. Let's go someplace we *can* be sure.'

Evelina knew she shouldn't. She'd been unfaithful once and she could forgive herself for that; it had been a moment of shock and bewilderment to find him alive. She'd lost her mind and acted on impulse. It had been wrong, but she could justify it, at least to herself. Now, however, she was of sound mind and the shock and bewilderment had dissolved into joy and gratitude. There was no excuse, no justification – even to herself. What she was about to do was wrong. Yet, she accompanied him back to his apartment all the same. As soon as they were through the door she was against the wall and he was kissing her and slipping off her coat and she was unbuttoning his. There was no stopping. The dialogue in her head went quiet. The arguments ceased. The rights and wrongs of the situation melted into a feverish urgency to be close. As close as two people could get. She wanted to wrap herself around him.

Afterwards, they lay on the bed as they had done the day before, and talked. They reminisced about Villa L'Ambrosiana, remembering that summer of 1943 before the war had cast its shadow over their golden part of Italy, plunging them into danger and finally heartbreak. They remembered the bicycle rides, the picnics, the long afternoons in the sunshine lying on their backs in the poppy field, gazing up at the clouds. They remembered the meals they'd eaten at Fioruccia and Matteo's apartment and the snatched moments in the shop when his father wasn't looking. Their shared memories ran deep like secret rivulets far beneath the ground where no one else could see them. They belonged to the two of them alone, and through their speaking of them they were brought to the surface to shine ever brighter.

They made love again, this time slowly. Evelina felt like a young woman, making love with Ezra in the chapel, exploring each other's bodies for the first time. Delighting in every touch. Feeling aroused by the smallest caress. When it was time to part, Evelina didn't ask what they were going to do. She didn't try to fix the future. She knew that, somehow, they would see each other. Somehow, they'd muddle through.

Evelina returned to her apartment in Manhattan and Ezra to the workshop and the violin he was repairing. Evelina told herself that the distance between them didn't feel so far, since before they had been parted by death. She was grateful that he was alive. Grateful that he was in New York. Grateful that they had found one another.

Evelina had a sudden yearning to play the piano. She hadn't touched a key since Ezra was arrested, but now he was back she felt the flow of energy once again, pulsating from her heart to her fingertips, and they twitched with longing to give expression to her deepest feelings. However, the apartment wasn't big enough to have a proper piano.

The following day she met Ezra outside Gandolfi's and they went straight to his apartment. After making love, Ezra lit a cigarette and Evelina made them both espressos with the aluminium cafetiere, just like they had done back home. The smell of ground coffee filled the apartment with a pleasant sense of nostalgia and she sat cross-legged on the bed to enjoy it. 'What do you do with your days, Eva?' Ezra asked.

'I paint.'

'I'm glad you still do that. Fioruccia always said you had talent.'

'She was being kind. You know, I sketched Fioruccia

from memory. It's quite a close likeness. I framed it and put it by my bed.'

'She'd have liked that.'

'I wonder if she knows.'

'You didn't sketch one of me?' He grinned at her over his coffee cup, and once again Evelina was surprised at his humour, how he made so little of the years they were apart and the fact that she'd thought he was dead.

'No, I didn't sketch one of you.'

'Why?'

She shrugged. 'I don't know. Perhaps I thought it would be disloyal to my husband.'

'God forbid you're disloyal to Franklin.' He chuckled and his grey eyes twinkled with mischief.

'Ezra! That was then. This is now. It's different.'

'I don't think there's much harm in a sketch of your old boyfriend, your *dead* old boyfriend. As for what we're doing now . . . well . . .'

She lowered her eyes. 'It was too painful.'

'You can sketch me now, from life. I look better alive.'

She couldn't help but laugh. 'You always looked good in my memory, Ezra. You were never dead there. Only in my nightmares.' She didn't want to think of those. 'I'll sketch you,' she suggested. 'I'd like to. I've drawn my family so many times, I need a new face.'

'Do you still play the piano?'

'I haven't played since you were captured.'

'Why ever not?'

'Because you were gone.'

'Now I'm back, you must play again.'

'I don't have a piano.'

'You can get an upright.'

'No room.'

'How about a console piano? They do some good ones in a shop around the corner from the workshop. I'll arrange it if you like. They can send it to your house.'

Evelina was excited. 'I'd love that!' she exclaimed happily. 'Of course, I'll pay.' Or rather, Franklin would pay, she thought. Would it be unfair of her to suggest it be her Christmas present?

'It's a deal,' said Ezra. He got up and started to dress. 'Come, I want to show you something.'

Evelina put on her clothes and followed him to the kitchen window. He lifted it and climbed through to the fire escape. 'This better be good,' she said, taking his hand and scrambling out.

'It is,' he replied with a smile.

Once on the fire escape she followed him up to the roof, wondering what on earth it was that he wanted to show her. The top of the building was flat and scattered with leaves which had been carried there on the wind. Evelina looked about her in delight. The roofs and skyscrapers of Brooklyn spread out around her like another world of concrete and glass. Ezra lay down. He patted the space beside him. 'Come, you have to lie on your back.'

Evelina was glad it hadn't rained. She did as she was told. Ezra took her hand and squeezed it. Together they gazed into the sky as they had done in Piedmont. Evelina took a deep breath. The sight of blue sky and clouds brought it all back to her like a long-lost melody, and she felt the familiar warmth spreading in her chest as it filled with happiness and love. She could forget her surroundings and disappear into the faraway blue, which was the same wherever one was. Finally, Ezra spoke. 'I like to come up here. I just let myself go, like a balloon, and float up into the clouds. Sometimes it's clear, other times it's cloudy, but every time, I leave myself behind. It's in these moments that I feel truly myself.'

Evelina could hear the rumble of traffic on the streets below and the distant wail of a siren, but she felt detached, as if they belonged to a different time and place. 'What do you mean by truly yourself?' she asked.

'Attached to nothing. Not my name, my body, my history, my experience, my story. I'm just in a state of being. It's peaceful. I can feel the wind on my face, the sun on my skin and I'm not thinking of anything . . . It's hard to explain. But I feel the energy that is me.'

'Do you still go to synagogue?' she asked.

'No. I haven't been since Vercellino.'

'Did the camp make you question the existence of God?' Evelina had heard survivors talk about how the evil they witnessed there made them lose their faith.

'God wasn't there. If He exists, He was looking the other way. But I'm not going to allow Hitler to beat me. The greatest revenge is my happiness and I intend to find joy in everything. In *life*. In the sky, the clouds, the birds, even in the sound of lorries and sirens and drills. There is beauty in everything if you look for it. Every day that I find enjoyment is a celebration of our people's defiance. A triumph of good over evil. A confirmation of my aliveness. God or no God, the only way I can find purpose in what I have lived through is to have learned something from it. That's what I have learned. To *live*.'

Evelina brought his hand to her lips and kissed it. Then they remained a while in silence, staring into the blue.

Evelina slipped into a new routine of seeing Ezra every

lunchtime. It was easy, taking the subway to Brooklyn and meeting him at his apartment. The console piano, Franklin's Christmas present to Evelina, arrived and she began to play. Her fingers had not forgotten and settled back into the old chords and harmonies as if they had never left them. Once again, Evelina drifted off on her imagination, just like Ezra had taught her to do. She was a bird, wings outspread, soaring over the mountains of Piedmont, dipping the tips into the rice fields and diving between the rows of neatly planted vines and olive trees. Her melodies took her home again, to the mossy grottos at Villa L'Ambrosiana, and Ezra was there, for he belonged in those gardens too, with her.

Evelina took her sketchpad and drew him. She relished tracing the lines of his face with her charcoal, caressing his features with her focused gaze. He lay back against the pillows, cigarette smoking between his fingers, watching her with heavy lids and sleepy eyes. She followed the line of his lips, the curve of his chin, the sensual contours of a face that she had kissed a thousand times in her imagination and hundreds more since he'd come back from the dead. His hair was receding and greying prematurely. It had once been thick and curly, the colour of soil. But experience and trauma had left their footprints all over him. Evelina was afraid to look too deeply into his eyes unless she saw his suffering there, suffering that she didn't have the stomach to face. But Ezra did not want to talk about the past. He was living in the moment, cherishing his freedom and his life; how else does one live when one has but by the grace of God stepped back from the abyss?

Months passed and this new routine became a part of life. Although Evelina knew she was betraying Franklin, it didn't feel like a betrayal. She had loved Ezra first. They were two halves of the same whole. An outward breath and an inward breath, one unable to exist without the other. Franklin was increasingly busy with work. His job was forever expanding. The responsibilities growing with each step forward that he took. Evelina was always home when he returned at the end of the day. She cooked him supper, listened to him talk about himself, then brought a mug of hot chocolate to his desk when he continued to work long after she had finished washing up. If it hadn't been for Ezra she would have felt unloved and ignored, but because of him she accepted her husband's compulsiveness, and Franklin was grateful for her understanding, without questioning from where it came.

Then one weekend the following spring, when Franklin had to go up to Boston on business, Evelina spent the afternoon with Ezra, leaving her children with Zofia. They walked around the park beneath plane trees whose leaves were just beginning to unfurl. Blossom was scattered on the breeze and birdsong filled the air. Life vibrated keenly in every border and the air was thick with the sweet smell of fertility and regeneration. They sat on a bench and looked out over the river. A few boats moved slowly across the water like ducks, and the sunshine, bright and golden, bounced off the ripples in their wakes.

'I want to tell you what happened to me after my capture,' he said.

Evelina braced herself. 'If you're ready,' she replied, knowing that it wasn't going to be comfortable returning to a place of such darkness.

Ezra glanced down at the numbers tattooed on the inside of his arm and took a breath. 'I'll tell you what happened, Eva, because I need to tell you. And then I will never speak of it again.'

CHAPTER EIGHTEEN

In June, Evelina received a telephone call from home. It was her mother calling to tell her that Nonna Pierangelini had died. Although Evelina had known it was unlikely that she would see her grandmother again, the finality of her death hit her hard. She remembered her as she had last seen her through the back window of the car, a squat figure dressed in black, waving a white handkerchief. *The world is full of traps*, she had said. *The devil puts them in your way to test you.* Had her grandmother known that Evelina might be tested? Could she have somehow known that Ezra was alive and foreseen the trouble ahead?

Franklin was sympathetic. He took off his glasses and looked at his wife in a way that he hadn't looked at her in months. Really seeing her and understanding her needs. 'Why don't you go pay your family a visit?' he suggested. 'Zofia can take care of Ava-Maria and you can take the boys. I'd come with you if I didn't have so much on.'

Evelina was grateful for his sympathy. 'Oh, I don't know. It's a long way . . .'

'You haven't been home since we got married. You should go see your parents, and Benedetta.'

Evelina thought about it for a moment. Her reluctance

had nothing to do with the voyage, but with Ezra. If she went back to Italy, she'd have to go for three weeks, at least. She knew she couldn't be parted from him for that long. She wasn't sure she could be parted from Ava-Maria, either. But her grandmother's death brought into sharp relief the fragility of life and she knew that, if she wasn't careful, years would go by and one by one the people who meant the most to her would grow ever more distant and finally follow Nonna Pierangelini into the next world, leaving Evelina with a searing regret at not having made the effort to visit them while she had had the chance. Italy wasn't that far away, after all.

When she mentioned it to Ezra, he made an audacious suggestion. 'If you wait until August, Giuseppe shuts the store for the whole month, being so hot in the city, and takes his wife to Tuscany. I could come with you.'

Evelina trembled at the suggestion. It was dangerous and yet, irresistible. 'You'd go back to Vercellino?' she asked, surprised.

'No, I'd go to Tuscany with Giuseppe and meet you in Florence. You could visit your family and then take the train south to spend time with me. A week, ten days, two weeks? Just you and me.'

The more she thought about it the simpler the idea sounded. If she went in August she could take the boys with her. Ava-Maria was too small and Zofia would be happy to look after her, but the boys were old enough to appreciate the trip and she could leave them with Benedetta while she went to Florence. She began to feel excited. It would be a dream to spend some time with Ezra where she wasn't constantly aware of her infidelity and the ticking of the clock.

*

A couple of months later, Evelina was on a steam ship, sailing across the Atlantic with Aldo and Dan. It had been hard kissing Ava-Maria goodbye, but Franklin had reassured her, holding their little girl in his arms and telling Evelina that he and Zofia would keep her busy so she didn't miss her mother. Ava-Maria had lifted her hand and waved as the ship had vibrated like an awakening beast and moved slowly out of the harbour, and Evelina had had to turn away for the sight was unbearable.

The crossing was rough at times, but the boys thought it great fun, rolling about in their bunks. Evelina felt sick, but focused on Florence and envisaged herself walking down the cobbled streets, hand in hand with Ezra, just like she had once visualized she'd do in Vercellino, until the war had shattered her dreams. As she lay in her first-class berth she thought about what Ezra had told her on the bench. He had shared his story without emotion, impassively, as if it had happened to someone else. Now, as she lay there, trying to hold back the shadowy images that crept out of her imagination – terrifying in their sketchiness, for how could anyone who wasn't there fully understand? – she realized why; because the only way to survive it was to separate himself from it. What he had been through and witnessed in Auschwitz was so terrible it defied comprehension. But what he wanted was to be listened to. Evelina couldn't give him much in terms of comfort, but she could give him that; her full attention.

After Ezra was captured, he'd been taken to Fossoli near Carpi, a camp run by Italians for Italian Jews, and English and American prisoners of war. He had been detained there for a month. From Fossoli he was sent to Monowitz, one of the camps in the Auschwitz complex. He endured eleven months of hard labour before the Russians liberated them. The Germans, in the light of the Allied advance, had attempted to evacuate all the prisoners, sending them on a death march from Auschwitz to Buchenwald and Mauthausen, intending to kill all those left behind who were too sick to be moved. But the speed of the Russian advance had forced them to change their plans and flee. Because Ezra was in the sick bay with scarlet fever, he was saved. However, it had taken him nine months to make his way home across Europe on foot and by train.

Evelina had listened. Ezra had not tempered his story with humour, but told it in a factual way, his fingers knitted, his eyes gazing over the river. He hadn't wanted sympathy, only recognition of what he had lived through. He'd spared her none of the horror and she had held herself together, straining her throat and jaw so as not to cry for him and his family, for she hadn't wanted *him* to have to comfort *her,* she who had lived out the war in the safety of Villa L'Ambrosiana. How could she show emotion when he showed none?

She, too, had focused her eyes on the river, allowing Ezra time and silence in which to speak. When he'd finished, she'd taken his hand and they'd sat there together, staring at the light bouncing off the water, without saying a word. After a long while he had held her against his chest, the only person he had left in the world, and murmured, 'Thank you.'

Now, in the darkness of her berth, Evelina cried. She cried for Ezra, for Ercole and Olga, Fioruccia and Matteo, and for their entire family. She cried too for the millions of souls swallowed into that vortex of evil. Then she questioned the God that had allowed it to happen.

Dan and Aldo were excited to be in Italy. Everything was new and different, and their questions were like gunfire, loud and unceasing. Tani picked them up at the station in Vercellino. He was older now. His hair had thinned and his face acquired a gauntness it hadn't had before. He ruffled the boys' hair and spoke to them in Italian, and then chided his daughter for not having taught them their native tongue. 'I tried,' she explained, watching him lift her suitcase into the trunk. 'But it's easier to speak the language everyone else is speaking.' When at last they arrived at Villa L'Ambrosiana her mother and Benedetta rushed out of the house to welcome her home. Artemisia's hair had turned grey. It was still long and curly, but time had stolen its thickness and lustre. Her face, however, had grown more handsome with age. She looked like a beautiful bird of prey with her aquiline nose and incisive gaze. The women embraced and then Evelina introduced her sons to their grandmother and aunt. Artemisia crushed them against her perfumed chest. Dan pulled a face, but Aldo was polite and tried to remember some Italian from the little his mother had spoken to him. Benedetta took the boys off to find her children who were playing in the garden.

Costanza was sitting on the terrace dressed in black, smoking a cigarette and drinking a glass of wine. Evelina had never seen her wear black. She looked unfamiliar, like a vulture perched there on her own, hunched over her wine glass. 'She wants to die,' Artemisia told Evelina out of the corner of her mouth. 'She says she cannot live without her sister.'

'I'll go and talk to her,' said Evelina, walking over to greet her.

Costanza lifted her heavy eyes to her great-niece and managed a sad little smile. 'Ah, Evelina. So you haven't forgotten us, after all.'

Evelina pulled up a chair and sat down beside her. Costanza took her hand in her old one. Evelina noticed that she hadn't even bothered to paint her nails. Her hair looked as if it hadn't been brushed in a long time and was pinned onto the top of her head simply to keep it off her face rather than in any particular style. It was slate grey with wide streaks of white, as pale as ash. Her eyes were still a beautiful shade of hazel and the light within them had not yet dimmed. 'I would never forget you,' Evelina reassured her. 'I only regret that I never got to see Nonna again.'

'She passed away peacefully in her sleep,' said Costanza, patting Evelina's hand. 'I'm sure she's waiting at the Gates of Heaven for me to join her before stepping inside. That's the sort of sister she was, you see. Always thinking about others, especially me. I never married because I didn't need to. I always had her. And I didn't want anyone else. She was my soulmate, you see, and I'm nothing without her.'

'That's not true, Costi. She wouldn't want you to be sad. She'd certainly wonder why you're wearing black.'

'I'm waiting for the Grim Reaper to reap me,' she said, flicking ash into the ashtray.

'But you've never worn black before.'

'I'm wearing it in honour of my sister.'

'She died two months ago. I'm sure she'd like to see you wear colour again. You've always looked so glamorous in colour.'

'I think those days are over, darling. I'm old and tired. Yes, I'm very tired. I'd like to lie in a cool grave and sleep for eternity.'

Evelina laughed. 'I'd like to give you a manicure.'

'Would you?' Costanza frowned. 'There's really no point anymore. When you're past it, you're past it and there's no going back. Who's to care whether my nails are painted or bare?'

'I care.'

Costanza let go of her hand and ran her fingers down Evelina's face. 'You're sweet. You were always sweet. Though, a little naughty. Tell me, how is life treating you in America? Is it true that the pizza is better there?'

'No, it's not better there, but it's pretty good.'

'What is your husband called?'

'Franklin.'

'That's it. He was handsome, I remember.'

'I've brought two of my children with me. Aldo and Dan. I can't wait for you to meet them.'

'I wish your grandmother had met them. She loved children.' Costanza sighed. 'Children loved her too. They've always been a bit suspicious of me. But they always loved her. How many do you have?'

'Three.'

'Yes, that's right. I forget things, you know. They go in one ear and out the other and only the odd thing stays in the middle. Usually the least important thing. That's the way it is. Your grandmother never forgot anything. She was particularly good at cards, right up to the end. She was as cunning as a fox. She didn't look cunning. Oh, she fooled everyone because she was round and soft with a sweet smile. Everyone thought *I* was the cunning one. But she was far more cunning than me. I had lovers, many lovers, and I don't regret one of them.' She screwed up her nose. 'Well, that's not quite true. One or two I could have done without. But if I told you that your grandmother had had a lover during her marriage to your grandfather, would you believe me?'

'I don't think I would, Costi,' said Evelina, wondering where this conversation was heading.

'You see. A wily fox was your grandmother and she

managed to fool the lot of you.' Costanza laughed. She stubbed out her cigarette and fumbled in her purse for another one. 'Did you bring . . . what's his name again?'

'Franklin?'

'Franklin. Did you bring Franklin with you?'

'No, just the boys.'

Costanza arched her eyebrows. 'Are you a good wife, Evelina?'

'Yes, Costi, I am.'

'Good. I don't want you getting ideas now that I've spilled the beans about your grandmother.'

'I won't.'

Costanza puffed on her cigarette as it caught the flame of her lighter and glowed crimson. She looked at her nails. 'You think you could do something with these?'

'I'm sure I can,' said Evelina. 'I think Nonna would want you to have red nails.'

'Maybe. But first, where are those children of yours?'

'Good question,' said Evelina, getting up.

'They're finding their roots,' said Costi, and noticing that her wine glass was empty, she looked around for the maid to bring her another bottle.

Evelina took more pleasure from this trip than she had when she'd come with Franklin just after they were married. Now that Ezra was back in her life she did not mourn him. She did not cycle into town and search for his ghost through the glass window of Ercole Zanotti's old shop. Nor did she venture with trepidation into the chapel and remember, for Ezra was no longer in the past, but in her present and her future. She was able to enjoy being at Villa L'Ambrosiana, liberated from the burdens of loss and regret, from the weight of memory and sorrow, anticipating her trip to Florence with a heart full of joyful expectation.

She went to visit her grandmother's grave. Nonna Pierangelini was buried in the family crypt in the cemetery in Vercellino, with Bruno, her husband and the sons she had lost when they were small. Evelina had picked a bunch of flowers in the garden, wild flowers, the kind she knew her grandmother would like. She put them in a vase, replacing the wilted ones which were already there. Then she closed her eyes and said a prayer. She realized, as she read the inscriptions on the plates, that her name would never be among them. When she died, she'd be buried in New York somewhere. The first Pierangelini, she imagined. Far from home.

Benedetta had agreed to look after the boys while she was away. No one questioned why she should want to go down to Florence and visit friends she had met in New York. The secret of a good lie is to give a half-truth. This is what Evelina did. She explained that she had a friend who worked for a luthier in Brooklyn. She, the luthier and his wife were going to be in Tuscany and had invited her to join them. Evelina had been to Florence a few times in her youth and she was very keen to go again. However, it wasn't the time to take the children as they were too young to appreciate it. There was an awful moment when Artemisia suggested she might join her, but that idea was quickly snuffed out by Benedetta who thought it impolite of her mother to invite herself, and besides, a week without their mother would give Artemisia time to get to know her American grandsons, and teach them some Italian.

Evelina had arranged to meet Ezra in a small *pensione* in the centre of Florence, near the Piazza del Duomo. She took the train from Vercellino to Milan and then from Milan to Florence. Her stomach was churning with nerves and it was tremendously hot. She wasn't able to concentrate on her book, so she fanned herself and looked out of the window instead, imagining how her life might have been had Ezra not been arrested. This week in Florence would give her a taste of the path not taken.

Florence was busy with tourists. Sensible Italians had left for the beaches, but foreigners braved the heat to see the famous Duomo and Medici treasures. Evelina took a taxi to the *pensione*. She looked down at her dress, creased from her travels, and wished she had chosen to wear something other than linen that crumpled so. It was early evening, but the sun burned with intensity, baking the buildings to a rich golden colour so that even the shady parts where it couldn't reach sweltered and gave no relief. Evelina wiped her face with a handkerchief and fanned herself madly. Florence was beautiful in the copper light but she was too distracted to notice, thinking only of Ezra and hoping he'd be there. She thought of Franklin then. But now was not the time to dwell on her infidelity. If the devil had set her a trap, she'd stepped right into it.

The taxi drove down a narrow street and pulled up. Evelina paid the driver and thanked him as he lifted her bag out of the trunk. She stood in front of the brown door, built into an elaborately decorated stone arch. On the right was a list of bells. She was about to press one when she felt a hand on her shoulder. She spun round. There, smiling down at her, was Ezra.

Relieved, she threw her arms around him. He lifted her off her feet, squeezing her so hard she could barely breathe. 'You made it!' he laughed.

She gazed up at him, drinking him in, every precious detail. 'I can't believe we're here,' she said. 'Just you and me and for a whole week!'

He lifted her suitcase. 'Come, let me show you where we're staying and then we're going to wander around Florence and watch the sun set over the Arno.'

The door opened into a pretty courtyard adorned with pink bougainvillea and faded pots of olive trees. In the centre was an old well, now a charming ornament filled with geraniums and a large black-and-white cat that watched them warily. An old lady in an apron was sweeping the cobbles in the sunshine. She stopped her labour to greet them. 'Good evening, Signor Zanotti,' she said, then nodding at Evelina, she added, 'signora.'

'Good evening, Signora Bianchi,' said Ezra cheerfully. 'My wife has arrived at last.'

Evelina was struck by the ease with which he referred to her as his wife. She felt her cheeks redden from the lie, and yet, with all her heart, she wished that it were true.

Signora Bianchi smiled. 'Good. Florence is not a city to enjoy on one's own.'

'It so lovely to be here,' said Evelina, following Ezra up the stone stair. At the top, Ezra put his key in the lock and pushed open the door. Inside was a simple bedroom and bathroom, with views onto the street and over the rooftops of Florence. 'It's perfect,' Evelina gasped.

'And so are you,' said Ezra, dropping her suitcase and taking her in his arms. 'Florence can wait.'

That evening they strolled around the city, hand in hand, just as Evelina had imagined they would. It felt wonderful to be in this magical place together, far from home. Here, she could pretend she was married to Ezra. She could forget herself and her attachments, and live a different life. Perhaps this is what it might have been like had Ezra not been captured. They would have held hands and kissed for all the world to see. There would have been no hiding, no sneaking about, no guilt. They would have been free to love each other openly, just like this.

They wandered through the Piazza del Duomo, admiring the cathedral and Brunelleschi's famous dome. Then they sat at a table beneath a parasol, ordered dinner and shared a bottle of wine. Ezra played with her fingers as they talked. He ran his thumb over the soft skin on the back of her hand and traced the lines on her palm, all the while looking at her with love and disbelief. The fact that they were here together was both intoxicating and astonishing, and they gazed at each other with intensity, conscious that every moment was a gift that wouldn't last, and there was no need for words.

They were too late for the sunset over the Arno, but they watched the moonlight instead, and the glow of the city's lights reflected on the water in dazzling streaks of gold. Ponte Vecchio, the iconic bridge that straddled the river, was still and quiet beneath the canopy of stars. Ezra lifted Evelina onto the wall. He put his arms around her waist and kissed her. She brushed his hair off his face with her hands. 'I love you, Ezra,' she said.

'I love you, Eva,' he replied.

And they both knew that the healing power of love and only love could penetrate those dark and troubled places and transmute them into light.

CHAPTER NINETEEN

Time moved slowly as if the Universe conspired to give Evelina and Ezra endless days and nights in which to enjoy one another. They didn't stay in the city, but took a bus out into the countryside to lie on the grass and make shapes out of clouds, just like they had done before the war turned those clouds to ash. They swam in a lake, made love on the bank and ate spaghetti in a small trattoria where the only other customers were a pair of old men playing chess.

On the final day, Ezra took Evelina to the market in Florence to buy her a gift. He wanted to find a keepsake that would always remind her of this week. They knew they would never get the chance to do this again. They would return to New York. To snatched moments in Ezra's apartment in Brooklyn. To the odd walk in the park, perhaps, but their wings would once more be clipped and their lives would reclaim them.

They wandered down the aisles between stalls selling leather goods, fruit, cheese, jewellery and religious icons. Evelina's hand was in Ezra's. He held it tightly as if they hadn't a care in the world, yet both sensed the time running out. They tried not to waste a moment of their last day worrying about parting. They stopped at a stand selling gold jewellery. Evelina began to browse. Everything was so pretty, but nothing felt personal. Evelina didn't want him to give her an ordinary bracelet or an ordinary necklace, she wanted something that would make her think of him.

Then Ezra spotted it, tucked away behind other pendants hanging on chains. 'Can we try this?' he asked the seller.

The man popped his cigarette between his lips and unhooked it. 'Twenty-four-carat gold,' he told them. 'The only six-pointed star I have.'

Evelina lifted her hair so that Ezra could fix the clasp. Then she looked at herself in the little mirror the seller had placed on the counter. The star rested against her chest and she ran her fingers over it in delight. 'I love it,' she said happily.

It was such a simple thing. No diamonds, no engraving, just a plain Magen David, a symbol of Judaism. 'We'll take it,' said Ezra.

Evelina put her arms around him and kissed him. 'I'll wear it always,' she told him. She did not think Franklin was the sort of man who would notice a new necklace, certainly not a simple one such as this.

'If we'd married I would have bought you one made of diamonds,' said Ezra.

'I wouldn't want one made of diamonds. I'd want one just like this.'

Just then Evelina heard someone call her name. She sprang away from Ezra and turned to see who had spoken.

'Evelina!' A plump woman with grey hair and a big smile was making her way towards her. 'It is Evelina Pierangelini, isn't it?'

Evelina recognized her at once. It was her mother's friend Giulia Benotti, the one she'd classified as a goose, with her honking laugh and pushy nature. Evelina felt herself go red. Had Giulia seen her kissing Ezra? 'Giulia, what a surprise!' said Evelina, walking towards her in the hope of putting some distance between her and Ezra, and kissing her sweaty cheek.

'What are you doing in Florence? I thought you lived in America.'

'I do. I'm just here visiting.'

Giulia settled her sharp eyes on Ezra, who was paying for the necklace. 'And who's the handsome young man?' Ezra turned and smiled nonchalantly. Giulia gasped. 'Ezra Zanotti?' She narrowed her eyes and put a hand to her breast. 'Madonna! It's not possible!'

Ezra took her hand and brought it to his lips. 'Signora Benotti,' he said.

'You were a boy when I last saw you. Before the war ... before ...' She looked at him as if he'd just stepped out of the grave. 'I thought ...' She turned her feverish gaze to Evelina, searching for an explanation.

'I thought so too,' said Evelina calmly. 'I'm here visiting friends and we bumped into each other. Such a coincidence.'

'I settled here after the war,' Ezra lied. 'After what happened, I couldn't return to Vercellino.'

Giulia gasped again, as if she understood the full horror of what he had been through. 'Of course you couldn't. Terrible, just terrible. What they did to ... I mean, your family. Terrible. Words cannot express ...' She smiled uncertainly at Evelina, a wild look in her eyes. 'It's lovely to see you, my dear. What a delightful surprise. You must come for dinner ...'

Evelina feigned disappointment. 'I'm afraid I'm leaving tomorrow morning. I've left my children with Mamma and

Benedetta, so I must go and collect them before heading
back to America.' She took Giulia's hand, hoping that she'd
managed to convince her with her story. 'It's such a bonus
to see you, Giulia.'

'A coincidence. I do love coincidences. I don't suppose
I'll see you again, now you live on the other side of the
world. I suppose you came back because ...' She hesitated.
The furrows on her forehead deepened with sympathy. 'I'm
sorry about your grandmother. Nonna Pierangelini was a
very special lady.'

'Thank you.'

'Very hard for Costanza. They were always a pair, always.
Well, I'd better hurry. Eugenio will be wondering where I
am.' She glanced at Ezra then back to Evelina. 'You didn't
bring your husband with you?'

'No, he couldn't leave work. It's lucky that I bumped into
Ezra, otherwise I'd have been wandering around this market
on my own.'

Giulia disguised her confusion behind a wobbly smile.
'Oh yes, very lucky.'

'Well, we must find the rest of our party,' said Ezra. 'It's
been a pleasure seeing you again, signora.'

'And you too.' Giulia put a plump hand on his arm.
'I'm glad you've ... you know, that you've settled here in
Florence. Lovely, just lovely.' She bade them goodbye and
then bustled off, disappearing into the crowd.

Evelina took a deep breath. 'Do you think she saw?'

Ezra scratched his head. 'Perhaps. She was certainly
electrified.'

'That's because she thought you were dead.'

'Resurrections do tend to put people off balance.'

'She was like a rabbit in headlights. Poor thing.'

'She'll scuttle back now and tell your mother, so you'd better think up a good story.'

'Hopefully she'll be too taken up with your survival to make a story out of seeing the two of us together.'

'Don't count on it. That woman's a gossip. I remember her from the shop. Giulia "*bocca*" Benotti.'

Evelina laughed. 'You called her "*bocca*"?'

'We had the odd nickname for our clients. "Mouth" suited her rather well.'

'What did you call my mother?'

'We didn't.'

Evelina wasn't convinced. 'Really?'

'She was too beautiful to have a nickname, and a good client. My parents only had the greatest respect for her.'

Evelina linked her arm through his. 'Thank you for the necklace, Ezra.'

'It's a pleasure.' He smiled down at her. 'I don't know about you, but I'm hungry. What do you say we find a nice restaurant and have some dinner?'

'I need a drink,' said Evelina.

'So do I.' They set off across the square. 'I should think Bocca Benotti needs one too!'

The following morning Ezra accompanied Evelina to the train station. Evelina was wearing her gold star, it lay against her chest above a heavy heart. 'I'll see you back in New York,' he said, holding her tightly.

'I can't believe it's over.' She closed her eyes, squeezing back tears.

'It's not over. It's only just begun.'

'You know what I mean.'

'No, you mustn't think like that.'

'But I want more.'

He smiled down at her with tenderness. 'You'll always want more.'

'Don't you?'

He shrugged. 'I'll accept what I'm given.'

'I suppose when you've been resurrected, any kind of life is a gift.'

'*You're* in my life, Eva. I never thought I'd see you again. *That* is a gift.'

Evelina cried quietly as the train pulled out of the station. She watched the city through the glass and wondered whether she'd ever see Florence again. It had been a perfect week and now it was over. Her heart ached so much she put a hand there to soothe it. She pictured Ezra as she had last seen him, waving at her on the platform, and knew that she should be grateful, as he was, for the fact that they could see each other at all. The trouble was, it wasn't enough. She wanted to wake up with him *every* morning and kiss him goodnight *every* night. She'd had a taste of it now; snatched lunch breaks in Brooklyn would no longer satisfy.

As the train steamed through the Italian countryside, Evelina thought of divorce. She'd never even considered it before, but now she'd spent a week with Ezra, the word floated into her mind like bait on the end of the devil's rod. Franklin would survive. He was pretty much married to his job anyhow. As for the children, well, children were resilient, weren't they? As long as they were loved, they'd be fine. Evelina tried to convince herself that they would survive anything too.

Evelina arrived at Villa L'Ambrosiana in the late afternoon. Aldo and Dan were waiting on the steps with

Benedetta's children, jumping about like frogs. When they saw their mother, they flew into her arms. Neither could stop talking, eager to tell her what they'd been up to while she was away. Aldo proudly showed off his Italian. Dan had learned to swear.

Evelina had done what Ezra suggested and worked out a convincing story to tell her mother, in anticipation of Giulia Benotti reporting that she'd seen them. She slipped it out over dinner with a vague and careless expression on her face. 'Do you know who I bumped into in Florence?'

'Who?' said Artemisia.

'Ezra Zanotti.'

'No!' Artemisia gasped. Tanni put down his wine glass.

Costanza uttered, 'Madonna!' Her hand with its perfectly manicured scarlet nails shot to her mouth.

Benedetta looked at her sister and narrowed her eyes. 'What happened to him?'

'He survived Auschwitz,' said Evelina evenly. 'He was the only one in his family to survive.'

Tani shook his head. There were no words for the barbarity of what the Nazis had done.

'How terrible,' said Artemisia, sounding like Giulia Benotti.

'I remember him as a little boy,' said Costanza. 'Handsome.'

'You were once in love with him,' said Benedetta. She was watching her sister carefully.

'I was,' Evelina replied with a laugh and a shake of the head, as if she couldn't imagine what she had ever seen in him.

'Did he marry?' Artemisia asked.

'No,' said Evelina. 'I didn't ask whether or not he had a girlfriend. I thought that would be prying.'

'He lives there, does he, in Florence?' asked Tani.

'Yes.'

'I suppose there was nothing left for him here,' Tani added.

'Ercole Zanotti is now a café,' said Costanza. 'It was better as Ercole Zanotti.'

'What does he do?' Tani asked.

'I don't know. I didn't really see that much of him. We bumped into each other at the market. I also bumped into Giulia Benotti.'

Artemisia smiled. 'How nice. They have a house down there. Although, I can't imagine what they're doing in Florence in August. Much too hot, I would think.'

'They have a lovely villa with a pool,' said Costanza. 'She told me all about it. I'm sure she sits in the water like a hippo and heads into town in the cool of evening.' Costanza laughed through her nose. 'Just like a hippo.'

Evelina was satisfied that she had diffused any suggestion that Giulia Benotti might make about her and Ezra on her return from Florence. She could just see her at the card table with her mother, causing trouble. Now her mother would be able to explain that it was an innocent encounter. Evelina was safe.

Benedetta, on the other hand, was not so easily fooled. Evelina knew that love emanated from her like perfume and that Benedetta could smell it. But she did not react to her sister's arched eyebrow, or to the way her eyes lingered on hers in the hope of catching a glimmer of guilt or a gleam of admission. Those days of shared confidences were long gone. But if Benedetta remembered anything of Evelina's affection for Ezra she would know that it was a flame that had never been extinguished.

*

The voyage back to New York was an easy one. The boys loved being on the boat again and played happily with the other children. Evelina had been sad to say goodbye to her family, especially as she didn't know when she would see them again. Costanza had waved her off from the villa steps, just like her sister had done, but unlike Nonna Pierangelini, Costanza was wearing colour again. Benedetta had hugged her fiercely and Evelina had wished suddenly that they had wandered arm in arm around the garden like they had done in their youth, and shared their secrets. She wished, now that she was leaving with no plan to ever come back, that she had shared her secret with Benedetta.

Artemisia had cried. In the old days Evelina would have accused her mother of putting it on for dramatic effect, but this time she had looked genuinely sorry, and Evelina had felt a lump in her throat, a lump which had grown thicker when she'd said farewell to her father at the port. Tani had embraced her fondly, holding her for longer than usual. 'You take care of yourself now,' he'd said. 'And write. We love to hear your news. Your letters keep us entertained for days.' Far from hiding in his study as he'd always done in the old days, during Evelina's visit he'd barely been there at all. It seemed that, with age, he'd finally recognized the value of family.

Evelina was excited to see Ava-Maria. She was less excited to see Franklin, who now stood between her and Ezra like an insurmountable obstacle. But he was happy to have her home and had bought her a beautiful bouquet of flowers as a homecoming present. He kissed her cheek and took her in with shiny eyes, full of affection. He had clearly missed her, perhaps more than he'd expected. He'd missed the boys too and delighted in the way they rushed into his arms, fighting over one another to tell him about their adventure. Ava-Maria, jealous of the attention her brothers were receiving, stamped her foot and wailed before storming out of the room and sobbing on the stairs, loudly, so everyone could hear. Evelina pulled her onto her knee and held her close. 'I've brought you some presents,' she told her and Ava-Maria immediately stopped crying.

Life swiftly returned to normal. Evelina went to see Aunt Madolina and Uncle Peppino for Sunday lunch the following day with Franklin and the children. Taddeo was there, as usual, and Alba without Antonio. Alba's children behaved badly, jumping up and down from the table and interrupting the adults when they were trying to talk. Alba was tense. She drank too much wine, smoked one cigarette after another, and made snide comments about her husband which were intended to go over her children's heads, but Evelina noticed the anxious look on the face of her eldest and knew that Chiara, at least, was much too smart not to be aware of the acrimony between her parents. Evelina looked across at Franklin who was deep in discussion with Peppino, and then at her children. The word 'divorce', which had seemed so bold with possibilities on the train back from Florence, now lost its potency as Evelina sensed the onset of resignation. What sort of mother would she be if she put her children through such a thing? She glanced across the table at Alba. It seemed inevitable that Alba would leave Antonio. Evelina did not want to be like her.

Evelina didn't see Ezra until the next day, but she sneaked out that evening and called him from the payphone, just to make sure he had arrived safely back in New York. On Monday morning she left the children with Zofia then headed into Brooklyn. The final days of August were punishing, the heat intense. She wore a light dress and sun-glasses and put her hair up in a ponytail. By the time she reached her station she was hot and perspiring.

Gandolfi's was closed for Giuseppe was still in Tuscany. Evelina wished she were still in Tuscany too, but Ezra seemed not to be concerned. Evelina found his lack of frustration hard to understand. After making love they sat on the bed to drink the coffee she'd prepared. Ezra had bought pastries from the shop around the corner and tucked into one with relish. 'This is so good!' he exclaimed, closing his eyes and savouring the taste.

'Ezra,' she began.

'Yes?' he replied slowly, a wary tone in his voice.

She smiled. 'Why are you saying it like that?'

'Like what?'

'Like you know what's coming and you don't want to hear it.'

'How can I know what's coming? I'm not a mind-reader.'

'I think you're pretty good at reading mine.'

'Oh no. You, Eva, you're as cryptic as the Sphinx.'

She laughed. 'I wish we were still in Florence. I wish we could walk around the city together, like an ordinary couple.'

He shook his head. 'You're like the woman in the vinegar bottle.'

'Who's she?'

'The woman who lives in a vinegar bottle. She gets given a wish from a frog.'

'It's always frogs,' said Evelina, biting into a croissant.

'Well, at least she doesn't have to kiss it.'

'It's not about a prince then?'

'No, it's about greed.'

'Oh.' Evelina stopped chewing.

'So, she asks for curtains because everyone can see into her vinegar bottle. When she returns home, her bottle has curtains.'

'You're going to tell me she's not satisfied.'

'She is for a while, but then she thinks it would be nice to have a bed.'

'Of course. Every woman needs a bed.'

'She goes back and asks the frog if he wouldn't mind giving her a bed. This he does, and, for a time she's very grateful for her bed.'

'But she wants more.' Evelina could see where this was going.

'She does. She summons the frog from his pond and asks for chairs and a table and perhaps a kitchen too.'

'He gives her all of that? He's a generous frog.'

'It's magic, so it's really nothing for him.'

'Okay, so then what does she ask for?'

'She demands clothes. I mean, how can she entertain her new friends in her new vinegar bottle, if she hasn't got nice clothes to wear?'

'He falls for that, does he?'

'*She* falls for it, in fact.' Ezra grinned at her. 'The frog tells her to go back to her vinegar bottle and she will find everything there that she deserves. She returns to find only the bottle, as it originally was.'

'And the frog?'

'I think he packed his bags and hopped off to find a different pond.'

'So your point is that I should be happy with what I have.'

'Yes. Accept life as it is and be grateful for what you have. Appreciate that we're here in this fantastic city, together. We might never have found each other.'

'Don't you want to be with me?'

'Of course I want to be with you. But I can't marry you. You're already married. Therefore, it's futile to wish for something I cannot have. It will only make me unhappy, and I decided when I emerged from Hell that I would never again take my freedom for granted, or any of life's other gifts.'

'What if I divorced?' Evelina hadn't planned on mentioning this to him, but she was curious to see his reaction. However, he did not give her the one she wanted.

He looked at her seriously. 'You have to think very carefully about that, Eva. You'll hurt four people in the process, and yourself as well. Divorces are minefields with mines in the places you least expect them.'

'Are you putting me off?' Evelina was affronted.

'I'm opening your eyes to the consequences.'

She folded her arms. 'Don't you want to be with me?'

'Eva, I'd marry you tomorrow if you were free.'

'I can become free.'

He sighed, unconvinced. 'You can—'

'Didn't those months in the camp teach you also that life is short?' she interrupted. 'That you need to live it as you want to, not as other people want you to, but for yourself? That sometimes you have to be selfish? That life is too short to waste being unhappy?'

'You're *not* unhappy, Evelina. You have three beautiful children, a comfortable home and a husband who loves you. I imagine that, before I appeared, you loved him. I think you still do. There are many ways of loving.'

'You cannot love me if that is how you feel! If you loved me you'd be desperate for me to divorce. You'd be begging me!'

'I *do* love you, Eva,' he insisted. 'I can't imagine *not* loving you, because you're part of me. But I'm not going to ask you to destroy the lives of your family just so that I can have you for myself. I would have once, but that's not who I am now. We cannot build our happiness on the pain of others.'

Evelina felt like Ava-Maria. She wanted to stamp her foot and run out of the room in tears. But she didn't. She drained her coffee cup and climbed off the bed. 'So, how do you see us in ten years' time?' she asked, taking her cup into the kitchen for a refill.

'I don't want to look that far ahead,' he said, lighting a cigarette.

'Okay, six months from now. Is that too far ahead for you?'

'A bit.' He blew out a cloud of smoke.

'Do you see us living like this? Snatching moments to be together? Is this what our lives are going to be like? Sneaking around like thieves?'

'Accept the vinegar bottle, Eva,' Ezra said and he wasn't joking.

'You're not a frog!' she retorted crossly.

'That's because you've kissed me and turned me into a prince.'

His smile was irresistible. She padded back into the bedroom and curled up in the armchair in the corner, hugging her knees. 'Before you appeared I was happy,' she reflected. 'Franklin is self-obsessed. His life is his work. Me and the kids, we're secondary. But that was fine. It was the way it was and I didn't question it. But now you're here, I can see a better way to live. I'm not like the woman in the vinegar bottle. I'm not wanting material things. I don't care about fine clothes and jewellery ...' She touched the star at her chest. As she predicted, Franklin hadn't noticed it. 'Except for this, of course.' She took a breath, surprised at the anxiety building in her chest. 'I care about *you*, Ezra. That's all I want. I just want to be with you, always. It's what I wanted when I was seventeen and it's what I want now. It's what I'll always want.' She looked at him with longing, hoping that he'd say he wanted her too. 'What do *you* want?' she asked and she felt her throat tighten. 'And don't say you want nothing. That you have everything you want. That your experience has taught you that you only need freedom to be content . . . I want you to tell me that you want *me*.'

He smiled indulgently. 'I want you to come over here so I can make love to you.'

'That's not an answer.'

'It's the only answer I can give you.'

'It's not good enough.'

'Eva—'

'It's not fair. You come back into my life and turn my world upside down and yet, you can't even tell me what you want. Where this is going. I'm being unfaithful to my husband, sneaking into Brooklyn every day to see you. I have a right to know what's in your head.'

Ezra sighed and stubbed out his cigarette. Then he looked at her steadily, holding her gaze with his honest, open one. 'I *do* want you. I want you and I love you, Eva. But I don't *need* you. That's the truth.'

'But *I* need *you*, Ezra,' Evelina said tearfully, wounded by his words. 'If the war taught me anything, it taught me to hold on to those you love because you never know when they might be taken away.'

Ezra got up from the bed and went over to hold her in his arms. 'Don't misunderstand me, Eva. I'm trying to tell you that I'm satisfied with the gift that is you. I'm not asking for more.' He kissed her temple and then cupped her face and looked into her eyes. 'I'm not going anywhere, Eva. I'm here. I'm always going to be here, waiting for you.'

CHAPTER TWENTY

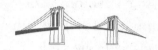

Evelina could not get Ezra's words out of her mind.

I don't need you. That's the truth.

How could he love her and not need her? Didn't the two go together? Evelina loved him and, because she loved him, she needed to be with him. She couldn't live without him, it was as simple as that, and yet, *he* seemed able to live without *her*. As if he could take her or leave her.

I don't need you. That's the truth.

That lack of urgency and craving was incomprehensible to Evelina who was consumed by both. The more she tried to get used to it, the less she made sense of it. How could he not need her? What did he mean? Was his love less intense than hers? Or was she simply weaker in the face of it?

But I can't marry you. You're already married.

If she were no longer married, would he marry her? Was it because of Franklin that he refused to fight for her? Was he afraid of being the reason for the break-up of her marriage and the splintering of her family? Afraid of having the weight of other people's unhappiness on his shoulders? Is that what he meant: I don't need you because I don't *want* to need you? As a result of losing everyone close to him, was he afraid of being dependent? Was his apparent detachment from need simply a way of protecting himself from the dependency of love?

Then Evelina would divorce Franklin without telling him. He'd be free of responsibility.

However, Alba got there first. She announced at Sunday lunch, when the children had got down from the table to play, that she had asked Antonio for a divorce. Madolina went white. Peppino asked her whether it was absolutely necessary. 'Have you tried?' he said.

'Of course I've tried, Daddy,' she retorted, looking at him in astonishment. 'The question you should be asking is, has *he*? The answer to that is, no, he hasn't.'

'I'm sorry,' said Evelina gently, feeling as if the wind had been taken out of her sails. 'I know how hard you've tried.'

'Thank you, Evelina,' Alba said pointedly. 'I appreciate your understanding.'

'I'm just sad for the children,' said Madolina. 'It's always the children who are wounded in the crossfire.'

'They'll be fine. They're robust,' said Alba carelessly.

Franklin caught Evelina's eye. She knew that he was thinking the same thing she was. That children are never robust enough to come out of a divorce unscathed, they just carry on in spite of their wounds. She looked back at Alba. Alba with her red lips and short blonde hair, fashionably curled. Alba with her conspicuous gold jewellery, diamonds and expensive clothes. Alba, the woman in the vinegar bottle. Was divorce one wish too many?

'Children appear to be fine because they have no other choice,' Madolina continued. 'What can they do but accept what they're given? Then they spend a lifetime fighting the feelings of worthlessness and instability, not to mention issues with trust and even love that divorce heaps upon them.'

'Lots of people divorce and the children survive,' Alba argued.

'But surviving is only a basic requirement of life. We can all survive most things,' said Madolina in her forthright manner. 'Whether we can still find a way to enjoy ourselves and prosper is another matter.'

'Alba needs to prosper too,' said Taddeo sensibly. 'There is always the saying, life's too short. In which case, what is the point of spending the best part of one's life being miserable? And sometimes kids pick up on their parents' misery and that affects them too.'

Alba laughed bitterly. 'Oh, me and Antonio, we shout at each other all the time. The kids need earplugs.'

'I think Alba knows what's best for her and her family,' said Evelina. Alba grinned at her, grateful for her support.

'No, she doesn't,' said Peppino firmly. 'Sometimes a person is too close to see the situation clearly.' He looked at his daughter. The same look, Evelina imagined, that he gave his employees in the air-conditioning factory. 'You have a nice life. Most girls can only dream of the life you live. You have a nice home, a nice car, nice clothes and jewellery, nice holidays and a nice family. You want for nothing, Alba. So, Antonio strays a little here and there and you don't like it. How about you turn a blind eye and see if the problem doesn't go away by itself.'

Alba sucked in her cheeks. 'What do you think I've been doing for the past five years, huh? Turning a blind eye! He has no respect, Daddy. None at all. Oh, he's all over me when he needs to be. I'm rolled out like a trophy when he needs to show off his wife and kids, all done up to the nines. He thinks another diamond necklace will keep me sweet. Well, I've got enough diamond necklaces to sink a ship! I don't need any more and I don't need him.'

That word 'need' again, Evelina thought bleakly.

'What did he say when you told him you wanted a divorce?' Franklin asked.

'That he'll fight me all the way.'

'That's what I feared,' said Peppino. He shook his head. 'You don't want to fight with the Genovese family.'

'They're rich, so what?' said Alba crossly.

'They're Mafia,' said Peppino.

There was silence. Even Taddeo had nothing funny to say about that. Again, Franklin caught Evelina's eye. He gave her a look, the kind of look that indicated support, conspiracy and perhaps gratitude that Alba's problem was not theirs.

'I think you need to tread with care,' said Madolina.

'Madolina's right,' said Taddeo. 'There's no reason to rush into anything.'

'I need a good attorney,' said Alba. 'A fierce one. You should know me by now. Once I've got an idea into my head, I run with it. And there's no stopping me!'

Evelina and Franklin waited until they were home, alone, before they discussed Alba and Antonio's divorce. With the boys safely out of earshot and Ava-Maria in front of the television, they went into the sitting room and closed the door. 'I think it's selfish,' said Franklin, settling into an armchair and lighting a cigarette. 'I couldn't say it at the table. It's not my place. But Alba has always been selfish.'

'Doesn't she deserve to be happy?' Evelina asked, sitting on the sofa and crossing her legs.

'She made her vows before God. I think she's throwing in the towel without much thought for those around her who are going to be hurt.'

'Maybe she's right. Children are resilient. They survive.'

'But at what cost?'

'I don't know.' Evelina tried to think of someone who was divorced, but she couldn't think of anyone. 'I just think there has to be a way out.'

'Marriage is for life. It's not always easy, but one has to work at it and overcome the difficulties, not only for the sake of the children, but also for the sake of the family as a whole. I think I'd put up with a lot to keep my family together.' He looked at her and smiled. Evelina felt guilty. How little he knew her.

She averted her eyes. 'I don't think you'd be happy with me running around with other men.'

'Of course not. No man wants to be a cuckold. But freedom within a marriage is an important, if not vital, component. Jealousy debases a person. Alba should turn a blind eye, in my opinion, and find a way to work with the situation instead of breaking herself against it.'

'Or maybe take a lover of her own.' Evelina chuckled at the irony.

'Perhaps.' Evelina was surprised that Franklin agreed. He noticed her bewildered expression. 'As I said, marriage isn't always easy. They need to find a solution that works for both parties. I somehow doubt Antonio would allow Alba to take a lover.' He smiled. 'I wouldn't want *you* taking a lover, either, so don't go getting any ideas, now.'

Evelina laughed uneasily. 'Of course not.'

'I just think in Antonio and Alba's case, they need to give each other certain freedoms.'

'It's a very unusual person who would agree to that.'

'The French,' said Franklin, drawing on his cigarette.

'Not the Italians,' said Evelina firmly. She sighed. 'I think it's going to be a long-drawn-out fight, and we're going to hear a lot about it.'

Franklin flicked ash into the tray. 'I'm glad it's not my problem. Life is hard enough without having to go through a divorce.'

It was then that Evelina realized that the idea of divorce for Franklin was as remote as the idea of building a house on the moon: it had never crossed his mind. She watched him open the newspaper and lose himself in an article. And she knew that Ezra was right. She wasn't unhappy. She loved Ezra and she needed him, but she wasn't unhappy with Franklin. There were, indeed, many different ways of loving.

A few days later, Evelina was at the kitchen table, listening to the radio while she mended Franklin's old coat, when she heard the familiar music of the *Mamma Forte* weekly show and then Aunt Madolina's unmistakable voice. Evelina put down her sewing and listened.

'Today I'm going to talk about divorce,' she said in her warm Italian-American accent. It sounded like tiramisu, Evelina thought. However, there was nothing sweet about her subject.

'I worry that the younger generation works less at making marriage work because it's easier to get out of and divorce carries less of a stigma nowadays than it once did. In my day divorce was not an option. It is still not recognized by the Catholic Church. "What therefore God hath joined together, let no man put asunder."' Madolina chuckled and took a breath. 'Divorce is like amputating a diseased limb. It's drastic, painful, and in marrying again you don't grow a new limb and there's always the chance that the disease will recur. What should be advised is to take time to work through one's differences. To give it a chance. Sometimes, if one hangs in there, one moves past the problem.

'We can all imagine how unsettling a divorce must be for children, but there have been various studies carried out recently that have concluded that the effects of divorce on children are far worse than any of us can imagine. The fear of future abandonment and rejection, emotional disturbance, maladjusted social behaviour, poor performance in school and the difficulty in forming attachments are just some of the problems these studies have highlighted. The trouble is we live in a society where people no longer have the sense of duty they once had, and pleasing oneself is increasingly becoming the Holy Grail – being happy is an attainable goal and must be pursued at any cost. Well, as you know, my lovely listeners, Mamma Forte says it like it is and I don't hide my meatballs under a mountain of spaghetti. Happiness *isn't* the Holy Grail and we *don't* all have a right to it. Sometimes we have to accept that we cannot have everything we want. Sometimes we have to put the welfare of others above our own selfish desires. Sometimes we just have to say, "No, I can't." It's about doing the right thing and living one's life with a sense of responsibility towards those little souls you have brought into the world.

'Now I know some of you aren't going to like hearing this. I don't mind being unpopular; someone has to say unpleasant truths. I'm a Catholic, but this isn't about religion, it's about basic human respect and love which applies to everyone. Before you dive headlong into divorce, ask yourself three questions: Have I really tried to resolve our differences? Do I really want to put my children through this? What is life going to be like for me on the outside? You loved each other once. If you look hard enough, I'm sure you'll find that love is still there.'

Evelina wondered whether Alba was listening to this. If she was, she had probably thrown a shoe at the radio!

That night when Evelina kissed her children, she remembered Aunt Madolina's words. *Do I really want to put my children through this?* Looking into their innocent faces, the answer was emphatically no.

Evelina couldn't sleep. She listened to Franklin breathing beside her and wished that he were Ezra. Her whole body ached for him; her arms ached to hold him; her legs ached to wrap themselves around him; her lips ached to kiss him. She tossed and turned, fearful that her restlessness would awaken her husband. The last thing she needed was for him to ask her if she was okay.

Eventually, she climbed out of bed, slipped into her dressing gown and scaled the fire escape to the roof. She lay on her back and looked up at the sky. It was a clear night. Stars glittered and a sickle moon shone with eerie radiance. She began to make patterns out of the stars. She could see the eyes of wild animals, lanterns of weary travellers, lights of distant ships. Then she was among them, floating in the darkness, weightless in space. She lost sight of the city around her and the feeling of the roof beneath her. She lost sight of who she was and where she was. She had no name, no history, no experience, no story. She was out of her body in the blackness, as light as a speck of dust, as tiny as a star. She savoured the marvellous sensation of just being, as Ezra had taught her to do.

At last Evelina's head cleared and a serenity came over her. With all her heart she wanted to be with Ezra, but she didn't want to hurt her children and she didn't want to hurt Franklin. When all was said and done, she did not resent Franklin, as much as she wanted to have someone to blame. Franklin loved her, even if he didn't show it very often. Theirs was a marriage that had moved swiftly into the familiar comfort and routine of domesticity and children. There was no romance anymore, or passion: there were no more long nights making love. But there was mutual respect, friendship and affection. No, she didn't resent him. Franklin had rescued her when she was lost in New York, and he had listened to her as she had struggled to come to terms with losing Ezra and leaving Italy. Franklin had been kind at a time when kindness had been more valuable to Evelina than gold. How could she even contemplate repaying that kindness with divorce?

When she thought about the future, it looked like a straight grey road ahead of her, disappearing into fog. She couldn't live like this for ever, taking the subway into Brooklyn, stealing an hour or so with Ezra and then returning home to be a mother and a wife. She just couldn't. And yet, there seemed to be no other way.

Confused by these thoughts, she called Taddeo the following morning and asked to meet him for lunch. Taddeo, as sharp as a pin, knew something was afoot just by the tone of her voice. No sooner had they sat down in the restaurant than he put his napkin on his knee, ordered a bottle of Pinot Grigio and said, 'Okay, Evelina, what's going on?' He spoke Italian, which he refrained from doing in Madolina's house. Madolina did not like to be drawn back to the Old Country after having spent so many years trying to shake it off. But Taddeo considered himself an Italian living in America and had cherry-picked the best of both cultures to suit his tastes. The language, in his opinion, was one of the best things about the Old Country, along with the food. Not even the best hamburger in America could beat a simple *spaghetti al pomodoro*.

'I have no one else to turn to but you,' Evelina said.

'You can count on me to be discreet,' he reassured her.

The waiter poured a little wine into Taddeo's glass. Taddeo didn't bother to taste it but waved his hand and waited while the waiter filled both their glasses then left. Evelina took a breath. 'I need to tell you about Ezra Zanotti,' she said and from the look on her face Taddeo knew that she was going to share something deep and intimate and ultimately painful. He did not make a joke, even though he had a gift for finding the comedy in the most dire circumstances. They ordered food and then he listened intently without saying a word.

Evelina told him the story from the beginning. How she had fallen in love in Vercellino, how Ezra had got engaged to Bruno's nanny, how they had finally come together when she was on the point of leaving for America. Then she told him of Mussolini's racial laws, the German occupation of the north of Italy, the round-up and exportation of Jews and of Ezra's capture and captivity in Auschwitz. Finally, she told him of the morning she'd been in the café waiting for Alba when he had walked in. Taddeo was astonished. 'Madonna!' he muttered. 'Risen from the dead.' Then Evelina confessed their affair. When she finished, she took a gulp of wine.

'I've told you everything,' she said with a sigh. She did, in fact, feel lighter for having shared it. 'Now I need your advice.'

The waiter brought their food and refilled their glasses. Then Taddeo leaned forward with his elbows on the table and rested his chin on his hands. 'I suppose you're thinking of divorce,' he said.

'It's crossed my mind,' Evelina confessed, ashamed to admit something so selfish. 'But I can't go through with it.

I don't want to hurt Franklin or the children. As Ezra said, we can't build our happiness on the pain of others.'

Taddeo nodded pensively. 'You can't have both Ezra *and* Franklin.'

'I know.' Evelina chuckled bitterly. 'I need two lives, two of me.'

'You can't have that either. What does Ezra say?'

'He told me that he loves me, but that he doesn't *need* me.' Evelina shrugged in confusion. She watched Taddeo's frown deepen. 'Does that make sense to you?' she asked.

'After the story you've just told me, I think it does.'

'How?'

'What does the word "need" mean to you?'

'That I have to have it. That I can't live without it.'

'I think it means something different to Ezra. I think it's about survival and acceptance. For Ezra it means that, after what he has lived through, which no human being should have to do, not even in Hell, he can survive being without you.'

'You mean, he can take me or leave me?'

'No, you're missing the point. You must try to understand him. He loves you, Evelina, like he said. But he's philosophical. You're married. He can't have you.'

'He's not going to fight for me.'

'What would be the point of that? He sounds like a good person, Evelina. A man who embraces life and is grateful for what it gives him. A man who has seen the ultimate pain and sacrifice and has moved beyond it to a place of acceptance and appreciation.'

'That sounds like Ezra.'

'He's not going to break up your marriage.'

'I want him to *want* to break up my marriage. I want

him to *want* to tear down the world for me. Even if he does neither, I want him to *want* to. I want him to *need* me like *I* need *him*.'

Taddeo smiled sympathetically. 'Evelina, real life isn't like the movies where the swashbuckling hero kills everyone who stands in his way and carries his beloved off into the sunset on a white stallion. Life isn't like that. People aren't like that. They're more complicated. You have to put this man into context. You have to understand what he's been through.'

'I'm stuck, aren't I?'

'You're *married*, Evelina,' he said with emphasis. 'Madolina's right. Sometimes you just have to say no.'

Evelina looked at him steadily, tears stinging. 'I can't live without him, Taddeo,' she whispered, her throat constricting again with emotion.

'No one's saying you have to live without him. He can be a part of your life, but you need to tell Franklin about him.'

Evelina's eyes widened in horror. 'You mean confess to an affair?'

'No, I wouldn't share that part of the story with him. But you need to let him know that Ezra is here and that you want him in your life. Not as a lover—'

'I can't have him as a lover?'

'But as a friend.' He took her hand across the table. 'As a dear, old friend.'

Evelina thought about this for a minute. 'I'm not sure I can live like that,' she said.

'It's either like that, or not having him in your life at all,' said Taddeo.

'I'm sure *he* could walk away without a backwards glance.'

'I wouldn't be too sure about that, Evelina.'

'I know *I* couldn't.'

'Then you have to compromise.'

'I hate that word.'

'We all do.'

'I'll think about it.'

'You do that.' Taddeo smiled and tucked into his gnocchi. He glanced at Evelina. 'And by the way, I'd be careful wearing that necklace if you're going to tell Franklin about Ezra. He's no fool.'

'Is it that obvious?'

'It's a Star of David. Who else but Ezra could have given it to you?'

Evelina did not want to make a decision. How could she choose to give up Ezra? She couldn't. How could she choose to divorce Franklin? She couldn't. So, she left the questions hanging in the air, unanswered, to think about at another time, when she *had* to think about them. She did not have to think about them at this moment.

Christmas came and went. It snowed in New York. The city looked beautiful draped in a sparkling white quilt, twinkling with fairy lights and ringing with the sound of carols. Evelina thought of Ezra on his own – not that he celebrated Christmas, being Jewish, but it was a time of family, of being together, and he had no one. Evelina wished she could include him in her family life like Madolina included Taddeo. Perhaps that was why Taddeo had suggested it, she wondered, because it was a situation that worked for him. Then Evelina was struck with a thought. Had Madolina and Taddeo been lovers? It was an outlandish thought, but suddenly it made sense. Madolina's aversion to divorce, the way she included Taddeo in every aspect of her life, the touching way they spoke to each other. Taddeo had told Evelina that she didn't have to live without Ezra. That he could still be a part of her life as a 'dear, old friend' – only not as a lover. That in itself was a strange suggestion. Anyone else would have told her to give Ezra up and to devote her time and attention to her husband and family. Only Taddeo would tell her that she could have both, if he had managed that kind of compromise himself.

Hadn't Taddeo and Madolina used the same phrase: Sometimes a person just has to say no? Was *that* the compromise that needed to be made? Evelina could no longer be Ezra's lover, but she could be his friend and embrace him into her family. If she loved him, wasn't that enough?

Evelina was going to ask Taddeo about it. She was certain he would give her an honest answer. However, she soon realized that she did not have to ask him, because she already knew. The veil had been lifted and Evelina saw the affection between her aunt and Taddeo displayed before her in all its simple joyfulness and she wondered whether it was possible for her and Ezra to ever reach such a beautiful compromise.

CHAPTER TWENTY-ONE

Alba was granted a divorce in spite of her parents' protestations. Evelina lived through the bitter feuding as Alba fought for more money than Antonio was prepared to give her. She telephoned Evelina at uncivilized times of the night and met her for coffee and lunch during the day to take her through the latest developments, using her cousin as a sounding board, a therapist and a shoulder to cry on when she felt overwhelmed. Evelina was putting so much energy into Alba and Ezra that she hadn't noticed how deflated Franklin had become. He was remote, as usual, working long hours at the university and in his study, but he was fundamentally tired. Evelina should have noticed and she should have encouraged him to go and see a doctor. But she hadn't. Franklin, therefore, took it upon himself to make an appointment without telling her – he didn't want to worry her with what he believed to be a minor concern. The doctor took his bloods and carried out other routine tests. The results were not dramatic. Franklin was anaemic and lacking in vitamin D. The doctor thought he might be fighting a virus. What would do him a lot of good, he said, was rest. 'The doctor has prescribed me a holiday,' Franklin told Evelina when he got home.

'You work too hard, that's the trouble,' said Evelina. 'That university works you to the bone.'

'I want to go away, just the two of us,' he announced with a smile.

Evelina's mind turned to Ezra. The thought of leaving him made her breathless.

Franklin sat down with a heavy sigh. There was something about the sigh and the way he sat down, like an old man, that diverted her attention from Ezra. She looked at her husband closely. He was pale, drawn and there were purple bruises under his eyes. He did not look well. Evelina was ashamed that she hadn't noticed before. 'Where shall we go?' she asked gently, sitting beside him on the sofa.

'Utah,' he replied. Evelina had never been to Utah. 'I want to see those famous mesa mountains. There's a retreat I know of. It's basic but I think it'll be just what I need. What we both need. You could do with a vacation too, Evelina.'

'When shall we go?'

'Next month. April's a good time weatherwise and it's reading week and exams at the university, so I can arrange cover.'

'I don't think you should work your health around the university. The college should work around your health. This is important, Franklin.'

Franklin smiled his appreciation. 'It'll be nice to spend time with you, just the two of us.' He patted her knee. 'We've been like ships in the night. I've been neglecting you.'

'Oh, you haven't been neglecting me,' she lied. The truth was that it suited her to be neglected. His neglect gave her the freedom to spend time with Ezra. 'I've been busy with Alba,' she added. 'She's a full-time job.'

'To be honest, I haven't felt myself for some time now.' He

inhaled deeply. 'I wasn't going to say anything. I didn't want to be a bore. But it'll be good to have a break.'

'On doctor's orders,' Evelina added firmly.

He chuckled. 'That makes it okay.'

Nothing could have prepared Evelina for the extraordinary beauty of Utah. It was like stepping back into the prehistoric world of the dinosaurs. The desert stretched out for miles and miles, and from that arid ground rose giant orange mountains in strange, otherworldly shapes, moulded by winds and, millions of years before, by water. Yawning canyons opened into the earth like vast, jagged mouths and above them the canopy of sky was bigger and bluer than Evelina had ever seen it. How could anyone not believe in God when faced with such magnificence, she thought as she stood on high, gazing about her in wonder.

The retreat was a series of lodges built at the foot of a flat-topped mesa mountain with a spectacular view of the desert plain. On that flat terrain, rabbits lolloped among broom snakeweed and desert sage and unlikely marigolds turned their yellow petals to the sun. Their room was a wooden cabin with a simple bedroom and adjoining bathroom, decorated tastefully in geometric Navajo fabrics. Double doors opened onto a veranda where they could sit and enjoy the sight of those distant hills that reflected the light in ever-changing shades of pink and blue as the sun travelled slowly across the sky.

There were other people staying there too, but neither Evelina nor Franklin felt like being sociable. They kept themselves to themselves, reading the books they'd brought with them, walking in the desert and lounging in the sunshine, talking. Evelina realized that the last time they had been alone like this was on their trip to Italy, fourteen years before. It was astonishing that they had never thought to arrange a vacation without the children. Perhaps if they'd taken more trouble with each other, Franklin wouldn't have become so engrossed in his work and Evelina might not have needed Ezra in the way that she did. As the days passed in peaceful tranquillity, Evelina watched the colour return to her husband's cheeks and a calmness settle upon him, as if he was gradually, with each day that passed, shedding some of the load that weighed him down. He didn't have his work to distract him and Evelina didn't have the children, Alba or Ezra to divert her. For the first time in years they gave their full attention to each other.

'I don't think I could have asked for a more supportive wife,' he said as they sat atop a mesa mountain one evening and gazed out over the vast horizon. The sun was sinking in an indigo sky, setting the mountains aflame with a fiery amber pink. Evelina wrapped her cardigan around her for, as the shadows lengthened, the temperature dropped. Soon it would grow chilly. She turned her face to the sun and shut her eyes, inhaling the faint smell of wild herbs that rose from the dry scrubland below and savouring the golden rays on her skin. There was something magical about this place, something deep and ancient that resonated with the deep and ancient part of her. Up there, on the top of the world, she felt part of eternity as if there had never been a time when she had not existed, when she had ceased to be. The feeling was powerful and it caused a fizzing sensation in her chest, filling it with love. Right now, there was nowhere she would rather be but here, on this prehistoric mountain, in synch with the timeless vibrations of nature.

'You've been good to me, my darling,' Franklin said, and

he looked bashful, knowing perhaps that he had fallen short in his duties towards her as a husband and friend.

'I've only done what any wife would do,' Evelina told him. 'What wife would not support her husband in his career? I've been happy to do it.'

'You're a selfless woman and I'm fortunate to have you. I know I've been distant and distracted and you've never complained. I should have been more attentive to *your* needs. I realize that now.'

'I don't have many needs, Franklin. You've given me everything I want.' Which was true, he had. Her children were her greatest pleasure and materially she could not have been more satisfied. She looked at him and no longer saw an obstacle to her and Ezra's happiness, but a dear friend. The man she had chosen to spend her life with. The man she loved. She realized now as this strange expansion was taking place inside her that she did, indeed, love him. It was a different love to the one she felt for Ezra. There was no urgency to it, no passion, no fire, no deep root embedded in tragedy. But there was a steadiness and a sense of security about it which she recognized now for its value.

He took her hand. 'I really need you, darling. When I was in the doctor's surgery, a thought floated across my mind. I could have something serious, like cancer. You know what the mind is like. It spins off in all directions, seeing the worst-case scenario. Well, I knew that if I had something drastic like that, at least I had *you*. That you'd be there to help me through it. I wouldn't be alone. It was a reassuring feeling. I'm grateful that I don't have something serious, but I'm grateful too that that small scare shone the light of my awareness onto you, the one person who has quietly stood beside me all these years and never once asked for acknowledgement.'

'You make me sound like a saint,' Evelina said, thinking of Ezra and wanting suddenly to tell Franklin about him. It wasn't okay anymore to deceive him. He deserved the best of her, not the worst of her. The sun edged a little further towards the horizon and the pink deepened to an orange gold. 'I'm not a saint, Franklin.' She squeezed his hand. 'There's something I need to tell you.'

'Okay.' He looked at her with understanding and Evelina wondered whether he was feeling the expansion too.

'Do you remember I told you about Ezra Zanotti?'

'The Jewish man who died in Auschwitz.'

'Yes, that's the one. Well, I was waiting for Alba in a café in Brooklyn a short while ago and he walked in.'

Franklin stared at her in surprise. 'My God, he just walked in?'

'Yes. I thought he was dead. The rabbi in Vercellino had told me that he was dead. He had made a mistake. Ezra had survived. He'd gone to Israel and finally emigrated here. He makes violins in Brooklyn.'

Franklin sandwiched her hand in his as if aware suddenly that he might lose her. His face creased with concern. 'What did you do?'

Evelina shrugged. 'What could I do? I embraced him. My old friend, back from the dead.'

'How do you feel about him now?'

Evelina looked into his eyes and smiled. 'I love him. I love *you* and I love *him*.'

Franklin nodded, trying to understand what sounded incomprehensible. 'I see.' His gaze fell to the Star of David at her chest. 'Did he give you that necklace?'

The fact that Franklin had noticed it took her by surprise. She had gravely underestimated him. She stared into his earnest face, pleased, suddenly, that he had. 'Yes, he did,' Evelina replied, touching it with her fingertips.

Franklin sighed and said nothing.

Evelina's chest expanded with feeling. How could she have ever entertained the idea of divorcing him? She brought his hand to her cheek and closed her eyes a moment. Now more than ever she needed him to be wise. 'I want Ezra in my life, Franklin. As a dear, old friend. He's not married. He's alone. He has no one else in the world but me. No one from his past. No family. No one. He lost everyone. I can't let him lose me too, now that he's just found me again.'

Franklin put his arms around her. She felt him squeeze her hard. Relief, perhaps, that she hadn't said she was going to leave him, or the wonderful expansion now taking place in his own heart and filling it with compassion. 'Then he must be a part of your life, my darling. And if he's a part of your life then he must be a part of my life too. A part of our family.'

Evelina was not prepared for the wave of emotion that crashed against her. It came out of nowhere, assaulting her from behind, filling her eyes with tears. 'Oh Franklin. I don't deserve you.' She pressed her face into his chest. He kissed the top of her head.

In that moment of tenderness, Evelina realized that not only did Franklin need her, but *she* needed him too. It was only now that she realized quite how much.

Evelina and Franklin returned home. The break had been good for both of them, but Franklin knew that he needed more than a vacation to make him well. He needed to cut down his workload and he needed to spend more time with his family.

Evelina arranged to see Ezra in the café around the corner from his workshop. She knew if she went to his apartment they'd end up in bed and she'd made a decision on the plane back to New York: she was going to end the affair.

Ezra smiled when he saw her through the window. Evelina felt nervous. She wasn't sure she could carry out her plan. It was going to take a great deal of self-restraint – self-restraint that ebbed away the moment she saw him through the glass. He pushed open the door and walked over to her table. She stood up and he embraced her, pressing his face to hers in a lingering kiss. They sat down. 'The break did you good,' he said, running his eyes over her, taking in every detail. 'You look well, Eva.'

'Thank you,' she replied. Then she took a breath. She wasn't ready to tell him yet. 'Shall we order something? I'm famished.'

'You have the appetite of a Jew,' he said with a chuckle. 'We're always hungry.'

'You could do with eating a bit more, Ezra. You're on the skinny side.'

'Skinny side? I eat all the time. I never stop eating. I don't know where it goes.'

'You're lucky. You have a fast metabolism. I wish I had a fast metabolism like you.'

'You're lovely just the way you are.' He grinned. 'Let's order a feast and give my metabolism a run for its money.'

They ordered a mound of pastries and coffee. Ezra lit a cigarette. He asked her about Utah and Evelina told him how beautiful it was. 'I don't think Franklin's any better, though,' she said. 'It did him good but he has to slow down now and give his body a chance to fight whatever it is that it's fighting.'

Ezra frowned. 'What's wrong with him?'

'I don't know. The doctors don't know. He's just tired.' Evelina noticed the concerned look on Ezra's face. 'Oh, it's nothing serious. He works too hard.'

Ezra blew smoke out of the side of his mouth. 'Then he's doing the right thing in taking a rest. How old is he?'

'Fifty-eight.'

'Not old.'

'Not young, either. He needs to look after himself. He needs *me* to look after him.' Evelina hadn't meant that sentence to sound loaded, but Ezra narrowed his eyes. The waiter brought their coffees and pastries, then left them alone.

Evelina sighed heavily and dropped her gaze into her coffee cup. 'I had a lot of time to think while I was in Utah,' she said.

Ezra stubbed out his cigarette then dropped a sugar lump into his coffee.

'Franklin needs me,' she continued, without looking at him. 'I can't go on betraying him like this. It's just not fair. It's not who I want to be.'

Ezra nodded. He stirred his coffee thoughtfully. 'What do you want to do?'

She raised her eyes to see that he was gazing at her with a serious expression on his face. 'I want to have both of you in my life. But something has to give, because while I'm married to Franklin, I can't sneak about sleeping with someone else.'

'I understand,' he said, in the resigned way of a man determined to accept whatever life throws at him.

She reached out and took his hand. 'I don't want to lose you, Ezra. I've lost you once already and I'm not going to lose you again.'

He tightened his grip on her hand. 'You won't lose me, Eva. I'm not going anywhere.'

'I told Franklin about you turning up.'

Ezra raised his eyebrows. 'How much did you tell him?'

'Just that you're here in Brooklyn and that I want you in my life.'

'What did he say?'

'That he wants to meet you. Any friend of mine is a friend of his. He wants you to be a part of *both* of our lives. That's the only way it's going to work.'

Ezra nodded. 'I need to think about that.'

Evelina withdrew her hand and lifted her pastry off the plate. 'Sure, take all the time you need.' She glanced at him. He seemed distracted suddenly, as if his mind had been called away to somewhere else. She chewed in silence. When she could take the silence no more, she said, 'Ezra? Are you okay?'

'Sure,' he replied, as if waking from a trance. 'How's your coffee?'

'Cold,' she answered, trying to rouse him with a smile.

She hoped she hadn't ruined it.

Evelina didn't know how to proceed with this new arrangement of not sleeping with Ezra. Their liaisons had been routine, every lunch hour, Monday to Friday. She'd met him at his apartment and they'd fallen on each other with the passion of two people who, denied each other for so long, were determined to savour every moment as if it were their last. Take that out of their relationship and what was left? Coffee in cafés? Lunches in diners? Holding hands across a table, gazing at each other with longing? It was like trying to reduce something massive into a tiny box; their love was too big for the small space Evelina wanted to give it.

Yet, it was all she was able to give.

*

Over the next few months Franklin's health deteriorated. Evelina spent more time at home, caring for him. Some mornings he couldn't get himself out of bed. Dr Shaw took more tests, yet nothing came up that suggested he was sick. He was referred to one specialist after another, but no one could get to the bottom of it. Eventually, he stopped work altogether. The university agreed to give him a sabbatical, and he resigned himself to a quiet life at home, reading.

It was then that he decided they should move out of New York. Evelina wasn't keen. How would she see Ezra if she moved further away from him? But Franklin was adamant that Greenwich would be a healthier place for him to live and, for that matter, for Evelina and the children too. They could buy a bigger house with a garden, and they would meet their neighbours. They barely even saw their neighbours in Manhattan. And Franklin could work at one of the local colleges.

Evelina went through the motions of looking at real estate with a heavy heart. In America she had only ever known the city. She'd got used to the noise of traffic, nights that never grew dark, the smell of petrol fumes and the embrace of buildings. It was familiar and had, over time, begun to feel like home. She wasn't sure she wanted to swap it for the quiet life, far away from Ezra.

Yet Greenwich was leafy and pretty and the houses were big with lovely gardens. She thought of the children cooped up in their apartment and remembered the boys' excitement at being at Villa L'Ambrosiana with all that space to run around in. She remembered the joy she had derived from the trees and flowers and secret gardens, hidden in the far corners of the estate. She'd be able to paint outside again. She'd have room for a proper piano. Maybe they could even have a dog. The more she saw the houses through the eyes of the children, the more her enthusiasm grew. It would be a proper home.

They settled on a white clapboard house with green shutters and a grey-tiled roof. It had a large garden with a swimming pool and an orchard of apple trees. To the right of the building stood a maple tree, to the left an enormous plane tree. At the back was a cedar that looked like it had been there far longer than the house. Evelina wondered whether they could hang a swing from one of the branches for Ava-Maria. With dormer windows in the roof and chimneys for winter fires, it looked like something out of a children's story book.

Evelina told Ezra of their plans to move over coffee in the café. Again he went quiet, lost in thought to a place where Evelina could not reach him. It seemed that ever since she had ended their affair a distance had opened up between them. The more her life changed, the greater that distance grew. Holding hands across the table was an inadequate bridge when they had been used to the intimacy and warmth of making love. Ezra hadn't wanted to end it even though he had said that he didn't need her. He had told her that he was satisfied with the gift that was her, and that he did not ask for more; but she had given him less. There was a great danger that less would dwindle to nothing.

Franklin and Evelina moved house in the spring of the following year just as the maple tree was turning green and the branches of the apple trees hung heavy with pink and white blossom. The children were ecstatic about their new home. Dan declared that he was going to build a tree house. Aldo wanted to climb the cedar tree to the very top. Ava-Maria wanted to swim in the pool. Franklin was delighted with his study and Evelina with her piano. Madolina, Peppino and Taddeo were the first guests at their dining-room table. Alba was the first to cry on their sofa. The only thing that was missing was Ezra.

Evelina took comfort in her music. Yet every time she closed her eyes and imagined she was flying, she felt Ezra beside her. She set up her easel in the garden, but when she put her brush to the paper she ceased to see the trees and flowers and saw Ezra, his eyes full of longing, lonelier than ever. And when she went out at night to look at the stars, so bright now that she was out of the city, she wondered whether Ezra was lying on his roof, seeing them too. After having mourned him for fifteen years, she couldn't bear to mourn him again. It was unthinkable that after finding each other they should be apart.

Then Ezra called her. He wanted to see her. 'I have something I want to tell you.'

Evelina took the train to Brooklyn and met him at the café. They ordered coffee. Ezra was unshaven. His curly hair had grown long and unkempt and his eyes were red. He smiled but he could not hide the unhappiness behind it. 'I've missed you,' he said. He did not reach out for her hand, but she took his all the same.

'I've missed you too,' she replied.

He shook his head. 'When I said I didn't need you, I was wrong.' He looked at her in defeat. 'I need you, Eva. I need you in my life. If I can't hold you, then at least I can look at you.' His smile grew more animated. 'If Franklin will accept me, then I'd like to meet him. I'd like to meet your family. I'd like to see your new house. Perhaps I can come and visit.'

Evelina wrapped her hands around his. 'Oh Ezra.'

He brought her hands to his lips and kissed them. 'When can I come?'

Evelina was in the kitchen cooking when the doorbell went. Franklin went to open it. Evelina heard him talking and then Ezra's voice as Franklin invited him in. She untied her apron and hooked it over the back of the door. When she saw Ezra, her face softened into a tender smile. He had shaved and trimmed his hair and even though his clothes looked too big for him, they were clean. She kissed him affectionately, aware that she was trembling with nerves. 'What have you got there?' she asked, looking at the box he was carrying. It had holes punctured in the top, which suggested that whatever was inside was alive.

Franklin called the children in from the garden. Dan had made a tree house and he and Aldo seemed to spend every free minute inside it. Ava-Maria had been in the playroom and came running into the hall. 'I want to introduce you to a very special friend,' said Evelina.

The children didn't look at Ezra. They looked at the box. Ezra put it on the floor. 'Go on, open it,' he said.

'Carefully,' warned Franklin as they began to tear the cardboard.

Little by little a cage emerged. 'What is it?' Evelina asked, frowning at Ezra.

'A friend,' he replied with a shrug.

'It's a mouse!' cried Ava-Maria in excitement. 'A mouse, a mouse, a mouse!'

The mouse stared up at the faces staring in.

The boys wanted to take it out and play with it. 'I think you should give it time to get used to you,' said Franklin. 'Thank you, Ezra. What a thoughtful present.'

'*Un topino*,' said Evelina with a sigh. A little mouse. 'Really, you shouldn't have.'

Ava-Maria threw her arms around Ezra, which took him as much by surprise as it did her parents. 'Thank you, Topino,' she said, mistaking that for his name.

Evelina laughed. She looked at Ezra. 'Something tells me that's going to stick,' she said. 'Come on in, Uncle Topino, and let's pour you a drink.'

PART FOUR

Greenwich, New York, 1982

Evelina sat at Franklin's bedside, his thin, bony hand in hers, and smiled at him with affection and sadness. She knew how disappointed he was not to be able to celebrate Thanksgiving. 'We'll celebrate it together, just the two of us,' she said softly. 'And next year, maybe . . .' but that was a futile thing to say. Franklin wouldn't make it to next year.

'Will you read to me?' he asked.

'Of course.'

'I like the way you read. I like your voice. You've always had a beautiful voice.'

'What would you like me to read?'

'*The Count of Monte Cristo.*'

'That's one of my favourites too.'

'I never tire of it.' He looked at her, his blue eyes deeper suddenly. 'But I'm tired of life, my darling.'

His resignation frightened her. 'Don't say that, Franklin.'

'It's true.' He sighed. 'I'm ready to go.'

Evelina's vision blurred with tears. 'I'm not ready for you to go.'

'We've had a good life together. We've travelled, we've enjoyed our children, we've laughed. We've always got on, haven't we?'

'We have,' she agreed. 'We got on from the very first time we met. Do you remember?'

'How could I forget? At Alba's wedding. Her *first* wedding.

That woman gets through men like most people get through bars of chocolate!'

'She does. I fear she's heading for number four now.'

'Why doesn't she just live with them? Why does she have to marry them?'

'If we start that conversation, I won't get around to reading to you.'

'You were seated next to me. You were dating that young man who was desperate to marry you, yet, you were reluctant to commit.'

'Mike, he was called.'

'Yes, that's it. Mike. He was nice enough, but he wasn't right for you. I liked the look of you, but it wasn't until we were in the café, talking, that I saw something special in you.'

'I was so cold, and cross.'

'Yes, Mike had just announced to the whole party that you were engaged.'

'I was mortified.'

'You were dignified. But I felt your embarrassment.'

'It was a foolish way to propose. You can't force a person to marry you.'

'He lost you then.'

'He had already lost me, Franklin.'

'We were in the café and I ordered you a hot chocolate. You must have been in your late twenties, but you looked younger. You looked like a girl, shivering with cold and fury.'

'I can almost taste that hot chocolate.' Evelina smiled wistfully at the recollection. 'It was delicious.'

'You said you could never love again.'

'Did I?'

'Yes, you told me about Ezra. You told me that he had

been killed in the war. Your big eyes filled with tears and you looked so unhappy, I almost believed you.'

'Almost?'

'I wondered whether I could make you love *me*.'

'Oh Franklin. You didn't even know me at that point.'

'Yes, but it crossed my mind. There you were, a beautiful young woman, with these pink cheeks and shiny eyes, telling me about a young man that you had loved and would always love, and I felt jealous.'

'Jealous of Ezra?'

'Jealous that you'd given your heart to him and that he'd taken it with him to the grave. I liked the look of you, you see. I wondered whether you could ever love *me* like that.'

Evelina shook her head. 'I never thought I would love again. But I did. I loved *you*.'

His smile turned tender, as if in the face of a golden sunset. 'You have loved me, my darling Evelina. But not in the way that you have loved Ezra.' Evelina made to protest, but Franklin stopped her by sandwiching her hand between his. 'There are many ways to love, and many degrees of it, Evelina. When you told me that Ezra had walked into the café in Brooklyn, I was fearful that you'd leave me. I understood the feelings you had for him, you see. The depth of them. You both shared roots, experience and tragedy. There's nothing more romantic than that. But you didn't leave me. You chose to stay.'

Evelina was crying now. 'Because I loved you too, Franklin. I still do. I love you very much.'

Franklin brought her hand to his lips and pressed it against them. 'And I love you, Evelina. Which is why, when I'm gone—'

'Don't speak of it.'

'When I'm gone,' he persisted with emphasis, 'I give you my blessing to share your life with Ezra.'

'Oh Franklin . . .'

'I don't say this out of self-pity, but out of gratitude and respect for your loyalty and love. I want you and Ezra to live the remainder of your days together, knowing that I gave you my blessing.'

'I don't know what to say. I don't want to think of you not being here.'

'I'm an old man, my darling. My time is up. I'm all right with it, so you should be too. I've had a good life. I'm ready to go. But I won't be happy, wherever I end up, knowing that you tried to honour my memory by making a shrine for me. When I'm gone, I'm gone, and I'll be happy knowing that you're with Ezra and that once a year, at Thanksgiving, you raise your glasses to me in a toast.'

Evelina was unable to speak for the emotion clogging her throat.

'The children will be surprised, I imagine. So I suggest you write your story for them to read and digest. Then they will understand. They need to know how you met, what you went through, how Ezra turned up out of the blue after you'd given him up for dead. It's an amazing story in itself, but it's *your* story and they should know it.'

'You've given this a lot of thought.'

'I've had a lot of time.' He smiled and there was no sadness in it. It was the smile of a man who had made peace with his fate. 'I want to go knowing there are no loose ends.'

'There are no loose ends, Franklin. You've thought of everything.'

'Come, let me kiss you.' Evelina gave him her forehead. His lips felt strangely cold against her skin. 'Read to me, will you.'

Evelina opened the book and began to read. ' "On the 24th of February, 1815, the lookout at Notre-Dame de la Garde signalled the three-master, the Pharaon, from Smyrna, Trieste, and Naples . . ." '

When Franklin passed away, his family were at his bedside: Aldo, Dan and Ava-Maria, and Evelina, of course, who held her daughter's hand while they quietly cried. It was a peaceful departure. Franklin gave no resistance. He just closed his eyes and slipped away. Evelina lit a candle and they prayed. 'Where is he now?' Ava-Maria asked.

'Somewhere nice,' Evelina replied. 'Franklin deserves the best.'

'I hope Heaven is real,' Ava-Maria added. 'I hope he's opening his eyes to find himself in fields of poppies and buttercups.'

Dan laughed through his tears. 'I think Dad would rather be in the great heavenly halls of learning.'

'Do you think there are such things?' Ava-Maria asked.

'Of course there are,' said Dan. 'I think Heaven is like earth but without all the bad things, like litter and Halloween.'

Aldo, who had remained lost in thought, laughed then. 'Halloween?'

'I hate Halloween,' said Dan, screwing up his nose. 'It's highly overrated. Dad hated Halloween too. Do you remember how he made us turn off the lights and pretend we weren't at home to stop all the kids coming knocking on our door?'

Evelina smiled. 'I do remember that. But you kids loved dressing up and going out.'

'Only because you made us,' said Dan. 'I was with Dad on that one.'

'So, no litter and no Halloween,' said Ava-Maria with a sigh. 'Only great heavenly halls of learning and a telescope so he can keep an eye on us down here.'

'And he *will* keep an eye on us,' said Evelina, feeling grief's familiar hand squeezing her hard on the inside. 'Because he loved us all so much.'

Topino came round as soon as he heard the news. Evelina let him into the hall. He didn't take off his coat and hat, but gathered her into his arms and held her tightly. Neither spoke. They didn't need to. Topino knew how much Evelina's heart was hurting and Evelina knew that Topino shared that hurt, because they were part of each other.

Aldo, Dan and Ava-Maria were in the sitting room with hot drinks and a boisterous fire, not knowing quite what to do with themselves. The atmosphere was heavy with sorrow and a strange awkwardness, because each had their own way of grieving and they weren't necessarily compatible. When Topino entered, Ava-Maria burst into tears again. Topino did what he did best: he sat beside her on the sofa, put his arm around her so that she could rest her head on his shoulder, and listened as she told him all the things she would miss about her father, and then all the things she was grateful to him for. The awkwardness melted away in the warmth of Topino's compassion and even the boys began to share their memories and release the occasional laugh.

The children offered to stay the night so their mother wouldn't be on her own, but Evelina told them she was fine, that she wouldn't be afraid, and they departed after dinner, leaving Evelina and Topino in the hall.

Topino put on his coat and hat and took Evelina's hands in his. He looked at her intensely, his grey eyes heavy with emotion. 'I don't want to leave you alone either, but it wouldn't be right for me to stay,' he said.

Evelina put her arms around him and pressed her face into the crook of his neck. 'I loved Franklin, Ezra. I loved him dearly. Give me time to mourn him and then I will come to you.'

Topino closed his eyes and held her for a little while longer. 'I'll always be here, Eva,' he said, 'waiting for you.'

Franklin's funeral was a large affair. A number of his old students and colleagues from Columbia and Skidmore turned up to pay their respects, as well as friends and family, of which he had many. The sun shone through the trees, turning the remaining yellow leaves golden, and a lone cloud moved slowly across the sky like a great ship carrying Franklin's soul to Heaven.

Topino, Taddeo and Madolina sat at the front of the church. Topino wore the same old coat he always wore, and a felt hat tipped low over his eyes. Taddeo wore colour because he did not believe in wearing black to funerals – why make a miserable day all the more miserable by dressing like the Grim Reaper, he argued. Madolina wore black but had chosen a hat adorned with rich purple feathers to please Taddeo. After all, it was more important to please the living than the dead. 'It should be me,' she said, shaking her head at the unfairness of it.

'Has it crossed your mind that God might not want you?' said Topino with a grin.

'Not until now,' Madolina retorted with a sniff.

Taddeo chuckled. 'Topino has a point, Madolina. Heaven isn't ready for you yet.'

'God didn't want me either,' Topino added. 'Just as well.'

'So what happens now?' asked Madolina, looking at Topino slyly.

'We give thanks for a precious life.'

'No, I mean with you and Evelina. What happens?' She grinned, presuming that he wasn't going to answer that question. 'I suspected long ago and then I knew, because Taddeo told me. When Peppino died, Taddeo and I could have moved in together, but the moment had passed and I was too old—'

'Rubbish,' Taddeo interrupted. 'Too old! My ass.'

Madolina ignored him. 'The moment hasn't passed for you and Evelina,' she continued. 'In fact, I'd say your moment is just beginning.' She patted his knee. 'Don't worry, you don't have to answer me. I'll find out in due course. All I will say is, don't waste it. I'm sure Franklin knew too, and if he didn't, he's not going to mind now. I'm sure one gains a certain perspective after death. You and Evelina belong together, like a pot and its lid.'

'Franklin is still warm,' said Topino quietly.

'So give it a week or two. At your age you can't afford to waste time. Every second is precious. I don't need to tell *you* that.'

Evelina sat at Franklin's desk. She ran her fingers over his things: his leather blotter stained with ink, his black Montblanc fountain pen and his empty filing tray that was once filled with documents, bills and letters, and felt his presence as if he were still there, peering over her shoulder. She swept her weary eyes over the bookcase, her gaze lingering on the photographs in silver frames displayed among the books. They celebrated a long chapter of family life, but now Franklin was gone and that chapter had come to an end as all chapters eventually do. With every end there sprouted a new beginning. Evelina had survived many new beginnings in her life; this was just one more. However, her heart reeled from sorrow, for in spite of experience the heart never learns to withstand grief's pain or to rise above it, it only learns what to expect.

Evelina put a pad of lined paper on the blotter in front of her and lifted a blue biro out of Franklin's pen holder. The page gleamed dauntingly white and clean beneath the biro. She wasn't sure she knew how to begin. She had never written anything like this before. She thought of Franklin and sighed with frustration; he'd know exactly what to do. Franklin had had a way with words that Evelina had found quite magical. She didn't have that talent. She wished he were here to advise her. *How do I start?* she asked, sending her thoughts out to him, wherever he was. She closed her eyes and inhaled slowly. In that space she heard Franklin's voice. It was as clear as if he were speaking directly to her, planting the words in her head: *Tell your story from the beginning*, he said.

And so she did:

Northern Italy, July 1934
  Villa L'Ambrosiana

Evelina Pierangelini inhaled deeply. The scent of rosemary filled her nostrils. How she loved it, this shrub with evergreen needles and purple flowers that grew in every border of the villa. The estate was bursting with flowers; there were vast terracotta pots of bougainvillea, heaps of thyme, an abundance of oleander, and jasmine that covered the limestone walls of the villa, exhaling its sweet perfume into the rooms, and yet, the smell that defined the place was rosemary. It was woody, aromatic and sensual. To seventeen-year-old Evelina, it was the smell of home.

It was a warm day in March. Evelina had invited her family and Topino for Sunday lunch. The scent of spring saturated the air, blossom was just beginning to flower on the apple trees and phosphorescent green shoots were rising out of the earth and emerging tentatively into the light. Evelina had cooked a sumptuous feast. They sat around the dining table. Madolina complained of the din. Taddeo refilled her wine glass and told her to dull her senses, because that was the only way to cope with a family that was never going to talk quietly. Ava-Maria announced loudly that she was expecting their first child. Jonathan blushed with pride. Dan had asked Lucille to marry him and they held hands beneath the table. Aldo, who was sitting in his father's chair, raised his glass and gave a speech just like Franklin used to do, and Lisa glanced down the table at her children who were listening to their father, their faces aglow with admiration. Evelina caught Topino's eye and smiled. Topino smiled back; a tender smile full of wistfulness.

At the end of lunch Evelina went into the study and collected three parcels wrapped in brown paper and tied with string and brought them to the table. 'What are they?' asked Ava-Maria, her shining eyes narrowing, sensing something unusual in her mother's demeanour, but not knowing what it was.

'These are for you,' Evelina replied. She handed one to Ava-Maria, passing the other two down the table to her sons.

Madolina frowned. Not even she, with her sharp powers of observation, could work out what the parcels contained. Ava-Maria was the first to unwrap hers, tearing at the paper impatiently. She lifted the manuscript out and her mouth fell open with astonishment. *Of Time, Tomatoes and Love, by Evelina Pierangelini*. 'You've written a book?' she exclaimed.

'I have written my memoirs,' said Evelina. 'For the three of you.'

'Wow!' said Dan. 'I didn't know you wanted to be a writer.'

'I don't,' Evelina replied.

'I don't understand,' said Aldo. He knew there was more to this than just his mother's recollections of where she grew up.

Evelina took Topino's hand. He gave it a reassuring squeeze. 'Your father suggested I write it after he gave me his blessing to start a new chapter of my life with Ezra.'

'Ezra?' said Dan, looking at Topino and then back at his mother in confusion.

'Ezra,' said Ava-Maria slowly, settling her gaze upon him with the light of a sudden dawning.

'Ezra and I are going to Italy. While we are away, I want you to read my memoirs. Then you'll understand.'

'About time too,' said Madolina with a smile. 'Are you going to Vercellino?'

Aldo, Dan and Ava-Maria stared at their mother and Topino in bewilderment. 'When you say you're going to Italy together, do you mean as a couple?' Aldo asked.

An awkward silence fell over the table. Lisa glanced at Aldo with concern. Lucille and Jonathan said nothing. Ava-Maria's eyes shone with tears. For a moment Evelina panicked that her daughter was going to scold her for being insensitive. But to her surprise she pressed the manuscript to her chest. 'If Daddy gave you his blessing then who are we to withhold ours?' she said. 'There's only one man I love enough to take my father's place at my mother's side, and that's you, Topino. You might be Ezra to Mom, but you'll always be Uncle Topino to me.'

The boys looked less thrilled. Their father hadn't been gone a year and their mother was setting off to Italy with his best friend. When it was time to leave, Evelina embraced them fiercely, hoping they would eventually understand and accept her decision. 'Just read the story,' she said. 'It's more complicated than you can imagine.'

Madolina kissed her niece goodbye. 'You enjoy Italy,' she said, patting her shoulder. 'And don't cut your honeymoon short for anything. Not even my funeral. You understand? You've waited over forty years for this.'

Ezra and Evelina sat outside on the swing chair. The sun was sinking slowly, setting the sky aflame. 'What do you see out there?' he asked.

'I see a burning orange,' Evelina replied.

'I see melting ice cream.'

Evelina laughed. 'You would see ice cream,' she said.

'Don't you?'

'No, I see a burning orange.' She turned to face him. 'How do you think that went?'

'It couldn't have gone better.'

'No, seriously. I think the boys were shocked.'

'Perhaps. That's understandable. I'm not as handsome as I once was.'

'Oh Ezra. You're still handsome to me.'

'And that's all that matters.' He slipped his hand around the back of her neck, beneath her hair, and kissed her lips. Evelina felt the old familiar stirrings as if her nerves were waking from a long sleep. His kiss was deep and tender, growing increasingly passionate as they rediscovered each other again. Gradually the years fell away and Evelina felt young again. Young and in love, and able at last to see a future where she and Ezra could be together.

Villa L'Ambrosiana, 1982

Evelina's eyes misted as Villa L'Ambrosiana came into view at the end of the avenue of cypress trees. It hadn't changed in all the years she had been away. It still had an air of neglect, of quiet watchfulness, of permanence. In the forecourt, the ornamental pond gleamed in the sunshine and the fountain of Venus was still dry. The marble statues of naked men in contrapposto stood on their pedestals as they had always done, their limbs mottled with moss and lichen, gazing blindly at the pots of purple bougainvillea and yew hedges clipped into uneven balls. Evelina's heart stalled then and she squeezed Ezra's hand ever tighter. There, on the steps to greet her, was her mother in a large sunhat, her grey hair falling wild and unkempt over her shoulders, a wide smile upon her handsome face, and Benedetta and Gianni, their children, sons- and daughters-in-law, and their grandchildren and dogs. The emotion caught in Evelina's throat and she began to laugh through her tears. Time stood still at Villa L'Ambrosiana as it always would, only the generations moved through it like the changing seasons, one after the other. Those walls remained as witnesses to life's transience and fragility, and perhaps, also, to its apparent lack of purpose – for what did walls know of the human heart?

Evelina climbed out of the taxi and ran to embrace her mother and sister. She didn't notice the lines time and tragedy had drawn into their faces, but she did notice the tears for they were tears of joy. Evelina would only see the light now for the shadows of the past had finally been laid to rest; she and Ezra had come home, at last.

Ezra looked at Gianni. The civil war seemed like another lifetime now. They had both taken different roads and yet, here they were, in the same layby, at the end of a long journey. The two men embraced and in their hold was a vigour that transcended words, for how could they possibly communicate in syllables the emotions rising in their hearts? They remained there for a long moment. In Italy it is not considered unmanly for men to cry.

Ezra and Evelina stood before the altar in the little chapel where they had first made love. Evelina did not think of Bruno's death or Ezra's arrest. She was aware only of the sunshine streaming in through the big windows, falling onto the crispy leaves and stone floor in shafts of gold. Ezra cupped her face and ran his thumbs over her cheeks, gazing into her eyes with tenderness. 'Evelina Pierangelini, will you take a simple Jewish boy, the son of a cloth merchant and a seamstress, to be your husband? I promise you that, with the little I have, I will love you and cherish you and allow nothing, ever, to come between us again. The river of life that separated us once has brought us back to the place where we started, and I vow to honour this moment for the gift that it is. I love you with all my heart, as I always have.'

Evelina nodded because she could not speak. She gazed upon the face she had held on to even when her head had told her to let it go, and felt an expansion in her chest; gratitude for a second chance, for an opening chapter, for love that survived the greatest odds, and for Franklin, for giving her this moment to enjoy without self-reproach.

Ezra bent down and kissed her, and with that kiss the years fell away and they were young again, stepping into a future that belonged to them.

ACKNOWLEDGEMENTS

Many years ago I was at a dinner party in London, seated next to the host's father, a very charming and charismatic man called Jonas Prince. He was wonderfully entertaining and we chatted for the duration of dinner. When I told him I was a writer he shared an incredible story with me; his mother's story. After hearing it, and being moved to tears, I told him I would give anything to write it. That story stayed with me and over the years I often thought about working it into a novel. However, Jonas's mother was Polish. I have never been to Poland and know nothing about the culture. She was also imprisoned in Auschwitz during the war, which is something I could never presume to write about, not being Jewish (I converted in 1988, but I wasn't born Jewish). However, the twist in the story was so powerful that I knew I had to find a way of making it work. Then, last year, I stumbled upon an idea. It was inspired by an old university book of mine that was sitting gathering dust in the bookcase: *The Garden of the Finzi-Continis* by Giorgio Bassani. I would set my novel in northern Italy, I decided, rather than Poland, and my heroine would be Italian and the young man she falls in love with, Jewish Italian. That way I would not write Jonas's mother's story, but would wrap my own story around the small but crucial twist I had found so compelling.

This book would never have been written had it not been for that fortuitous meeting with Jonas. Therefore, I owe him an enormous debt of gratitude. I will not spoil the story by revealing the twist, but you'll know it when you get to it, and that is the nugget of truth in the book which my imagination could never have conjured up. Thank you, Jonas, for your kindness in sharing your mother's story with me and I hope that one day we will meet again.

I like to invent my own towns and villages so that I can make them my own. I get letters from readers asking where exactly Incantellaria is on the Amalfi Coast, or Ballinakelly in County Cork, because they would like to visit them, and I have to write back and tell them the disappointing truth: they can get close, very close, but they'll never find them. In the same way Vercellino is also invented. There is a town called Vercelli in Piedmont which inspired Vercellino, but I have not misspelt it. If you do want to visit Vercellino, Vercelli is as near as you'll get!

I would like to take this opportunity to thank the people in my life who enrich it. Writing is a solitary occupation, so having a cup of London's most delicious coffee at Rino's at 40a Kensington Church Street gets me out of the house and that brief morning chat with the proprietor, Rino Eramo, and his vivacious wife Morgana, while I sit at the little round table in the sunshine, is one of the highlights of my day. Twice a week I work out with Carl van Heerden at Core Collective in Kensington – he is brutal but brilliant and were it not for him I'd just sit at my desk all day long eating biscuits; he saves me from myself, and I am very grateful for that! The charming Artan Mesekrani manages the Ivy Kensington Brasserie which is the best local restaurant and my favourite hang-out. He has a great team and they always make me feel welcome. On weekends we head to The Yard Café near Alresford. The Moon Roast coffee is delicious and Ted 'Longshot' Longden knows just how I like it. The cake is excellent too!

I'm grateful for my parents, Charles and Patty Palmer-Tomkinson, my brother James, sister-in-law Sos, and their four delightful children, Honor, India, Wilf and Sam, and my aunt Naomi. The older I get the more I realize how important family is. It is everything!

I would like to thank my wonderful friend and agent, Sheila Crowley, at Curtis Brown, and the dynamic team who work with her: Luke Speed, Anna Weguelin, Emily Harris, Sabhbh Curran, Katie McGowan, Grace Robinson, Alice Lutyens and Sophia MacAskill. A big thank you to my eagle-eyed and expert editor, Suzanne Baboneau, and my boss, Ian Chapman, and their brilliant team at Simon & Schuster UK: Sara-Jade Virtue, Richard Vlietstra, Gill Richardson, Dominic Brendon, Polly Osborn, Sabah Khan, Matt Johnson, Sian Wilson, Louise Davies and Francesca Sironi. Simon & Schuster Canada have worked so hard and with great enthusiasm to make my novels a success over there, so I would like to thank them too: Nita Pronovost, for whom no detail is too small, and her fabulous colleagues Kevin Hanson, Cali Platek, Mackenzie Croft, Shara Alexa and Jillian Levick.

Books rarely become successes on their own. In my case it's a delicate alchemy where many ingredients – the work, the agent, the editor, the sales, creative, marketing and publicity teams, and the retailers – all come together in harmony to produce something special. I couldn't do without a single one of those ingredients and I am truly grateful to all of them for their hard work and enthusiasm. Indeed, Ralph Waldo Emerson said that nothing great was ever achieved without enthusiasm; those passionate people are the wind beneath my wings! I would also like to thank my readers, because without them I would not have a job! Having travelled around the world and met many of them, I believe I have the nicest readers in the world.

Thank you to my husband Sebag, our daughter Lilochka and our son Sasha, for their patience, laughter and love. They inspire me every day and remind me constantly of what I love best about my life.

Santa Montefiore

Stories that stay
with you forever

Stay in touch with Santa for monthly updates
on her latest books.

Sign up for Santa's newsletter at
santamontefiore.co.uk

You can also connect with Santa on social media,
or follow her on Amazon for new book alerts.

🐦 SantaMontefiore

📷 SantaMontefioreOfficial

f /SantaMontefiorebooks

a bit.ly/FollowSanta

Also available by

SANTA MONTEFIORE

The Deverill Series

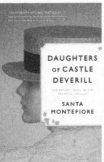

"Everything she writes, she writes from the heart."

Jojo Moyes, *New York Times*
bestselling author of *Me Before You*

Read more
SANTA MONTEFIORE

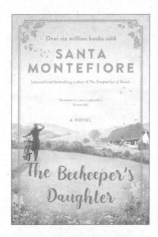

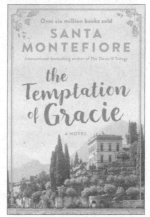

"A pleasure to read. . . .
A new Montefiore novel is always a major event."
Toronto Star